EVERYONE
LOVES YOU BACK

Louie Cronin

Gorsky Press
Los Angeles • California
2016

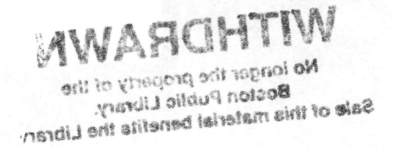

Published by
Gorsky Press
P.O. Box 42024
Los Angeles, CA 90042

ISBN 978-1-941576-22-9

For Jim

CHAPTER 1

Bob Boland is surrounded. Yuppies everywhere. Goddamned professional women with their blunt cuts and power suits, their wimpy men, pale faced and narrow shouldered, their PhDs, MDs and JDs on proud display in their book-lined studies.

The neighborhood has always been full of snobs — half of it belongs to Harvard, the other half to Harvard professors, grads, and wannabes, the type who donate buildings and gymnasiums, who endow symphony chairs in perpetuity — but there used to be room for the little people, who deliver the mail, plow the driveways, clean the teeth, fix the burners. Now the new rich are crowding them out, throwing around so much money that the neighborhood is barely recognizable. Slate roofs, copper drains, specimen trees, heated driveways — nothing is too good for them. If there's a beautiful front yard, they put up a fence. If there's a fence, they tear it down and put in a hedge. Blacktop becomes lawn; lawn becomes groundcover; groundcover becomes brick. And God forbid the house should peel. Bingo! An army of painters descends, airlifted from the latest Third World country in collapse, sanding, scraping, hanging like bats under the eaves, risking their lives to try out matching trim colors.

Bob never thought he'd be singing the praises of the horsefaces, stingy old bastards with their patched tweed jackets and homely gray-haired wives, wearing the same frayed shirts and resoled shoes year in and year out, living in their gloomy mansions, driving their ten-year-old Mercedes, riding their three-speed Raleighs with the cracked leather seats and rusty wire baskets, scarves wrapped around their necks like they were in merry old England, the motherland, the well from which their bottomless coldness must have sprung. But now he feels something approaching affection for them, for mannish old Pricilla Sutton, lurching down the street in her Wellingtons and worn flannel shirt, her white hair escaping from a headband. Even she looks a little uncomfortable now, unsure where she belongs in this new world of conspicuous consumption.

At eleven-thirty at night, when everyone else in the neighborhood is getting ready for bed, clicking off the TV after an IQ-lowering dose of local news, turning down the covers, slipping between the six-hundred-thread-count sheets, curling up with a *New Yorker*, a mystery, a spiritual how-to, Bob is heading to WJZY. His shift starts at midnight, but he likes to get to the station a few minutes early, pull some CDs, set up the breaks, clean up the studio after that pig BJ, who will watch him clean, never once getting up from his chair. BJ is so lazy he will roll to get another CD, to program the computer, to read the log. He has mastered the soundboard push off; he's the gold medallist of the chairbound. Every night the trashcan overflows with fast food wrappers, crushed coffee cups, old newspapers, spent ketchup packets. And BJ has the body to show for it. He has grown into the chair; his hips and ass seep girlishly over the sides. Like nearly everyone in radio, BJ has a good voice, deep and round, with a butterscotch finish; you picture James Earl Jones, maybe Gregory Peck in *To Kill a Mockingbird*, but what you get is a pale, fat, thirty-five-going-on-fifty-five white guy who is obsessed with jazz.

Bob is obsessed with jazz too, but he doesn't look the part. He still has the broad shoulders and muscled upper body of the athlete he was supposed to be. His sports career foundered his freshman year at UMass, when he discovered jazz and pot. The coach threw him off the team. His father stopped talking to him. His mother slipped him tuition money and he graduated with an individually crafted degree in Altered States of Consciousness and the Evolution of Bebop. Find a job with that.

Bob always gets to the station before Riff, who is out in the parking lot smoking a joint. Now that it is forbidden to smoke in the studio, Riff makes do with a before-show toke and a pick-me-up in the men's room during breaks. Back when Bob started in radio everybody smoked, cigarettes and marijuana, ashtray right next to the microphone, helped your voice get that nice gravelly touch, gave men the balls they might lack, and women the balls they almost certainly did.

Riff is another little white guy pretending to be black, but at least he was one of the first. He's been around forever, snuck into clubs to see Miles and Coltrane when he was a teen. He has a very low maintenance approach to his appearance: shaves his head once a year, ignores it for the rest. He wears nothing but jumpsuits, which he designs and his third young wife dutifully sews. His only regular upkeep is his pointy little goatee, a must for white guys pretending to be black. After twenty years in radio, Bob could write a treatise on white guys pretending to be black. Like you didn't already fuck over black people, you have to steal their culture, appropriate their blue moods, envy them their suffering. Most of these white–black guys ended up with drug problems, the only surefire way to shed their middle class privilege and get down with the brothers.

But Bob respects Riff. Back when he decided to become a black man, it wasn't the thing to do. And Riff still likes white people. He and Bob started working together when WJZY was mostly jazz; now it's mostly news. They have been together for thirteen years, longer than any of Riff's marriages, longer by far than any of Bob's relationships. Occasionally they socialize on the weekends, getting together after midnight. Riff's wife Sue cooks dinner, and they drink and talk until dawn. Riff always manages to find a woman who will cater to his schedule, breakfast at 4 p.m., lunch at 11 p.m. Sue is up when he rolls in. *Maybe you were a little hard on the guy who didn't know who Johnny Hodges was. You should have let the old lady finish.* Riff does a kind of hybrid jazz/talk show. When he feels like it, he plays music; when he gets bored, he takes calls from the audience. Old people, insomniacs, sick people, shift workers, drug addicts, musicians — they're the ones who are up all night, roaming their houses, spinning the radio dial. They talk about music, sleep, God, food, sex. Bob will cue up a CD — Pharaoh Sanders, Ron Carter — and sneak it in under the conversation. Some nights Riff awakes with a song or artist under his skin, and they play CDs all night, Riff's head bopping, Bob's foot tapping out the beat. He used to get stoned with Riff. It made a fairly easy job into a challenge. The control board turned into a cockpit, the *On Air* light a beacon, the music a message from the other side. But now pot makes him paranoid. He starts reconsidering everything. Why do men wear pants? What if his last relationship was his last relationship? What if there were no heaven and this life mattered? Now Riff smokes alone, and Bob relies on the roiling chemicals his own brain makes to keep up with him.

This fall has been hell for Bob. He can't seem to sleep. The neighborhood comes back to life in the fall, after the relative quiet of the summer. Students return to their dorms, scientists to their labs, the goddamn squirrels start fighting, designer dogs barking, school kids singing and laughing. And worse, the renovations begin anew. Contractors, plumbers, roofers, landscapers arrive in a convoy of earthmovers and pickup trucks. Bob prefers the winter, the days as tight and silent as the night, the ground frozen, the air forbidding, doors and windows shuttered against the cold. Although snow is a mixed bag for the daytime sleeper. At first it muffles everything, swaddles you in a lovely white cocoon, but then the snow blowers start and plows crash onto the asphalt and roaming bands of kids ring your bell and ask if you want them to shovel. Snow is almost worse than fall.

Bob has tried sleeping pills, ear plugs, a mouth guard, room darkeners, a white noise machine, a fan, an air conditioner, a contoured neck pillow, melatonin, kava kava, St. John's Wort, acupuncture, vodka, beer, wine, warm milk, and chamomile tea. Nothing works. He has asked the neighbors to keep their workers quiet. He has pleaded with the workers to have pity on a fellow working man. He has stayed up whole days to make himself tired. But something new is happening. Thirteen years on the overnight shift and he can no longer sleep.

Riff has no such problem. He and his wife live in the woods on their own ten acres and they sleep all day, stay up all night. Their house smells like mildew and is developing a mossy green tint. Vines grow over the windows; huge pine trees dwarf the front porch. The backyard has reverted to forest. Wisteria has wrapped itself around an entire patio set so that it is now green and impenetrable. On the weekends Riff will smoke a joint and go out in the yard in the late afternoon and think maybe he should hire someone to hack away at this jungle. Then the light will fade, and the place will morph into an enchanted fairytale of vines and primeval forest. Luckily they live in a rundown part of town. Their neighbors have cars up on blocks, boats that will never again float, motorcycles in pieces, and broken down refrigerators on their back lots. So they are not about to complain.

Riff glides into the control room a few minutes before air. "My man," he says. "How're things? You sleep?"

Bob shakes his head. "No. Today the city got into the act. They're re-bricking the sidewalks. Do you have any idea how loud a brick cutter is?"

Riff shrugs. "That's a drag, man."

"Who the fuck wanted new bricks anyway? Some stupid historical commission, I'm sure. Did I tell you, this woman rang my bell the other day at eleven a.m.? Complaining that my trim color was not historically correct. Eleven in the morning!"

"Should be against the law. I think it is against the law."

"And she had the nerve to give me the name of some historically correct painter, who will come over and do some founding fathers juju on the paint scheme. Probably cost a fortune. My neighbor Abigail's probably behind it. She left me another message this afternoon."

Riff is flipping through the CDs, pulling out Billie Holiday, Carmen McRae, Betty Carter. "You should sell that place, Bobby," he says. "Move out with me and the masses. Relax. That neighborhood is taking years off your life, man, and between you and me, you haven't got that many left."

"I was there first. Why should I have to move?"

"Cuz there's one of you and lots of them, and plenty more where they came from. Sell that place. You could buy a cool pad, doesn't have to be out in the boonies with me. Could be in the city, Roxbury. Black people wouldn't give you all that shit."

Riff hands the CDs to Bob, walks into the studio, sits down at the mic, puts on his headphones, and waits for Bob's cue.

"Thirty seconds," Bob says into the talkback.

"Plus those ugly women in your neck of the woods..."

Bob cuts his mic, holds up his hand to silence him, watches the digital clock trip from 11:59:59 to 12:00:00. He starts Riff's theme music and cues him in.

"Hey, Riff here, Oliver Nelson in the background, you're up, you're listening, we're cool. It's a nice night out there. Saw some deer on my ride in, heads down, grazing on the yellow line, felt like stopping my car and giving them a lecture, when will you boys learn about highways and automobiles, anyway the moon was pink, pink, that's cool, the sky was kind of charcoal gray, and I got to thinking what would it be like to be an animal, roaming around this messed up world that humans created, how are they supposed to know about yellow lines and why shouldn't they snap the heads off all your tulips? They were here first." He cuts his mic and motions for Bob to bring up the music. Then he speaks into the talkback. "You could make a lot of money on that old haunted house of yours, Bobby. You could live on a boat. You could buy yourself a penthouse. You could fucking retire."

"Yeah, yeah, yeah," Bob says into the talkback.

Riff cues him to lower the music. "Tonight we're going play some

Billie, and maybe some Ella, and whoever else you want to hear. If you feel like talking, give me a call. If you don't, that's cool. Me and Bob will just groove out for the whole evening."

Irene, the overnight newscaster, bounds into the control room and hands Bob a script. "Hey, Bob, you hear about Omar?"

Bob spins his chair around to face her. "No."

Irene leans against a tape deck, pushes a strand of dark hair off her face. "They caught him falsifying health insurance claims and fired him!"

"Omar? He seems like such a straightlaced guy."

"Yeah. Well. Some insurance company dumped them when his wife got sick. So he was exacting his revenge. Took them for thousands and thousands of dollars over the years."

"Really? Omar? But how'd they find out?"

"Kathy. Who else? Omar had lied about when she started here, so she could get covered sooner. Do you believe it? He did her a favor and the little bitch turned him in!"

"Doesn't make sense. Why would she do that? "

"Beats me. Phase one in her scheme for total world domination? I tell you, though. You should never, ever, trust a woman who wears makeup in the middle of the night."

Bob looks more closely at Irene. Is she wearing makeup? He doesn't think so, but what does he know? Her cheeks and lips are pale. Her eyes are large and dark, but so are the circles under them. "She'll be our boss some day," he says, and turns to load the cuts for Irene's newscast into the computer. Kathy is just like the people in his neighborhood, claiming the moral high ground as long as it keeps them on top and little fuckers like Omar on the bottom. "Her type always wins."

Kathy is the new morning drive newscaster, imported from Cincinnati or Cleveland, some place in the Midwest, which she flies back to every three weeks to get her hair cut. She and Bob had gotten into it her first day on the job. She wanted him to record a spot. "Get O'Mara," he said. "I'm off the clock."

"News doesn't follow a clock," she said.

"But I do. And I get time-and-a-half plus night shift differential."

She changed her tack, smiled at him, shook her carefully cut blonde hair. "Please? I don't understand all that union stuff. I'm under the gun. And I don't know O'Mara."

He'd stayed and recorded the spot, then edited and mixed it before leaving. The next day he was called into his boss Mitch's office. "What the fuck are you staying overtime for? No one okayed that."

"Kathy was supposed to."

"Well, she didn't. And she filed a complaint about your attitude, said you were uncooperative, and *slow*."

Oliver Nelson finishes. Riff hands off to Irene who starts her newscast. Riff gets up and wanders into the control room. "Something going on between you two?"

"What?"

"Irene likes you, man. I can feel the pheromones right through the glass."

"Me?"

"Who else is she going to go for, BJ?"

Bob shrugs. "We were talking about Omar. Did you hear they fired him?"

Riff smooths his goatee. "Bet Irene looks great without clothes on."

"There's nothing going on between us. Believe me."

Riff snorts. "You handsome guys are all the same. Never had to work hard to get women, so you never learned how to read them. But I did, and trust me, Irene likes you."

Bob looks at Irene, her hand poised over the control board, ready to trigger a flood of haranguing ads for excess stomach acid, muscle aches, white sales, and spreadable cheese. She catches him watching her and breaks into a shy smile. Bob smiles back. For the first time in days he feels like he could sleep.

CHAPTER 2

10:45 a.m. The workers are shouting in Spanish next door. Bob strains to make out what they are saying. Are they cursing him, his mother, and his offspring for all eternity? He had called the noise abatement unit of the mayor's office the day before to complain. A lot of good that did. Some brain-dead clerk told him, they have rights too, you know. Why don't you get a day job? As if it were that easy. They are so close it sounds like they are in his bedroom. Bob lurches to the window, raises his room-darkening shades. The new neighbors, Tom and Abigail Greenough, are digging a foundation. A three-story, twelve-room house isn't big enough for them. They need a conservatory.

The trench looks awfully close to his property line, wherever that is. He doubts his parents ever had a plot plan. He is wondering whether he should look upstairs in their bedroom closet for the deed — he thinks his mother kept it in a lingerie bag to fool thieves — when the front doorbell rings. Bob can feel the jarring notes at the pit of his stomach. He throws on a t-shirt and jeans, slides into flip-flops, and runs a hand through his hair to push it back off his face. A stubborn brown curl springs onto his forehead as he opens the door. Abigail Greenough herself is standing there with a friendly looking guy in a sweater vest, rimless glasses, and work boots. "Bob," she says and steps forward. "Bob, do you have a minute?"

Bob takes out his earplugs. "What?"

"I want you to meet our arborist, Johan."

Who the fuck has their own arborist?

Johan extends a large but well-manicured hand and they shake. Not a bad guy. He looks embarrassed to be there. Abigail smiles her winning smile, tilts her head of close-cropped auburn hair. Bob can tell she wants something; her body vibrates with energy. She is some kind of bigwig at Harvard, the type who walks around in a flowing cap and gown during graduation — which is a terrible time in Cambridge — parents and family and alums strolling six-deep down the brick sidewalks, clogging the narrow streets, taking up all the good parking spots. "Did you get my messages? Would this be a good time to talk about your trees?"

"Not really." Bob leans against the doorway, folds his arms in front of his chest. "I was asleep. You know, I work nights."

Abigail and Johan exchange a look. Movers and shakers do not work nights. "Oh, so sorry. But I dragged Johan all the way out here. He's actually the arborist for the Botanical Gardens." Abigail juts out her chin. "Could we show you something out back?"

Bob looks over his left shoulder into his living room. The couch beckons.

"It'll just take a minute."

"Oh, all right." Bob pulls on a jean jacket and follows them out to his backyard, which is overgrown, but not in an epic Riff way, just overgrown. It still looks like a back yard, but the grass seed never took, the ground is compacted and dry, and only a few heroic weeds show through the cracks. The mock orange bushes — his father's pride, though he had called them by some other Latin name — are gangly and misshapen, and some boring insect has had its way with their leaves. The brick patio his father painstakingly laid has sunk and is covered with leaves, and the roots from the old trees have heaved up the bricks in places so it looks like an earthquake has struck. Bob picks his way through the sticks and rotting leaves — I should have worn shoes instead of flip flops, he thinks — and feels a strange crunching underfoot. Peanut shells! The damn squirrel lady is at it again, feeding the little rodents so they can go forth and multiply in the eaves of his house.

Bob joins Johan and Abigail at the base of the largest tree. "Hmmm," Johan says, and looks up.

Abigail shades her eyes with a hand and follows his gaze upward. "Hmmm," she says.

Bob looks up at the tree, sees nothing out of the ordinary and then looks down at the profusion of peanut shells. "Hey, it's not my fault about the squirrels," he says. "It's Maureen, the whack job in the apartment back there." He points to the fence that separates his yard from the overpowering brick apartment complex behind him.

"We're not worried about the squirrels." Abigail smiles and the skin around her eyes crinkles. Even her crow's feet are attractive.

"Wait 'til they get into your attic."

Abigail looks to Johan, who smiles and enunciates slowly, as if hosting a public television program for children. "Well, if you trimmed the trees back, Bob, they wouldn't be able to get into your attic."

Bob rolls his eyes. They dragged him out of bed for this?

"What we're really concerned about," Johan smiles again, "are the trees themselves."

Abigail nods upwards. "They're Norway maples, an invasive species, and they are killing my trees."

"What?"

"They are what we call 'phytotoxic,'" Johan says. "They are actually poisonous to other plants."

"Oh, come on." Bob sways on his feet, feeling almost dizzy. He yearns for a cup of coffee, but if he has one now he will never get back to sleep.

"No, really. They're an urban blight," Johan says. "They grow like weeds. They leech all the moisture out of the soil. And they form such a dense shade cover that nothing can grow under them. Look at your own yard." He points. "That's because of your trees."

Bob looks at the hard-packed ground. "Really?"

"And you see Abigail's cryptomeria radicans over there? They're not going to make it. Because of your Norway maples."

Bob looks guiltily into Abigail's yard. The three evergreens near the fence do not look good. In fact, the one closest to his property looks dead already.

"Sorry about your trees, Abigail." He shakes his head, shrugs his shoulders. "But I don't know what you want me to do about it."

"Well." Abigail looks at Johan. "We're going to have to replace them."

Bob pats the back pocket of his jeans where he keeps his wallet and then folds his arms over his chest. "Yeah?"

"And, while we have the earthmovers in the back yard anyway, it would make sense, if you took your trees down at the same time." Abigail smiles and nods her head. "They might give you a discount."

"What?" Bob looks up at the trees, which dwarf his three-story house. "You want me to take down my trees?"

"And time is of the essence. We need to plant now before it gets too cold. Johan, you're free on Fridays, right?"

Johan takes out his date book. "This Friday?"

Bob shakes his head, rubs his eyes. "Look, I told you. I don't have time for this right now. I work for a living."

"Next Friday then?"

"That's actually better for me." Johan starts scribbling in his date book.

"Let me think about it." Bob turns to leave them.

"Love to get an answer by the weekend, Bob." Abigail lays a hand on his forearm. "I'll need to book the earthmovers."

"I'll think about it."

"Super." Abigail turns and trots down his driveway, Johan drafting in her wake.

Bob tries to remember what she does at Harvard. Something in the arts? Or was she some kind of dean? He feels around in his jacket pockets for his keys. Not there. Of course. Now he will have to climb through the narrow window over the sink. He has the presence of mind to wait for Abigail and Johan to disappear around corner of the house, before he attempts it, then drags a trash barrel out of the garage and places it under the window. He steps up onto the trash barrel, which buckles under his weight and threatens to topple, but catches himself on the splintery windowsill. He pushes the old black screen up and out of the way and checks on the window. Unlocked, thank God. He hoists his upper body onto the ledge and plunges headfirst into the kitchen sink. Not too bad for his forties.

Of course there are dirty dishes in the left side sink — he hadn't quite gotten around to them the day before — so he aims for the right side, but as he squeezes his long legs through the window, he pushes the cold water spigot to the *on* position and a jet of cold water sprays the front of his jeans. He pulls himself fully in, climbs out of the sink, turns off the spigot, and slams down the window. To hell with Abigail and her precious trees, he thinks, and grabs a dishtowel to blot himself dry.

CHAPTER 3

———◦———

Riff and Bob are standing in the kitchen at JZY. It's 5 a.m. and Riff is about to go home. Bob has three hours left on his shift. "Relax, man," Riff says. "They can't take away your trees. No matter what that bitch says." He stirs a packet of Swiss Miss with Mini Marshmallows into his coffee. "Presto, mochaccino!" He takes a sip. "Delicious."

"Yeah, but she can make my life miserable." Bob pours a packet of instant chicken noodle soup into his mug and fills it with hot water. He looks at the dehydrated specks of green floating at the top and wonders if parsley counts as a vegetable. After Abigail's visit, he couldn't get back to sleep so he searched the closet for the property deed, to no avail, though he did find a Little League trophy, his blue cub scout kerchief, and a light-up Infant of Prague.

Then he tried working on his "piece," about the new generation of jazz players, the Young Lions, who were supposedly reviving the form. Reviving it? Ha! They were killing it. He'd started it as a letter to the editor of *Downbeat*, but it quickly outgrew that forum and over the years it has morphed from a rant, to an article (published in *JazzIs*), to a treatise, to an unwieldy jazz manifesto. He works on it whenever he can't sleep, and now it is over three-hundred pages long.

Usually the concentrated effort tired him out, but this time it riled him up. Who anointed them the Young Lions anyway? A bunch of moldy old white jazz guys, casting about for something to say. Finally he had abandoned the piece and crawled back into bed around 9 p.m. and then overslept, and hadn't had time to make a lunch, so he's subsisting on soup, peanut butter crackers from the vending machine, and some string cheese he stole from the staff refrigerator.

Riff snaps a to-go lid onto his mochaccino. "Don't think about it too much. I find things always get better if I ignore them." He hefts a satchel full of CDs and music magazines over his shoulder.

"But she wants an answer by the weekend." Bob sits down at the stained Formica table and leans over and blows on his hot soup.

Riff puts a hand on his shoulder. "Now that's your mistake, Bobby. Letting people like her set the agenda."

Bob looks up at Riff. "Should I tell her I need more time?"

"No, fuck her. Tell her you're flying to Paris this weekend, for a date with Catherine Deneuve."

Bob laughs. *Catherine Deneuve.* Riff is so out of date, he makes Bob feel young.

"See you on Saturday?" Riff says.

"Yeah, what time?"

"Uh, we got to do it on the early side. Omar's coming too. Around ten?"

"Since when are you so friendly with Omar?"

"Hey, the enemy of my enemy is my friend."

"Is your enemy management or the insurance company?"

"Both."

Bob takes a sip of his soup. He used to love this kind of soup when he was young, thought it was the best tasting stuff he had ever eaten. His mother had been a meat and potatoes, mid-century American cook, with a twist. She couldn't eat seafood or dairy. So on top of the well-done meat and canned vegetables, they'd had dry potatoes and butterless white bread. Instant chicken noodle soup with its powdered garlic, autolyzed yeast extract, and dehydrated chicken fat globules had seemed like haute cuisine. Now it tastes gritty and MSG laden to him, and insubstantial. He thinks he will raid the fridge for the last of the string cheese.

Riff begins to say something else, but he is drowned out by the intercom. "Bob Boland to Studio 3. Bob Boland to Studio 3."

Bob looks at his watch, shakes his head. "I've still got ten minutes on my lunch."

"The lovely Katherine awaits thee." Riff heads for the door. "Good luck."

Bob grabs the last of the string cheese and stuffs it in his mouth as he walks to Studio 3. Kathy is standing at the door. "We have a lot to do today." She snaps her fingers. "Let's get to work."

Bobs walks slowly across the studio. He adjusts the lights over the control board and then switches out the chair for a more comfortable one. He lowers it until his arms just rest on the control board. He turns on the computer and then gets up and walks over to the thermostat. "Is it hot in here or is it me?" Kathy exhales loudly, bites her lip and pulls up a chair close to the computer. She crosses her leg and swings her foot up and down. Stockings, at five in the morning. Nice legs but the jittering foot is disturbing. "I had ten minutes left on my lunch break," he says.

"Oh, Christ," she says. "I wish I could just edit this myself."

"Well, you can't," Bob says.

"Yeah, well, Larry is breathing down my neck to get it on the air." She hands him a mini disc player. "Go to seven minutes in and dump the whole thing into the computer. And there's a minute of room tone at the end. Don't forget the room tone, like you did last time."

"What do you want to call it?"

"'Japanese Maple,'" she says and jumps up out of her seat. "Back in five."

Bob doesn't usually listen as he dumps audio into the computer. "Don't fill your head with that nonsense," an old timer had counseled when he first started. "You'll run out of space." Now it's second nature to him to pay no attention to content. He's about two minutes in, though, when something draws his attention. They're talking about his neighborhood in Cambridge, his street. Something about a tree? Could it be his tree? Is the whole neighborhood against him? He hears a woman's voice, a rising note of hysteria. "I look at that tree every morning as I drink my coffee." A male voice. "We'll fight this with everything we got."

Kathy plunks down on the seat beside him. "Someone ate all my cheese. I can't believe it. I'm on the Zone and that's the only protein I can eat this week."

Why the hell is she on a diet? Probably trying out for TV, where, in fact, she belongs — she's good looking and would mow down her own grandmother for a scoop. Bob exhales into his shirt to see if his breath smells of cheese. It smells of lack of sleep, gingivitis, and institutional coffee, but not necessarily of cheese. "So they're trying to save some tree?" he asks.

"Yeah, they sold this old house with a big tree on the lot and the developer wants to take it down and put in condos. The neighbors went ballistic. But what's cool is, it's Cambridge. So they've got a global warming expert, a judge, and two Nobel Prize winners who've signed the petition to save it."

"Really?" Bob smiles for the first time that day. "Do you have a contact for them?"

"Why do you want it?"

"I live in that neighborhood."

"You do?" Kathy looks him up and down. "Funny, I wouldn't have pictured you there."

"No, you wouldn't," he says. "I was grandfathered in." He changes the file name to "Save My Maples" and pulls his chair closer to the screen.

He calls the number Kathy gave him when he gets home that morning. "Is Leonie Marshall there?"

"Speaking. Can I help you?" Her voice is cultured, wary.

He tells her he's a neighbor, would love to sign the petition.

"Oh." Her voice changes. "Great. I thought you might be with the developer or the press. They're driving me crazy! Where do you live?"

Bob gives his address.

"The red house?"

"Yeah, the red house."

She lives one street over, but their backyards sort of touch.

"I know your house," he says. "You painted it purple."

"Periwinkle," Leonie says. "But I know, it's too San Francisco for this neighborhood. My next door neighbors hate it."

"I like it." Bob only noticed the new color because he tried to bribe the painting crew with a six-pack to keep their radio down.

"I'm on my way out to teach a class. I can drop the petition off for you to sign, or you can come over here later this afternoon."

"Well, actually, I was hoping to get more involved than that," Bob says. "Do you have some literature?"

"No, but we're meeting Saturday afternoon. At Mabel's."

"Mabel?"

"I thought everyone in the neighborhood knew Mabel. She's such a character. She's a brilliant astrophysicist, and one of the first female Morris Dancers!"

Bob cracks his neck. Everyone in Cambridge is brilliant. And they've got plenty of spare time for asinine hobbies. He takes down Mabel's address and tacks it to the refrigerator with a heating oil company magnet. Then he pulls down the shades, unplugs the phone, puts in his earplugs, and tries to sleep.

§

The meeting is at 3 p.m., early for Bob, but he sets his alarm, drinks two cups of coffee, and arrives at Mabel's sprawling Victorian right on time. "Come in! Come in!" Mabel says. She's a wholesome looking woman, with curly brown hair hanging in a long braid down her back. She shakes his hand with a firm, muscular grasp. Bob can imagine her hefting a Maypole over her shoulder and strapping Morris Bells to her ankles. "How fun to meet one's neighbors," she says. "I've seen you before, shoveling your walk!" Bob nods. He likes to shovel. When he started as an engineer there was more physical activity involved. He rarely sat. He jumped from tape deck to control board, edited tape with a grease pencil and a razor blade, cued up records with one hand and stretched to slide the faders with the other, bounded down the hallways with a last minute spot and slapped it on a tape machine for air. Now everything is digital. He edits on a computer screen, saves to a hard drive, and rests his wrist on a gel cushion to prevent carpal tunnel syndrome. For the first time in his life, he worries he'll get his father's stomach.

Mabel leads him into her living room, where a few people from the neighborhood are gathered. He looks for Abigail, but luckily, she's not there. A wormy looking bald guy, whom Bob has seen hitting on women at the grocery store, is shoving a brie-loaded cracker into his mouth. "Arthur," he says through the brie and holds up his other hand to wave. The guy on the couch with the bushy gray hair looks familiar too, but not from the neighborhood. From television, Bob thinks. A poet? A filmmaker? He thinks he saw those sad, raccoon eyes on "Charlie Rose."

"Everyone," Mabel says. "This is Bob Boland. He wants to join our little band of eco warriors." She pours herself a glass of white wine and holds it aloft. "To the ramparts!"

Bob pours himself a glass of seltzer and sits down next to the sad looking guy, who shrinks back into himself and manages a weak smile. "Richard," he says. "Nice to meet you." He folds his hands in his lap and looks down at them.

A few other familiar people from the neighborhood show up. The rabbity woman from the antique house behind the apartment complex sticks her head into the living room and blinks, then retreats to the hallway. A tall woman with flowing brown hair and a deranged-looking smile, whom Bob has seen picking through his garbage, takes the seat next to Arthur and leans close to hear what he is saying. A short little guy with a compact body, dressed in jeans and a Yale sweatshirt, whom someone refers to as "The Judge," inches toward the center of the room.

The doorbell rings again. "Leonie!" Mabel opens the door. Bob has noticed Leonie before, hurrying down the street when he is heading to work. She is tall, thin, and straight-backed, dressed in an oversized sweater that covers her wrists; her short dark hair is pulled off her face. Her very pretty face. She smiles into the room. "Have you seen the Metro section? Page 1!" She holds up the paper. A picture of a spreading purple tree above the fold, under it the headline: *The People's Republic of Trees.*

Everyone cheers.

"Bravo! Bravo!" the wormy guy shouts.

Leonie puts the paper on the coffee table and scans the room for a seat. She sits down cross-legged on the floor, in front of Bob, folding her long legs under her. One easy motion. She must do yoga or something. She grabs a cracker from the plate on the table and spreads it with brie. "Richard!" she says to the guy next to Bob. "So nice to see you here." She offers him the brie, but he holds up a veiny hand to ward it off. She takes a bite of the cracker, licks her lips, turns to Bob, extends her hand, every movement measured, elegant. "I don't think we've met," she says. "I'm Leonie."

Bob puts out his hand. "Bob, from the red house?"

"Oh, Bob, I'm so glad you made it."

Mabel taps the side of her wineglass three times. "All right, people, shall we get started?"

Leonie smiles and nods her head and mouths, "Later."

The little guy in the sweatshirt starts to speak. "Okay, as far as I can tell, we don't have a legal leg to stand on."

Everyone groans. Bob sits up, wishes he has brought a pen and paper. He leans over and touches Leonie's shoulder. "Anyone taking notes?"

She takes a notebook and a pen out of her purse and hands it to him. Their hands touch briefly.

"The tree is completely on his property. It's in the back of the house; it's not a street tree. He has every right to cut it down. But that doesn't mean we're not going to fight."

"Hear! Hear!" Mabel puts two fingers in her mouth and whistles.

Bob writes down, *private property, not a street tree.*

"What we've got going for us is the rareness of this particular tree. There are reports that it's the oldest living Japanese maple in captivity."

Appreciative laughter.

"And it's growing right here in our neighborhood. So we make the argument that it is historically significant. It can never be replaced. The whole community stands to lose if they cut it down. We have a civic duty to preserve it."

Bob looks at Leonie. She nods her head in agreement. Her eyes are shining, her lips slightly parted.

The Judge finishes up. "Now I think my eminent colleague from the Ethnobotany Department, Staunton Chase here, can speak to the specific botanical issues."

Staunton Chase stands up. He is a small man, with a neatly trimmed gray beard, and tortoise shell glasses. He's wearing a brownish corduroy jacket with leather elbow patches and a sweater vest. He clears his throat as he approaches the center of the room. "Not only may it be the oldest living Japanese maple in this part of the world," he says. He has the kind of deep, confident voice, that could command a lecture hall of sleepy students. "But I believe it may have been the first Japanese maple taken out of Japan, when it opened up to the rest of the world in the 1850s." He looks around the room to let this fact settle in. "Just think of it. When Japan opened up to the West. Think of the effect that had on art, literature, design, religion, history. This tree is a living embodiment of a cultural moment, of a huge shift in geopolitical forces. This tree harkens back to a time of emperors, naval fleets, East meets West. And it's still here. It's still here!"

Staunton pauses for a moment, removes his glasses, and cleans them on his vest. "Now," he continues. "It may have only survived due to benign neglect." A few people in the room chuckle. "But we are older and wiser now, and we can't let it be mowed down to put in underground parking! This is not a decision to be left to the marketplace. This is a moral imperative. Like the monks in Ireland who saved the manuscripts, and let's face it, Western civilization, from the barbarian hordes, we must band together to save this tree!"

Another cheer. Mabel stomps her feet. The Judge yells out, "Go Staunton!"

Wow, Bob thinks. Western civilization. These people have an elevated sense of their place in history.

Professor Chase goes into detail about the species and the available techniques to determine the tree's exact age, and Bob drifts off. Couldn't you just chop it down and count the rings? Of course there must be a more high tech way to determine that, without chopping it down. It is 1997 after all. He looks around the room. Nice oriental rugs, a dark polished sculpture that looks like a donkey with a hard on, a music stand covered in sheet music. Staunton is now speculating about who planted it — that's easy, Bob thinks, some Harvard professor, back from sabbatical in Japan — these people are always on sabbatical. And they get summers off so they can flock to the Vineyard or Woods Hole or Europe, while Bob sweats it out with his K-Mart air conditioner, accumulating his 1.33 vacation days a month. He is feeling sort of sleepy so he straightens himself up. Staunton is winding down. "... This spectacular specimen is a piece of our heritage, a living link to the past."

That's good. Bob writes down, *A living link to the past*. He tries to remember who planted his maple trees. He never paid much attention to that kind of stuff when he was growing up, and neither parent is around to ask. They weren't interested in preserving their heritage — his mother's father was a drunk, skidding in and out of work, drinking up the rent money. His father's parents ran a grocery store, which is how they could afford the house. They bought it when his father was still a teenager and gave it to him when he got married. By then they had moved to a ranch house in Belmont — two and a half baths, everything on one floor, a deep freeze in the garage.

Staunton hands off to Leonie, who stands up and moves to the center of the room. "So, we've already gotten on the radio and in the paper. And I think the six o'clock news is ready to bite. The other two things we need to do are leaflet the neighborhood and meet with the Zoning Board. Anyone available to go to City Hall during the day?"

Hands go up all across the room. Fucking academics. Everyone is available. Of course so is Bob. And his cousin Mary Elizabeth works at the Zoning Board. He raises his hand.

Leonie looks around the room and picks him. "You want to go to the City Hall or leaflet?"

"Both." He'll run his phytotoxic trees by Mary Elizabeth while he's at it.

"Perfect!" Leonie says. "And I can help you leaflet. We want to plaster the neighborhood. Tomorrow work for you?"

They agree to meet at four at Bob's house. Leonie will supply the leaflets.

Bob slips out of the meeting while they are discussing a letter-writing campaign and a possible bake sale. Damn, he thinks, as he walks the short block home, what'd I just get myself into? City Hall? Leafleting? And two early days in a row. He'll pay for it next week at work. But he can't wait to impale a "Save the Tree" flyer on Abigail Greenough's antique wrought iron gate.

CHAPTER 4

It's surprisingly warm on Saturday night, so after dinner they sit outside on Riff and Sue's screened-in porch. Sue has flung white lights around the back yard, looping them over the wisteria-covered patio set, the grill, the lawnmower, and the clothesline. In the dark, you can almost imagine it's some kind of illuminated topiary. Bob leans back in his chair and sighs. "It's so quiet out here," he says, stomach full, beer buzz holding. "So peaceful." Riff's black and white cat curls around his feet.

"And warm," Sue says. "So far I am really enjoying global warming." She and Riff are nestled on a wicker loveseat that is really not big enough for two people. Sue has her bare feet tucked under her; she's dressed in a long hippie skirt, could be 1970 as far as she is concerned. Was she even born in 1970?

"Me too," Irene says. "In fact, I'm thinking of buying land in Nova Scotia. I predict it's going to be the next Miami Beach."

"Nova Scotia?" Riff shakes his head. "Too Anglo." He fishes a joint out of his breast pocket, lights it and passes it to Bob, who is about to say no, but then he thinks, what the hell, I'm among friends. I can always crash on the couch. He takes a puff, holds it in for a short time and exhales.

"So did I tell you what I did today?" Bob passes the joint to Omar who shakes his head and passes it on to Irene.

"You sleep?" Riff asks.

"No, I infiltrated enemy camp. I went to a neighborhood meeting, about saving a tree."

"Fuck, Bobby, you still worrying about your tree?"

"Trees," Bob says. "Trees. She wants to take down *all* of them."

"Oh fuck your trees. You could pitch a tent here in my back yard and have all the trees you want."

"Not in the city. They're like gold in the city."

Irene takes a hit off the joint and holds up her hand. She has something to say but she has to wait until the smoke has infiltrated her lungs. "Bob, I hate to break this to you," she finally gasps out. "But your trees are basically weeds."

"Traitor! That's what they say!"

"And they're right. Norway maples are weeds."

"If you buy into that distinction." Riff gestures to the dark woods behind them. "I don't. And neither does Mother Nature."

"Mother Nature would have wolves roaming your back yard," Irene says.

"You wouldn't believe my neighborhood," Bob says. "They had the head of the ethnobotany department at Harvard there."

"Aren't those the guys who discovered psilocybin?" Riff asks.

"No, no," Omar says, "they find plant-based drugs to cure cancer." He is wearing khakis, a sweater, and slip-on leather shoes, polished. Funny to see him without a tie. That had been one of Bob's enduring life goals. Not to wear a tie. Look where that got him: pushing buttons in the middle of the night, taking orders from the likes of Kathy. The joint has come back around and he is stoned enough to want more. He takes a long hit and passes it to Omar again, without thinking.

"Sorry, but I can't smoke." Omar shakes his head. "Not in my present frame of mind. I mean, I'm being investigated by the insurance company. They're threatening to press charges. I've got no job. And I don't have a reference."

"I'll give you a reference," Riff says. "A great one."

Irene exhales a long plume of smoke and coughs. "Me, too."

"Ditto," Bob says, his voice sounding surprisingly high to his own ears.

"Thanks, but references from coworkers only go so far. They know you're hiding something."

"So, Omar." Sue sits up and shakes her head as if to clear it out. "I don't really get it," she asks. "You fudged some kind of coverage dates?"

Omar draws himself up. "Oh, no, Sue. Much more than coverage dates. I double, triple, sometimes quadruple billed them — for the exact same procedure, or visit. I always stayed within the benefit structure though. I didn't want to raise any red flags. I would have never gotten caught, if it weren't for Kathy."

Omar seems almost proud of his accomplishment. Bob rubs his temples; his brain feels bruised. He wishes he could reach right inside and massage the soft gray matter, but all he can do is rub the bony cage around it. "But why would Kathy turn you in?" he asks.

"That's easy. To make herself look good," Irene says. "What I don't get is why you would ever do her a favor."

Omar rolls his eyes and looks down at his hands. "She reminded me of my wife."

"Oh." Irene takes a sip of her red wine, glances sideways at Bob.

"She reminded me of my ex, too," Riff says. "So I knew she'd be a conniving bitch!"

Everyone laughs. Bob leans back in his chair and surveys the room. Riff has a stain on the front of his jumpsuit. Sue is running her fingers up and down his arm. Oscar Peterson is playing in the background. Irene's red top shows off her breasts. And her hair looks shiny and long. Did she do something with it? This is probably a setup, Riff's way of getting them together. But what about Omar? Maybe he's supposed to be with Irene. Surely it's been long enough since his wife died. Imagine being attracted to Kathy — even Bob isn't that fucked up. Now, he could go for Leonie. He's always liked tall, dark women. And yes, that WASPy face. Nice bones. Like a real estate ad for a fixer upper. But would she ever go for him? Riff thought him handsome, and his mother said his eyelashes were wasted on a man, but he was a union guy, at the top of the scale to be sure, cost of living increases every year, the occasional overtime bonanza, but no big windfalls in his future. Of course he could sell the house, but where would he go? Someplace like this, out in the middle of nowhere. Miles from a quart of milk.

"I guess your boss won't give you a recommendation?" Sue asks.

"Are you kidding?" Omar says. "He fired me! And he's on his way out anyway. He already gave notice."

"Wonder who they'll get to replace him?" Irene asks.

Bob's eyes feel scratchy; his throat is vaguely sore. He feels like he is about to come down with something, with everything. He lets his eyelids flutter closed.

"Hey, Bob," Irene taps his shoulder. "You okay over there?"

"Oh yeah." He shakes his head. It's been a long time since he's smoked pot. "But I think I might just lie down for a minute." He gets up and walks into the house, toward Riff's cavelike living room.

Irene follows him. "You sure?"

"Just tired," he says. "My neighborhood's a construction zone, and I was up early today." He sinks down onto the soft leather couch. He wonders if someone like Leonie smokes pot. Probably not. She seems too healthy. Some kind of dancer or something. Maybe a yoga teacher. Nah, a yoga teacher couldn't afford that house. Unless she's married to some Wall Street guy, who makes money reproduce in their bank account. But he doesn't remember a ring. Surely he would have noticed a ring. Irene turns on the lamp next to the couch, sits down beside him. He can smell her shampoo, something familiar and flowery. He can feel the warmth of her thigh through his jeans. He puts his head back. He feels sleep is close. Something in his body has released, and he's not quite there yet, but he knows it will come and he can stop worrying and let his mind drift over the day. Mabel. The botanist. The bandy legged judge. Imagine doing all this for some fucking tree. He feels a hand running up and down his thigh. "Jesus!" He bolts upright.

Irene pulls her hand away as if from a hot stove. "Sorry," she says. "Sorry." She jumps up off the couch. "I better go." She rushes out of the room.

Bob gets up and follows her to the hallway, touches her arm. "No. Don't go, Irene. I was just dozing off, and you startled me." He leads her back into the living room. "Sit down. Here." He pats the couch.

"No, I better go. I'm pulling an early shift tomorrow." Her face looks so pained, so embarrassed, that Bob can't stop himself. He leans over and kisses her on the lips, softly. "No, stay." They fall back into the couch, and he is no longer tired and his hand moves to her breast and he kisses her again, and the thought of Monday at work crosses his mind, but he banishes it, lets himself fall into this other place, not sleep, but much better.

CHAPTER 5

Leonie rings Bob's doorbell at four sharp. She's wearing dark tights, clogs, a short skirt, a scarf around her neck, and a suede jacket. Bob feels underdressed in his green t-shirt and jeans, though he picked them out carefully; they are his best fitting jeans and his most comfortable t-shirt. Leonie's hair is pulled up and back, but strands of it are falling down around her face. She's got a stack of neon orange flyers in her arms. "Come in," he says, and leads her into the living room, his mother's room. He has never changed the furniture: the Ethan Allen couch, the leather-top coffee table, the thick brocade draperies with the sheer curtains beneath, the fussy lamps.

Leonie takes it all in, looks at Bob for a moment and then up at the ceiling. "Wow," she says, "high ceilings! What are they? Ten feet, twelve feet?" She puts the flyers down on the mahogany table his Aunt Claire had given his parents as a wedding present.

Bob shrugs. "I don't know." Tall ceilings are all he has ever known. Even the tiny apartment he rented in Somerville had high ceilings. When he goes to other people's houses he can't imagine how they live like that. Bent over, cramped.

"Could I get you something to drink? Water? Coffee?" He gestures vaguely to the kitchen.

"Oh no, too late for coffee. I'd never get to sleep tonight. And I teach tomorrow morning."

"So, what do you teach?" Bob sits down on the couch. The springs are shot, and he sinks down too low.

Leonie sits in his father's reading chair. Bob winces as she leans back into the stain left by his father's hair cream; there's still a jar of it in the medicine cabinet. He makes a vow to clean all that out next weekend. What has he been waiting for? "I teach dance to Harvard kids who will never be dancers."

"Why? Not good enough?"

"Oh no. Harvard kids are good at everything they do. But they don't become dancers. They become Supreme Court Justices who appreciate dance." She uses her whole body when she talks. Her long neck sways.

"And you? Where'd you learn to dance?"

"Barnard," she says.

She must be good. You don't teach dance at Harvard if you're not good. Then again, what does he really know? He has lived among Harvard people his whole life, shoveled their walks, delivered groceries for their Christmas parties, even once attended a pot luck block party, but this is really his first incursion into their world. Maybe Harvard was like the media. You imagine these golden beings on the inside, then you finally break through to find some undeserving slob like BJ, or worse Kathy, unremarkable in every way except her oversized ambition.

"And you? Have you lived here all your life?"

Trick question. *Yes* and you're a townie. *Yes, but*, and you're ashamed of being a townie. "Most of it," he says. "I went away to New York, then I came back."

Leonie nods. "Nice place to come back to." She looks around the room. "What a beautiful house." Once again he is saved by real estate.

Leonie opens a large suede shoulder bag with a mouth like a boa constrictor and takes out a map on which she has drawn a vaguely rectangular shape in highlighter. "I thought we would start here at your house, then work our way to the Quad, but we'll skip the married student housing. They're all on the way somewhere else."

Bob watches her long thin fingers trace the area on the map. Her skin is darker than his; she might even get a tan. No wedding ring, just two oversized silver rings. She's got a large silver bracelet on her thin wrist. She is a beautiful woman. Does she know that? Leonie looks from Bob to her wrist and back again. He sees something register with her. She watches him watching her and neither of them looks away.

The phone rings. She looks around the room to find the sound. Damn phone. Bob gets up and walks to the hallway to his grandmother's old phone table and chair. Imagine, separate furniture for talking on the phone. How did it happen that things from his own lifetime are now curiosities? He suspects it is Irene. Of course it is Irene. He has almost forgotten. They kissed for a long time on the couch and who knows where it would have ended, but Sue came looking for him. "Bob, Bob, are you okay?" she had called, and they pulled apart. He knows he should answer the phone, by all the laws of sex and kindness and mutual respect, but not now, not with Leonie here. He lets the call go to voice mail.

Leonie has gotten up from the chair, gathered her stuff and the stack of neon colored flyers. "Shall we do this then?" she asks. He grabs his jean jacket and the industrial stapler he recovered from his father's junk drawer and ushers her out the front door.

Bob is stapling a flyer to the large ash tree that blocks the end of his driveway when Leonie lays a hand on his arm. "Uh, Bob, not sure we should be stapling flyers to trees. I mean we're pro tree, right?"

"Oh, right, of course," Bob slaps himself on the forehead. "What was I thinking?"

"I brought tape." Leonie fishes a roll of bright pink masking tape out of her bag and hands it to him. "Maybe there'll be some bulletin boards you can use your stapler on at the Quad."

"Fine." He wraps the flyer and the tape around a nearby utility pole and stands back to look at his handiwork. *Save Our Tree!* is lettered in large black print.

"You know, Mabel wanted to include that Joyce Kilmer poem. *I think that I shall never see a poem lovely as a tree.*"

"Really?" Is this a bad thing, Bob wonders, or a good one?

"These science types are so literal." Leonie laughs.

Bob walks down his neighbor Bryce's walk and slips a flyer into his already stuffed mailbox. Must be out of town, on another book tour.

"You know Bryce?" he asks Leonie. "The big Buddhist?"

"Not personally. But I know of him, of course. In fact I use one of his meditation tapes." She pauses. "It really helped when I was going through my divorce." Her face colors.

Bob squints at Bryce's putty-colored Victorian. Good news! She's divorced. Though he's not sure about her taste. If he were going to buy a meditation tape, he'd buy one from someone who seemed happier than Bryce.

They pause in front of McMahon's house, the only derelict house left on the block. "All yours," Leonie says. "This place scares me."

Bob walks up the steps to the lopsided porch. There's no mailbox, or mail slot, so he leans over and slips a flyer under the louvered door. He can hear a dog barking in the rear of the house. The porch obscures two large bow front windows surrounding a carved wooden door. Bob remembers the windows from when Mrs. McMahon was still alive, before McMahon and his sons slapped on the porch and paved over the entire yard to park their dump trucks.

"I don't know why I bothered," Bob says when he returns to the sidewalk. "Old McMahon would just as soon chop down a tree as save it."

"I can tell. His place is such an eyesore." Leonie looks at the porch and shakes her head.

"Well, he's not really such a bad guy," Bob says. It's okay for him to criticize McMahon, but not some Harvard person. "He let the house go after his wife died." He remembers McMahon at his father's and then his mother's wakes. They went one right after the other. Both from cancer, like McMahon's wife. Was it something in the water, the air, the ground beneath their feet? Bob had returned within a year to the horrible front parlor of Hanify's Funeral Home, across from the church and his old grammar school. McMahon had dragged his ungainly figure up the stairs and come straight for Bob. "You're all alone now, Bobby. Better get married. Life's no good alone. No good at all."

Leonie hands him another stack of flyers, and they continue walking. "So, do you know everyone in the neighborhood?"

"Not everyone." Bob nods towards the next house, a large brown-shingled mansion with an intimidating high stockade fence. Leonie bends down to slip a flyer under the latched gate. "Now these people are old-style Cambridge," Bob says. "They don't want to know you, and you don't want to know them. They'd build a moat around their house if it were practical."

Leonie laughs. "You're funny," she says. "I like funny men."

A warm glow spreads over Bob's chest. He smiles. She smiles back. "Let's cross the street," she says. "See if we can get a glimpse of the Japanese maple." She grabs his hand and pulls him across the street.

There is a huge old tree in front of the house with roots so large that they have heaved up bits of the brick sidewalk. "This it?" Bob asks.

Leonie looks at him strangely and lets go of his hand. "Weren't you listening at the meeting? It's a Japanese maple, in back of the house."

"Oh right." He cranes his neck to get a look around the old Victorian, but all he can see is another high stockade fence and some overgrown evergreens. "Maybe I could lift you up and you could see over the fence?"

"You sure?"

Bob shrugs. "Of course."

They walk to the side of the house, and Bob kneels down and makes a step with his hands. Leonie puts her bag down and steps onto his hands, and he lifts her up. She is not as light as she looks, but her balance, even on his two shaking hands is perfect. "Can you see it?" he asks, straining under her weight.

"It's beautiful! Absolutely perfect. I can't believe anyone would want to cut it down."

Bob lowers her to ground, and she rests her hand on his shoulder. He has the urge to kiss her but hesitates, and she pulls away. "You really should see it," she says. "But I don't think I could lift you up."

"I'll take your word for it."

Bob takes her hand again and pulls her across the street to the Quad where he finds some large bulletin boards, and Leonie finds some environmentally minded students who agree to wallpaper their dorms with flyers.

"There," Leonie says after she has handed her last flyers to the students. "I feel like we've earned ourselves a cup of coffee."

Bob looks around Starbucks. Each year a new crop of fresh-faced overachievers arrives in Cambridge. They seem to be getting taller, broader; at the counter he had stood behind a tall, well-built Indian kid, must have been 6'6", a specimen of breeding and feeding, with wide swimmer's shoulders and a loping athletic walk. At 6 feet, Bob had towered over his parents. But soon he will be dwarfed by this young super race. This Starbucks feels more like a Harvard student lounge than a coffee shop; wires snake from laptops to wall outlets. The kids type soundlessly, fingers flying over their keyboards in some new way — not how Bob learned to type, banging away at his typewriter, hitting the return carriage with a triumphant resounding "thwap!" A bottle of Wite-Out at his side. Not that he ever got really good at typing. He's a two-finger guy, though he has improved during these last years at work.

Leonie is at the counter getting honey for her Awake tea. She turns to smile at him. She has gorgeous white teeth, pink gums. Bob has kept the area dentists busy keeping his teeth. He knows them all: the orthodontist, the endodontist, the periodontist, the oral surgeon. He has bounced from one office to another, referral in hand. He doesn't want to lose his teeth like his parents' generation did, in their forties, his age!

Leonie walks to the table, takes a seat, unwinds her scarf, blows on her hot tea, which is now pale with milk. She takes a sip. "Well, that went a lot quicker than I thought," she says. "I pictured us debating the tree issue with everyone on the street. And no one even said, 'Hi.'"

She shrugs off her jacket. Bob would like to reach over, help her, but he keeps his hands to himself, one on the slightly sticky table, the other wrapped around his warm coffee mug. "Hey, this is Cambridge," he says. "You don't want to be the first one to say 'Hi.' You could be left standing there with your mouth open."

Leonie laughs and takes a sip of her tea. "God, it's all so exhausting. In California, you just say 'Hi, have a nice day,' and get on with your life."

"Sounds nice. What part of California are you from?"

"Marin County, north of San Francisco."

Bob had visited San Francisco in mid winter, expecting California sunshine, the Beach Boys, surfboards, flip-flops. It rained the whole time. He remembers running from a bookstore to a dark, brocaded bar, huddling under the awning of a tattoo parlor, the Day-Glo Victorians garish against the gloomy gray skies.

"My Dad taught at a small college in Marin."

"So, you're part of the intelligentsia."

"I wouldn't say that. He taught statistics."

"Still. And what's your background?"

"I'm a dancer. I studied at Barnard."

"No. What nationality are you?"

"Oh." She shrugs her shoulders. "Uh, American?"

"No, like what ethnicity are you?"

"I don't know. English, Irish, German? I'm not really sure. I think there's some Native American in there too."

"You don't know?"

"No, it's not a big deal in California. I'm white. Anglo. My family has been there for generations. So what are you?"

"Irish. Of course. Boland's an Irish name. Lots of Irish people settled in Cambridge, though believe me, they weren't welcomed."

"I don't get the East Coast. I mean, that's ancient history. Who cares about all these old prejudices?"

"Oh, a lot of people still do," Bob says. "Believe me."

Leonie takes a cellophane-wrapped packet of chocolate covered graham crackers out of her pocket. "I almost forgot," she says. "I bought us some cookies." She unwraps the cookies and offers one to Bob. He feels like he is in some complicated dance. He could watch her move forever.

He takes one and bites into it. "Mmm, these are good."

"Yeah, aren't they? I hate giving Starbucks any more money, though."

"Oh everybody complains about Starbucks. But you know what was here before they came? Nothing. Absolutely nothing. You couldn't get a decent cup of coffee in this town."

"Funny, I would have thought you, of all people, would hate Starbucks."

"No, I was glad they showed up." He wonders what she means, *You, of all people.*

Leonie looks down at the Graham crackers. "Want the last one?" She pushes it toward him.

"Nah, we'll share." Bob breaks it in two and puts the smaller half in his mouth.

Leonie takes a piece of the larger half.

"Funny, you don't sound like you're from Boston. How come?"

"I got rid of my accent." He shrugs to make it seem easy, though of course it hadn't been. He leans in over the table. "I can tell you the exact moment when I decided to lose it. I was singing in the high school choir, actually I was listening to the rest of the class singing, and they were dropping all their 'R's, and suddenly it just sounded stupid to me. I thought, there's a goddamned 'R' in there. Pronounce it!"

Leonie is leaning in, too. He can tell she likes him. But she needs to make him into an acceptable love interest, a townie with a brain. He will help her. "So I practiced at home. I stood in front of the mirror and pronounced my 'R's. *Forty four. On the corner. Tomorrow morning.* My mother said I sounded like a snob. The other kids made fun of me. But I didn't care. I didn't want to sound like them." Now he slips in and out of the accent, most times on purpose — when he's trying to get the DPW to pick up a couch or talk his way out of a parking ticket — but sometimes by accident. A middle 'R' will ambush him. He'll say ent*uh*tainer or insp*uh*ration. Or he'll add an extra 'R,' pizzer instead of pizza. He avoids the word parka all together, a total mindfuck for a Bostonian to pronounce. Almost as bad as khaki.

Leonie is playing with the cellophane wrapper, rolling and unrolling it like you would cigarette papers. "So, you don't really fit in here, do you?"

Bob thinks for a minute. He finishes the dregs of his coffee. "I used to," he says, though he is not sure that was ever true. "And you, do you fit in here?"

"Yes and no," she says. "I like my job. And I love my old house and the brick sidewalks and the architecture. But it's all too Puritanical. I'm from California, and deep inside I don't believe life has to be this hard."

Bob laughs. He leans in and rests his chin on his fist. Usually he would side with the Puritans in this debate. And with his inborn Irish melancholy and drummed-in Catholic guilt, he might do them one better in the gloom-and-doom department. But at this moment, life doesn't seem that hard at all. It seems easy and flowing, and he pictures the California sunshine again, the Beach Boys, surfboards, flip-flops, and a dark-haired woman with perfect white teeth.

CHAPTER 6

Bob is pacing back and forth in the windowless staff lounge. "It's a goddamn feast or famine," he says. "I mean, years I've been wandering in the desert and now two women. Two women! Can you believe it?"

"The light must be hitting you right." Riff takes off his jacket and hangs it on the coat rack. He sinks down onto an old orange couch.

"I mean I like Irene a lot, but this woman Leonie. She is so..."

"Out of your league."

"You think so?"

"I know so."

"You never met her."

"I know her type." Riff pulls his shoulder bag up onto the couch, extracts a thermos, unscrews it, pours some hot coffee into the lid and takes a swig. "She's slumming, Bobby. Or she could be crazy. Lot of these smart women are totally fucking bonkers."

"She's not crazy." Bob walks across the hall to the control room door and peers in, checks the clock. BJ is cleaning his fingernails with his Swiss Army knife. Not the first time Bob will have to brush fingernail clippings from the control board. They've got two minutes before the closing theme starts. He turns to Riff. "She is definitely not crazy."

"And what the fuck are you doing to Irene? You're going to hurt her. For what? Some anorexic dancer who is always going to look down on you?"

"I don't know. Fuck." Bob runs his hand through his hair. A few strands come out in his hands. He had always taken his full head of hair for granted. Is that what aging is about? Watching your assets disappear?

He hears the door to the newsroom bang open, and Irene emerges and starts downs the hall towards the studio, script in hand. Bob flashes Riff a sign. He straightens up on the couch. Irene stops at the door to the lounge. "What are you two talking about? You look guilty."

"We were just saying how pretty you looked," Riff says. "Nice top. Really brings out your eyes."

Irene colors, then laughs. "You are up to something!"

Bob punches Riff on the arm, "Riff, I can't believe you, man. Ever heard of sexual harassment? You could get fired for saying something like 'nice top.'"

"Don't worry." Irene smiles at Bob. "I'm not going to sue someone who says I'm pretty."

Irene does look pretty. Her face seems softer, rounder. Her cheeks are glowing, her eyes bright; even her hair looks shinier. She is blooming, and it's all his fault. He is making a mess of everything. "Actually," he says, "we were talking about something one of my neighbors said."

Irene leans against the doorjamb, arches her back to scratch it against the molding. "The one who wants to cut down all of your trees?"

"No another one. She moved here from California. And she told me she doesn't think life has to be this hard."

"Someone from the tree group?"

"Yes, one of the organizers."

Riff laughs, then pours himself more coffee. "I need to wake up for this conversation."

Irene shakes her head. "Well, I don't buy it. I spent six months on unemployment in San Francisco. Life's just as hard out there. Everyone goes to California because it's supposed to be easy, and then they jump off the Golden Gate Bridge."

Riff stands up, gathering his thermos and his bag. "I once read an interesting article about that bridge," he says. "Turns out most people jump towards the city, not towards the ocean. Strange, huh? Even when they are ending it, they leap towards the known." He walks to the doorway, turning sideways to squeeze his small potbelly past Irene. "Because it's never about jumping off into the great unknown, is it? It's all about leaving this crazy shit behind!" He walks to the studio door and stands there waiting for the On Air light to go out, then he pushes in the door and shouts, "Hold on, the cavalry is here!"

As soon as the door slams shut, Irene turns to Bob and says, "So, did you get my messages?"

"No? When'd you call?" He had forgotten to check his messages, so wrapped up had he been in Leonie and the leaflets.

"I don't know. Late afternoon?"

"I must have been asleep. I was tired."

Irene smiles. "Me too. But a good kind of tired, like I spent the day hiking." She reaches out and touches Bob's arm.

"That was fun," he says and instantly regrets it.

"Yeah, it was." Her voice has a new sultry edge. Of course she's in radio; she can do things with her voice that most people can't. It's an occupational hazard. Lots of radio people develop these vocal tics: weird pronunciations, over-long pauses, sliding words together, enunciating a little too forcefully, as if they had stripped words of all meaning, leaving only the sound of their own booming, sexy voices. She leans in closer. "Want to go out some time?"

Jesus! When did women get so forceful, so self-assured? "Sure," he says. "That would be great." He bends his head toward her and in doing so, catches a glimpse of the clock. "Damn!" he says and straightens up. "Look at the time!"

Bob pushes open the door to the control room. Irene follows him in. BJ points to the clock on the wall. "You're late. We're already into the break."

"Sorry about that," Bob says. "Sorry."

BJ looks past Bob and notices Irene. "Hi, Irene," he squares his shoulders and sucks in his stomach.

"Hey, BJ. Did you have a nice weekend?"

"What weekend?" He gets up from his chair, still holding in his stomach, looking like he might explode from the effort.

Bob slides into the still warm chair. He can't wait for BJ to leave so he can clean the console. He sets up Riff's opening theme. Irene hands him his copy of the news script. Their hands touch for a second, and she winks. Her hand is so soft and so small. His own are rough and callused, though he can't really claim it's from physical labor. He can't decide if this is excruciating or fun. He fires the last commercial in the break and lifts his hand to cue Riff in.

Riff looks from Bob to Irene and back again. He shakes his head at Bob, almost imperceptibly, but Bob sees it. He opens his mic.

"Riff, here, Oliver Nelson there, the sky's so dark we need to crack it open, what happened to the stars, man? It's only September. I mean, sure the leaves are starting to turn and the birds are saying adios, but it's too early to feel the weather closing in. So tonight we're going to shake things up, let Mother Nature know we're paying attention. Enough of this darkness, we want warmth and sun and rhythm. Tonight, we're heading south."

Bob makes a mental note to play some Israel "Cachao" Lopez, then grabs the logs to set up the next break. Always have it ready, in case you drift off. Irene leans against the studio wall. "Want to hear the latest on Omar? He cheated on all of our health forms. Not just his or Kathy's. All of ours."

"I thought they covered a lot more of that last crown than I expected." Bob's tongue searches out the strangely smooth surface of his new porcelain crown. "But I never said anything."

"And rumor is, we might have to pay them back!"

"No! Do you think Omar lost his mind when his wife got sick? Or maybe he wasn't all there to begin with?"

"Well." Irene leans over the console and lowers her voice. Bob leans in to hear. "Supposedly they found a way to declare her cancer a pre-existing condition, and they threw her off his insurance. They had to change doctors, go to County hospital, where they cheaped out on everything. Left her lying on hospital gurneys unattended. Wouldn't spring for MRIs. Made her beg for painkillers. Omar was buying them on the street at the end."

Bob shakes his head. "Forget what I said. That's enough to drive anyone crazy."

Riff has moved on from the weather. "Hey, before the show started, me and Bobby and Irene were talking about whether life had to be this hard, and to tell the truth, I don't think so. I subscribe to the late, great Art Blakey's philosophy: We're here to have a ball."

"Like it matters what we think." Irene says.

Bob turns down the monitors. "You know what my next door neighbor the Buddhist would say? That life is suffering. But once you accept that, it gets easier."

"See, that's what I hate about religion. Full of loopholes!" Irene's voice rises. "Just accept that it's hard, and it no longer is! Life sucks, but you'll get your reward in heaven."

"I believe in heaven."

"You do?" Irene raises her eyebrows.

"Yeah, I think so. And hell. I mean, hell's not a stretch for me at all."

"You know what I think? I think you die and that's it. Party over, oops, out of time."

Bob shakes his head. "Doesn't make sense to me. I know my parents are still out there somewhere. I can feel them."

Irene speaks softly. "Sure, your parents are somewhere, Bobby. But they're in your head. Not out there."

"You're up." Bob motions to the clock.

Irene heads into the news booth. Riff hands off to her and then takes off his headphones and saunters into the control room.

"So, I see you two are getting along."

"We were talking about heaven and hell."

"Whatever floats your boat. Look, Bob, this could be good for you. Irene's a really nice woman. And I hate to see you fuck it up."

"I'm fine, Riff."

Riff raises his eyebrows. "No, you're not. You're juggling two women, when you can't handle one. I tell you what, I'm going to tell you my secret to success with women."

"Oh God, I can't wait."

"I've never told anybody this, but I have an absolutely foolproof way to win any woman's heart."

"Really?" Bob says. "I'm all ears."

"Treat her nice."

Bob laughs. "That's it?" he says. "That's your big fucking secret?"

"Yup. Flowers, dinners, candles, compliments. Women like to be treated nice."

"Unbelievable." Bob turns back to the script and loads the first news cut into the computer, looks into the news booth, and waits for Irene's cue. She smiles up at him and he smiles back and wonders if "nice" would work on Leonie.

CHAPTER 7

The morning commute traffic has died down by the time Bob turns onto his street, and he is lost in thought when some yuppies and their designer dog dart out in front of his car. Jesus! He slams on the brakes. The yuppie woman starts, and then waves at him. "Bob, is that you?" It's Abigail Greenough, with her husband, Tom, and their dog. She motions for him to join them on the other side of the street.

Bob pulls his car over to the curb and gets out.

"How perfect to run into you," Abigail says, smiling.

"No, I almost ran into you," Bob says. "You didn't look at all."

"You were going awfully fast for a residential neighborhood," Tom says. He is dressed in a long cowboy duster and a wide-brimmed suede hat, his thick, black hair curling under the brim — the cowboy look is all the rage with urban academics this season.

Bob sighs. He wants to be home in bed.

"This is quite a coincidence," Abigail says. "We were going to call when we got back from walking Kiki." Kiki pulls against the leash, then lunges at Bob.

"Kiki!" Tom snaps her leash back. "Down, girl!"

"You're not afraid of dogs are you?" Abigail asks. "She's just so excited to meet a neighbor."

"Oh no," Bob says. "Not at all." He is not exactly afraid of dogs, though he has never been exactly comfortable around them and in general he avoids any contact with their mouths, tries not to approach them when they are eating, crosses to the other side of the street when one appears, and was never so happy as when Cambridge passed the leash law. He leans over to pat Kiki on the head and she snaps at his hand.

"Sorry," Tom says. "She's just a puppy." Bob takes a step back.

"So have you thought anymore about your trees?"

"I don't know," Bob says. "I'd hate to lose the shade." He is trying to remember the points he cribbed from the meeting at Mabel's. Something about street trees?

"Shade!" Abigail says. "You've got all the shade you need back there. What you need is light."

"No, Abigail, what you need is light. I'm happy with the shade."

Kiki starts licking his left thigh. He can feel her hard wet tongue right through the fabric. "Hey, stop that!"

Abigail narrows her eyes for a moment and then flashes Bob one of her big smiles. "Maybe we could sweeten the pot?" She looks at Tom and he looks back at her and some understanding passes between them.

"What if we paid to remove your trees?" Tom says.

"You'd pay to remove my trees?"

"We're not getting any younger you know." Abigail smiles coquettishly, as if she in fact were getting younger. "We want to enjoy our back garden now."

Bob shakes his head. "No, I don't think so."

"What?" Abigail's smile fades.

"Why in the world not?" Tom asks.

"Because they're my trees. And it's not just about the money."

"Oh come on," Abigail says.

"I don't care how much money you have. You can't make me take down trees on my own private property." That's it. Is there another point he's forgotten to make? He should have prepared for this meeting.

Abigail rolls her eyes and sighs. "Bob, we'd be doing you a favor."

"We'd be really grateful if you'd think about it again," Tom says.

"Sure," he says, though he has thought about it all he intends to. He turns to leave.

Tom clears his throat. "What if we had your trees thinned out, instead?"

Bob turns around. Do these people never give up?

"We could thin them out. Might help with the light situation."

"I don't know." Bob shakes his head. "I have to think about it."

Tom nods and then puts his free hand on the small of the Abigail's back, like a ballroom dancer, and guides her off down the street.

Bob gets back into his car. He thinks for a moment of just leaving it there, but it's parked in a two-hour visitor parking zone and all he needs is a ticket or far worse a tow, because despite his protestations to Tom and Abigail, money is very much an issue for him and probably always will be.

There's a notecard in his mailbox from his neighbor, Bryce. Probably trying to borrow his driveway for his meditation workshop again. Bob has plenty of parking spaces. In fact, maybe he should start renting them out. Bring in a little extra income. But it all seems so mercenary.

Dear Bob, the note reads. *Got an idea for a fabulous gardening project, but I would need your help to bring it to fruition. I want to create a community meditation space in my back yard. I've got a great designer (from Japan no less!) all lined up and ready to go. The catch is, in order to put in a privacy gate, I would need to borrow a foot or two at the back of your driveway. In exchange I could give you a foot or two at the front of the driveway.*

What do you think?

With loving kindness,

Bryce

Bob places Bryce's note on the mahogany entrance table and walks over to the living room window to survey the driveway. The foot or two in question is presently covered in tangled weedy growth. At one time his father had planted some rose bushes in there, but they had never taken hold. Now Bob occasionally attacks it with a weed whacker, but only when it's threatening to take over the driveway. He's inclined to just let him have it, but he should probably run it by someone sensible before he agrees. One more thing to ask Mary Elizabeth when he goes to the Zoning Board.

CHAPTER 8

Buddy "Guitar" Lewis, Bob's old college roommate, is playing at the Pink Pearl on Sunday. Bob reaches across the breakroom table to grab Riff's pen, circles the listing in the Arts Section, then puts it back without Riff noticing. Maybe he should ask Leonie to go with him? He could call Buddy ahead and get front row seats. He'd suggest it to her casually. *Friend of mine's in town, jazz guy. You doing anything?*

Of course he's having dinner with Irene on Saturday. Some fancy place in the Square. He kind of hates going out to dinner because it's always too early for him; he is never hungry enough, and he is still in the mood to drink coffee and not wine. But Irene seems really excited about it. Has some gift certificate she's been saving up. What if something happens with her? Could he really go out the next night with Leonie?

Riff leans across the table and squints at the upside-down listing. "Hey, we should have him on the show," he says. "He's a great guitar player."

"You know he's a friend of mine?"

"Yeah, you told me. About a million times." Riff leans back in his chair and balances on one leg.

"What would we do with him?" Bob asks.

"I don't know," Riff says. "Let him program a set. Talk about his influences?"

"*I'm* his influences!" Bob jabs a finger in his own chest. "I introduced him to the blues and jazz. Before he met me he was listening to the Eagles! He's exactly the kind of opportunist I'm writing the piece about."

"How's that going?"

"I'm kind of stalled right now."

"You should let me read it."

"I will. When it's done." He looks back down at the Arts Section. "I'm thinking of going to see him on Sunday."

"You taking Irene?"

Bob hesitates.

Riff slams back down onto both legs of the chair. "You're a jerk, you know that? A real jerk." He gets up to leave the breakroom.

"Come on. I didn't plan it this way. It just happened."

"Well, you can't just let everything happen. Time you did something. You're not fucking helpless."

"I have to be sure."

"You're sure. You're just hedging your bets. Women aren't like us, man. They are sensitive and monogamous to a fault. A guy's still trying to figure out if he's interested and they're picking out china patterns. They got different plumbing, man; they are hardwired to connect. Even someone who plays tough, like Irene."

"If you worked with Leonie, would you be rooting for her?"

"I wouldn't be working with Leonie."

"You could be. If you got that Harvard gig."

Harvard is appointing a director for their newly founded Louis Armstrong Jazz Archive. Riff is a natural candidate. A living, breathing jazz archive himself. Well liked, loved, in fact, in the jazz community. A fixture on the local jazz scene. But he's not black, and Bob thinks that might be a sticking point. They need someone black, since a bunch of rich white guys is behind the archive. Bob closes up the paper and tosses it in the trash and walks over to the coffee maker. Pours himself a cup. "I got to brace myself," he says. "I got a meeting with Peralta this morning."

Riff pauses in the doorway. "What's that bastard want?"

"Probably trying to change my shift again. Take me off nights."

"Maybe you should, if you want to have a social life." Riff tries hard to look selfless.

"No, I like nights. Too many suits around during the day. Plus I'd have to pay those bastards to park during the day. I'm not management, or talent."

"You could afford the parking."

"And I don't really care about the news and all those talk shows. I just like jazz and you."

Riff smiles. "You want me to put in a word then? Tell them I can't do the show without you?"

"Yeah."

"Consider it done." Riff turns to leave. "And it's true. I don't want to do the show without you. I'm too old for that shit."

"Thanks," Bob says.

"But make up your mind about Irene, okay?" He pats Bob on the shoulder, a little too forcefully. "Don't keep leading her on."

Mitch Peralta's the chief engineer. He was a great sound engineer in his day, so they promoted him to management, something he is truly awful at. He was tall and lean when Bob first met him, but over the years he has filled out. His face has grown jowly, his neck full, and the buttons of his shirts strain at the middle. He has a picture of his wife and three daughters on his desk, the wife seated, the three daughters standing, a tropical looking sky behind them. Probably had it done at the mall. We'll take the Maui Sunset, thank you. His wife is a babe, though. Tall like Mitch, with long blonde hair and long legs. Bob has never understood what she saw in him. They have of course produced three blonde daughters, all of them blessed with her good looks, though Bob thinks he sees a hint of Mitch's cretinous brow in the youngest one.

Mitch is reading email when Bob comes in. He motions for Bob to sit down, while he stares at the screen. He holds up one finger. Bob closes his eyes. He could sleep right here, though the buzz of the fluorescent lights is disturbing. The station is noisy at night, but much worse during the day. The sales staff is on the phone; reporters run back and forth into the studio; the elevator creaks through the floors; the intercom cackles out the latest meeting. He opens his eyes and looks around Mitch's office. It is suspiciously neat, the sign of an inferior mind. The studio schedule has been push-pinned to the wall, perfectly aligned with the engineering schedule, the vacation tallies, and the list of official company holidays.

Mitch closes his email and turns to face him. He rubs his eyes and massages the eye sockets. "I got to take you off nights for a while, Bobby."

"Oh come on. You know I hate days."

"O'Mara's extending her leave."

"How long?"

"Another month, supposedly. But let's be honest. Once they have a kid, they don't give a shit about this job."

Amazing this guy hasn't been sued. "That's not true," Bob says. "What about Sally? And Beth?"

"Trust me. This is just the beginning. Next it'll be mother's hours, a four-day work week, sick days, snow days, doctor's appointments, fucking nanny gets arrested. Deported."

Bob laughs, in spite of himself. Mitch had been their shop steward before he was management, had fought long and hard for sick days, maternity leave, mother's hours. Now he has switched sides. He is a creature totally without self-doubt. If Bob were Mitch, he would be so plagued with self-doubt he'd never leave the house.

"And besides that, Riff and I are a team."

"Riff can handle a month without you. We'll put BJ on overnights."

"Put BJ on days."

Mitch shakes his head. "Nah. He's too weird for days."

"So am I."

"No Bobby, you can pass." He looks at Bob's faded black t-shirt and jeans. "Barely." He flattens his own tie, which is clipped inside his shirt, military style. "You up to speed on EditPro?"

Bob considers his answer. If he says no, then Mitch might rethink the shift change. He and Riff and Irene will have their blessed nights. If he says yes, he'll be on days and it will be a lot easier to see Leonie. But what is he thinking? Nothing has happened with Leonie, yet. And Riff doesn't want to do the show without him. But what if he did get the jazz archive gig? Where would that leave Bob? Working the overnights with some sex therapist?

He decides to gamble on Leonie, hopes that Riff will forgive him. "Yeah, I'm good enough at EditPro," he says. "And I'm sure I'd get better."

"Okay. Let's start next week." Mitch smiles at Bob. "I'll talk to BJ this afternoon. And try not to piss off Kathy, okay? She's already complained about you once."

Bob nods and stands up. "Hey, you think they're really going to make us pay back the insurance company?"

"Hope not," Mitch says, turning back to his computer. "You wouldn't believe how much of my daughter's braces they covered." His eyes glaze over, and his mouse hand starts moving, and Bob, dismissed, turns and walks out of his office.

CHAPTER 9

Bob's cousin Mary Elizabeth has not lost her Boston accent. In fact, to Bob's ears, it has gotten even stronger over the years, perhaps from working in City Hall, surrounded by people whose livelihoods depend on keeping their accents.

"Are you fucking crazy?" she asks, after Bob tells her about Bryce's request to borrow a foot of his driveway. They are sitting in her cramped and cluttered office, drinking Dunkin Donuts coffee, which he picked up on his way over. "Don't let him build onto your property. You'll want to sell sometime, and you'll be tied up in court. And believe me, the jerks always win."

Bob does believe that, and he is about to tell her so when he starts to sneeze, uncontrollably. "Jesus, Mary Elizabeth," he says. "How can you stand working around all this dust?" He gestures toward the floor-to-ceiling bookshelves piled haphazardly with yellowed paper files. "This place should be condemned."

Mary Elizabeth looks around, waves her hand dismissively. "After twenty-five years," she says. "I'm immune to dust. Either that or it's my own dust." She takes a sip of coffee and makes a face. "Those morons put too much sugar in this again."

"Supposed to be a regular," Bob says.

Mary Elizabeth walks across her office to a battered Mr. Coffee machine and tops off her coffee. She is dressed in a skirt, blazer, heels, and stockings. Her legs are still nice, but she has thickened around the middle and her face has the square jowly look that Bob's aunts all developed in middle age. From the back he can see the dark roots in her blonde hair. Mary Elizabeth is a few months younger than he. Does he look that old?

"What if he gives me land in the front of the driveway in exchange? The part he wants is of no use to me, and it wouldn't be of any use to a buyer, either."

"No, Bob, listen to me." Mary Elizabeth walks over to where he is sitting and leans down. "You don't want to mess with property lines. Ever. Your father would be turning in his grave!"

Bob leans back, away from her. "Okay, okay. I get it."

"What else?"

"Abigail, my neighbor on the other side." He tells her about his phytotoxic trees.

"Phyto what?"

"Phytotoxic trees. They kill other trees."

"Spare me. Are they growing onto her property?"

"No."

"Are they threatening any structures?"

"No."

"Then she doesn't have a leg to stand on. They're your trees. You can do what you like with them." Mary Elizabeth sits back down at her desk and reaches in her desk drawer for a cigarette.

"Can you really smoke in here?"

"No." She takes a lighter out and lights a cigarette, takes a hit, and then exhales the smoke. "God, what is it with your neighbors? One's trying to steal your property, the other wants to cut down your trees? I'm so glad I moved to Somerville when Jen moved out. I mean, my next door neighbors paved over their back yard, and installed flood lights that shine directly into my bedroom window, and they've got this horrible pit bull, chained up out back, who never stops barking, but you don't hear me complaining, do you?"

Bob laughs. "My God, you sound like me. One more thing." He tells her about the Japanese maple and the plans for the development on his street. "So, I'm supposed to find out. Aren't there some zoning laws about density that would stop it?"

"I don't know," Mary Elizabeth says. "I'll have to look that one up. But I don't get it. Which side of this one are you on? The tree huggers' or the developer's?"

"Neither, really. You can't even see the tree from street. I just wanted to get some pointers on how to fight for *my* trees. And," he coughs out some more dust. "I've kind of got a thing for one of the organizers."

"Really?" Mary Elizabeth leans forward, puts out her cigarette in the Dunkin Donuts cup. "This is much more interesting. Which one?"

"Never mind. I don't want to jinx it."

"Now I really want to hear." But she backs off and asks him a few more questions about the group and their arguments. "Well," she says, "from what I can tell, they don't have much of a case. Then again, this is Cambridge, so they could probably drag it on long enough for the developer to give up."

"So they'd win just by exhausting the other side?"

"You got it."

"Wow. Bet they don't teach that kind of law at Harvard Law School."

"No, Bobby, that is exactly the kind of law they teach at Harvard Law School. God, you are so naïve!"

Bob shrugs. "One more favor?" he asks. "Would you help me sort through my parents' stuff?"

Her face softens. "You still haven't cleared all that out? Of course I will."

They make a date for a Saturday in late October, and he leaves. October already, he thinks as he hurries down Mass. Ave., hoping his parking meter hasn't run out. He has just gotten used to September.

He is just drifting off to sleep, after a few hours of tossing and turning — he should never have drunk that Dunkin Donuts coffee — when he hears the sound of a saw starting up. He gets out of bed and steps to the window. He can hear workmen shouting somewhere behind his house but he can't see them. He puts on the jeans and t-shirt he so recently removed and heads out onto his back porch. His neighbor Tom Greenough is standing in Bob's back yard, dressed in a cowboy hat and LL Bean barn jacket, directing a crew of chainsaw-wielding landscapers. One of them has already climbed up the tallest of Bob's trees and is poised to hack off a large bottom branch. There's a fresh cut lower on the tree, and an even larger branch on the ground.

Bob runs to Tom's side and yells to be heard over the chain saw. "What the hell is going on? Are you cutting down my trees?"

"No, no, no," Tom shouts. "Of course not! We mentioned thinning them, right? You said you were okay with thinning then."

"No, I didn't."

"I distinctly remember that you did, Bob. You said you didn't want to take them down, but didn't mind us thinning them out a bit to get some light."

"I said I'd think about it," Bob says.

Tom shrugs his shoulders. "Well, I don't want to quibble about it."

"Those are huge branches you're taking down." Bob sees Abigail coming around the corner of their house, picking her way around the sawhorses and piles of lumber for their conservatory addition.

"Hi, Bob." She smiles her dazzling white smile as she crosses into his yard. She looks to Tom. "Is there some kind of problem?"

Tom sighs. "Now Bob doesn't want to thin the trees, either."

"Oh." Her face falls. "I thought we had agreed." She scrunches up her forehead as if trying to understand his sudden change of heart.

"No, we didn't agree," Bob says. "I said I'd think about it." His voice sounds petty and churlish, even to his own ears.

Tom holds up his hand and waves for the tree guy to climb down. "What?" The tree guy removes his ear protectors.

"We got a little misunderstanding here," Tom yells, tilts his head in Bob's direction.

"Jesus!" The tree guy glares at Bob, shuts off the chainsaw, and unhooks himself from the tree.

"Look, Tom, you can just send this crew home right now," Bob says.

"Well, they'll have to clean up first." Abigail nods toward the large branches and wood chips on the ground.

"Fine, then send them home. And we can talk about thinning them some other time." Bob turns to head back inside.

"Wait!" Abigail calls out. "What if we remove that pile of debris over there by the garage for you? While we're at it?"

Bob turns to look at the untidy pile of leaves, grass, and branches leaning against the garage. Some very aggressive vine has started to wind its way over and around the top, so that it almost looks like a bush. "That's my father's compost pile." His father used to remove the rich black dirt from the bottom of the pile and work it into the soil around his roses.

"Bob, that's not a compost pile," Tom says. "That's a pile of yard debris."

"Which is compost."

Tom rolls his eyes at the tree guy, who has made his way down the tree and joined them. "No, that's what I'd call a rat's nest," the tree guy says.

"In fact, the people in the condos complained about it," Abigail says, nodding in the tree guy's direction. "They wanted to call the city. You know they had that rat problem." She shivers and her nostrils flare out.

"I'm pretty sure it's illegal to have an uncovered pile like that," the tree guy adds.

Bob narrows his eyes at the tree guy. Where's his sense of solidarity? Of course Abigail and Tom are paying him, while Bob is trying to cut his wages short.

"It's really a public health hazard," Tom says.

"Spare me!" Bob says. "You know you don't have a leg to stand on. Send them home, and we'll talk about it later."

"All right, Bob." Abigail smiles stiffly and puts her hand on her husband's forearm, as if to forestall him. "Let us know when you're finally ready."

Bob goes inside, removes his clothes, and gets back into bed. He strains to hear the sound of the chainsaw starting up again, but all he hears are the sounds of the crew shouting and finally, their truck starting up. Had he really given Tom and Abigail permission to thin his trees? He doesn't think so. But he's not really sure. From now on, he's going to have to write everything down. Like Mary Elizabeth said, these people are just trying to exhaust him until he quits.

CHAPTER 10

On Saturday night, Bob and Irene walk from his house into Harvard Square for dinner. Their reservation is for nine thirty, the latest the restaurant could offer. Provincial Boston, everything closes up early. You could die of starvation after ten o'clock. They walk side by side, occasionally brushing against each other, but resolutely not holding hands. Irene's hands are in her coat pockets. Bob's are at his sides, though they are cold. The weather is changing. He had fished a warm wool jacket out of his hall closet, only to find that the moths had gotten at it, near the collar and on one of the sleeves. What the hell, he thought, it's only Cambridge, and took a black scarf out of the closet, and wrapped it around his neck to camouflage the damage. Irene is wearing a skirt, a skirt! – he didn't even know she owned one — and some kind of chunky high-heeled shoes. She has to walk carefully over the uneven brick sidewalk, but she looks good and he is flattered at her effort.

"You look nice," Bob says.

"And so do you. You should dress up more often."

"So, where are we going again?" Bob asks.

"Prana. It's the new cool place. Haven't you heard about it?"

"Nah," he says. "I'm not cool. What is it, Indian?"

"No, it's some kind of Asian–American fusion place, with a Buddhist vibe. I don't really know. I did some voice-over work for their advertising agency, and they gave me a gift certificate."

"It's not vegetarian, is it? It pisses me off to pay a lot for rice and vegetables."

"No, not vegetarian. And you're not paying, Bob. I am, or more exactly, the advertising agency is."

Bob smiles. "Okay." He is actually getting hungry, and he can almost imagine drinking something alcoholic, though he could still use another cup of coffee. Early in the afternoon someone had rung his bell, a kid probably, guilt-tripping about the environment or selling candy bars so his school could afford books, or a Fed Ex guy, trying to deliver a package to one of the pashas in the condos behind him — the bastards, trying to blame their rat problem on his compost pile. He had woken up at the sound of the bell and felt the familiar lurching in his stomach that meant that he would not get back to sleep. Everyone says that insomnia starts in your head, but Bob knows differently. It starts in your stomach, and only then does the mind get into the act, recycling the day's horrors, worrying about the next day's, almost drifting back to asleep, then waking again with an adrenaline-producing jolt.

"So." Irene pats his arm. "Peralta put you on days?"

"Yeah. To cover O'Mara's leave."

"Her baby is so cute. Did you see him when she brought him in?"

"No." Bob shakes his head. He likes babies but he has learned to avoid talking about them with women with whom he'd like to have sex. The whole topic is too charged and awkward and fraught. Next thing she'll be talking about her nieces and nephews and asking Bob whether he ever wanted kids and noticing if he walks on the traffic side of the sidewalk, protecting her and her unhatched eggs from the automotive onslaught. "Did O'Mara say when she'd be coming back?"

"I got the feeling she's having doubts about coming back at all." Irene says.

"Damn."

"Yeah, you shouldn't have let him change your schedule," Irene says.

"No, it's just that I hate the idea that that moron Mitch Peralta might be right. He predicted she wouldn't come back."

"Doesn't take a psychic to see that a new baby is a lot more fun than a boring engineering job."

"So that's what you think about my career, huh?"

Irene stops short on the sidewalk, puts her hand to her mouth and backpedals. "Sorry, I didn't mean you. Bob. I, I meant..."

Bob puts his hands in his pockets and keeps walking.

"It's just that. I always think of you as different."

"How's that?"

"Well, you've got a passion, jazz. You and Riff are a team."

It's pathetic, really. Sure he's got a passion, but it's not like he's a jazz player or even a jazz critic. He's an engineer who writes a treatise on jazz when he can't sleep. He'll probably never finish it. How many degrees of separation is that from the real thing? His friend Buddy may not be an original, but he can play, and lives and breathes the music. "You don't have to make me feel better, Irene. I just fell into the job. And I never fell back out."

"Well, what did you really want to do?"

"Listen to music," Bob says. So far this night is not going as planned. This was supposed to be light and fun and involve a little too much wine and hopefully sex. Not a career counseling session.

"What did you major in?"

"Pot."

Irene laughs.

"With a minor in coke," he says. "What did you major in?"

"I never went," Irene says. "I got a temp job as a receptionist at a radio station and worked my way up. But I am always afraid when I have to look for work again. I never went to college."

"You didn't miss much."

"Easy for you to say."

"No, it's true. But why are we talking about college? See, it's living here in Cambridge. Everything is about where you went to school and how smart you are and how many degrees you have. In the rest of the country people don't even talk about it."

"No kidding. I felt like a Rhodes Scholar in California. I was the only one at my radio station who could spell."

"Yeah, radio is full of morons. Big blustery morons with deep voices."

"And funny bodies. Man, the men in radio are butt ugly."

"Thanks." Bob hip checks her and she hip checks him back. He grabs her hand. They walk in silence for a while. Bob has forgotten how nice it is to head out for a night, holding hands, nothing to worry about except what to order. Is he in the mood for fish, or is that a romance killer? Nah, he thinks he'll stick to something safer, chicken maybe, or pasta. He swings Irene's hand and she swings back.

It's always takes longer than he allows to walk into the Square, so they are ten minutes late for their reservation, have to run the last couple of blocks, and arrive at the door breathless and laughing. The door is carved and heavy, imported from somewhere in Asia. Some Buddhist temple gave up its front door so that a bunch of self-centered

Americans could eat out. They are met by an extremely thin woman in loose pants and a white sleeveless blouse. She seems impervious to the cold. She looks down at Irene's calf length skirt and chunky shoes and then back up again quickly. Her gaze barely takes in Bob at all. "Welcome to Prana," she says and holds her hands in front of her in the prayer position and bows. Irene rolls her eyes at Bob. He tries not to laugh.

She escorts them to a similarly clad hostess who looks down at her reservation book and frowns. "Is there a problem?" Irene asks.

The young woman smiles a big smile. "Oh no, we'll fit you in, even though you're late." She leads them up a flight of stairs. There's a waterfall at the head of the stairs and a huge Buddha that seems to levitate above it. "You're lucky," she says, flipping her long healthy hair over her shoulder. "We were just about to give your table away." She places two oversized brown menus on the table and takes an oven lighter out of her pocket and lights several candles.

Bob looks around the restaurant. The clientele is young and well heeled. The woman are very dressed up and revealing quite a bit of skin. The men are dressed predominantly in black — black blazers and collarless black shirts and dressy black pants. Where do these kids get all the money? Everyone seems to be drinking fancy cocktails in martini glasses. The lighting is low, lots of candlelight, and the décor is bamboo, rattan, and carved heavy wood. Their waiter glides over to him. He too is dressed in black including a black apron he has wrapped around his substantial middle, Paris bistro style. Like the door girl, he bows, hands in the prayer position. "Namaste," he says.

"Namaste," Irene says and nods her head.

"Hey," Bob says.

"Is this your first time at Prana?" His eyes flick over Bob's moth-eaten shoulder and then quickly away. "Let me tell you a little bit about us. Our chef, Amelia, takes inspiration from what's fresh and local, but she's not afraid to combine these ingredients in a global fashion. She's been greatly influenced by her travels in the East and her Buddhist practice." He pauses here for effect. "Actually, she is more of a conceptual artist than a chef, and food is her muse. The results, if I do say so, are spectacular. For example, do you like popcorn?"

Bob shakes his head. "What?"

The waiter produces a basket of popcorn from behind his back and puts it on the table. "This is organic corn, air popped and then tossed with herbs de Provence, parmigiano reggiano, and a just a hint of truffle oil." He pinches his forefinger and thumb together to illustrate.

Irene takes a kernel. "Delicious. Bob, try some."

Bob takes a handful, tips it back into his mouth, while the waiter holds his breath. "A revelation!" Bob says.

Irene sneaks a peak at her menu. "Could we order a drink?"

"Of course. Are you interested in the wine list or the cocktail list?"

"What do you have on tap?" Bob asks.

The waiter shakes his head. "We have an extensive selection of bottled beers. I would recommend Tiger; it's Malaysian."

"You got it."

"And for you, ma'am?"

A look of irritation flutters over Irene's face at being called "Ma'am." Bob checks out the waiter again. His hairline is receding, but his face is unlined, his cheeks full. He's young, impressed with himself and this ridiculous restaurant. He and Irene are oldsters to him, marginal, like his own parents had become. Bob remembers taking them out for Chinese food. His father had gamely ordered sweet and sour pork and egg rolls, and had eaten heartily, while his mother nibbled at her fried rice, then lit a cigarette. Bob had ordered some scary sounding seafood dish, just to impress them, and then struggled to get it down, his eyes tearing up at the heat, his throat closing around the rubbery fish tentacles.

"Got any tequila?" Irene asks.

Their waiter blinks. "We have a great selection of margaritas. Let me bring you the cocktail list."

"No, just give me a shot of Cuervo Gold, and one of those Tiger beers."

"Make that two shots," Bob says, though he can't remember the last time he drank tequila, or to be exact he can remember the last time, he just can't remember anything about it.

When the waiter has gone, Irene picks up a kernel of popcorn and throws it at Bob. "Truffle oil!" she says.

"So how much can we spend? " Bob asks.

"Don't worry." Irene waves her arm. "I got it covered. No way we're going to spend it all."

"Great." Bob leans back in the booth. He picks up a kernel and tosses it at Irene. She tosses one back and he catches it in his mouth. He aims for her mouth but she misses it, and the popcorn lands on the man sitting behind her, who turns and brushes it off like a flake of dandruff.

Their waiter arrives with their shots and beers. He grins and rocks back in forth on his toes, his fingertips tapping together. "Let me know what you think of the Malaysian beer," he says.

Irene takes a sip. "Wonderful," she says and then lifts her shot to her lips and knocks it back. Their waiter looks over his shoulder at another table and excuses himself.

Bob tries to do the same with his shot but can get less than half of it down. "My God." he says. "How'd you do that?"

"Practice," she says. "I drink a shot every morning when I get home from work. I mean it's daylight out. I need something. Don't you drink yourself to sleep?"

"Nah, never worked for me." Bob says. "Plus I'm afraid of alcohol, afraid I'll become a drunk."

"Did your parents drink?"

"My mother drank a bit. My father never took a sip. But my grandfather was a drunk, and my Uncle Gene, too. It's in the blood. Just waiting for me to slip up." He sips at the tequila, feels it burning its way through his body. He remembers the first time he drank whiskey, at his Aunt Mary's house. He was still too young to drink legally, but his aunt had made him a rye and ginger and the alcohol had coursed through his body, and he felt good all the way down to his toes and thought, "Grandpa! Now I understand!"

"And you? Did your parents drink?" He realizes he knows very little about Irene. She worked in California; she didn't go to college. He thinks she used to be married.

"Yes," she says. "They did. And they still might. I don't know. We don't talk much."

"And you don't worry about the tequila?"

"If it becomes a problem, I'll worry about it then."

"But then it may be too late."

"But what if it never becomes a problem, and I waste all that time worrying about it?"

Bob wonders what percentage of his life he has spent worrying. Definitely a good part of every sleepless night and several hours before he attempts anything new, and several hours after he has attempted anything new, and weeks before his doctor's appointments, because, like alcoholism, he fears that cancer is also lying in wait: the lump, the bleeding freckle, the telltale headache in his frontal lobe.

Irene sips her beer and opens the huge brown menu. Her neckline is low enough that Bob can just see the swell of her breasts. Not large breasts, but nice breasts. He wonders if he could get a kernel of popcorn to land between them.

"Everything sounds so fucking weird," she says. "We better hurry; our waiter is about to pounce."

Bob opens his menu. Smoked salmon and rennet-less cheese cannolis. Shitake mushrooms and candied ginger scallops. Squab liver pie.

The waiter sidles over to their table. "Would you like to hear about our specials?"

Bob and Irene nod. "Our chef tonight is working with some fresh local seafood. She only buys from the docks and from one organic brook trout farm. She has married the flavor of the trout with Turkish ground chickpeas and a drizzle of EVOO…"

"Hey, isn't that Kathy?" Irene cranes her neck around her menu. "Over there by the bar?"

Bob looks over his shoulder. Sure enough Kathy is leaning against the bar, a shimmery blue drink in her hand, a tall man at her side. She notices Bob and Irene. "Oh!" She mouths. She waves, grabs her date's hand, and leads him to their table.

"How to ruin an expensive dinner," Irene whispers.

Kathy walks over to the table. "Jason," she says to the waiter.

Jason smiles. "Did you like your fruit kebabs?"

"Loved them."

Irene points to their tequilas and holds up two fingers. Jason nods and leaves the table.

Kathy looks from Bob to Irene and back. "What are you two doing here?" She raises her eyebrows. "Is there something I should know?"

"No." Irene shakes her head. "We have to hang out together. Who else stays up so late?"

"Sure, sure." Kathy turns to Bob. "Isn't the food here fabulous?"

"So far we've just had popcorn."

"I love that popcorn. I have to stop myself from filling up on it."

"Can you eat popcorn on the Zone diet?"

"Well, I always go off it when Anthony is here!" Kathy winks at her companion and squeezes his hand. "Let me introduce you all. Bob and Irene work at the station. Bob's a sound tech. He works with Riff — remember that old jazz guy we talked about? And Irene's a newscaster, too, but on the overnights."

Anthony nods his head and sticks out his free hand to Bob. His hand is cold, his handshake a bit too firm. "Nice to meet you both."

"Anthony is my fiancé." Kathy takes a sip of her blue drink.

Oh, good, Bob thinks, maybe she'll get pregnant and fall in love with her little baby and never come back to work.

Irene clinks her beer with Kathy's cocktail and says, "Wow, that's great news. Congratulations!"

"Oh, we've been engaged forever. We've just been waiting until we could both find a job in the same market."

Bob's ears perk up. *Market?* Anthony must be in radio. Kathy beams, leans into him. The waiter puts down two more brimming glasses of tequila. Anthony purses his lips. "Who's driving?"

"Oh, neither of us," Irene says. "We walked."

"Bob lives in the neighborhood." Kathy turns to Bob. "Actually, we drove by your house. You're not looking to sell, are you?"

"No, I'm not selling," Bob says.

"If you ever change your mind..."

"You'll be the first to know," he says.

Irene catches Bob's eye. He turns away so as not to laugh.

"Well, it's late," Anthony says, eyeing their shots of tequila. "Some of us have to get up early."

After they're gone, Bob throws another piece of popcorn at Irene to get her attention. "What a jerk," he says.

"He seems okay."

"He's engaged to Kathy. How okay could he be?"

"Come on, give the guy a chance."

Bob shakes his head. "No, while I'm giving him a chance, he'll be plotting against me. You can't let people like him get a head start."

Irene shakes her head and laughs. "You're so paranoid."

"There's a fine line between paranoid and prepared."

Their waiter returns to the table and smiles. He thinks better of them now that they know some regulars. "Have you decided yet?" He folds his hands over his apron.

Bob looks at the menu. Irene turns to the waiter. "What do you recommend?"

"Well, since it's your first time here, I would recommend the tasting menu. You get to sample what our chef is excited about today."

Irene shrugs. Bob says, "Sure." Much less work than deciphering the menu.

§

The first course is a miniscule salad with squid and ouzo custard served with a fizzy white wine from the Alsace region. They are both hungry so they dive in and the first bite is pretty good, but then the strange mixture of tastes and textures catches up with them. Luckily the portion is so small that it's gone before they are really turned off. The next course is a steak tartare with a raw egg on a bed of cold cellophane noodles, served with a Macedonian red. Irene pushes her raw steak towards Bob. "All yours."

Bob pours his finger of Macedonian wine into Irene's glass. "All yours." Bob punctures the raw egg, which slithers over the clammy little squares of highly seasoned steak. Oh well, he thinks and takes a huge forkful and lets it slide down his throat. Irene puts her finger down her throat and mimics gagging. He finishes off both plates in two more mouthfuls, then washes it down with water. "Someone's got to eat it," he says.

Next is Chilean sea bass in a miso–ginger marinade. Jason puts the dish down in the middle of the table and then takes out a flashlight and shines it on three chiclet-sized pieces of sea bass.

"You're kidding, right?" Bob says.

Jason shifts the flashlight to a pile of greens next to the fish. "This is lamb's lettuce," he says, "imported from France. It wasn't on the menu but Amelia spotted it at the farmer's market this morning."

Bob spears a piece of fish with his fork and swallows it whole. It is salty and has the texture of roasted garlic. He wonders for a minute if it *is* roasted garlic.

Irene takes a piece and swallows. "Thank God we aren't paying for this!" she says.

The main course is a lobster tail with drawn yak ghee, curried lentils, and savory bread pudding, served with a greenish looking Portuguese white. Bob has never understood lobster. He never ate it growing up and it seems difficult to approach now, with all those tentacles and claws and the bibs and crackers and drawn butter. He did try a lobster roll once at the beach and thought he'd be just as happy with a hot dog. He gives his lobster tail to Irene, who takes the cracker and attacks it expertly. He downs the lentils and bread pudding and dunks some bread into the yak ghee, which tastes to his uneducated palate like butter. He likes the Portuguese wine even less than the Alsatian and the Macedonian, but he drinks it nonetheless. Obviously things are not going to get better.

Dessert is an innocent looking pudding with pistachios, chocolate chips and a green sauce drizzled over the top, served with a sauterne. Irene takes a spoonful of the pudding then spits it out. "I give. This dessert tastes like fucking pesto! This place is just too weird." She gets out her purse and slaps the folded up gift certificate on the table. "Let's go get something to eat. I'm hungry."

On the way home they stop at the Leaning Tower of Pizza for two cheese slices and two Diet Cokes and sit in the corner of the restaurant reading the Want Advertiser. Bob buys them a dollar's worth of M&Ms from the candy machine, for dessert. "So Kathy and her fiancé want to be your neighbors," Irene says. "She must make a lot more than I do if she can afford Cambridge."

"Don't go there," Bob says. "It will only make you feel bad."

Irene folds her slice in half and lets the oil puddle onto her paper plate. She drains her Diet Coke. "Boy, am I thirsty."

"Another round?" Bob walks to the refrigerator case. He looks out the picture window at the dark street. The pizza parlor is around the corner from Leonie's house. Bob wonders what she is doing now. Meditating, stretching, practicing back bends? Or is she already in bed? Resting up for their night out at the Pink Pearl? Bob had called her in the middle of the week to ask how the tree campaign was coming along.

"Pretty good," she said. "We've got the Historical Commission on board and an inspector from the zoning board has promised to make a site visit, and oh, wait 'til you hear this, the Associated Press is going to interview me over the weekend!"

"The Associated Press? That's unbelievable." Wars were raging, babies dying of cholera, typhoons wiping out whole subcontinental villages, and the Associated Press was going to do a story about a tree? "Good for you," he said. He launched: "Hey, I was wondering, if you're not too busy. A friend of mine is in town this weekend, jazz guy, and I have two tickets. Any chance you'd be free on Sunday night?" His face was hot and burning, the words had come out in a rush. Had they even made sense?

"Sure. Sounds like fun. What time?"

She said yes. Unbelievable. He'd pick her up at seven. They'd get a drink first. Amazing how it fell into place, just like he had rehearsed it. Was this the way other people's lives always worked?

Irene finishes off the second Diet Coke. "You got anything to drink at your house?" she asks.

"I've got wine," Bob says. "A witty California red."

"Sounds perfect," Irene says, and they link their arms and head up the street to his place.

CHAPTER 11

Bob wakes up with a start, and momentarily doesn't know where he is. The windows are misplaced. Light is streaming in from the wrong direction. His neck and back ache; his hand is asleep; his head throbs. He opens his eyes and looks around. He is in his living room, on the couch. His clothes are in a heap on the floor, his belt snaking out of his pants. There's another little pile of clothes next to his: Irene's chunky heels and skirt. The night comes back to him in a rush. He jumps up, pulls on his pants, and runs into the bathroom. Irene is asleep on the floor, by the toilet, in a nest of towels, another towel bunched up under her head, the afghan from his parents' bed wrapped around her. Poor Irene! He kneels down and strokes her cheek. "Hey," he whispers. "Are you feeling better?"

Irene opens her eyes and moans. Her breath is awful. "No," she says and falls back onto the towels.

Bob stands up and brushes his teeth. It must have been the lobster. He doesn't feel all that great himself, but he chalks it up to too much drink, too rich food, and perhaps a guilty conscience. Not food poisoning. He kneels down again, shakes Irene's shoulder to wake her. "Let's get you into bed," he says. "You'll be a lot more comfortable there."

Thank God the bed is made, the sheets are clean, the floor is swept. He had even opened the windows and aired the room out before they went out. He leads Irene to the bed and sits her down, then swings her legs over the side. She lies back down and sighs and immediately falls back to sleep. Bob walks to the kitchen and gets a glass of water, and the big pot his father used to soak his feet in. Just in case. "Here you go," he says as he enters the room, and puts the pot and the water on his bedside table. How easy it is to slip into the cheerful patter of the sickroom. He had nursed his mother when she got sick. He converted the dining room into a bedroom, so he could hear her, from her hospital bed in the living room. Even after she died, he hadn't had the heart to move upstairs to her room, or even worse, his. Moving back home was deflating enough.

He gets a washcloth and wets it with warm water and a little bit of soap. He washes Irene's pale face. He can see the pulsating blue veins under the skin of her forehead and her eyelids. She twitches as he washes her but doesn't wake up. He assumes the worst is over, but what does he know? Perhaps the lobster will come back for a rematch?

In the afternoon he dials Riff's number and leaves a message. "Hey man, you want to go see Buddy Guitar Lewis tonight? Irene got food poisoning. Call me back."

Irene calls out from the bedroom. "Go!" she says.

"You're alive." He enters the room and sits down on the side of the bed.

Irene lifts her head. "Ouch!" She rubs her head. "I'll just go home, to sleep. You should go."

"No," Bob says. "You're too sick."

"I'm not sick anymore. Just embarrassed."

"I'm not leaving you alone."

"What are you going to do, watch me sleep?"

"I've got plenty to do. Now, do you want some toast or something? Some tea? You must be starving."

"Oh God, no." Irene's face pales. "No food." She falls back onto the pillow.

Bob cleans up the living room, folding their clothes and placing his on the arm of the couch, and Irene's on the coffee table. He takes the half empty bottle of Merlot into the kitchen and puts it in the fridge. He knows it's not supposed to be cold but what the hell, no one is looking. While there, he inventories the fridge. He needs milk, butter, and ginger ale. More bread. Maybe a can of chicken soup. Some saltines. Easy re-entry food. He looks at the clock and figures he might as well call Leonie. He takes the phone out onto the back porch so Irene won't hear. Leonie answers on the first ring. Was she sitting there, waiting for him to back out? "I hate to do this," he says, "but a friend of mine is sick."

"Oh no," she says. "Is he going to be okay?"

"Oh yeah." It's easier not to correct the pronoun. "Just food poisoning. But I was really looking forward to seeing you."

"Me too."

"Maybe you should go, you should use the tickets. Buddy is really good. And the seats are great."

"No, that's okay."

He insists she try and she calls back a few minutes later. She's found someone to go. Should she come over there and pick up the tickets?

No! He tells her he'll drop them off. He has to go out and do some shopping anyway.

He checks in on Irene before he leaves. She is sleeping, moaning occasionally, but sleeping. He looks at himself in the bathroom mirror, *You bastard*. He smoothes down his hair, brushes his teeth again, puts on a coat, takes it off, then puts it on again, slips the tickets into his breast pocket, and heads out the back door. He stands on his porch for a moment. It's one of those beautiful New England fall days when the heat buzzes the air and the leaves are falling and everything is kind of hazy and orange. When he was little, the air would have smelled of burning leaves, but of course now burning them is illegal. He had loved wandering through Cambridge on those fall days, kicking his way down the brick sidewalks through piles of leaves, hunting for bright yellow ones, or red ones, or perfectly formed ones to bring into school, though he can't imagine now that the nuns put up with much of that. He can't remember any crafty nuns, any decorations in the schoolrooms at all, only the statues and the crucifixes and the cursive ABCs marching above the blackboard.

He hears a rustling in the corner of his yard and looks over and sees two squirrels chasing one another down the partially thinned Norway maple. He winces at the still fresh cuts on the trunk and the residue of sawdust around the base. How much of the tree would be left if he hadn't stopped them? His neighbor, Maureen, from the condo building, is leaning over the fence and throwing peanuts into his yard. "Hey," he yells. She freezes. "Hey!" He strides over to the fence. "I thought you weren't going to feed them anymore."

"Well the little creatures have to eat, too," she says, glancing from side to side. "You'd let them starve, would you?"

"No, but you're throwing the peanuts into my yard. If you want to feed the squirrels, do it somewhere else."

"But I haven't got a yard, have I? I've only got this back alley and the poor squirrels have nowhere else to go either."

"Spare me," Bob says. "Go to the park and feed them."

"But those aren't my squirrels," she says.

"Well, your squirrels are getting into the eaves of my house and running through my walls when I am trying to sleep." Bob looks at her closely. She is about his age, maybe a few years older. Her hair is cut short, her clothes neat, and her face could almost be pretty were it not so pinched, but she's obviously not all there. Her eyes dart from side to side. She can't quite make eye contact. He has seen her walking multiple dogs and talking to herself. Why is he wasting his time arguing with her?

"You know Abigail wants me to cut down these trees."

"No!" Her eyes go large and round. She looks up and down the length of the tree. "Over my dead body!"

"And I am trying to save them."

She eyes him warily.

"But I can't have this fucking rodent problem, or I'll just let her." He turns to walk away.

She stands there lips pursed, hands gripping a couple of peanuts. "We'll see what the city has to say about that."

Bob walks down the length of his driveway and turns around to look. She is standing at the fence, her hands closed around the peanuts, and he knows she will feed them again the minute he is out of sight. Was she feeding the rats, too?

Oh well, he thinks. At least it's warm and the squirrels are not in the house yet, and at least he and Irene did not have sex the night before. They had come home and opened the bottle of wine and sat down on the living room couch and Irene kicked her chunky shoes off and tucked her legs up under her — amazing how women could fold their bodies into such small bundles — and they sat talking and drinking for a while, and at one point Irene leaned over and kissed him and he kissed her back and they put their wine glasses down on the coffee table, and kissed some more, hands roaming up and down each other's bodies, and then they lay down on the couch and their clothes came off and Irene did look great naked. She is just muscled enough, just soft enough, just curvy enough, and things were getting a little steamy when she suddenly sat up and asked for water. "I'm not feeling that good," she said. And Bob got up and went to the kitchen but before he could get back to the living room, she had charged into the bathroom. They'd been up most of the night, Irene curled up on the bathroom floor, Bob dozing on the couch. Occasionally he would wake up to hear her retching and cursing the restaurant, the lobster, the freaking ad agency. She was embarrassed, but he assured her it was nothing, though several times he had to leave the bathroom to regain his composure, and once he came close to puking himself.

But now on a beautiful Sunday afternoon as he is heading over to Leonie's, Bob thinks that maybe it was meant to be. He and Irene weren't meant for each other. He and Leonie were meant for each other. How convenient to have fallen for someone who lives around the corner. This is the great thing about Cambridge — it's in walking distance to everything. You can walk over to see the woman you're interested in, then walk to the grocery store to shop, and she can walk to the club to listen to Buddy, the guy you've known since you were eighteen, when you both were virgins, though he seemed a bit more worldly, coming from New York.

Bob kicks through a pile of leaves on the sidewalk in front of McMahon's. Funny how no one rakes anymore. The landscapers come during the week, leafblowers on their backs, while the overlords earn the money to pay them. Let's face it, if you can't afford a landscaper you can't afford Cambridge. Everyone Bob knows has been priced out. The bohemians, the artists, the druggies, the eccentric radical politicos with the multiple buttons on their jean jackets have all decamped for somewhere less pricey. Bob remembers when Cambridge felt like a hotbed of revolution, when peace signs covered the windows, and the big old houses were turned into communes and ashrams, when there were love-ins on Cambridge Common, and Harvard Square smelled of pot. He remembers walking barefoot to the river, picking his way over the brick sidewalks, trying to toughen his tender feet so he could show everyone just how relaxed he really was.

Leonie is waiting for him on her porch. She reaches up to pinch the flowers off a potted geranium. Her arms seem elongated, maybe from years of dancing; her back is unbelievably straight. Her hair curls at the back of her neck; the label from her sweater is poking up and Bob has the urge to flatten it for her. His night with Irene has emboldened him; the whole world now seems open to his touch, but he holds back.

"Nice day, huh?" Leonie sinks into a wicker porch chair.

Bob sits down across from her. "Beautiful," he says.

She puts her feet up on a glass-topped wicker table. She is wearing scuffed-up suede boots and black pants and the same oversized sweater he had seen her in the first time.

"So who'd you get to go with you?" Bob asks.

"My ex, Gary."

Bob snaps to attention "Your ex-husband lives here?"

"Oh, yes, we came out here together. Actually, he got the job first. Then I followed. By that time he had met his new wife, but he didn't know how to stop me."

"Someone younger?"

"Of course," Leonie says. "Another linguist. It was love at first declension."

Bob laughs. "And she doesn't mind your going out to hear music together?"

"Oh, no. They're soul mates. Gary and I are still good friends. And our parents in California have remained friends. We even spend the holidays together."

"Really?" Bob can't imagine being friends with any of his exes. Too many hurt feelings, too much jealousy, anger, betrayal, disappointment, bitterness, and that's just on his side.

"Would you like something to drink?" Leonie asks. "Wine, or beer?"

"Beer," Bob says, trying not to picture Irene sleeping back at the house.

"Come on in."

He follows Leonie into her living room — very clean, very Zen, there's a polished baby grand piano in one corner, some kind of filmy curtains over open shades — and then in through a pantry to her kitchen, which even this late in the day, seems filled with light. One corner has been expanded to create a sitting area/sunroom. There's a comfortable-looking chair almost enveloped by green plants, hanging from baskets, arching toward the sun, winding over the window frames.

"You have a green thumb?"

"Not really," Leonie says. "Gary does. And he left them behind. But plants love this room so much, even I can't kill them."

She opens her refrigerator, which like the rest of her house is clean, spare and uncluttered, and takes out a beer. "Would you like a glass?"

Bob shakes his head.

Leonie pours herself a glass of red wine and sits down at the kitchen table. Bob pulls out a chair and sits next to her. "Sorry about tonight," he begins, "I feel like…"

Leonie holds up her hand to stop him. "No problem. We'll do it another time."

He relaxes, takes a long sip of the beer. He hasn't really eaten and he can feel a buzz coming on. It's so nice to be out of the house, away from the sick room. Poor Irene. What is he doing? "I shouldn't stay long," he says. "I need to get to the grocery store before it closes."

"Your friend's back at your house?"

Bob nods, then tries to steer the conversation away from Irene. "Have you ever been to Prana?"

"No, but I have been wanting to. Maybe we could go sometime."

Bob can't believe it. She is asking him out. He smiles. "I'd love to go out to dinner with you, Leonie, but I don't think my stomach can take another dinner at Prana."

"Of course!" She laughs. "What was I thinking? Your friend got food poisoning there. What did he eat?"

"I think it was the lobster." Bob takes a sip of his beer. "When do you want to go to dinner? I've been moved to the day shift. Wednesday?"

"Can't. Teaching that night."

"Thursday?"

She hesitates. "Sure… sure. Thursday would be fine."

Bob finishes off his beer and gets up to go. Leonie gets up too. She is almost as tall as he is. He feels like she is pulling him toward her. He leans in a bit and she leans in a bit and their lips meet. He puts his hand on her upper arm. He can feel her muscles through the bulky sweater. She turns her head sideways, kisses his bottom lip, then pulls at it with her teeth. Bob kisses her back and feels a clench in his stomach, followed by a warm flush all over his body. She is the first to break off. She nods her head and smiles and looks at the door. "I guess I'd better get going," he says and walks through the living room to the front door and onto the porch. "Oh," he stops, and walks back into the house. "I almost forgot. The tickets." He hands them to her and kisses her on the cheek. She waves goodbye as he walks down the porch stairs.

He takes a couple of steps and sees a man hurrying down the sidewalk towards the house. He has long curly blonde hair and horn-rimmed glasses, and is dressed in a denim jacket, plaid scarf, baggy corduroys, and clogs. Bob sort of smiles at the man and the man sort of smiles back, but slows his pace so they won't intersect. How very Cambridge. Bob reaches the sidewalk and turns in the opposite direction and hurries down the street to the grocery store, whistling under his breath.

CHAPTER 12

How the hell is Bob supposed to shift his schedule by eight hours? Daylight Saving Time rolls around and normal people moan about that lost hour of sleep for weeks. One measly hour. Plus Irene is still there. He has not had a woman sleeping in his house since his mother died. The whole ecology of the house is off; he can feel the estrogen upsetting the balance. He makes up a bed on the couch for himself and lies there awake, staring at the ceiling and at the headlights of passing cars. There's a gap between the shades and the window sashes and light from the streetlight slashes across his face. No way he is ever going to sleep. He could get up and make a cup of tea. He could watch TV. He could try the jazz history book someone gave him for Christmas. He could call Riff.

Riff answers on the second ring. Ornette Coleman is playing in the background "My man. What are you doing up?"

"Can't sleep."

"Why don't you come in early then? You could show BJ how to do your job. He's bad, man. Slow. I had to go out in the parking lot and smoke another joint to keep myself from strangling him. Even stoned, I have more get up and go than that fucker. How does he keep his job?"

"More work to fire him than to keep him."

"Yeah, well. You got to come back. I can't take it. How long is this going to last?"

"I don't know. I haven't even started." At the idea of starting a new shift, of working with Kathy and the rest of the news department, of skulking around the halls, trying to avoid Mitch and other managers, Bob suddenly feels sleepy.

"You hear about the new General Manager?"

"No!" Now Bob's wide awake. "Did they finally hire someone?"

"Yeah, they're announcing it today. At the station meeting."

"It's not Peralta, is it?"

"No, somebody from out of town. California, I think."

"Of course."

"And how's Irene?"

Bob lowers his voice "She's still here. Asleep. But she's going to be fine."

"And that other woman?"

"I canceled. Of course."

"Good."

"Well…" Bob tries to untangle the phone cord as he talks. He holds it over his head and ducks under it.

"You're going to see her?"

Bob doesn't answer.

"Come on man, you got to tell Irene."

"You want me to wake her up after she's been sick all day and all night?"

"Fucking trees."

"What?"

"You'd have been happy with Irene if it weren't for those fucking trees."

Bob changes the subject. "So, are you sticking around for the meeting?"

"Wouldn't miss it," Riff says. "We got to block this asshole off at the pass."

"My thoughts, exactly."

"It's a shame about Irene, Bobby. A damn shame."

Bob hangs up and looks at the pile of his clothes on the couch. They'd be fine for overnights, but they are not quite good enough for the daylight. Especially if he has to go to this meeting. All the reporters and admins and middle managers will be there, jostling each other to kiss up to the new GM. Nothing in his upbringing had prepared him for the sycophantic pandering of the work world. His father had been his own boss. His income may have been unpredictable, dependent on how low he could price his merchandise, how much money people had to spend, how much the landlord upped his rent, but he didn't have to suck up to idiots to survive. Bob was not good at it. Neither was Riff. They had so far survived by showing up, doing their jobs, and being safely out of the way by the time the decision makers rolled in every morning. And there wasn't, to be honest, a lot of competition for the overnight shift.

He will have to go into his room and get something clean and presentable to wear, risk waking up Irene. He had gotten her to sip some ginger ale and to eat a couple of crackers around 9 p.m. and then she had fallen back to sleep. He puts on his dirty jeans and opens the door, which creaks on its antique brass hinges, and tiptoes across the scarred oak floorboards. "Bob? Is that you?" Irene's awake.

"Who else would it be?"

"Is something wrong?"

"Can't sleep," he says. "Thought I'd just go in early, hang out with Riff, and make myself really tired for tomorrow night."

"Do you want your bed? I feel so guilty." She sits up, pulls the covers up to her shoulders. Bob can't help but notice her delicate collarbones, and pale neck. "Hey, do you have a T-shirt or something I could wear?"

Bob walks over to his dresser and takes out a clean T-shirt and throws it to Irene. He turns his head while she puts it on. It hangs off her narrow shoulders. She pulls her dark hair back and twists it around and piles it on top of her head. "Wish I had a hair clip," she says.

"You seem much better."

"I feel much better," she says. "Maybe I should go in with you?"

"Nah, Riff already made a big deal about you being sick. So you can't go in now. You'll make him look bad."

"Who's he told? BJ?"

"And, they've hired a new GM." Bob says. "They're going to announce it this morning."

"I have to go then. Why don't you stay? We could both go in together. There's room in here." Irene pats the side of the bed. "I promise I will leave you alone."

Bob smiles. He sits down on the bed. Irene snuggles next to him and puts her head on his shoulder. His hand starts rubbing her arm reflexively. Her breathing slows, but Bob is wide awake. It may be his own comfortable bed, but there is a semi-naked woman in it. He is not about to sleep.

He leans over and kisses the top of her head. "No, I think I'll go in." He finds a clean pair of jeans and underwear and ducks into the bathroom to change. When he emerges, Irene is standing in the hallway. His T-shirt comes halfway down her thighs. She goes up on her toes to kiss him. "Thanks for the lovely evening, Bob. Sorry I got sick and ruined it."

Bob kisses her back, puts his arms around her waist. "Oh you didn't ruin it," he says. "We had fun. And we got Prana out of the way. Now we never have to go there again." It feels very good and very bad to be doing this. All those lonely nights when he dreamed of someone kissing him off to work, when the idea of a woman in his clothes had seemed so very far away. But now he thinks he can still smell Leonie's clean hair on his shoulder and taste the cinnamon and minty taste of her mouth in his. Surely Irene must taste it too? But Irene sighs and smiles and disentangles her arms and patters back to bed. She walks with a slight wiggle at the end of every step, in the way that some shorter women do. Her legs are not long, but just long enough, emphasized by her bare feet. "Good night," she says as she pulls the covers back up.

Bob wishes Riff understood. He needs someone to talk to. He puts his spare set of keys on the kitchen table and calls out, "See you later," as he slips out the back door.

Bob and Riff take seats in the back of the cafeteria. There's a table of bagels and pastries and urns of fresh coffee set up behind them. The staff is filtering in and slowly waking up to the coffee and bagels. Riff lifts his sunglasses, rubs his eyes and yawns. "Who are all these people?"

"Beats me," Bob says. "Sales? Marketing?"

"Can you imagine dressing like that every day?"

Bob looks around at the men in suits, the women in heels and stockings; he shakes his head, closes his eyes. They are sitting directly under the cafeteria speakers. He can hear Kathy droning out the local news, the inevitable mix of the tragic and the trite.

Mitch hovers behind them, adjusting the lights.

"Hey turn those down, man, they're way too bright." Riff shades his eyes with his palm. Mitch sighs and turns them down.

"He's got a pole up his butt today," Riff whispers

"Didn't get the job. Now they're making him do the PA for the coronation of the guy who did. How would you feel?"

Riff nods. "Very sensitive of you, Bobby."

"At least with Mitch we would have known how bad it would be. Now the sky's the limit."

Larry, the program director and acting GM, enters the room. Following him is someone who looks a lot like Anthony, Kathy's fiancé. Bob stands up to get a better look. Oh fuck. It *is* Anthony.

"Oh, no. This is bad."

"What?"

"See that guy behind Larry? That's Kathy's fiancé. We met him the other night at Prana. Kathy's boyfriend is the new GM."

Larry and Anthony turn to greet the staff like politicians on the stump, smiling into the air in front of them, occasionally locking eyes with an actual human being, and winking. Anthony has a certain glow about him. He looks to be in his late thirties, early forties at the most, the age of the new conquerors. Bob's generation has somehow skipped the In Charge phase, segueing directly from immature fuckups to over-the-hill budget busters. It's humiliating really, but Bob can't quite muster the indignation to protest. He never really wanted to be in charge.

Larry picks up the cordless microphone Mitch and his staff have conveniently set up for the event. He gestures to Mitch to turn down the regular speakers in the room. Mitch switches them off abruptly, cutting Kathy off before she has finished giving out the call letters. Anthony looks up from his notes and frowns. Mitch folds his hands in front of his chest and widens his stance.

Larry stands up. "All right everybody, let's get started." He looks like a lounge singer working the room. "I have some great news. After much consideration and a nationwide search, we have hired a new General Manager. I would like to introduce you to Anthony Di Tucci. He comes to us from KLPP in Sacramento. Before that he was with the ABC affiliate, WBNG, in Cincinnati, and before that he started the all-news format for an FM/AM combo in Tallahassee."

"Whoop de do!" Riff whispers.

"'Nationwide search,'" Bob says. "That's code for: 'Fuck you, Mitch.'"

Bob is that rarity in radio, someone who has stayed put. Radio is full of nomads who pull up stakes and move across the country, yanking their children out of schools, their spouses out of careers and houses. They pull into a new town whose name they can't pronounce, whose politics they don't understand, whose traffic nightmares are just grids on their Triple A maps. They rent expensive furnished apartments, and immediately find a dry cleaner, a gym, and good takeout within an easy commute to work. The only people they know are at the station, so they make friends there, fall in love there, cheat on their spouses there, and re-marry and reproduce and drag the ensuing unhappy family all around the country to start the cycle again. Their worlds get narrower and narrower with each move. They leave everything behind for their careers, though Bob has always suspected they didn't have much to leave behind in the first place.

Larry wraps up his introduction. "So let's give a great big welcome to our new GM, Tony Di Tucci!"

The cafeteria explodes with applause, a few catcalls, even a whistle. Roger Michaud from Advertising pounds his fists on the table. Anthony stands up, and takes the microphone from Larry. "That's *Anthony* Di Tucci," he says. "But thanks for the generous introduction."

Larry sits down and promptly starts biting his lip. Anthony scans the crowd. "I am happy to see so many of you made it to the meeting," he says. "I realize that for some of you that meant coming in on your own time or extending your shifts, and I know how hard that is. I started out on morning drive at my college station, so I know what sleep deprivation is all about!" The audience laughs. Bob rolls his eyes. College fucking radio.

"And it's doubly important that you are here, because I plan to outline a new path for the station. And for that to work, we're going to need all of you to get on board. We know it's not easy to accept change, but it's really the only way to keep an organization vibrant and growing in the crowded media environment that we live in."

"Where's this going?" Bob whispers.

"Can't be good," Riff says.

"The main reason that the company hired me for this job is that they have a vision for this station going forward, and they believe I have the experience to realize it. If we look at the station's ratings over the last couple of books, it's clear that we are losing audience share whenever we stray from our stated mission, which is to bring news and information to the Boston area. So," he stops and smiles at the audience. "We are going to stop straying from that mission."

The cafeteria is silent. No more catcalls, only a few nervous sounding coughs.

"The company wants to commit us to an all news and information format by the end of the year. To that end, we are going to start phasing out all non-news programming immediately."

There's a mumbling and a shifting of chairs across the cafeteria. Several people turn all the way around in their seats to stare at Riff.

One of the more intrepid reporters raises his hand, press conference style. "Are you saying that you are going to get rid of all the music, sports, and entertainment shows?"

Anthony takes a step back, as if the question was exaggerated, extreme. "Not all, and not right away."

"But eventually you're going to ax them?"

Anthony looks at the reporter for a few moments before answering. He's trying to memorize his features, Bob thinks, so he can retaliate later. "Eventually we are going to be an all news and information station. Yes."

"And the company has decided this, sir, without consulting any of the staff?"

"The company has charted a course for the station in the coming years that is practical and I believe visionary. We are going to concentrate on news." He looks around the room, a faint smirk on his face. "And by the looks of our indefatigable reporting staff, we have a bright future ahead."

The audience laughs. The reporter remains standing. "So you can guarantee that no one is going to lose their job?"

Anthony pauses. "I can guarantee that this station is going to be stronger place for all to work."

"This guy's the devil," Riff whispers. "But who else would fuck Kathy?"

Bob laughs and looks at his watch. 9:45. Di Tucci's been in charge for fifteen minutes, and he's already turned their world upside down. He feels a yawning pit at the bottom of his stomach. Sounds like his and Riff's days are numbered. And what other station is going to take them on? Riff is old and the jazz audience is older. Bob is worried, but he also feels the tiniest bit exhilarated. Perhaps this all will end. Maybe there is something else out there for him. He could move to California with Leonie and massage dancers' feet or carry around ice packs and biofeedback machines for their torn ligaments. Leonie could get a teaching job, and he could keep house. They could buy a farm and raise organic goats. He'd plant Japanese maples, or palm trees and whatever else grows out there. Prickly pears?

Anthony is talking about Phase 1 of his plan, which sounds like some kind of Soviet-style soul searching on the part of the staff and then assignment to their various gulags for reeducation.

The door to the cafeteria opens slowly, and Irene slides in. Her face is pale; her hair looks stringy and unclean. Damn, he should have directed her to the extra bottle of shampoo in the linen closet, given her a bath towel. But he didn't expect for her to arise, Lazarus-like, to attend this stupid meeting.

Anthony looks over at the sound of the door opening and squints. Irene's eyes widen at the sight of Anthony. Bob watches as the realization that he is the new general manager sinks in. She starts to frown, but quickly hides it and gives Anthony a big smile. "Sorry," she mouths and hunches her head into her shoulders as if to make herself disappear.

Riff stands up slightly and waves her over. She hurries to the vacant seat beside Bob. "Oh my God," she says, as she sits down.

Bob shrugs. "Don't worry, you'll be fine. You're in news." He takes her small warm hand and places it on his lap. "But we jazz dinosaurs are on the way out."

CHAPTER 13

"I guess you don't edit much on the overnights." Kathy looks at her watch. "Can you pick up the pace? Please?"

Bob has been struggling to move a chunk of audio from the front to the back of a piece, and he keeps on losing little bits in the process. There must be a better way to do this, but he doesn't have time to poll his fellow engineers to find out. Instead, he goes on the offensive. "Well, if you'd make up your mind..."

"That's how I work. I need to hear the edit first. O'Mara doesn't have a problem with that. Of course, she's really fast."

He will get faster on EditPro, eventually. But today he feels like he is wading through peanut butter. He is so tired he could put his head down and sleep right there on the console. His nerves are jangled from dealing with so many people, his stomach soured from too much coffee and donuts, his mind buzzing with Anthony's plan for their future. He forgot to pay in advance for the parking lot, and now he is probably getting towed while Kathy goes back and forth with this piece about endangered fish.

"Should we open with the Gloucester fisherman? Or the chef at La Mer?"

"Who cares! They're both full of it. Where'd you get them anyway, central casting?"

"Or how about the retired school teacher? She's good, and we got great sound of her frying up catfish. We could open with the oil sizzling in the pan."

"Why is she even in the piece? Because she's black?"

"No! Because she's retired, on a fixed income, and she can't afford swordfish. That's an important demographic, you know."

"See, that's what I hate about the media. Demographic. You come up with some story line, and then you go out and find the right demographic to prove it. It's all made up."

"I got news for you, Bob. You're part of the media, too."

"Not really," Bob says. "I'm a fluke."

"Lots of people would kill for your job."

"Lots of people are insane."

She turns back to the computer screen. "Let's open with the oil in the frying pan and move the fisherman to the end."

Bob selects the segment with the retired school teacher and moves it to the front of the piece. Then he selects the segment with the fisherman and moves it to the end. Then he closes up the space between them. Presto! He feels like a surgeon with a mouse. He hits play.

"What happened to the sizzling oil?" Kathy shrieks.

"I don't know. I thought I selected everything."

"Was it on a different track?"

"Damn. I forgot about the effects track. Give me a minute. I got to think this through."

Kathy looks at her watch. "This is supposed to air at four! Should we get someone in here who knows what he's doing?"

"No," Bob says. "Just give me a minute." Should he do three "undos" or is it faster to grab that sizzling oil sound effect and move it? Or will that mess up the placement of all the other sound effects? He should zoom out and look at the whole piece. Get some perspective. But he needs to see the effects track, too. How does he resize the tracks? He knows there's a button somewhere. Over there? No — definitely not that one.

Kathy leans over the console, grabs the mouse out of his hand.

"Hey," Bob says. "Give me that!" He reaches for the mouse, but Kathy holds firm.

"Let me show you how it's done," she says.

"You're not supposed to touch my equipment. Union rules."

Kathy clicks on a little box under the track name. A drop-down menu appears with the different available sizes. "There," she says," that's how you resize a track."

Bob grabs the mouse out of her hand. "Thanks, but don't let anyone ever see you doing that, or I'll have to write you up."

Kathy rolls her eyes. "I used EditPro at my last job. These union rules are from the dark ages."

"So, is your boyfriend going to get rid of the union, too?"

Kathy gives him an exasperated look. "We don't talk about work at home."

"But you are going to get rid of Riff's show, right?"

Kathy sighs. "No one listens to the radio for music these days, Bob."

"We've got plenty of listeners."

"Have you looked at your last book? You're way down."

Bob has never paid much attention to ratings. During station meetings when Larry got out the overhead projector and flashed the ratings graphs on the wall, Bob usually napped. There were basically two facts you needed to know to understand the whole ratings business. 1) People listen to the radio on their drives to and from work, and 2) A whole class of consultants makes a living theorizing what could bring in listeners for the rest of the day. Bob has lived through many waves of consultants and their formats — happy talk, news you can use, shock jocks, dance tracks, easy listening, all request, disco lunch.

"Maybe no one stays up late anymore," he says. "Everyone's on Ambien."

Kathy looks at him carefully. "No," she says. "Other stations' overnight numbers are just fine. Especially news and talk stations."

"I was being sarcastic. So, when's he going to can us?"

"I'm sure he'll keep as many people as he can, shift people around, make use of everyone's talents."

"Shit. Then I'm getting laid off, for sure." Bob turns back to the computer, resizes the tracks, and realizes he shouldn't just move the sizzling oil. He hits undo until he is back at the original version and starts all over again. He bends closer to the screen to make sure he has selected every bit of audio, and as he does so a drop of perspiration slips down off his nose. He will get better at this eventually; he's just not sure if eventually will be soon enough.

CHAPTER 14

Leonie suggests they meet at a restaurant downtown, after work. She's heard good things about it. Bob is nervous and can't find a place to park. Where the hell is he supposed to park downtown anyway? He should have paid for a lot. He has driven around Chinatown four times looking for a space, and on the fifth he tried an unfamiliar alley and ended up on the expressway. He looks at the clock on the dashboard; he is late and he is on his way to Cape Cod. He could call the restaurant, something vaguely Middle Eastern sounding? Arak? Aral? He knows it's in the old Leather District. On one side of the expressway is the ocean, on the other the marsh where the Irish mob dumped their bodies. Bob looks at the bucolic scene and wonders how many bodies are still there, waiting to be found. He wonders if everything is as corrupt in California. He can't imagine a city that isn't full of crooked cops, lying politicians, homegrown mobsters. It's all he has ever known. Now he is stuck in rush-hour traffic. Rush hour must last two or three hours these days. He is used to gliding along the highways in the dark. If he feels like going slow, he goes slow. If he feels like going fast, he goes fast. Why did he let Leonie convince him to go downtown? When they both live in Cambridge, for God's sakes. When they could have walked.

It had been another hellish day at work. A live interview with a station in New York, and he had mistakenly dropped the line. Mitch had been all over him. He called him into his office and shut the door. "How could you do that, Bobby? How could you do that?"

As if anyone could explain why he made a mistake. Bob eyed the chair opposite Mitch's desk. He would have liked to sit down, but instead he stood with his hand on the doorknob, ready to bolt. "I fucked up, Mitch. Okay? I fucked up."

"Tell me you'll never do it again." Mitch stood very close.

"I can't promise you I'll never make another mistake."

"Sure you can."

"No, it's out of my control. I am going to make more mistakes."

"Now that's where your negativity comes into play. Can't wait to shoot yourself in the foot. Make the promise and be done with it."

Bob turned the door knob to leave. "This is crazy."

"Just make the promise, Bobby."

"All right, I'll never make another mistake."

"Good." Mitch sat down behind his desk. "Now we can both get back to work."

Leonie is sitting alone at a table by the door, sipping a glass of red wine and reading. She looks up when he enters and her face relaxes into a smile. She starts to get up and he says, "No, no, sit. Sorry, I'm so late."

"I was beginning to think I was getting stood up," she says, smiling, as if this would never happen. "Where were you?"

"I made a wrong turn and ended up on the expressway, stuck in traffic."

Damn, Bob thinks, what a way to start off. "I should have taken the subway. It's just, I don't mind taking the subway to get somewhere, but I hate taking it back, you know? It's like okay, I'm done, and I want to go home now, not wait in some dank hole for a train."

She raises her eyebrows, shrugs. "I don't mind the train," she says. "Gives me time to read."

He sits down and motions for the waiter, who has been hovering by their table with menus. He points to Leonie's glass of wine and tries to get comfortable. He can't think of anything to say to her. *How was your day?* seems too familiar. Another apology would just draw attention to his lateness. He picks up the menu and scans it, not taking anything in. "Have you been here before?" he asks.

"No, I just heard about it. My colleagues rave about it."

He tries to imagine calling Peralta a "colleague." Or Riff. This is a mistake. A colossal mistake. He's jeopardizing things with Irene for someone with whom he has nothing in common.

When the waiter brings his glass of wine, Leonie says, "Let's order an appetizer. I am starving. I am always hungry on days when I teach. Do you eat mussels?"

I do now, he thinks. He takes a sip of wine. It's good. Of course she would order something good. He can feel the alcohol spreading relief through his veins. He takes another sip, then another. He is still jetlagged from working days. He looks out the window at the gates of Chinatown. Maybe they should have gone there. The food is good enough. Maybe not as authentic as San Francisco's. Not as impressive as New York's. It's just boring old Boston, and he is boring old Bob and what did he ever think someone like Leonie would see in him?

"So did you have a nice day?" she asks.

"Not really." He smiles and starts to tell her about the line he dropped and the confrontation with Mitch, but then he stops himself. It doesn't put him in the most flattering light. "I am not really happy working days," he says instead. "I am not all that into the news. I'm more into jazz."

"Oh my God," she says. "I almost forgot to thank you. Buddy! I went to see Buddy. You're right. He's really talented. We loved the show!"

"So was that your ex, with the clogs and the long curly hair?"

"Yes." She laughs and takes a sip of her drink. "He saw you too. I think he was a bit jealous."

Bob leans back in his chair. So this really is happening. This really is a date, and this beautiful woman really is interested in him. Don't fuck it up, he thinks. "I thought he was remarried."

"When did that ever stop someone from getting jealous?" She loops a piece of dark hair behind her ear. "I haven't really been with anyone since he left me."

"He's an idiot."

"Thank you," Leonie says.

"No, I mean it. He's an idiot."

Leonie leans over the table and kisses his cheek. "And I mean it," she says. "Thank you."

Bob picks up the menu and smiles down into it. "Did Buddy come over to your table?"

"No," she says. "Was he supposed to?"

"Just thought he might come looking for me. I called him to get the tickets. We went to college together, you know. I introduced him to jazz and blues. He didn't even start playing until after college."

"That's amazing. He seems like he's done it his whole life. And you, did you never play?"

"I tried piano, when I was young." He had taken a couple of piano lessons from one of the nuns, who hovered so close he could smell her talcum powder, and he would get distracted by the idea that nuns needed talcum powder, that they had bodies under those robes, nooks and crannies where sweat might accumulate. And he would lose his place in the piece and wham! A ruler would come crashing down on his fingers. "Pay attention!" He'd run his throbbing fingers over the keys and scramble to find his place in the wavering line of little black notes, and even then he suspected this was no way to master an instrument.

"And did you never think of going into music?"

"I was a jazz DJ for a while. And I've written record reviews and several articles. Right now, in fact, I'm working on a piece that grew out of an article I published in *Jazzis*. Actually, it's getting so long that now it's more like a book. I don't think any magazine would publish it."

Leonie leans forward. "A book? What's it about?"

"See that's my problem." Bob shifts in his seat, takes a sip of wine. "When I started, it was about the new generation of jazz musicians. How they were going to kill jazz. Because they just didn't have the heart. You know? I mean, Like Buddy. He's good. And he's got an awful drug problem, so he has suffered a bit. But he's just repeating something that was already done. And done to perfection. He's not adding anything to the form. But the trouble is, I've been working on the goddamned piece for so long, that jazz is almost dead. So now I am revising it. Less a warning, than a long-form obituary!"

"Wow, you are amazing. I would love to read it."

"Yeah, sure," Bob says, "if I ever finish it." He is flattered despite himself. Is he really amazing or is it just amazing to her that a guy like him has a brain?

The waiter returns to the table with their mussels. Bob watches Leonie unfurl her napkin, her long thin fingers smoothing out the creases. She takes a mussel and opens it and spears the orange flesh inside and forks it into her mouth. "Mmm," she says. "I love mussels."

Bob takes one onto his plate and imitates what she has done. It is delicious, garlicky and buttery, with just the right amount of bite. How has he lived his whole life in Boston and never tasted mussels? They were just one of the many things his parents didn't eat. Lobster, mussels, shrimp, clams, crab, cheese, olives, avocados, artichokes, garlic, butter, chives, shallots, peppers, veal, sausage, mushrooms, sour cream, pizza, lasagna, ravioli, sweet potatoes, clam chowder, clam chowder for Christ's sake! Oh to be Irish in Boston. Holding onto some outmoded version of Irishness — eating corned beef and cabbage on St. Patrick's Day, dyeing your beer and your cupcakes green, offering up your daughters for step dancing lessons, your sons for the priesthood, nursing your bitterness against the British, the Protestants, the Orangemen, fearful of the Italians, Jews, and Gypsies, suspicious of the French — not real Catholics at all, with their mistresses, snooty wines, and indigestible food. Bob's father always claimed that the Irish digestive system craved a nice well-done piece of steak. Let your bowels chew on that for a while, he said, and all will be right.

Bob takes another mussel and washes it down with the spicy red wine. One thing his parents did right, though; they stayed in Cambridge and left him the house, so he could grow up and meet someone like Leonie.

After dinner they walk hand in hand through Chinatown to retrieve his car. Now he's glad he brought it. He can drive her home; they can sit side by side in this private dark bubble; he can turn off the car, and they can linger in front of her house. Though there is a lot of pressure in a car: memories of awkward high school kisses, furtive groping, long pauses while neither he nor his date could think of anything to say. But Leonie makes it easy. As he pulls into her driveway, she leans over, puts her hand on his arm, and asks, "Would you like to come in?"

They sit at her kitchen table and sip more wine. It's getting late and he has to work in the morning and she has to teach in the morning, but neither makes a move to go. Bob puts down his wine glass and stands up and pulls her to her feet and starts kissing her, and to tell the truth it is a little strange, a little awkward. She is almost as tall as he is and their noses bump. And they pull apart and laugh, but then come together to try again. She loops her arms around his shoulders and he wraps his around her muscled back. He squeezes the muscles up and down the side of her spine and then lets his hand rest on her hip. "Wait!" she says and disentangles herself and walks over to the window and lowers the shade. "I don't want all of the neighborhood to start talking. You know how that goes." And he says yes, though really he doesn't. He hadn't realized the neighbors talked, because he has never been part of their conversation.

They move into Leonie's bedroom and she dims the light and he says, "No, I want to see you," and she turns it up a bit, not as bright as he would like, but soon his eyes adjust, enough so that he can see her golden, still tanned, skin. Ah skin! How has he lived so long without the touch of it? How soft her arms are. How gentle her features. He lifts her shirt over her head. She unclasps her lacy black bra. "You'll never figure this one out," she says. "The hooks are in the front." Her breasts are small but perfectly shaped, the nipples large and brownish. He cups one of her breasts in his hand and rubs his finger over the nipple, which stiffens to his touch. She moans. Perhaps it has been a long time for her, too? She lifts his shirt over head, places her hands on his shoulders. "Such nice shoulders," she says. "You could have been a dancer." She steps out of her pants and underwear. He shrugs his quickly to the ground, checking his back pocket to be sure the pack of condoms is still lodged safely there, and they are finally on her bed when she suddenly stops him and says, "Wait, I have to tell you something."

Oh no, he thinks. She's really a man, she has a month to live, her ex-husband is in the closet, videotaping them. "What?" He runs his hand down the length of her body.

"I'm not using birth control."

"That's okay," he says. "I've got condoms."

"No," she says. "I don't want to use birth control. I wouldn't mind if I got pregnant."

Bob sits up. "But you don't really know me. I don't really know you."

Leonie sits up and props herself up against the headboard. "But you were ready to sleep with me?"

"Of course, I've been ready for that ever since I met you."

She smiles. Compliment noted. "But you see, I'm getting older. And I want a baby. If it happens, it happens. I won't put any pressure on you."

"But that's not what I want," he says.

"You don't want children?" She leans away from him.

"Not now. I want to get to know you and you to get to know me and we go out to lots of dinners and we have lots of sex and then when we are good and ready, we think about having children."

"By then maybe I won't get pregnant," she says. "I don't have that long."

"Would you really want to raise a child by yourself?"

"Sure," she says. "I'd rather do it with someone, but time is running out."

Bob nods. Time is running out for him too. He is no longer young. He is no longer young middle aged. He is on his way out, genetically speaking. He wanted children, of course, but he wanted them in some indefinite future when things got easy for him, when he had something left to give. So far his life has been a struggle. Just enough money to survive, to pay the taxes and keep the house heated, just enough to fix the roof and maintain his car. How did his parents ever do it? Did they just close their eyes and plunge? Which frankly is what his hormones would like him to do right now. Jump, Bobby, jump. She wants to get pregnant. No strings attached. But he can't just jump.

"I can't do this," he says. "I don't want to be your sperm donor."

"I'm not thinking of you as a sperm donor." Leonie walks her fingers up his arm, lightly. The hairs on his arm stand on end. "I like you. A lot. I just don't want to stop myself from getting pregnant anymore. I did that for twenty years and sometimes I think I would have been better off being careless. At least I would have a child. I wouldn't be so alone."

He puts his arms around her. "But you're not so alone. I would like to see you. I would like to see a lot of you."

"Then why don't we just let nature take its course? If we're meant to be together, we'll stay together. If I'm meant to get pregnant, I'll get pregnant. Let's just see what happens."

He pulls his shirt back over his head and pulls the covers to his waist. He is no longer aroused. "You know, Leonie, this is really crazy. What if I had HIV?"

"Do you have HIV?"

"No, but we should use condoms anyway, and then both get tested. Just to be sure."

"And then wait for the tests to come back and another month is gone, another egg rolls down the shoot, maybe that was the last month my body would ever get pregnant. Maybe that was *the* egg. I have watched my girlfriends struggle with this, month after month, and then suddenly it's over. You're done. You guys don't understand."

"But I do. That's why I'm an only child. My mother spent her thirties trying to get pregnant, and didn't have me until she was over forty."

"See! Things happen very quickly once you're forty. I don't have much time."

"Really, you're over forty? I thought you were younger."

Wrong thing to say. She gets out of bed and finds her underwear on the floor and pulls them up over her muscled thighs and slender hips, stamping one foot at a time as she does so. He can't help but notice the dark triangle of her pubic hair as it disappears beneath the lacy fabric of her underwear. She turns up the lights. "I just meant you look so young," he says. "I'm much older than you."

"Look," she says. "Maybe you're right. We hardly know each other."

Bob leaps out of bed and pulls on his underwear. "Oh, Leonie, I'm an idiot. I'm sorry. Can we please start over again? We'll turn out the lights, get back into bed and start all over again?"

Leonie smiles, but folds her arms over her chest, and shakes her head. "Not tonight," she says.

Bob finds his pants on the floor. Leonie walks out of her bedroom as he puts them on. When he emerges she is standing in the hallway, his coat in her hand.

He starts to say something, but then he looks at her face and knows it is time to be silent. She has revealed way too much. He should leave now, quickly, while there is still a chance she can face him again.

He grabs his coat and walks to the door without turning back. "I'll call you," he says, and he closes the door gently behind himself and plunges into the cold night air.

CHAPTER 15

His phone is ringing when he lets himself in the back door. "Wait 'til you hear the latest about Omar," Riff says. He can hear a tenor sax in the background. Dexter Gordon, maybe Lester Young?

Bob shuts the door behind him, takes off his coat and throws it on the kitchen table. "They hire him back?" He looks at the clock. 1:30 a.m. He's booked at 9 for an editing session with Kathy and then at 9:30 for a mix with Irene.

"Far from it!" Riff snorts into the phone. "The insurance company wants its money back. All of it. They want us all to repay the money we saved, or they'll throw Omar in jail."

"Oh no." Bob sinks down onto one of the kitchen chairs. "How much?"

"Depends on what you owe. I just got a bill for $11,765.33. Remember all that physical therapy Sue had for her back?"

Bob gets up and wanders into his bedroom, looks at himself in the mirror. He's got that disheveled, just-out-of bed look; his face is flushed. "But we didn't even know it was going on."

"They want their money. Can you imagine Omar in jail?"

"How far back does this go?"

He hears Riff shuffling papers. "I got charges here going back eight years."

"Damn. This is just what I needed tonight."

"Oh yeah, how was your date with the Radcliffe broad?"

"Harvard," he says. "Radcliffe doesn't really exist anymore." He tells Riff about Leonie's plan to get pregnant, his reluctance.

"No wonder she was interested in you."

"Thanks."

"No really. It didn't make sense. No offense Bobby, but she was way out of your league. Don't feel bad. It would never have worked out anyway."

"I'm not giving up."

"Are you crazy? Forget about her. See how things develop with Irene. I told you. She really... Oh shit. Hold on. I got to give BJ another CD. He let the music run out!"

BJ has committed the cardinal sin of radio, dead air! Bob hears shuffling in the studio, Riff shouting over the talkback, and then Miles Davis starting up in the background.

"So I guess BJ's not getting any better?" he says.

"No, worse," Riff says. "Can you believe it? This could be my last days on the radio, and I have to spend it with him? He's sucks all the joy out of the room. Even the music can't cheer me up. I've lost my will to live, man. I try to get into a groove and then I look across the glass, and there he is, with that big dumb mug of his. And he'll probably keep his job. He's union!"

Bob checks that his alarm clock is set, then walks into the bathroom to brush his teeth. "Look, I got to go to bed. I got to be there in less than eight hours."

"Hey, did you talk to Buddy Guitar Lewis about being on the show?"

"Not yet."

"Well please do it. I got have something to keep me going until you get back."

Bob promises he will call Buddy, though he doubts that getting Buddy on the show will be enough to keep Riff going.

There is something crawling in the walls over his head. He can hear it scratching and clawing away, so close that it seems to be in the room with him. Damn squirrel lady. Of course it's a squirrel. It must have found a soft spot in the fascia board and chewed its way in. He should have checked the flashing, but he hates getting up on the ladder. He is not that comfortable with heights. He no longer trusts his body to make the right decisions, to put weight where it should put weight, not to lean too far out. But most of all he fears he will come face to face with a squirrel or a raccoon and lose his balance and crash down three stories to his death. Local man. Dead, at forty-eight. After a brave struggle with a squirrel.

Worst thing is, there is nothing he can do. He can't rout it out now in the middle of the night. He can't ask it politely to keep it down. He could get up and find his earplugs, or put on a fan. But the insistent scratching and scrabbling would cut right through the fan's reassuring drone.

He gets up and makes himself a cup of coffee. Two nights in a week when he hasn't been able to sleep. He wonders if you can die from lack of sleep. Surely something must happen at a molecular level. Perhaps the cancer cells crest or some cellular sentry meant to keep them at bay falls asleep at his post. It can't be good.

He gets out his headphones and tunes into Riff's show. Coltrane. He closes his eyes and sees Leonie's long curving torso. His nerves are still lit up with her touch. If only he could have stayed the night. Should he have gone ahead, not worried about her getting pregnant? No, that was not right. They barely know each other. But should two people who barely know each other make love in the first place? Of course, they are in their forties. Their bodies know what to do and how to do it, and stopping short seems almost perverse. But put yourself in her place. All those years of preventing something and now time is running out. Perhaps she is right. Let nature take its course. Don't stop something you want desperately to happen. But they are already a long way from nature. Natural was getting pregnant in your teens. Or having some girl's father march you to the altar with a gun to your head. Or courting for years and then getting married and realizing your spouse hates sex.

There is something very unnatural in letting yourself get pregnant by a neighbor, going it all alone, taking matters into your own hands. What shocks him most though is how much Leonie has thought this through and how it has never occurred to him at all. Was Irene thinking the same thing? Was she another ticking time bomb?

He could imagine marrying Leonie; they could raise children and goats. He could be a stay-at-home Dad. He is tired of the Mitch Peraltas and the Anthony Di Tuccis of the work world. He would be happy to stay at home and change diapers and do laundry, to plant seedlings in cups in the window and ride the sit down lawnmower over the grass the long-haired goats hadn't already gotten to, a little boy or girl in his lap, but maybe that was dangerous, child abuse, you didn't put a baby on a sit down mower, but he's sure they would love it, as he would have, but what does he really know?

There is more scrambling overhead. Definitely more than one squirrel. Probably a family of squirrels. Animals do not live solitary existential lives. Only humans do. Bob thinks he will have to hire somebody to get rid of them this time. He has never felt quite comfortable hiring people to work on his house. He feels he should do the work himself. It's the Irish way. He is supposed be the one with the chimney soot and raccoon shit in his hair, not the rich guy with clean khaki pants and soft leather shoes. It is imprinted in his DNA. The meek shall inherit the earth.

He gets up and finds the yellow pages and looks up pest control, then exterminators, then wildlife control. There it is. Bay State Trappers, a picture of a raccoon in a 'Havahart' trap. He writes down the number to call them in the morning. Then he locates his earplugs and attempts once again to sleep.

CHAPTER 16

Bob is waiting for Mitch when he arrives in the morning. He has been perched on the corner of Mitch's desk, drinking coffee for fifteen minutes. Mitch barely has time to put his briefcase down on his desk, when Bob starts. "I want off days. Riff can't work with BJ. It's hurting the show. It's going to kill his ratings."

"No," Mitch says. He hangs his beige raincoat up on his coat rack. Wife must have bought it for him. It's regulation Middle Management. Probably bought him the briefcase too. What the hell does he have to put in a briefcase? A baloney sandwich? An extra pair of socks? "Since when did you care about ratings?"

"Why not?"

"I need you on days." Mitch makes a shooing motion with his hand to get Bob off his desk.

"Riff needs me on nights. Why don't you let me do something I'm actually good at?"

"Bob, I'm doing you a favor." Mitch sighs as he settles into his chair. "You need more editing experience. And you need to show your face around the newsroom, to make an impression on the people who matter. Know what I'm saying?"

"So Riff's show is really on the way out?"

Mitch straightens his tie, switches on his computer. "You don't have to go down with the ship, Bob. The union will fight for you. You've got seniority. But they got to have a reason. You got to give them a reason."

"Well, how long do you think this day shift is going to last? When's O'Mara coming back?"

"Never."

"What? You know that for a fact? When were you going to tell me?"

"Relax. I just found out. But right now my hands are tied. I can't hire anyone. I got to shift people around, until we get a better picture of the, uh, staffing needs of the station."

Bob sighs. This is not the first upheaval he has been through. He's survived format changes. He's gone through several different general managers. He's walked the picket line, twice. Both times he emerged scarred and scathed. Before his first strike, he had asked one of the old timers how he was supposed to survive. "You don't," the old timer said. "You never recover."

It had taken him years to work down the balance on his credit cards. He had to borrow money to pay his real estate taxes. He had lived through a long cold winter with the heat turned low, wearing a down vest and a hat to bed. But for some reason, this change feels worse. It seems like it is happening in slow motion, with plenty of forewarning, plenty of time to agonize or plan ahead. And that is almost more painful. He almost wants it to be over, and quickly. Or maybe this is what it's like when you get older and your powers of denial wear thin. Perhaps it's just the lack of sleep, the unfamiliar shift, the strange hours. Perhaps it's that he has been thinking so much about Irene and Leonie in the last few weeks, that he has let all the signs of impending doom slip by.

Maybe it's the goddamned squirrels. He had called Bay State Trappers at seven a.m. Just a hunch. He figured a business like that might open early. A gruff voice answered on the second ring. Bob told him about the squirrels and asked if they covered Cambridge.

"Cambridge? No way! There's no parking. They'd just as soon tow you as look at you."

"You can park in my driveway. How much do you charge?"

"How many squirrels?"

"I'm not sure. A few."

"You want them dead or alive?"

"I thought you used 'Havahart' traps."

"Sure. We call them 'Luv a Rat' traps! We got them. But poison's cheaper. You block up their hole. They die in the eaves."

"I don't want them to die some horrible death."

"Hey, they don't give a shit about you, man."

"If you use the traps, where do you take them?"

"Out here, to the country."

Bob looked at the phone exchange. He wouldn't exactly call it "the country." But then again, his squirrels weren't exactly country either. They'd miss the overflowing trash cans, the fast food wrappers, the sooty Norway maples. He made an appointment with a trapper named Rusty, for that evening, after work.

Bob paces back and forth in front of Mitch's desk. "Sit down, will you? You're making me nervous." Bob looks down at the chair, which is covered in papers. "You can throw that crap on the floor," Mitch says. "It's next year's budget. I got to do the whole thing over anyway."

Bob sinks down onto the chair. He pushes the papers to the back. Riff will be okay financially, he thinks. He owns the house outright. He's never lived beyond his means. He's probably got a pretty good amount socked away. And he's got a young wife. Maybe she could actually get with the twentieth century and work. But he doesn't know how Riff will fare emotionally. He has his music. He has his pot. But is that enough? Men need some place to go, somebody to see every day, a schedule to keep, a word to describe themselves. DJ. Personality. Talent. Whatever. Women, Bob thinks, are different. They can busy themselves around the house. They can obsess about curtains or babies, or cousins, or bulbs for the garden. They can shop. What are men supposed to do? Build things? Mow the fucking lawn? His father never had time to retire. He worked and then he got cancer and he worked some more until he couldn't leave the house and then he died. Then his mother took over the store and worked until she got cancer. They sold the store to the guy who worked nights. Not that it was worth much by then. They hadn't owned the building and the rent was high and the grocery business was changing. Supermarkets were cutting into their profit on the low end, gourmet shops on the high end.

Bob finishes up his coffee and tosses the empty cup into Mitch's trashcan. "Kind of strange that the new GM is Kathy's fiancé, huh? What was she? An advance scout?"

Mitch shrugs. "Hey, everybody's got to work somewhere. Can you blame them for wanting to work together? Happens all the time."

"Still. She shows up here. Starts making trouble. Gets Omar fired."

"Omar got himself fired. He was the one who was stealing. By the way, did you get your bill? I put a call in to my lawyer the minute I got mine. I don't think they can make us pay."

"But Omar will go to jail."

"He deserves jail."

"Oh, he's a good guy. Just misguided."

Mitch snorts. "Never took you for such a bleeding heart, Bobby. Wait 'til you get your bill!"

Bob tries to think back over the last eight years. He's fairly healthy. Surely he couldn't owe that much? Of course there was all the dental work. And the MRI when he was having neck pain. And oh no, the wisdom tooth extraction that went so wrong he ended up in the emergency room. And that time he sprained his ankle. That couldn't cost much, could it? And the acupuncturist he went to for insomnia. For ten months.

Bob looks at his watch and then gets up out of the chair. "I've got a session with Kathy in fifteen minutes. I've got to set the studio up. Wouldn't want to waste any of her precious time."

"Good, good. Glad to see you thinking ahead."

"But, Mitch. Really. If Riff's show is on the way out, don't let him go out with BJ. Put me back on nights, at least for the end, okay?"

Mitch nods. "I'll see what I can do. For the end."

For once, the session with Kathy goes smoothly. Bob is prepared, her piece is short, and she is not in as much of a hurry as usual. He makes a good suggestion for a closing song and then makes a particularly difficult edit in the music. "That was brilliant, Bob." Kathy pats him on the back. "Absolutely brilliant." So he is feeling pretty good about everything when Irene walks into the studio.

She looks like hell. Her hair is pulled back off her face in a tight ponytail. She has dark smudges under her eyes. She's dressed in loose jeans and a shapeless sweater and scuffed up white sneakers. Bob stands up. "Hey, Irene," he says. "What's going on? Everything okay?"

She looks him in the eye and then shakes her head. "You don't know?"

"Did you get your bill from the insurance company?"

"Yeah." Her shoulders sag. "I owe them seventeen grand. But that's not why I'm upset."

"No?"

"Where the fuck have you been? Why haven't you called me? Jesus Christ, I spend the night at your house. After getting poisoned, I might add. And then we're all lovey dovey at the station meeting and holding hands and everything, and then, nothing! Nothing! What are you? Eighteen years old or something?"

"Oh no." Bob walks over. He takes her hand. "I'm sorry. I've just been so busy this week. You know with the schedule change and working days. And then on top of it, I got squirrels in my house. I haven't had time to think."

"Really?"

Bob sees hope in her eyes. He should just tell her the truth. He's in love with someone else. He didn't mean for this to happen. And he would never ever want to hurt her. He hopes they can be friends. In fact, maybe they could still date. They don't have to sleep together, not just yet. They could take it easy, like they were eighteen years old again. What could be wrong with that?

"Really." He puts his arms around her. She stands there rigid at first, but finally relaxes, puts her arms around him, and lays her head on his shoulder. "I've been so depressed," she said. "Waiting for you to call."

"You could have called me." He strokes her hair.

"No." She pulls away and looks him in the eye. "There comes a time when you have to wait for the man to call."

"In this day and age?"

"Yeah. Men have no problem calling if they're interested. If they don't, it's a really bad sign." Her eyes cloud over again. She pulls back further. "Listen to me." She smacks herself on the forehead. "What am I saying? You didn't call!"

He sinks down into his chair. "Irene," he says.

"You bastard!"

"What?"

"Did you meet someone else? That woman from your neighborhood? That's who it is, right, the one from California? Who thinks life shouldn't be so fucking hard?"

"Jesus."

"I knew it." She throws her bag and some papers down on the console. "You wouldn't give a fuck about a neighbor's philosophy if she weren't hot. What, is she? Tall, blonde, thin?"

"No," Bob says. He puts his head in his hands. How do women figure all this stuff out? Was he so transparent? He looks up. "But you're right. Her name is Leonie."

"You are such a fucking disappointment," Irene says. She grabs her bag and her sheaf of papers and turns to walk out the door.

"Aren't we going to lay down some tracks?"

"Fuck the tracks!" Irene throws her sheaf of papers up in the air and they fall all over the studio floor. "I'm out of here." She walks out of the studio, slamming the door behind her.

"Damn." Bob bends over and gathers the sheets of her script and puts them into the recycle bin. This is why you're not supposed to get involved with people from work, he thinks. Or your neighborhood. When everything blows up, you've got nowhere to hide.

Rusty has somehow managed to take up all four of the parking spaces in the driveway, so Bob has to drive around the block looking for a place to park. Not a good sign, he thinks, but at least he showed up. "Bay State Trappers" has been hand lettered across the side of his white panel van, but whoever did it ran out of space and the E, R, and S are crowded together toward the rear. Bob looks at the house as he approaches from down the street. Paint is peeling in several places — under the gutters, over the bay window on the second floor, in a long drip that runs parallel to one of the downspouts. It seems like he just got done paying for the paint job and it needs to be done again.

There's no one in the van so he looks around the yard and then up at the roof above his back porch. He sees something glinting in the fading evening light. "Hello?" he calls out. "Hello?"

Rusty emerges from the shadows of the garage, and Bob starts and puts his hand to his chest. "Jesus, man, you scared me!"

"Sorry." Rusty holds up a battered looking trap. "Had to fuck with the release on this one. I was looking for a hammer." He looks accusingly at Bob.

"I don't keep tools in the garage. This is the city."

"That's okay," he says. "I bent it with my hands."

Rusty's hands are large, dirty, and swollen around the knuckles. He is dressed in a bulky flannel shirt and worn out jeans. He has a long, thin, gray ponytail and is missing one of his eye teeth, something you never see anymore unless someone is in the middle of a getting an implant and for some reason neglects to put in the fake one. Bob is heading for an implant himself. One of his teeth is too far gone for a crown, or a root canal. He's got a referral for an oral surgeon and a dental cat scan, but he keeps putting it off because of the expense. When the tooth starts to hurt, he doubles up on the Sensodyne toothpaste and Orajel.

"So," he says. "Have you figured out where the squirrels are getting in?"

Rusty looks at him and smiles, revealing another missing tooth, further back in his mouth. "Ha!" he says. "Easy! You got a huge hole under that eave." He shades his eyes and looks up. "Come on up, I'll show you." He tramps through the bed of hostas that Bob's father put in and climbs onto the fire escape, holding onto the trap with one hand and the fire escape with the other. He scrambles up the fire escape and onto the roof of the porch. Bob follows him up the fire escape and steps gingerly onto the roof. "Watch out there," Rusty says. Bob teeters backwards for a second and Rusty grabs him by the jacket. "Careful, man! I got a trap right there. Just in case the little fuckers come up the fire escape." Bob nods and lets out his breath. Must be what he saw glinting in the light.

Rusty bounces up and down on the porch roof. "You got some soft spots here man. When's the last time you replaced the roof?"

Bob shrugs. "Never?"

Rusty continues up the next fire escape and climbs out onto the roof, which covers the back of the house. Bob follows him but stops at the top of the fire escape. The roof is pitched at a forty-five-degree angle and covered with wet leaves and pine needles. "Think I'll stay here," he says and looks around. Bob doesn't like heights. But he has to admit, the view is amazing. He can see the tops of Abigail's new trees, the tips of which are already turning a disconcerting brown. He looks to the other side of his house and into Bryce's backyard. There are piles of dirt and gravel and maybe woodchips. The meditation garden. He has forgotten all about it. He makes a mental note to call him, after he has called Leonie. He has learned his lesson about waiting to call.

Rusty scampers up the pitched roof, trap still in hand, and points with his other hand to a large hole under the eaves. "You see that? Surprised you don't have raccoons," he says. "It's big enough. But the good news is you get one or the other, squirrels or raccoons. They don't get along. And you got squirrels."

Bob nods and points to the apartment building behind him. "Well," he says. "No big surprise. There's a woman in that apartment building who feeds them."

"What the fuck!" Rusty sets the trap under the hole, and then makes his way down the roof to join Bob on the fire escape. "Then I can't guarantee the job. I can catch them. And then patch up their hole. But they'll be right back if she keeps feeding them."

"Tell me about it," Bob says. "But there's nothing much I can do to stop her. She's crazy. And you know, crazy people always win."

"We could poison her," Rusty says, talking out of the side of his mouth. "I got a van full of poison down there."

Bob looks at him closely. "What?"

"Just kidding. Just kidding." He hits Bob on the shoulder. "Man, I couldn't live here." He starts backing down the fire escape to the porch roof. "Too many crazy people. Crazy smart people. The worst kind."

Bob follows him and steps onto the roof, testing this time for soft spots under his feet. "How much is this going to cost?"

"Ah, I think we can give you a flat fee. Fifteen hundred for the lot of them. I'll put out two more traps tonight. And then check the traps every day and bring them back out to the country. But —" He leans in so close Bob can smell tobacco on his breath. He cups his hand to the side of his mouth. "Between you and me and the lamppost, I think the hawks just kill them, the minute we let them loose. They're so fucking freaked out after being in a cage, you know what I mean?"

Bob nods. Maybe he should just go for the poison?

"Once we get them all, we'll put some hardware cloth over the hole. But you probably want to patch it up better. You got a good carpenter? I'd say you got a lot of carpentry work in your future."

Bob glances over at Leonie's house. It looks to be in much better shape than his. Maybe he could move in with her and sell this house to another couple like Abigail and Tom who could replace the gutters and patch up all the rotten wood and cover the roof with thick pieces of slate and cap the turrets with copper and install whirlpools in every bathroom. "You take a check?"

"No, cash only. Half up front. And the other half when I declare you rodent-free."

Bob makes a move to the fire escape. "I'll have to go to the bank," he says.

"I can wait 'til tomorrow."

"You work Saturdays?"

"Of course," he says and laughs. "We're an emergency, on-call type business. 24/7."

Bob shakes his hand, climbs backwards down the fire escape to the porch roof and then down to the ground. He misses the last rung of the fire escape and crashes down onto one of his father's giant hostas, twisting his ankle in the process. He limps up to his back door and lets himself into his kitchen and sinking into a chair, remembers how as a child he had run up and down those fire escapes, nimble as a squirrel.

CHAPTER 17

By Sunday afternoon his ankle is better, and Bob is getting ready to go out and rake leaves. The day is blustery and gray, and the leaves have drifted into one corner of his front walk so that the house almost looks deserted. He puts on a heavy sweatshirt and work gloves and checks his answering machine once more before he heads outside. Leonie still hasn't called back. It's been two days. He's left three messages. Maybe, unlike Irene, she hadn't been waiting for his call? Maybe it was over, pure and simple. He had fucked it up. She had moved on.

He walks down the stairs to his basement, to get some lawn bags and a rake. How many years has he been raking this same tiny patch of real estate, first with his father yelling at him that he was doing it all wrong, and now with his neighbors giving him dirty looks because he has waited so long? He opens the back door of the cellar, pushing against a pile of leaves that have gathered in the stairwell and walks up the stone stairs and into the back yard. What a mess! The Norway maples are almost bare; only a few yellowed leaves still cling to the branches. Aren't maples supposed to turn red and orange in the fall? Put on a show? Not his maples, the antisocial killers. He looks up and sees one of his neighbors in the apartment building behind him looking out the window. She immediately draws her blinds.

He walks toward the driveway and stops short when he sees that a fence has been erected between his and Bryce's property. Damn. He had forgotten to call him. Now Bryce has just gone ahead and done it. Bob leans the rake and lawnbags against the garage and marches over to Bryce's front door. He leans on the bell and when no one answers, he leans on it again. Finally, Bryce appears, a blissed-out smile on his broad, tanned face. He is wearing sweatpants and sandals with wool socks. He bows his head when he sees Bob.

"What the fuck?" Bob says. "I didn't say you could build that fence on my property."

"You never got back to me." Bryce rubs his eyes. Has he been meditating or just napping? His hair is clipped short and combed slightly forward onto his forehead, at once concealing his receding hairline and giving him a monkish appearance. But his broad shoulders and slight gut ruin the effect.

"What, did you wait a week?"

"I waited ten days, Bob. Not a word from you." Bryce sighs.

"You got to take it down."

"Oh, come on. You don't even use that part of your driveway, and if I do say so myself, the guy did a great job. Kind of pagoda-like, isn't it?"

"Look, it's not a good idea to mess with property lines. I consulted with the Zoning Board, and they're dead set against it."

"Really?" Bryce raises his eyebrows and narrows his eyes, as if considering the idea. "Maybe we could write something up, stating exactly where your property line ends and mine begins. That should satisfy the Zoning Board."

"That's not the issue. You didn't have my permission."

"Well, as they always say, it's easier to ask forgiveness than permission." Bryce smiles his lopsided, little boy smile.

"You don't have that either!" Bob shouts. His face is getting hot.

"Bob." Bryce puts a soft hand on his forearm. "Let me show you the garden. It's a really special place. And you should feel free to use it any time you want."

"I'm not interested in your stupid meditation garden. You built something on my land. I could sue you."

"Maybe you *should* be interested in a meditation garden." Bryce has lowered his voice, he is speaking slowly. Does he think he can hypnotize Bob into accepting this?

"What would you do if I did that to you?"

"I would sit with it."

"Oh fuck you, Bryce."

Bryce holds both his hands up in front of him. "Please, Bob. That's enough cursing. We can dialogue about this again, when you calm down. But right now, I don't feel like we're making much progress." He moves to close the door.

Bob wedges his foot in to stop him. "That's it, Bryce, I'm hiring a lawyer."

"I bow to the light within you." Bryce bows his head to touch his clasped hands and then closes the door.

Bob walks down the Bryce's tidy brick walkway to the sidewalk. He has recently installed antique looking copper lights on the path and chunky cobblestones as edging. Some kind of orange flowers are still in bloom, in the midst of a glossy green ground cover. Super landscaping job. Not a stray leaf in sight. Meditation business must be booming.

After he has finished raking, Bob goes back inside to check the answering machine. He takes a beer out of the fridge, opens it, walks to the bay window on the side of the house, and stands there brooding. His neighbors have absolutely no respect for him. They do whatever they want regardless of what he says. Why do they even bother to ask? Of course, it's true, he had totally forgotten to get back to Bryce. He's got too much on his mind. Leonie, Irene, work, Tom and Abigail. They had gone right ahead and done what they wanted, too. There is no winning with these people. Maybe he should listen to Riff and get out of this neighborhood once and for all. There is nothing left here for him. The phone rings.

Bob rushes over to get it and then stands there and lets it ring again. It's a Cambridge number. He picks up.

"Bob?" Leonie's voice. "I am so sorry. I was away for the weekend. For a workshop. I thought I had told you?"

"No, you didn't." Bob takes another swig of his beer. "But that's okay. Nothing to be sorry about." Relief floods into his shoulders, down his back and his legs. He rises up on his toes. "I'm just happy to hear your voice." He walks to the window and smiles. Sand is seeping under the pagoda-like gate and onto his property. There's a new tree in Bryce's backyard, and he can just make out Leonie's kitchen window through its purple shimmering leaves.

"Do you want to come over?" she asks.

Leonie is waiting for him in her living room. He can see her through the window, sitting at the edge of her couch, a glass of red wine in her hand. She is dressed in a v-necked sweater that shows off her long neck. He can see the outline of her collarbone, the slightest hint of cleavage. She is wearing lip gloss.

She gets up and smiles and something inside of his stomach relaxes, like a fist unclenching, for the first time in three days. This is going to be okay, he thinks.

She opens the door and he leans over to kiss her. She kisses back and says, "Let's go back into my bedroom and start from where we left off."

"Really? Are you sure?"

"I'm sure." She takes his hand and leads him down the hallway to her bedroom. She stops in the doorway and turns to face him. "Look," she says, releasing his hand. "I've thought a lot about it all this weekend and you are right. We should use birth control. I was being crazy."

"No, I've thought it over too." He puts his hands on her forearms. "Maybe it is time we stop controlling every goddamned thing in our lives."

"No, don't you see? That's it. I was trying to control things. I mean, I'm so tense and wound up about having a baby, I probably wouldn't get pregnant anyway! I have to let go. Maybe I'll have my own child some time. Maybe I won't. But right now, let's just enjoy being together."

Leonie walks ahead of him into the bedroom, lifts the covers and slips between them fully clothed. Bob does the same. They lie in bed side by side for a few minutes and then he takes her hand and she rolls over and he rolls over and they start to kiss. He lifts up her shirt and runs his fingers over her belly. He can feel her breathing in as he does so. She slips her hands underneath his shirt and strokes his back. Every hair follicle seems to stand on end. He leans in to kiss her again. "Are you sure about the birth control?" he asks.

"I'm sure," she says and rolls over on top of him. From this vantage point she looks different, almost unrecognizable. Gravity is pulling her features down toward him in an unfamiliar way and for a moment Bob hesitates. Who is this person? Here he has hurt Irene, disappointed Riff, and gotten involved with someone from Harvard and a neighbor too. But then she leans over and kisses him deeply and his body takes over and he doesn't hesitate again for the rest of the night.

CHAPTER 18

The layoffs start on Monday. Fred Souza, the midday classical announcer, is first to go. Bob watches silently as Fred gathers his things from the staff lounge and places them in a cardboard box. "You know," he says. "It wouldn't be so bad if they replaced me with someone good. But they're replacing me with a shrink from LA."

"You get any severance?"

"Two weeks!" he says. "After ten years. I wish I was union like you guys."

"Yeah," Bob says. "We're lucky."

"They'll figure out a way to get rid of you, too, believe me. But at least they'll have to break a sweat."

"What about Riff?" Bob asks. "Heard anything?"

"He's safe for now. I mean, it's the middle of the night. Di Tucci's going to work his way through the daytime lineup first. Then he'll get to nights and weekends."

Bob knows he should be worried, but he is instead full of warmth and grace since he spent the night with Leonie. This morning they'd had coffee in bed. They fit so well together. Things mostly just seemed to flow. And when they didn't they laughed about it and talked their way through it. He was definitely in love with her, but he wasn't going to say that, not yet; that would scare her away.

Now he shakes Fred's hand. "Really sorry to see you go."

Fred shrugs. "I'm just the first," he says, not kindly. Bob lets go of his hand. "And what the hell, they make me leave in the middle of the day? They don't even let me finish out my last show, like I'm going to barricade myself inside the studio and seize the microphone?"

"They're just paranoid." Bob remembers the last strike. He was working on the Saturday night when the deadline for a settlement came and went, and Mitch Peralta had come to the studio with two armed guards and escorted him out the door. "See you soon, I hope," Mitch had said.

And he said, "Yeah, hope so," though it was six months before he got back to work, and by that time Mitch had grown a goatee and Bob was thousands of dollars in debt.

"Fuck, I think I'm going to get out of this business," Fred says. "I'm just too old for this drama. It's not like we're saving children's lives or making lots of money. It's only radio, for God's sake!"

But it's the only thing I really know how to do, Bob thinks. "Can I carry something out to your car?"

"No," Fred says, "I got it. I'll be in touch." Bob watches him walk out the door and thinks, I will never see him again.

He has an open hour; he was supposed to be recording a promo with Fred, and now he has nothing to do. If he were truly ambitious he would go back into the studio and start putting together his own audition reel, something he should have been doing all along. You can't get complacent in radio. It's a fickle business. But he doesn't really know where to start. So he walks down the hallway and sees Irene in the studio, recording a spot. She is safe, thank God. He can tell that she has seen him, something in the way her eyes widen and then quickly narrow, but she turns away and keeps on with her script and doesn't acknowledge his presence. He wanders into the kitchen and thinks he will sit down and have a cup of coffee and call Leonie.

Mitch is in the kitchen, rifling through the cabinets for something to eat. "Didn't we used to stock packets of instant oatmeal?" he asks as Bob walks in.

"Over there." Bob nods his head in the general direction of the cabinet over the sink. He walks to the coffee pot and pours out the last of the coffee, then adds a creamer. What is a creamer, anyway? Milk? Half 'n' Half? Some kind of creamy chemical effluvium? The coffee is lukewarm, so he walks over to the microwave.

Mitch is there ahead of him, a packet of instant oatmeal in hand. "Want to see something cool?" he asks.

"Sure."

"So this is supposed to take 50 seconds, right?"

"Yeah." Bob nods.

"Well, this is something I figured out. Put in 44. Two strokes, same number. Saves time."

"Cool," Bob says. But secretly he is thinking, how did it come to this? Wasn't I smart in school? How could someone like Mitch be my boss?

The microwave dings, and Mitch takes out the oatmeal and tastes it. He frowns and puts it back in for 11 seconds. "Old microwave," he says.

"So, they let Fred go. Filling the slot with a shrink from LA?"

"For the time being," Mitch says. "Eventually, we're going to develop a local program. Could be a good opportunity for you. Get in on the ground floor."

"Really, what kind of program?"

"Well, not jazz!" Mitch laughs. "That's for sure." He takes the oatmeal out and tastes it. "Perfect!"

"Another talk show?"

"I don't know. They got focus groups and a new consultant working on it."

Bob puts his coffee in. Presses 33.

"See how much faster that is?" Mitch asks.

Bob removes his coffee from the microwave, sips it and spits it out. It's so hot he burns his tongue. Next time he'll try 22. Funny how you can't get stupid stuff like that out of your head. He blows on his coffee and sits staring out the window of the kitchen. He is tired but his body feels energized. He can feel a stirring below. He could have sex again, this very minute. This is good. He was a bit worried. He walks over to the phone and is about to dial Leonie's number when Irene walks in. She stops short when she sees him. Bob puts the phone back in its receiver.

"Your new girlfriend?" Irene asks.

"Irene," Bob says. "I'm sorry."

"Don't start."

"No, really. I never meant to hurt you." He reaches out to touch her arm. She pulls back.

"And no touching me!"

"All right," he says. "Sorry."

She walks over to the coffee pot and finds it empty. "Just my luck," she mumbles.

"I could make you another pot."

"No." She takes the carafe over to the sink and dumps the last muddy drops of coffee out.

"You hear about Fred?" he asks.

"Yeah." She stands with her back to him, swishing the coffee pot violently with water. "I'm probably next."

"You? No way. You're a newscaster."

Irene turns around to face him. "But I'm not their kind of newscaster. I just want to do my work, get my paycheck, and go home to my tequila and joint."

"Don't let them hear you say that." Bob takes a step toward her and lowers his voice. "You never want to go home. You have to tear yourself away from work. You love it here. You wish you could live here. It's all you ever wanted. It's your whole fucking life. You'd mow down a toddler if it got in the way of a news story."

Irene laughs and then stops herself. "Don't even try with me, Bob."

"Sorry."

Irene opens two packets of coffee and dumps them in. "This crap is so weak," she says.

"Why didn't I think of that? Two packs."

Irene sighs.

"I heard they were putting a shrink from LA into Fred's slot," Bob says.

"No, I heard a talk show. With Kathy as a host. Watch out. They'll need an engineer."

"No way. And I've asked to go back on nights. I want to be with Riff for his last days."

"How noble. What's your girlfriend going to think of that?"

Bob shrugs, but she's right, if he goes back on nights it will be really hard to see Leonie. He has tried it before. Once he was involved with someone who worked normal hours while he was on nights. After three months, she called to break it off, told him she'd been seeing someone else — while he was asleep.

Irene looks at her watch and pulls out the carafe to grab a cup of coffee while it is still brewing. But the coffee maker is old and something is wrong and the stream of hot coffee keeps pouring onto the warming plate and then onto the counter and dripping down the cabinets onto the floor. "Damn! Damn!" Irene slams the carafe back down on the warmer. "Nothing's going right for me today. Nothing!" She bites her lip as if she is going to cry.

Bob grabs a clump of paper towels and mops up the hot coffee off the counter and cabinets. Then he bends down and cleans it off the floor. Finally he stands up and hands a towel to Irene.

"Thanks, Bob," she says, dabbing at the front of her sweater. Her brown eyes are watery and full. "I know you didn't mean to hurt me." She tosses the paper towel into the waste paper basket, grabs her coffee, and turns to leave. "But you did."

Bob nods and sits down at the table and waits a safe amount of time, before calling Leonie.

CHAPTER 19

On the way home from work, Bob stops at the Harvard Wine Shoppe to pick up a bottle of red wine to bring to another meeting at Mabel's. He and Leonie are going together. He has given himself plenty of time. He is not good at buying wine, but he doesn't want to ask the guys behind the counter whom he recognizes as townies like himself. What would they know? And he is not about to read the stupid little cards they have affixed to the shelves. *Chewy with hints of jam. Notes of earth and toasted tobacco.* Sounds like his mother's old freestanding ashtray, which is still in the attic. Bob hasn't had the heart to throw it away.

Bob decides he will select the wine by price and label. French, he thinks. French should be safe. Avoid the table wine. He knows that much. Man, there are so many fucking chateaus. And what's with the identical labels? Don't they have graphic designers in France? Maybe he should just go by price — fifteen bucks? Is that reasonable?

"Can I help you?" A good looking, young, blonde woman has materialized by his side. She must be new. He would have noticed her. "Hi, I'm Tina. Are you looking for a French red?"

Bob nods. "Yeah," he says. "Something good, but not too good if you know what I mean."

She narrows her eyes. "A Cotes du Rhone maybe? A Burgundy?"

"I don't really know. I don't drink a lot of wine."

"Do you know what you'll be eating?

"Cheese? Chips? It's just a meeting."

"Okay," she says. "Let's go for a crowd pleaser then. Would you consider an Italian? Or a New World wine? Does it have to be French?"

Bob shrugs, looks at his watch. "Whatever you think is good."

"Well, I've been drinking a lot of Shiraz these days." How many days can this very young woman have had? "Shiraz is hot right now. It's from Australia."

"Okay, sure."

Just then the door to the liquor store opens, the little bell attached to the top of the door rings, startling the large gray cat who has been sleeping in the window. His next door neighbor, Abigail, sweeps in. "Bob," she heads towards him. "I thought that was you." Tina excuses herself to find the wine. "What a coincidence," Abigail says. "I was going to call you later. More bad news about the trees, I'm afraid."

"Really?" Bob takes a step back. "Isn't it still too early to tell?"

"No, Johan was over the other day. He's afraid we'll lose the whole lot. Again!"

"Too bad," Bob says.

Tina has reappeared with a bottle of Australian red. He doesn't like the label, which is abstract, brightly colored, a little too modern. "I brought this to a party last weekend," she says. "Everyone loved it." Bob imagines a pulsating room of tattooed twenty-somethings, with stringy hair and low slung pants.

Abigail smiles. "You need a wine recommendation? Let me show you our favorite red. It's from the Gascogne." She marches down the French wine aisle and snags two bottles, hands one to Bob. The label is reassuringly French, very boring. "It's really very drinkable, and reasonably priced." Up close she looks younger than Bob previously thought. Her skin is firm and unlined. Her short red hair shows no gray. She may even be younger than he is. Her lines seem to be entirely about smiling.

"Great, I'll get them both," he says, not wanting to hurt the young woman's feelings. He should have some red wine on hand anyway. It's what Leonie drinks. Leonie. He is actually dating Leonie. He feels a tightening in his stomach. Tina takes his two bottles of wine and heads over to the checkout counter. They follow.

"I should really just buy a case," Abigail says. "But I'm not sure I like what that says about me, you know?"

"Yeah," Bob says. "I could never buy a carton of cigarettes when I smoked. It just felt like I was giving in to my addiction."

"Exactly! And besides, it's much more French to shop every day." She smiles and blinks her eyes.

Tina rings him up. "Next time you come in, tell me how you liked each of them, okay? That way I can get to know you."

"Sure." Bob hands her his credit card. This is what it's like to be in love, he thinks. Everyone loves you back, even in Cambridge.

He pauses after she hands him the receipt. Does he have to wait for Abigail now, walk her home? Sometimes he wishes he lived in a different era, when the codes of conduct were more clearly established, lengths of polite conversation predetermined, men's and women's roles solidly set. His father would have known what to do. He would have tipped his hat, picked up Abigail's bag, and held the door for her as she walked out.

"Wait up," Abigail cries, her credit card in her mouth, one hand on the bottle of wine, the other fiddling with the clasp on her briefcase. "We'll walk together."

He holds the door open for her, and they emerge together onto the sidewalk. A cold wind is blowing up Mass. Ave. Bob thinks he can detect a hint of salt and ocean on it.

"So, the trees," Abigail says. "I think we are going to have to replant them. But we were smart this time and got a guarantee."

"Great," Bob says. "But that won't be until the spring, right?"

"Not sure. I've got a conference call with Johan and the nursery guy tomorrow." Abigail pauses at the intersection and pushes the walk button. She taps her foot as she waits. "Ah, here we go," she says when the white Walk signal flashes. She launches into the crosswalk. Bob hurries to keep up with her.

"Of course, we'll do whatever Johan tells us to do," Abigail says, looking over her shoulder at Bob as they near the opposite sidewalk.

Suddenly a cab turns into the crosswalk, heading right toward them. Bob yells, "Abigail!" and instinctively pulls her back toward him and away from the cab. The bottle of wine slides out of her hands and onto the cab's hood and bounces and breaks on the pavement. The cab driver slams on his brakes and stops inches from them. He rolls down his window and leans out. "You morons!" he says. "I got a fucking green!"

Abigail points at the little white man in their walk signal and holds up her hand in her best imitation of a crossing guard. "And we've got a fucking Walk!" Her cheeks are flaming red.

Bob removes his hand from her forearm and pounds on the hood of the cab. "And you were going way too fast. You could have killed us."

"No such luck," the cabby says and drives off through the crunching glass and red wine.

Abigail bends over to pick up some of the shards of glass. "We can't just leave this here."

Bob bends down to help her, but keeps an eye out on the traffic and finally pulls her out of the intersection. "Never mind," he says. "It's not worth getting killed over."

"Can't they coordinate these traffic signals?" Abigail asks once they have safely stepped onto the curb.

"Yeah," Bob says. "Seems like it would be the first assignment in traffic engineer school."

"Actually I've complained to the city about this very thing." Abigail shakes her head. "There's a horrible intersection right under my office window. You wouldn't believe the accidents I've witnessed. While I am trying to write."

Is she concerned about the danger, or the interruption to her writing schedule?

"And the woman I talked to at City Hall, who told me not to worry, that it was a against the law to run over someone in a crosswalk, even if you do have the light."

Bob laughs. "What a relief," he says. "Our heirs could file a wrongful death suit."

Abigail throws her head back and laughs, too. She has a surprisingly full-throated laugh. "I am giddy with relief," she says, brushing a tear from the corner of her eye.

They stop at the next two intersections and though they are only small, side streets, they look first one way, then the other, and then the first way again. As they are approaching Abigail's house, she checks her watch and says, "Want to come in for a drink? I could really use a drink after that."

"Me too," Bob says. "But I'm meeting someone."

"Well, some other time," Abigail says. "We'll bring out the really good wine to celebrate our narrow escape from death."

"That'd be great," he says.

"And Bob." She lays her hand on his. "Thank you. I didn't see that cab at all."

"No problem." He reaches into his bag for the bottle of French red. "And here, take this."

"No, I couldn't."

"No, I've got two. And I don't even drink wine." He presses the bottle of wine into her hands.

"Well, all right then," Abigail says. She opens her wrought iron gate and starts down her brick and granite front walk. Bob had watched the bricklayers re-lay the bricks several times to get the pattern right. There's a granite medallion in the center, where Abigail pauses, and turns. "Bob," she says. "Thanks, again. You're a champ."

Bob waves and walks the few steps to his house and then turns into his own front walk. The bricks are sinking in places and burned out brown grass is poking up between them. He could pull out the grass, he thinks, or isn't there something that you pour on it to kill it? Vinegar? Hot tea? Soon enough the grass will die back anyway and the bricks will be slick with snow and ice. Maybe in the spring he will re-lay the bricks, a job he doesn't know how to do, but how hard could it be? His own father had laid these bricks when he was a teenager, while his grandfather stood over him and criticized. His father had never tired of telling the story. "The old man had to have a fucking herringbone pattern." Sometimes Bob thinks the ghost of his grandfather inhabits the house still. Once when he and his father had been painting a bedroom, one of the windows had gotten stuck, and his father had struggled to unstick it, while Bob stood by helplessly. Suddenly the sash had snapped and the heavy wood window had come crashing down, nearly crushing his father's fingers. His father jumped back and knocked over a can of China blue paint, which had spread out in a fast-moving puddle over the hard wood floor. "You miserable bastard!" His father shook his fist at the ceiling, at the walls, at the offending window. "Still trying to get me, aren't you?" Bob threw himself to the floor and tried to staunch the flow of blue paint with a drop cloth.

Bob lets himself in and gathers the mail up off the floor. The usual bills and catalogs. He puts it down on the mahogany table and waits for Leonie to arrive. No letter from the insurance company, yet.

Leonie rings his bell, and Bob meets her at the door and pulls her inside and starts kissing her. They fall onto the livingroom sofa and run their hands up and down each other's bodies. "Remind me," Bob says. "Why are we going to this meeting again?"

"I have to," Leonie says. "I have to give them an update."

"You could email it," Bob says, and kisses her neck. "Or fax it." He kisses her clavicle. "Or leave a long voice mail."

"No." Leonie laughs and sits up straight. "I do have to go. And anyway, we can't spend all our lives in bed. We'll get sick of it."

"I will never get sick of it." Bob sits up too. "Will the meeting last long?"

"We can leave after I give my report."

"Then they'll know we're together."

"Who cares?"

Bob smiles and thinks how much has changed in such a short time.

They go around to Mabel's back door. Bob is about to knock but Leonie tests the door knob and twists it to let them into the kitchen. "Hello?" She calls out. "Mabel?"

"In here, sweetie."

Bob looks at Leonie. He hadn't known she and Mabel were this close.

They walk into the kitchen, which opens out onto the living room, where several neighbors are gathered, though not as many as last time. The documentary filmmaker is not in evidence, nor the rabbity woman from the house next door to the apartment complex, but the judge, and the smiling woman who goes through Bob's trash are standing around the coffee table, and someone he doesn't recognize is chatting with Mabel by the piano. Mabel looks up from her conversation and walks into the kitchen to greet them. "How nice to see you, Leonie," she says and leans over to kiss her cheek. "And Bob? It's Bob, right?" Bob nods and hands her the bottle of wine.

"Thanks," she says and turns around. "Judge, we got another red!"

"Oh good," the judge says, walking into the kitchen. "I was just about to resort to white."

Mabel picks up a corkscrew from the kitchen counter and opens the bottle. She pours out a glass for the judge and hands it to him. He cups the bowl of the glass in his hand, then swirls the wine and sticks his nose in. Finally he takes a sip.

"It's a Shiraz, from Australia," Bob says. "Supposed to be good."

"It's fine," the judge says, without conviction. He takes another sip and nods. "Yeah, it's fine."

"Sorry," Mabel says. "I should have let it breathe."

Damn, Bob thinks, I should have given Abigail the Shiraz and kept the French red for myself. Why had he trusted a twenty-something?

Leonie takes a glass and sips it. "Oh, I like it." She moves closer to Bob and takes his hand, pressing into him.

"So Bob," Mabel asks. "Why haven't we met before? Did you recently move to the neighborhood?"

"No, I've been here my whole life," he says.

"He's from an old Boston family," Leonie says. "They've had that house for generations."

While what she says is technically true, it is not the truth. Irish people are not old Boston. They are new, immigrant, interloper, Catholic Boston. But Mabel does not seem to get the distinction. "Lucky you," she says. "I love that house. I've only been here since grad school."

"Harvard?" The judge asks.

"MIT." Mabel shakes her head. "Much better department." She takes a sip of wine and turns to Bob. "The judge grew up around here too. I think you might be the only two natives in all of Cambridge!"

The judge sidles up to Bob. "A fellow Cantabrigian, huh? Where'd you go to school?"

Bob looks at him more closely. They are around the same age. Somehow he still expects every authority figure to be older than he. "Immaculate Heart," he says. "You?"

"Giddings Prep."

"Right next door."

"Yeah. The kids from Immaculate Heart used to climb into our schoolyard and beat the crap out of us." The little judge puffs out his chest and draws himself up. "You don't sound like you went to Immaculate Heart. Where's your accent?"

"I got over it," Bob says, looking down into the judge's eyes in what he hopes is a menacing way. Let him think he was one of the tough kids who terrorized him, not one of the good Catholic boys who tried to call them off.

The doorbell rings and Mabel excuses herself to answer it. "Abigail!" She says. "So glad you could make it."

Abigail and Johan are standing at the door. "I brought my arborist," Abigail says, beaming, and then hands Mabel Bob's bottle of French red. Johan does a little bow to Mabel. Oh come on, Bob thinks. Where the fuck are we? A French court?

Abigail steps inside the threshold and spies Bob across the room. She squints and the skin over her neatly arched eyebrows knits together as she looks from Mabel to Bob and back again. Then she comes over to where he and Leonie stand. All smiles. "Bob," she says. "We have to stop meeting like this!"

Leonie raises her eyebrows. "Like what?"

"Leonie," Bob says. "This is my next door neighbor, Abigail. We just ran into each other at the liquor store. And narrowly escaped getting run over on the walk home."

"Bob saved my life," Abigail says.

Leonie smiles ands puts out her hand. "Pleased to meet you, Abigail."

"And Leonie lives in the purple house. Behind mine?"

"That's not purple. It's periwinkle. Love that color." Abigail turns to include Johan, who has migrated to her side. "And this is Johan. He's the arborist at the Botanical Gardens."

"Oh, you're the arborist!" the judge says. "We need your expert testimony in dealing with this developer. He's a slippery bastard. Now he says he'll move the Japanese maple to the back of the lot. Still cram in as many condos up front as he wants. Can he do it?"

"Well, actually, you can never be sure a tree of that size and age will survive a move. And Japanese maples are notoriously finicky."

"That's good. Tell me more."

Johan removes his glasses and takes out a cloth to clean them. "It would be quite risky."

"How risky?" The judge asks. "Can we talk percentages?"

"Not off the top of my head," Johan says. "I'd have to take a look at the tree and the site."

"When? The guy wants to do it soon. Isn't it too late?"

"No, we've still got a window," Johan says. "Couple of weeks though, at most."

"Damn!" The judge snorts and buries his nose in his wine glass.

Johan puts his glasses back on and smiles nervously. "By the way," he turns away from the judge to address Abigail. "Did you tell Bob about your trees?"

"Just this afternoon," Abigail says. "Actually, we had quite a day."

Johan interrupts her. "They really don't look good. I don't think anything will thrive there, unless we can get rid of your maples."

"What are we talking about here?" Leonie shakes her head. "I'm lost."

Johan turns to Leonie. "Bob's trees are killing Abigail's trees," he says. "We're hoping he'll let us remove them."

Leonie gives Bob a questioning look.

"And I just want to preserve all the big old trees in the neighborhood." Bob's hands are starting to sweat.

"Oh." Leonie screws her eyebrows together. "That makes sense. I guess."

"But it doesn't really," the judge says. "Not all old trees are created equal. A hundred-and-fifty-year-old Japanese maple that some yahoo wants to pull up and move is not equivalent to a Norway maple that sprouted out of a crack in your driveway. You have to take a more nuanced view of these things."

"But look," Bob says, his voice rising. "My trees are tall, taller than all the buildings around them. When you look out the window you see green. They move with the wind. They make a nice rustling sound. So you want to cut them down and replace them with what? Some spindly little tree that will never grow that tall again in my lifetime?"

"Putting in trees is a matter of trust in the future, of stewardship." Johan takes a sip of his red wine. "It's for the next generation. Not us."

"Actually," Abigail says. "I'm thinking of my generation. I want something to grow in my backyard next summer."

"And those trees shade the back of my house," Bob continues. "And they shade the building behind me." He can feel his face getting red. "Not sure they'd be happy about losing those trees either."

"That whole building is impossible to deal with. Just because you own a four-hundred square-foot condo doesn't mean you own the view out your window!"

"Hey, watch it!" The judge says to Abigail. "You're trampling all over our case."

"Look," Leonie says. "I think we all want the same things here. We're just quibbling over details. We want to keep the neighborhood green and beautiful. We don't want greedy developers to clearcut a lot, cram in as many condos as they can, and then move on to their next project. They don't care what they leave behind. But we have to live with it. We have to hold their feet to the fire."

Everyone nods in agreement. Bob nods too, but he actually feels a bit sorry for the developer. Who knows how much he paid for that property? Who knows if he's really greedy or just some hard working contractor trying to get a leg up? Maybe he's sending his kids to Giddings Prep. He can only imagine how much that costs. But all the same he is thankful to Leonie for smoothing things over. He is thankful to Leonie for not storming out on him right then and there.

Mabel opens the French red and starts to refill their glasses. Bob holds his hand over his. "No, thanks." More alcohol would only stoke his anger.

Mabel hands Leonie a plate of cheese and crackers. "It's time to move to the living room," she says, "and get this meeting started. Some of us have to work in the morning."

Bob follows Leonie into the living room and settles down next to her on the couch. While Leonie rustles in her bag for her notes, he puts his arm around her shoulder. He leans over and breathes in the scent of her clean hair.

"So you never really cared about the Japanese maple, huh?" she asks.

Bob is silent while he considers whether or not to tell the truth.

"You just wanted to win against your neighbor and that funny little arborist guy."

"Yes," he says finally. "But actually, when I ..."

"Stop." Leonie stiffens her back and pulls away from him. She runs her fingers through her hair and smoothes her skirt and sits up straight.

Bob retracts his arm. "Leonie, I'm sorry. Are you mad?"

"Which is it?" she asks. "Sorry that you lied or sorry that I might be mad?"

There is no good way to answer that question so Bob is silent again. He inches away from her and into the corner of the couch.

The judge walks into the room and places his wine glass on the coffee table and then plops down next to Leonie. Leonie shifts closer to Bob. "One thing for sure," the judge says, almost whispering. "We can't let Abigail anywhere near a courtroom or she'll blow the case for us. Hard to paint yourself as the underdog when you have your own prissy little arborist."

Leonie exhales and rubs her eyes and the bridge of her nose. "Now I know why I don't get involved in local politics," she says. "It just gives me a headache."

"Oh, don't take it all so seriously." The judge claps her loudly on the back. "It's all just a game. You fight as hard as you can to win, but if you don't, what the hell. It's only a damn tree."

Leonie looks out of the corner of her eye and smiles at Bob. Thank God for other boorish men, Bob thinks. They make me look good.

The judge takes a sip of the French red and smiles. "Now this is more like it."

CHAPTER 20

Bob puts his arm around Leonie as they walk home. It has gotten much colder out and Leonie is only wearing an oversized sweater. She leans into him for warmth. "I hate when the weather turns here," she says. "It makes me want to run back to California."

"Let's go then," Bob says. "I hate this weather, too."

"You would just leave like that? Walk away from where you grew up? From all this history?" Leonie gestures toward the cold street, the large humming houses, belching out warmth, light, and erudition.

"I think so," he says. He looks down the street, at the bare trees. All the leaves are gone now. One good rainfall usually knocks them out. The color is gone too, and it is still only fall. Months and months of gray winter ahead. He shivers and squeezes Leonie's upper arm. She puts her arm around his waist and squeezes back. "I used to like the winter," he says. "I liked the snow and Christmas, and snow days. Sledding. But now I dread it."

Both of his parents had died in the winter, his father in the middle of a blizzard. He remembers riding in the limousine, and watching the long black hearse in front of them fishtailing in the snow and thinking, could we really get into an accident in a funeral procession? Don't we have some kind of divine dispensation from the laws of physics?

His mother died within the year. Lung cancer, too far gone to treat. Couples often go like that. One after another. Can't live without each other. But what about him? They left him all alone. It was just as cold when she died, though not snowing. Almost worse. His father's death had been a spectacle, stage managed, earth shattering. But, there he was again, less than a year later, in the same cemetery — the frozen crunchy ground, the tattered American flag that they put on his father's grave for Veteran's Day. The empty space on the gravestone for his mother's name. Room below for his.

He brings himself back to the present. "Do you want my jacket?"

"No, but that is sweet of you. And so old fashioned." Leonie kisses him on the cheek.

"Look," he says, putting his hands on her forearms to stop her. "I did join the group because of my trees, not the Japanese maple. I was trying to win against Abigail and Johan."

Leonie nods and resumes walking. "I'm too cold to stop," she says. Once they are moving, she goes on. "You could have told me, you know. I would have understood."

Bob nods. "Really?"

They walk along in silence, heading back to Bob's house. Leonie touches his arm. "But she can't make you do anything you don't want to do. You own the house, right?"

"Right," he says. "But she can wear me down. She has so much money, and she's got a goddamned arborist on her side."

"True." Leonie laughs. "You are overmatched. And the really hard part is, they're right."

"Damn. You think I should let them take down the trees?"

"Of course."

"She's offering to pay."

Leonie withdraws her arm. "She offered to pay? What are you waiting for?"

"I don't know." Bob shakes his head, puts his hands in his coat pockets. "It's the principle of the thing."

"What? Private property?"

"No, more that these people have got to be told no, for once in their lives. Somebody's got to stop them. They can't have everything they want. There's just something wrong with the Abigails of this world. I mean they're smart, so they want all the right things — green space, beautiful trees, preservation of the environment, an end to clearcutting the rain forest. But, it's all for them, and God forbid you get in their way. They'll just mow you down."

"But they're not trying to mow you down."

"Oh yes, they are. They'd have me out of here in a minute if they could. Did you hear that judge? What a pompous ass!"

"He asked me out."

"What?" Bob stops short.

Leonie smiles. "You jealous?"

"When did he ask you out?"

"After the first meeting. He called me the next day."

Bob is thinking, the little bastard wasted no time, did he? "And what'd you say?"

"I told him no, that I was seeing someone."

"But you weren't."

"I was planning to," Leonie says. She takes his hand and puts it in her sweater pocket and they walk that way up the street to Bob's house. Bob can feel his face coloring. He smiles to himself. She had wanted him, too. Amazing really. He is flattered but just a little bit put off. Is Leonie just a more attractive version of Abigail? So assured she, too, would get what she wanted?

Bob lets them in the back door. He fumbles with the key on the dark porch. "I should put in a light," he says, "or a motion sensor. But once you start messing with the electricity in an old house, you don't know what you'll find." He opens the door to the kitchen and tries to see the place through Leonie's eyes. The floors are scarred and gouged and need to be refinished. They're so far gone he doubts they will even take another sanding. There's a cobweb in the corner near the ceiling. The furniture is not quite antique, nor is it vintage. It's more Mid-Century Left Behind. The rugs are oriental and worn, but not quite old money. They are too brightly colored, he thinks, the weave is too loose.

"I have a good electrician, if you want his name." Leonie follows him into the kitchen. "I got him from my next door neighbors."

"He's probably gouging you, living in this neighborhood." Bob takes off his coat and throws it on one the back of one of the kitchen chairs. He puts his keys on his key hook.

"Bob, you live in this neighborhood," Leonie says. She keeps her sweater on and wraps her arms around herself for warmth.

"I know, I know. But I know the secret townie handshake and they give me a break."

Leonie smiles and looks around the kitchen. "Beautiful doors. What are they? Gum wood?" She walks over and runs her hand up and down the grain of the wood. "You can't find doors like this anymore." She walks from the kitchen into the living room. "What happened to this one?" She points to the top of the door, which looks warped and discolored. "Water damage?"

"My dad always said that the previous owners threw wet diapers on top of that door, which discolored the wood and caused it to buckle and swell and then shrink."

"Wet diapers?" Leonie asks. "Who would throw wet diapers over a beautiful wood door like that? Probably the ceiling leaked and it dripped down on top of it."

Bob looks up at the door. Leonie's version makes more sense. But he had always taken his father's story for the truth. Why wouldn't he?

He follows her into the living room and moves to kiss her but she has moved to kiss him and their heads bump. "Ouch," she says. He puts his arm around her very narrow waist. Amazing how much more breakable women seem than men. Leonie is still looking around the room. "Oh God, I love that stained glass window." She points at a multicolored window above the couch, with jewel-toned pieces of glass arranged in a pattern of leaves and flowers.

"When I was little I used to think those were real rubies and emeralds," Bob says. "Abigail actually tried to buy that window from me. As though I'd just start stripping my own house and selling it off to her, piecemeal. I think it kills her that I have nicer stained glass windows than she does."

"You don't see yourself clearly. You know that?" Leonie pulls away from him. "You have led a very privileged life. But all you see is how much more everyone else around here has."

"And believe me, they see me that way, too."

Leonie looks skeptical.

"I'm telling you, it will never change." He thinks for a moment. "Let's do it, we'll go to California, start all over again."

"Bob, you are moving too fast. It's too soon to talk of moving to California."

"But not too soon to talk of having a child?" Once it is out of his mouth he regrets it. "Sorry," he says. "I didn't mean that. I really didn't mean that."

Leonie's shoulders droop. She sighs. "No, it's not the same at all, Bob. You're talking about us moving to California together. I was talking about raising a child by myself."

"You're right," he says. "I am rushing things. I don't know why I do that. We've got all the time in the world."

She cocks her head and looks at him. "I wouldn't go that far."

"No, really. Who knows what will happen." He pulls her down on the couch, kisses her and smoothes her hair. She sighs and relaxes into his arms. They lie there long enough for Bob to start falling asleep. He pulls her to her feet. "Let's go to bed, now, or we'll end up with cricks in our necks."

"I haven't given up, you know," Leonie says as they walk to his bedroom. "Just because we're using condoms."

"I know." He nods his head and pats her arm. He really doesn't know what she is getting at, but he is too tired to pursue it. It's been an awfully long day and he needs to sleep.

Bob wakes up to Leonie poking him in the ribs. "Bob," she whispers. "There's somebody outside. Something's going on. I think you should get up."

Bob looks around the room to orient himself. It's 6:15. Had he set the alarm the night before? Probably not. Good thing she woke him up. He gets out of bed, grabs his pants, which are draped over the doorknob, and puts them on. He walks into the kitchen. He can hear voices now, a man and a woman, arguing. He walks out onto the back porch, sees Rusty's truck. The voices are coming from above him. The door opens and Leonie steps out onto the porch in her sweater and jeans.

He nods towards the truck. "It's just Rusty, the trapper I hired to catch the squirrels. Must be talking to somebody."

"You call that talking?"

Bob and Leonie walk down the stairs into the driveway and Bob looks up and in the pale light he can just make out two figures on the roof of the porch, one male whom he assumes is Rusty, one female. They seem to be struggling with something.

"Hey," he yells. "Everybody all right up there?"

Rusty walks over to the edge of the roof. "No. Crazy woman is trying to steal my traps."

Bob climbs up the first few rungs of the fire escape until he can see clearly onto the roof. His neighbor Maureen is holding onto one of the traps, trying to wrest it away from Rusty. There is a terrified squirrel inside, clawing at the wire mesh.

"Jesus Christ, Maureen," Bob says.

"I am not stealing anything. I am trying to free this poor creature!" Maureen lets go of the trap and walks to the edge of the roof. She is dressed in an overcoat and sweatpants and bedroom slippers. "That poor thing has been trapped in a cage all night long, and you not doing a thing about it."

"Give me a break, Maureen," Bob says. "These are Havahart traps! I'm paying extra for them."

"Oh, I know all about your Havahart traps," Maureen says. She points at Rusty. "You just take them out and drown them. I've read all about you."

Rusty puts the cage down and rubs his eyes. He looks at Bob. "I told you I hated working in Cambridge. It's just not worth the aggravation."

"Then go back where you came from," Maureen says. "And leave the poor creatures be." She edges over the side of the roof and starts climbing down the fire escape, her broad flat behind coming at Bob at rapid speed. He starts backing down the ladder himself. One of her bedroom slippers falls off and lands on the ground in front of Leonie who runs to pick it up and then tosses it to Bob.

"Here," Bob says, and places the slipper on Maureen's dirty sole. Her heel is crusty and yellowed. He instinctively wipes his hand on the back of his pants and then touches the small of her back. "I'll help you down."

Maureen's hand comes down and flicks Bob's hand away. "Don't touch me!" she says.

Bob removes his hand and backs down the remaining steps, and into the garden. Maureen picks her way carefully down the fire escape and then turns to face him. "You didn't have to hire this murderer. I could have gotten the squirrels out for you. You catch more bees with honey, you know."

Bob can barely suppress a smile at the idea of anything about Maureen being honeyed. Leonie is smiling too, but covers her mouth with her hand.

Rusty picks up the trap again and swings himself over the railing and climbs down the fire escape. He drops the trap down and then jumps down the remaining few steps of the ladder.

Maureen runs to the trap and bends down to look inside. "There, there." She runs her fingers along the wire cage. "There, there."

"Been trying to reach you," Rusty shouts in Bob's direction.

"Sorry, man, I've been busy."

Rusty takes in Leonie, looks her up and down, and nods. "I found another nest," he says. "Way up on the back roof, closer to the trees. You got a regular squirrel superhighway there. The squirrels just come and go as they please. And the wood's all rotten. This is a bigger job than I thought. I'm going to have to charge you fifteen hundred more. And you're going to have to find a carpenter fast."

"I told him he neglected his house." Maureen turns to look at Leonie, as if noticing that there was someone else there for the first time. "He's just letting it fall down around him."

"Maureen," Bob says. "I'm going to take care of the squirrels and the house and everything is going to be fine. So why don't you go back to bed?"

She looks at Rusty and then his truck. "Is that you? Bay State Trappers?"

Rusty nods.

"All right." She narrows her eyes. "I'll be watching you." She turns and walks down the driveway.

Rusty shakes his head.

"You need another downpayment?" Bob asks. "I'll have to hit an ATM."

Rusty shrugs. "No rush. But I'd kill for some coffee."

"Sure," Bob says. "I was just going to make some."

"Hold on." Rusty picks up the trap and puts it in the back of his van and locks it. "I don't want her breaking in to free the little bastard."

The three of them head up the back stairs and onto his back porch. Bob opens the door and holds it for Rusty who nods to Leonie and says, "After you, Madame." Leonie ducks under Bob's extended arm and touches him as she does so and he turns and smiles at her.

Rusty walks over to the kitchen table and plops down on one of the wooden chairs. He folds his large weatherbeaten hands in front of him on the table. Bob takes the coffee out of the freezer and fills up the grinder with beans. Leonie takes a seat across the table from Rusty. "Bob," she says, her gaze fixed on Rusty's hands. "I read you shouldn't leave coffee beans in the freezer. It dries them out."

"Really? I thought I was supposed to leave them in the freezer." Bob puts the top of the grinder on. "See, they keep changing the rules on me."

Rusty leans his chair back and balances it on one leg. Bob can almost see the gouge beginning to form in the oak floor beneath him. If his mother were alive she would yell at him, "Sit up straight before you ruin my nice wood floors!"

Rusty looks around the room and then up at the ceiling. "Fuck," he says. "What is it with these crazy Cambridge broads?"

Leonie arches her eyebrows.

"I mean, is it hormones? Lack of hormones?"

"Hey, I'm from Cambridge!" Leonie says.

"Oh, sorry." Rusty sits up straight suddenly and the chair slams back down on all four legs. "No offense."

"Maureen's not your typical Cambridge woman." Bob leans onto the coffee grinder and then waits for its screech to subside before he continues. "She's the one I told you about, who feeds the squirrels."

"Right there, my friend, is your problem. You see, it's always the humans. The animals are never the problem."

Bob pushes the start button on the coffee machine, while Rusty and Leonie sit there not speaking, and switches on the radio under the kitchen cabinet to cover the silence. The dulcet tones of an NPR newscaster fill the room, talking about the latest atrocity in the Balkans. The announcer has just the right amount of gravitas to his voice, but he still can't keep from savoring his words, tasting each perfectly pronounced syllable.

"This okay, with everyone?"

"Sure," Leonie says. "That's my station. I always have it on. Oh, sorry. I didn't mean to offend WJZY."

"I listen to NPR when I feel like I'm going to fall asleep at the wheel," Rusty says. "Gets my blood going."

"Really?" Leonie asks. "Why?"

"Cuz they're full of shit. Bunch of rich liberals trying to tell us what to do."

"And what's wrong with being a liberal?"

"Nothing!" He winks at Bob. "If you don't mind giving half your paycheck to the government."

"What? You don't want to pay for highways? Or fire fighters?"

"Coffee's almost ready." Bob puts three mugs down on the kitchen table. "Does anyone want milk? Sugar?" He looks from Leonie to Rusty.

"I'll take some milk," Leonie says.

"And I'll take both," Rusty says.

Bob walks over to the refrigerator and turns off the radio as he does so. He returns to the table with a quart of milk and a box of sugar. "Uh, sorry about the presentation," he says. Then he gets the carafe and fills the mugs.

Rusty takes the box and pours an incredibly long stream of sugar into his coffee.

"How can you stand that much sugar?" Bob asks.

"I got a wicked sweet tooth," Rusty says. He takes a sip and smiles.

Leonie pours milk into her coffee and takes a sip. "Ah," she says. "Now I can talk politics. Never talk politics before coffee."

Rusty takes this as a sign to continue. "And I mean, half of these liberals are on the public tit." He pounds his hand on the table. "And they have the nerve to tell the rest of us how to live our lives!"

"No, in this neighborhood, they have tenure."

"I wish I had tenure," Leonie says. "It's not that easy to get."

"Really? Do you teach?"

"Yes, dance."

"Jesus!" He turns to Bob. "Where did we go wrong, huh? Here I am crawling up on rich people's roofs, fighting with raccoons, and getting covered in bat shit."

"Don't tell me there are bats up there, too?" Bob asks.

"No, no bats." Rusty gulps his coffee. "Just squirrels. A whole colony of them. But really," he says, taking another long sip. "Like I tell my kids. Get a degree and get some cushy job. That's where I went wrong. I got to work for a living."

Bob takes a sip of his coffee. "How many kids?"

"Three. You'll probably see my oldest one of these days. I got him checking the traps. Which reminds me. Our little friend is probably freaking out there in the back of my van. I got to go and take him to his new digs in the country." He pushes back the chair, scraping it against the hard wood floor and stands up. He reaches over to shake Leonie's hand. "Sorry to get into it back there," he says. "Not often I meet real NPR types in the flesh!"

Leonie shakes his hand back. "And you're the first trapper I've ever had breakfast with."

Bob walks him to the door and tells him he'll have more cash for him tomorrow. After he is gone, he pours himself more coffee and sits down next to Leonie.

"Where on earth did you find that guy?" she asks.

"The phone book?"

"He's so missing linkish."

"Hey, somebody's got to deal with raccoons. At least he doesn't have to sit at a desk all day or go to station meetings and listen to audience research."

"Or fight with the department chair about how to fund the pottery studio." Leonie exhales. "But really, how depressing. Teaching your son to check traps, in this day and age."

Bob sits and strokes her hair and tries to imagine having a child with her. Mozart in utero, gifted and talented preschool, bilingual nanny, wooden pull toys hand carved in Vermont, oboe camp.

"I had a really nice time," Leonie says finally and stands up to go.

"Me too," Bob says. "Want to try it again tonight?"

"Sure," she walks to the back door and turns with her hand on the door knob. "And the night after that."

She closes the door behind her and Bob remembers her comment about not giving up on children yet and vows to ask her what she meant later.

CHAPTER 21

———◦———

Friday night and Bob is meeting Riff at a jazz club at a hotel on the river. All the jazz clubs are at hotels in Boston; and the clientele is well heeled, mostly white couples who drive in from the suburbs in their Saabs, Subarus, and Lexi. Bob pulls into the parking garage, noting all the scrapes and gashes on the concrete columns, and is almost drawn to leave the mark of his champagne-colored Honda on the closest pole. He is bleary eyed and running late. He has spent every night this week with Leonie and wonderful though it has been, it is beginning to catch up with him. He has not slept much. And he is still not used to the day shift — the bustle of the staff, the buzz of constant rumors, who is going to get the ax next, who will survive? It is almost titillating, much more fun than working, in fact. Now the staff has something in common to talk about, a unifying force. Where will we all be tomorrow?

Bob is safe, for now. They'd have to lay off several more junior engineers to get to him. But that is little comfort. If they want to get rid of you, they eventually find a way. Or they make your life so miserable that you quit. He has seen it before.

Riff is waiting for him right where he said he'd be, outside the elevator. He is wearing a blue jumpsuit, a plaid scarf, and a black beret and sunglasses. Bob waves as he rounds the corner of the ramp, but Riff doesn't wave back. He probably can't see a thing in sunglasses, at night, in a poorly lit parking lot. Bob toots his horn, and Riff turns and smiles and waves him into a space. Riff walks over to the car and gets into the front seat.

Bob turns off the car and undoes his seatbelt. "Sorry I'm late."

Riff is already lighting up a long skinny joint. "Killer pot," he says.

He takes a hit and hands the joint to Bob. Bob hesitates for a moment. What will Leonie think? Will she smell it on him? Then again, she is from California. Wouldn't that make her open-minded about pot? He takes a hit and holds it in. Besides, what better way to hear jazz?

They take the elevator to the top of the hotel. Does it move awfully fast, or is it an optical illusion because one of the walls is glass and you can see a pool of water at the bottom? They walk down a long, winding, anonymous corridor to the entrance of Lady Day's, where a line is beginning to form. Riff glides past the line, right up to a woman who is seated on a tall stool by the door. She is heavily made up, wearing a low cut black dress and gold jewelry. She is dressed for three in the morning. As the night goes on, she will look better and better. "Diana, my love," Riff says and grabs her hand.

Diana jumps off the stool and throws her arms around Riff and kisses him on both cheeks. "So glad you made it!" She looks over his shoulder at Bob and smiles. "You guys are in for a real treat!"

She unhooks a velvet rope and leads them to a small table right in front of the stage. The club is completely empty. They sit down and Bob looks out at the Charles River and the lights of Cambridge on the other side. He leans back in his fake leather club chair, puts his hands behind his head, and closes his eyes. He can feel the pot coming on. Cocktail jazz is playing over the speakers, but not loud enough to block out the ambient sound of the room. He can hear the wind buffeting the tall windows, the windup and surge of traffic on Storrow Drive, the faint whoosh of the elevators, a rhythmic clanking from the bar.

"Don't worry," Riff says.

Bob sits up and looks over to him. "What?"

"This is energy pot, kind of like a cross between coke and pot. Give it a minute. You'll be right as rain." Riff takes off his sunglasses to rub his red-rimmed eyes, then puts them back on.

Bob closes his eyes. He feels a yearning in his gut for Leonie and wishes she were there. She has a student dance concert tonight, a must attend. "I wouldn't put you through it," she said, when he offered to come. "I'll meet you later, if there's time."

The manager of the club walks over to their table and pulls up a chair. "We've got a good grilled salmon tonight."

Riff pats his substantial middle. "Thanks, Gerry. But it's too early for me to eat. That would upset the delicate ecological balance of my gut. I'll just take a ginger ale. Bobby, you want something?"

Bob orders a burger and a beer. He knows the club will pick up the tab, but he doesn't want to overdo it. This club could be out of business in an instant, replaced by a karaoke or sports bar. Nothing in the jazz world is a given.

Gerry calls a waiter over to the table and gives him their order. "So, Riff, you going for that job at Harvard?"

"I got to 'go' for it?"

"Well, yeah. Throw your hat in the ring. You'd be perfect."

Riff shrugs. "How early you think I'd have to get up?"

"It's a jazz archive, man. And they're going to bring all the legends in to play. Late hours come with the territory. You'd probably have to escort all the old guys back and forth to their gigs."

"That I could do."

"You've got to hand it to Harvard. Trying to recognize these guys before they die. You should get in on the gravy train."

Bob knows that Riff is just playing it cool. He has already applied for the job. Bob edited his application. He read his letters of reference. He put together a "best of" jazz interview reel for him and dubbed it to cassette.

The waiter arrives with their drinks and the manager excuses himself and walks to the door. Diana is just letting the crowds in. First a group of young Japanese hipsters in large black glasses and tailored black clothing rushes in. They scan the club and settle for a round table in the back corner. Riff bows his head to them and they bow back, aficionado to aficionado. Next comes a couple, very dowdy, academic, Cambridge looking. He's dressed in a tweed sports coat and corduroys. She's got thin gray hair and wears a Guatemalan-looking black dress with a braided hem. They are carrying their winter coats on their arms. They hurry down the aisle toward the front, stop to glare at Bob and Riff, and settle for the bistro table right next to them. The man puts his hand on the chair Bob has saved for Leonie and asks, "This taken?"

"Yes." Bob pats the coat he left on the back of the chair. The man scowls at him and pulls a chair from another table.

The woman pushes the small bistro table away from her and steps on Bob's heel with her clog. They drape their coats and sit. They are so close that Bob can smell the mothballs coming off their clothing.

Riff whispers in his ear. "What is it with these Cambridge people? The whole fucking club is empty and they have to sit on top of us!"

Bob leans in. "They figure we got the best seats."

Riff shakes his head. "Anywhere else and people would leave a couple of open tables. I don't know how you live here."

"If you get that Harvard job, you'll have to do it, too."

Riff shakes his head. "I'm not going to get the Harvard job. They need a black guy or, even better, a black woman. They're a bunch of old white guys themselves."

Bob suspects Riff is right. It's like all these modern jazz and blues bands. Three middle class white guys like himself and one black dude they feature prominently on the album cover.

The tables around them fill up, one by one. Several times Bob has to guard Leonie's seat. Riff asks. "So is this Radcliffe woman really coming?

"Yes," Bob says. "And I keep telling you, her name's Leonie." Even the sound of her name makes him smile. "We've been together every night this week."

"Whoa! Maybe you should take it slow."

"Take it slow? I'm forty-eight years old. I've been taking it slow my whole life."

"Well if you come on like a panting dog, she'll think you're desperate."

"I think she feels the same way."

Riff shakes his head. "Things must be really bad out there for single women."

Bob punches him on the shoulder. "You're going to like her," he says. "Despite yourself."

The waiter delivers his burger. The club is full. The band members file onto the stage, first the drummer, then the piano player, and finally the bassist, who breaks into a big smile when he sees Riff.

Bob whispers, "You know him?"

"He's been around forever. Like me."

After the band tunes up, the lights go down and the singer walks on stage. She's a young white woman, with long dark hair, dressed in an off-the-shoulder black dress and high heels. She has a pretty face, with just a touch of something hard bitten to it. Something around her mouth, Bob thinks. She has seen hard times. Living in Cambridge has made him forget that white people have hard times, too.

A spotlight plays on her and she nods to the band and they all start as one. She has a full-bore, husky voice that she totally controls. She holds a note for so long — no quavering, just one long assured out breath — that the audience gasps in pleasure. She smiles to herself but doesn't make eye contact with the audience. The bass player nods his head up and down.

"Nice pipes," Riff says.

Bob closes his eyes and lets himself drift. The singer is not exactly an innovator, more of an interpreter, but she has a great voice and great taste. When she finishes her first song, the Japanese guys erupt into applause. She smiles at them and launches into her next song. Amazing, really, how much more the Japanese appreciate jazz than Americans. Perhaps it is just too available here. Bob and Riff can catch good jazz almost every night of the week, at small venues, and the tickets, compared to rock concerts at least, are a steal. So what if you have to buy a couple of drinks? So what if you're seated next to guys like Mr. Tweed, who is one of those irritating jazz fans who laughs along with the music, as though it's an inside joke only he and the players get.

At the end of the next set, Bob feels a tap on his shoulder and turns around to find that Leonie has arrived. He gets up and gives her a hug and a kiss. He breathes in the scent of her now-familiar shampoo and soap. Riff starts to get up out of his chair too, but Leonie pats him on the shoulder and he sinks back down. He removes his dark sunglasses. "You're even prettier than Bobby said."

"Thanks." Leonie smiles and turns to Bob. "Bobby?"

"You can't live in Boston without becoming Bobby." He motions to the seat they have been saving all night for her. She sits and as she takes off her coat, her chair rubs up against the tweedy woman's chair. The woman pushes back. Leonie rolls her eyes and sniffs at the air. "What's that smell?" she whispers. "Mothballs? I hate that smell. It's so toxic. It makes me sick!"

"You want to move?" Riff asks. "We could move."

Leonie shakes her head. "No, but could they cram us in here any tighter? That's one thing I hate about the East Coast. No sense of personal space."

"It's not the whole East Coast," Riff leans close. "Just Cambridge."

Leonie nods. "I know exactly what you mean. It's like at the grocery store. People stand way too close, breathing down your neck, like they'll get rung up sooner if they hover."

"I think it's because they're all academics who live in their heads," Riff says. "They're thinking about that next book."

"No, they're thinking about how to destroy their enemies in the department."

Riff laughs. "Let me buy you a drink." He motions to the waiter and turns his attention again to Leonie. "Do you like jazz?"

"Oh yes," Leonie says. "My Dad's a big fan."

Riff winces at the mention of her "Dad" but smiles and quizzes her on his favorite musicians. She tells him about a great concert she saw at Yoshi's in the East Bay. Riff asks about her work at Harvard and is surprisingly knowledgeable about dance. Has he read up on it to prepare? Leonie squeezes Bob's hand. This is going well. Bob is relieved. The band comes out and starts another set.

The bass player nods at Riff again, and this time the singer acknowledges him, too. Leonie whispers in his ear. "I didn't know Riff was such a big deal."

"Oh yeah," Bob says, feeling proud. "There's nobody like him, really."

"*Sui generis*," Leonie says.

"What?"

"One of kind. Like you."

Bob tries her compliment on for size, decides he doesn't like it. Is she implying that while he's an exception, it's perfectly fine to look down on all the other Irish Catholic townies? Or, maybe the pot is making him paranoid. He pushes the thought from his mind, puts his arm around Leonie's shoulder and settles in to enjoy the last set.

At the end of the night, Gerry comes over to their table. "Good luck with the Harvard gig," he says to Riff. "You got my vote."

"Speaking of Harvard." Riff introduces Leonie to Gerry. She shakes his hand and tells him how much she liked the band.

"We'd love to get them on the show sometime," Riff says.

Gerry suggests they go over to the bar where the band is autographing CDs, see if they can set it up. Riff gets up to follow him.

As soon as they're gone, Leonie leans over and asks, "Harvard gig?"

"Yeah, there's a jazz directorship opening at Harvard. Riff's going for it."

"Oh, right, the Louis Armstrong Archive. Are they really open to non academics?"

"They must be. Everybody's telling Riff to apply."

"Why don't you go for it?"

"Me?"

"You know a lot about jazz. And you're working on a book, right?"

"Well." Bob shrugs. "Riff's a big deal, like you said. I'm not. And yeah, I'm working on a book, but I've been working on it for ten years, and I'm not about to finish it soon."

"But you've published articles. And reviews. Publications are really important in the academic world. Does Riff have any?"

"No."

"I could help you with your application. Wouldn't it be great? We could work together." She grabs his arm and squeezes it. Her eyes are shining.

Bob shakes his head. "I'd love to work with you. And I'd love to work in the jazz field. But I would never go up against my friend for a job. That's Riff's gig. If he gets it, I'll be ecstatic."

"But if he doesn't get it, then somebody else will, right? It might as well be you!"

Bob can't quite wrap his head around this line of reasoning, why it rubs him so wrong, "No," he says. "I couldn't do it."

"Look," Leonie says. "I've gone up against friends for positions lots of times. It's just life in the arts. Everyone understands. I mean, didn't you go through this when you applied to college?"

"No, I went to UMass. If you got a certain SAT score you got in."

"But then somebody else didn't."

"No, we all got in."

"Bob, you're being naïve." Leonie laughs. "And passive. I mean what are you waiting for? Opportunities like this don't come around often."

"I'm waiting for the bride and groom to notice me and invite me up to the good table."

"What?" Leonie turns all the way around in her chair to look at him.

"Don't you know the parable about Jesus at the wedding banquet?"

"The water into wine?"

"No, another one. Jesus is at a wedding, and he sits at a table with all the slobs and riff raff. Only after the bride and groom personally invite him over does he sit at the table of honor. The nuns drilled that one into our heads. You're not supposed to push yourself ahead."

"And you're still waiting for someone to invite you to the good table?"

"I guess."

"Bob, you're in the wrong parable. How about the one about hiding your light under a bushel?"

"The nuns weren't big on that." He looks over at Riff who is now at the bar, talking to the lead singer and the bass player. He's got his arm around the singer's shoulders. She is laughing flirtatiously. Riff holds up his hand to indicate that he'll just be a few more minutes.

"Go for the jazz director job," Leonie says, as she gathers up her coat and purse and gets up to leave. "Riff will understand."

"I doubt it," Bob says.

Later, on the ride to Leonie's, Bob puts on a CD of Roy Hargrove. Wonderful trumpet player. He likes how jazz can transform any environment into some place mysterious and charged. He remembers how he used to drive home from college in his VW bug. Nothing worked but the radio. He would listen to a jazz show out of upstate New York and forget that his feet were cold. The inside of the little car would feel warm and lit up, like a club, in candlelight. All he has really ever wanted was to share this moment, this trumpet, bending off the walls of his car, these white lines slipping under his wheels, these dark clumps of foliage melting by. He doesn't need a jazz gig; he has this music, this night, this purplish sky.

CHAPTER 22

On Saturday morning, Leonie goes into the studio to critique the students' dance performance, and Bob goes home to prepare for Mary Elizabeth's visit. She's coming at noon to help him clean out the attic. He checks the mail and finds a letter from his HMO, SafetyNetInc, nestled among the catalogues, credit card offers, and grocery store flyers. He waits until he has made a pot of coffee and settled himself down at the kitchen table to open it. He owes a little over ten thousand dollars. Due immediately. He slams the letter down on the table so hard that coffee spills out of his cup. He jumps up to get a sponge and mops the coffee up. How could Omar have ever thought it was right to involve them in his own private vengeance?

He is tempted to call Riff, but he'll still be asleep. He thinks briefly of calling Irene, but decides that is an even worse idea. Instead he calls Omar, who answers on the second ring.

"What were you thinking?" Bob refills his cup of coffee, cradles the phone between his neck and shoulder. "I owe SafetyNet ten grand!"

"Sorry," Omar says, with a sigh. "I'm sorry." He sounds really depressed. Glum, in fact. "If I could undo it, believe me, I would. My father's been trying to borrow money to pay it back. I even tried to borrow it from my wife's family. They won't even talk to me."

"Have you talked to SafetyNet directly? Maybe you could cut a deal?"

"My lawyer won't let me."

"You have a lawyer?"

"Of course. I'm facing jail time!"

"Don't worry. We won't let that happen," Bob says. "We'll figure out something."

"Thanks." Omar is silent for a moment. "If only Kathy hadn't arrived. You know, I was just about to stop."

"What?"

"I kept a running tally. I wouldn't have gone over the amount they owed me. I was just evening the score."

"So, my ten grand? That was applied to your tally?"

"Of course."

"That's almost heroic."

Omar laughs. "Tell that to the judge." Bob's gaze is drawn by some movement outside his kitchen window. The gate to the meditation garden swings open, and Bryce appears. He carefully latches the gate behind him and steps into Bob's driveway — exactly what Bob objected to in the first place. What's to stop all his other guests from doing the same?

"Hold on, I've got a neighbor at my back door."

"They still trying to cut down your trees?" Omar laughs. "I'll let you go."

Bryce pads up the back staircase and raps on Bob's French door. When Bob doesn't answer immediately, he raises his hand to shield his eyes from the sun and peers in through the French doors. Bob gets up from the table. "Bryce!" he says as he opens the door. "What's up?"

"I came to apologize," Bryce says. "I shouldn't have put in the gate without your permission. I was caught up by my own plans and didn't have the patience to wait for your response. Sorry." He looks down at his feet. His hair is thinning on the crown, typical male pattern baldness.

Bob nods to himself. This is true. Perhaps this Buddhist stuff really does work?

Bryce looks up, continues. "I can take it down if you want."

Bob hesitates. He wishes Mary Elizabeth were already there, to bolster his resolve. He knows he should take it down. But it seems almost petty to insist upon it now. "Let me think about it," Bob says.

"Okay." Bryce smiles. "And if you have time tomorrow, there's going to be a blessing ceremony for the garden. Would love you to come. Might heal some of the bad energy between us." He reaches into the pocket of his barn jacket, takes out a printed card, and places it in Bob's hand.

"Thanks."

"Around three." Bryce waves and trots back down the stairs.

Bob puts it on the kitchen table next to the ten-thousand-dollar invoice. There's a wood cut of a maple tree and a koi pond printed on it, the pagoda-like garden gate silhouetted in the background, in four colors. Doesn't look like Bryce expects that gate to come down anytime soon.

He finishes up his coffee and heads upstairs to get ready for Mary Elizabeth's visit. He'll need boxes and garbage bags, maybe some tape. The attic is less like an attic than an unfinished room next to the chimney. The boards are wide rough planks. The ceiling is slanted. There's a large cedar closet on one wall, a selling point for the house, but Bob suspects the moths have long since adapted to the smell of cedar, maybe even grown fond of it. He opens the door and pushes a few boxes out of the way, then fumbles for the light switch over his head. Is it a pull chain, or just a string? He can't remember. He finds a chain and pulls it but nothing happens. Perhaps the bulb is burnt out? Then his fingers find a long piece of string and he pulls that and the bare bulb lights up the little room. When is the last time he was up here? Right after his mother died? He remembers lugging that heavy box of her clothes up the stairs. But that was years ago. He picks up one of the boxes, carries it to the corner of the room, and shoves it under the eaves, but as he does so, he notices a pile of chewed up insulation in the corner. Could be new or old, he can't tell. He'll have to bring Rusty up here, have him take a look. All he needs are the squirrels to start gnawing at his already substandard wiring.

He goes downstairs to get a broom and a boom box. He'll need music to get this done, something serious and beautiful, but not too sad. He's thinking Coltrane, Miles, Bill Evans. Or maybe Mary Elizabeth will have a more practical, up-tempo, suggestion.

She prefers silence, so they can catch up. And she is a lot less efficient than Bob expected. She keeps going off on sentimental reveries about the contents of the cedar closet. In response, Bob is finding it easy to be ruthless.

"My mother was so jealous when Aunt Peggy got this coat!" Mary Elizabeth takes a long mink coat off its hanger and slips into it. She twirls around. It's much too short for her. "How barbaric, huh? Wearing an animal pelt to church?"

Bob jerks his thumb toward the box labeled "Goodwill."

"Oh no, I'm thinking we could get some money for this," Mary

Elizabeth says. "I vote "vintage."" She points to another box, overflowing with brightly colored maxi dresses, vinyl records, and speckled plastic dinnerware. Bob frowns and looks at his watch.

"On second thought, we don't want PETA on our tails." She takes off the coat and drops it into the Goodwill box. "I think it's illegal to wear fur in Cambridge anyway."

Bob picks a box marked "Christmas" off a teetering pile of boxes, trash bags, and plastic bins. "Want to go through these?"

"Sure." Mary Elizabeth opens the box and reaches in, takes out a balled up wad of newspaper, and unwraps an old fashioned egg-shaped Christmas ornament.

"Oh, I remember that one." Bob takes it from Mary Elizabeth and sniffs it. "Is it my imagination or does this smell like Christmas?" He holds it under her nose.

"Smells like moth balls. Everything up here smells like moth balls."

Bob tosses it into the Goodwill box. "You think moth balls are poisonous?"

"Yeah, but it's too late for us. We've already been exposed. And to asbestos and second-hand smoke. I think my mother breastfed me with a cigarette in her mouth."

"Mine, too. But she never breastfed, bottle only."

Mary Elizabeth unwraps a figurine of one of the wise men. "I assume there's a whole set here," she says. "For the manger?"

"Yeah," Bob says. "Somewhere."

She unwraps St. Joseph and puts him on the chair with the wise man.

Bob finds a lamb and the Baby Jesus and puts them with the rest. The next ornament is a porcelain angel with an upturned nose, which he throws into the trash.

Mary Elizabeth holds up one of his mother's favorite ornaments. It's pale pink and the center is hollowed out and painted a shimmery gold. "Aunt Peggy always had such beautiful stuff."

"Take it," Bob says. "Take anything you want." He hands her an empty box.

Mary Elizabeth puts the pink and gold ornament into the empty box, then reaches into the storage box for another ornament. As she unwraps the innermost layer of newspaper a few shards of colored glass and some dark brown pellets drop from her hands. "Oh gross!" she says. "Mouse droppings!" She lets go of the ornament and it clatters to the floor.

"So much for my mother's beautiful stuff."

"We could catch Hanta Virus up here." She looks inside the box again. "But I hate to throw these all away. Do you have any rubber gloves?"

"Let me look." Bob heads down the stairs. On the second floor landing he pauses to look into his old bedroom: same twin bed with the saggy mattress and the plaid bedspread; same scarred wooden headboard, onto which he had pasted stickers of race cars and super heroes and then later had carved a peace sign. The drapes are the same depressing plaid as the bedspread and are pulled back at the sides with scraps of fabric. The nonsense women think up. The yellowed shades are at half mast, and one of them is missing its pull; fingerprints are visible along the bottom edge. Still, it is a nice room. He used to love lying there looking through the small diamond-shaped window panes, watching the wind blow through the tree tops, imagining that he was in a blizzard or a hurricane or even better, that he was on a sailboat and the wind was pushing him out to sea.

He hurries past his parents' bedroom, and continues down the stairs to the front hall and walks into the kitchen. He finds an unopened bag of yellow rubber gloves under the sink. His mother always wore them when she washed dishes. She was very proud of her slim fingers, her long, painted nails. He supposes he should have cleaned out this cabinet too, gotten rid of all vestiges of his parent's lives, but why? To put his own stamp on the household cleaning products?

He grabs two pairs of gloves and another large trash bag. "Got some!" he yells up from the second floor landing. Mary Elizabeth leans out over the third floor railing. His mother's lace wedding veil floats out around her head like a halo. "What?" she calls.

"Gloves," he hurries up the remaining stairs to hand them to her. "Where'd you find that?"

"In a garment bag way at the back of the closet. And I found her wedding gown, too." She motions for him to follow her into the attic. "Look." She holds up the gown on its hanger. "It's beautiful. All these tiny pearls. But so small. I don't think I could get one of my arms into it."

Bob fingers the slightly yellowed satin gown. It doesn't look like a grown woman could ever have worn it. His mother must have been so thin when she got married. Bob remembers her as always being short and stout. Until the end, of course, when she got sick. "What am I going to do with this?" He can't give his mother's wedding gown to Goodwill or worse to the trendy vintage store on Mass. Ave. where all the young ghouls salivate over fondue pots and console TVs.

"I could take it," Mary Elizabeth says. "For the girls. They love to play wedding."

"Let me think about it," Bob says, picturing the gown in a heap in the corner of the girls' room.

"Okay." Mary Elizabeth hangs the wedding gown on the neck of an old brass floor lamp. "On second thought, let's keep the fur coat, too." She dives into the Goodwill box and retrieves the coat and puts it on top of the wedding gown. Then she removes the lace veil and wraps it around the top of the hanger. The effect is eerie, ghostlike. Mary Elizabeth makes a face. "I'm not being much help, am I?"

Bob smiles. "This is harder than I thought."

"I know." Mary Elizabeth lays a hand on his arm, looks him in the eye, which makes him uncomfortable. He does not want to tear up in front of her. "We could finish up another time," she says. "There's no big rush. Is there?"

"No rush," he says. "But let's keep going."

She nods, turns to the box of Christmas stuff. "Ok, I'll focus on this. You tackle the cedar closet."

They work in silence for the next hour. Mary Elizabeth's box keeps growing. Bob clears out the cedar closet, tossing out summer dresses and light wool suits, several threadbare overcoats, and a wide-brimmed straw hat. He stops when he finds his father's blue seersucker suit. He remembers him wearing it to church on hot summer Sundays, the congregation fanning themselves with their prayer cards, the fans turning ineffectually overhead, the priest's voice droning. He can almost feel the sweat dripping down the neck of his own starched collar, and his stomach rumbling in anticipation of the powdered sugar donuts they would pick up on the way home. Where are his parents now? Are they old or young, is his father's hair black or gray, does he still have the white, untanned skin where he shaved off his sideburns? Is his mother fat or thin, and has she finally been able to quit smoking? No wonder he has put this off.

Mary Elizabeth finds a battered children's school desk. "Oh, look Bob," she says. "It's got a hole for an inkwell and a seat attached. Where on earth did this come from?"

"I don't remember. It's just always been here."

He looks around the room. Still so much to empty out. Hockey sticks and ice skates and several moldy old board games. Broken-down chairs, a broken tennis racket; a rolled-up needlepoint rug, a wall-to-wall carpet remnant in a depressing shade of baby-shit brown, and some rolls of wallpaper, curled and yellowed. His father always saved them for patching.

"Can I take the desk for the kids?"

Bob hesitates. Maybe he will have his own kids someday.

"We play Catholic school," Mary Elizabeth says. "And I'm the mean old nun, of course."

"Sure, go ahead," Bob says.

Mary Elizabeth tries to lift the desk but it is too heavy for her. "Want to help me get this down to the car?"

Bob picks up the other end. "I can do it myself."

"Yeah, but why do it alone?"

They carry it to the landing, reposition themselves and Bob starts to back carefully down the stairs. "Too bad we don't have two of them," he says.

"One is good enough. They are already spoiled."

They wind their way down the two flights of stairs, and then through the living room, and into the kitchen. Bob stops to unlatch the door and they continue onto the back porch, down the stairs, and around the driveway to Mary Elizabeth's Saturn wagon.

They set the desk down again, and Mary Elizabeth opens the lift gate. Bob angles the desk this way and that to get it into the trunk. Will she be able to see over it? He turns around to ask her, but her gaze is fixed on the end of the driveway. Leonie is approaching. She is wearing a pea coat, scarf, jeans and cowboy boots. Bob has always liked women in cowboy boots. She breaks into a smile and waves to them as she strides toward them. Once again Bob is struck by how effortlessly she moves.

He rushes forward to meet her, kisses her lightly on the cheek, takes her hand, and walks her back to Mary Elizabeth's car. "Leonie, this is my cousin, Mary Elizabeth."

Leonie puts out her hand to shake. She looks from Bob to Mary Elizabeth and shakes her head. "I don't really see a resemblance," she says.

"No," Mary Elizabeth says. "You wouldn't. Bob looks like his father. I'm from his mother's side."

Bob looks from Leonie to Mary Elizabeth. They are only eight years apart but Mary Elizabeth looks much older. Her mouth curves slightly downward and there are deep creases on either side that go almost to her chin. Her mother had those same lines, part disappointment, part iron will.

Leonie looks at the school desk. "So, am I too early? I didn't mean to interrupt."

"Oh no," Bob says. "Time for a break, anyway. Want some coffee?"

"How about a beer?" Mary Elizabeth says. "We could go to Finn's."

"Sure," Leonie says. "I have always wanted to go there. But I've been too intimidated."

"Don't get your hopes up," Mary Elizabeth says. "The beer's okay, but the food sucks."

Leonie smiles and shoves her hands into the pockets of her pea coat. "I'm game."

It's still early so they score a corner booth. An elderly waitress with dyed black ringlets piled on top of her head approaches them with water and menus. She is wearing a white blouse, black skirt, black apron, thick shiny stockings, and sturdy black tie shoes. Bob shakes his head at the menus. "We're just getting beers," he says. "I'll have a Bass Ale and oh, maybe some French Fries."

The waitress scowls and pivots, then pads slowly back to the waitress station to return the menus.

"And I'll get some onion rings," Mary Elizabeth calls to her back. "And a Heineken. And…" She turns to Leonie.

"Bass Ale."

Mary Elizabeth shouts out Leonie's order and then says, in a much lower voice, "They have the rudest waitresses here."

"Yeah, it's kind of a game with them." Bob says. "Who can be the meanest. Actually, Finn's was the first place I got served. I was fifteen."

The waitress returns in a few minutes with three bottles and glasses, which she places down in front of them and then carefully pours out the Heineken for Mary Elizabeth, letting the beer course down the side of the glass so it doesn't develop too much of a head. Then she pours out Leonie's and Bob's. "You want ketchup?" she says and turns around before they have time to answer.

Bob winks at Leonie. "Yes," he shouts at her back. He holds up his beer. "To a clean attic!"

Mary Elizabeth holds up her glass. "And a really cool desk!"

Leonie clinks her glass with both of theirs. "So, is the desk for your kids?"

"Oh no," Mary Elizabeth laughs and shakes her head. "Grandkids!"

"Grandkids? You have grandkids?" Leonie looks at Bob in surprise.

"Yeah. I have a daughter who's thirty. And you, do you have children?"

Leonie shakes her head. "Not yet." She looks down at her hands. Mary Elizabeth raises her eyebrows at Bob. He shrugs. There is silence at the table.

"We're going to play Catholic school with it," Mary Elizabeth says. "I play the mean old nun and my granddaughters are the students and I think up all sorts of horrible punishments for them. They love it."

"You both went to Catholic school?"

"Oh yeah," Bob says. "We were in the same class from first grade on."

"Remember Sister Theodora?" Mary Elizabeth asks. She turns to Leonie. "She made me sit in the trash, on top of the empty milk cartons and baloney sandwiches."

"That's awful!" Leonie leans her head back against the tall booth and takes a sip of her beer. She is laughing at them. This is exactly what Bob did not want to happen. Catholics as some sort of anthropological joke, his tribe on display. "What were you being punished for?"

"Talking, probably. I always was talking. Or wearing my bangs too long."

Or getting pregnant at the junior prom, Bob thinks, but doesn't say. Each year, a few Catholic school girls got pregnant at the prom. It was all too much for them. The gown, the punch, the beer, the boy, the joint, the car. Most of them had never even kissed or held hands. They had no experience saying *no, maybe*, or *yes, but*, and they got pregnant. Bob himself intended to have sex on the night of the prom, but his date, Catherine Malloy, threw up before he could press his case. Mary Elizabeth still never mentions the pregnancy or the fact that she had to leave school.

"The nuns were different to the boys," Mary Elizabeth continues, warming to the topic. "Even meaner. I remember them banging their heads against the chalkboards. They really hated boys."

Bob flashes his eyes to Mary Elizabeth to try to get her to change the subject, but she goes on. "Remember when you ran for class president and Sister Willamette set you up?"

Bob groans. He holds up his hand to catch their waitress's attention. She is heading to a table of loud young men with two sloshing pitchers of beer. He orders another round with a nod of his head.

"You were president of your class?" Leonie asks. "Somehow I just can't picture it."

Bob shakes his head. "No," he says. "I lost."

"Bob!" Mary Elizabeth breaks in. "He's not telling the whole story. He lost by one vote. His own. He voted for the other guy!"

Leonie looks at him. "Why on earth would you do that?"

"Sister Willamette lectured us about how it was the Christian thing to do, to vote for your opponent," Mary Elizabeth says. "Bobby was the only kid in school who took all that Catholic nonsense seriously. The other guy voted for himself!"

Leonie starts to laugh and Bob and Mary Elizabeth join in. The waitress puts three more beers down in front of them, Bass Ales for Bob and Leonie, a Heineken for Mary Elizabeth. Amazing, how she always gets the order right.

CHAPTER 23

It's getting harder and harder to communicate with Riff. He's asleep when Bob is up, up when Bob's asleep, and the few hours they overlap never seem to be the right ones to call. On Sunday afternoon, Bob waits until the respectable hour of 3 p.m. to dial his number, and although Riff claims that he's been up a while, he sounds groggy and slow witted. Bob can hear the whistle of a tea kettle, the clatter of a teaspoon in a cup, in the background. He must be making his morning cup of tea.

Bob tells him about the letter from SafetyNetInc, his conversation with Omar.

"Are they even the ones who threw her off the plan?" Riff asks.

"I don't know." It hadn't occurred to him to ask. Would Omar's vengeance be that diffuse? That he would hold an entire industry responsible?

"But get this. He was going to stop, as soon as he reached the amount they owed him."

"And how would he calculate that, exactly?"

"I don't know. But he would. He's a benefits specialist after all. He's probably got it all worked out, down to the very last penny. Deducted copays, out-of-network expenses, lifetime out-of-pocket limits. I mean, he's not a crook."

Riff slurps his tea. "More a bureaucrat gone mad."

"He's kind of heroic when you think about it," Bob says. "A Robin Hood figure. Here he was giving us all the benefit of his crazy scheme. Didn't matter to him whether the insurance company was paying for my gum surgery or Irene's orthotics."

"Or Sue's Seasonal Affective Disorder lightbox."

"Sue has Seasonal Affective Disorder?

"We both do. You probably do too. Working nights is like living in permanent winter. We use it all year long."

"Does it work?"

"I don't know. We'd need a control group who didn't use it. Hey, maybe you're the control group. We do seem happier than you. Everyone is happier than you."

"That's debatable. Anyway, I think Omar should be celebrated, not thrown in jail. What he did took guts and cunning. We should have a fucking parade in his honor. Or some kind of event, where we could collect donations, for his bail." Bob is getting excited. He pictures a Salvation Army style bell ringer and a cauldron full of twenties.

"Man, you're going a little crazy here. Are you not sleeping or something?"

Bob sees a flash of maroon and gold pass by his kitchen window. "Hold on a minute." He walks over to the window to check it out. A trio of monks in long robes is strolling down his driveway, heading for the garden gate. The Buddhist Blessing Ceremony. Of course. He had forgotten all about it. There's a multi-colored prayer flag strung between the gate posts. "Speaking of crazy. You won't believe what's going on next door." He tells Riff about Bryce, the Blessing Ceremony.

"Bobby, I got to say. Nights are boring without you. I never talk to BJ. Does he have crazy neighbors? Does he own a house, a cat? Who the fuck knows! He's as silent as the grave."

More and more people file down the driveway. The ceremony's going to be standing room only. "Jesus Christ," Bob says. "Bryce must have invited the press. There's a tall guy with a camera and one of those vests you put all the film in, and oh my God, here comes a limousine. Maybe it's the Dalai Lama?"

"The Dalai Lama's in your neighborhood?"

"Just kidding. You see this is where we got it all wrong. These people here, they have the glimmer of an idea and they snap their fingers and make it happen. And they make sure the press is there to document it. And they apply for funding from some foundation so they don't have to shell out any of their own money to keep it going. They aren't paralyzed by self-doubt like normal people are. In fact, they've been encouraged from an early age to think all of their stupid ideas are good. They've been overnurtured."

Bob watches as a couple of very pretty and relaxed-looking women approach the meditation garden. One of them is holding a bouquet of flowers, the other a wrapped fruit basket. So far these Buddhists are an attractive, prosperous-looking bunch.

"Well, I have to admit, it is kind of a good idea," Riff says, after a minute.

"The benefit for Omar?"

"No, the meditation garden. Wouldn't mind one out back in my yard."

The limousine door opens and a very thin, blonde woman in a short skirt, heels, and black stockings gets out and teeters down Bryce's side walk. She looks more New York than Boston. Maybe she's his publicist?

"But how about the benefit for Omar?" Bob asks.

"That's a crazy idea, Bobby. He broke the law. He defrauded an insurance company."

"How about that guy from Philadelphia? He's a cause célèbre, and he killed some cops!"

"Trouble is, what Omar did is not only illegal, it's also kind of boring. It's not like he's a romantic revolutionary figure, Bob. He's a fucking HR guy."

"But he is a revolutionary, in his own way. It's just the times we're living in that are boring."

Riff sighs loudly.

Bob stares out the window at the prayer flags fluttering in the wind. Does Bryce have to leave them there now until they rot? Or disintegrate? "What if the fundraiser were a concert?" he asks. "A jazz concert? I could ask Buddy to play. You could ask that woman from Friday night."

"Nobody wants to be associated with insurance fraud."

"But everyone hates the insurance companies. And rich people like my neighbors love to get behind an underdog. Makes them feel less guilty about their Brazilian cleaning ladies and Ecuadoran landscapers."

Riff laughs and takes another loud sip of his tea.

Bob knows he's onto something. Why can't Riff see? Is it because they are both so mired in lower middle class thinking?

Somebody is backing a Ford pickup truck into the driveway and stops in front of the gate. There's a huge metal gong in the bed of the truck. Bob tells Riff he'll call him back and runs out onto his porch. "Hey!" he yells. "Hey! You can't park there."

A tall skinny kid with close-cropped hair, a sweatshirt, and jean jacket, gets out of the truck. "No problem, man." He raises two fingers in a peace symbol. He's got wooden prayer beads wound around his wrist. "Just let me unload and I'll move it."

Bryce opens the garden gate wide for the gong-bearing kid, motions for some monks to come help him unload, and turns to Bob. "Hi neighbor," he says. "So glad you could make it."

"Bryce, I can't have everyone traipsing through my yard, blocking my driveway. This is exactly why I didn't want this gate here."

Bryce nods his head in an understanding way, while keeping an eye on the gong-moving crew. He pats Bob on the back. "Yes, sorry," he says. "That was unforeseen. Let's talk about it after I get through this event, okay? But in the meantime, won't you come see the garden? I am so proud of it."

Bob shrugs and follows him into the garden. "My next door neighbor, Bob," Bryce says to an elderly woman in a purple wool coat. "He gave a foot, so that the garden could happen." The old lady smiles kindly and bows her head to Bob. There is a path or rose petals strewn artfully on the ground leading up to the pond, where the kid and the monks are setting up the gong. The monks smile beatifically as Bryce introduces, "Bob, who gave a foot."

It is a beautiful place. No detail overlooked. The wooden stepping stones are arranged so that they get smaller as you approach the pond, probably to make the tiny yard look bigger. The fish in the pond look fat and healthy and swim energetically round and round, as if posing for a Japanese wood cut. The wind rustles the copper leaves of the miniature Japanese maple. There is a bench made of the same rough-hewn wood as the steps, but burnished and sculpted to accept the human form. People are standing around in groups of threes and fours, waiting for the ceremony to begin. There's a pot of burning incense on the ground. The grass is brand new and spring green, the topsoil rich and black. The requisite Buddha sits in the far corner in a kind of ivied grotto. "Wait until next spring," Bryce says. "My gardeners put in a thousand bulbs."

"What happens to the fish in the winter?" Bob asks.

"The gardener takes them out to an aquarium."

Sort of like Rusty, Bob thinks. Though his animal transport service is one way.

"Feel free to use it whenever you like," Bryce says. "Just remember to latch the gate behind you. It's actually state health code, with the pond and all."

Bob shakes his head. First time he has heard about the state health code. Yet another thing Bryce has just sprung on him. He turns to leave.

The two pretty women smile at him, and the one with the bouquet of flowers steps forward. "Thank you for helping realize this very mindful space," she says and hands him the bouquet.

He thanks her and rushes through the garden gate and into his own very mindless driveway. Whatever is burning in that incense pot is giving him a headache.

CHAPTER 24

Riff is waiting for him in the lobby when he gets into work. He is sunken into a modern, expensive-looking couch. On the wall above him, there's a framed print of the dunes of Provincetown. The light casts orange and purple shadows over the dunes, which coordinate perfectly with the orange and purple weave of the upholstery — so much for the last general manager's artistic taste. "I got an email from Anthony," Riff says. "He wants to see me at ten. He's going to can me."

"What?" Bob sits down next to Riff on the couch. "He said that?"

"No, but what else could it mean? Not like he's going to ask me about my lumbago."

"I don't know." Bob scratches the back of his head. He flicks his hand over his shoulders and looks for the telltale flakes of dandruff. "Maybe he just wants to get to know you? Do you have lumbago?"

"No!" Riff laughs and tries unsuccessfully to heave himself off the couch. "You want to get coffee? You booked for anything?"

"Come on, I'll check." He pulls Riff up off the couch, surprised momentarily at how skinny Riff's arms are, how insubstantial they seem. The skin is loose and even the bones of his arms seem small. They walk down the hall to the engineering section of the station. The corridor narrows as they approach Mitch's corner office; putty-colored PC's, broken DAT machines, and decommissioned reel-to-reels line the walls. Near the ceiling, there's a bookshelf full of old audio tapes, the cardboard boxes weak and chewed looking at the edges, the labels curling off. The engineering schedule is posted on a large bulletin board outside Mitch's office. It's a crazy quilt of color and patterns that looks impressive from a distance but is actually hard to read up close. "Looks like Mitch discovered Excel," Bob whispers to Riff.

"Bastard's got too much time on his hands."

Bob leans in close to find his name. "Shit! I've got to edit with Kathy," he says. "What a way to start the day. Walk me to the studio?"

Riff nods. They cut across the back of the station and take another long corridor, to the studios. "So how's everything with Leonie?" Riff asks.

"Great. Really great." Bob's voice sounds strange to his own ears. Only assholes say 'great.' "It all feels so natural."

"Well, natural's not always good for you," Riff says. "Cigarettes and booze and corn dogs feel natural to me."

Bob looks up and stops short. Kathy is standing outside the studio waiting for him. She's balancing a mini disc player, several CDs, and some DAT tapes in her arms. She is dressed in a narrow gray skirt and spiky high heels, the better to stomp on anyone who gets in her way.

"Riff," she says, "aren't you supposed to be home in bed by now?"

"Yeah," he says. "But your boyfriend has summoned me to a beheading."

"A beheading? Who's getting beheaded?"

"Me."

"Oh, you're being paranoid." She laughs and shakes her head. She turns to Bob. "Ever put together an audition tape?"

"Of course."

"Well, good, I am trying out for my own talk show!"

So Irene was right. They're replacing Fred with Kathy. And here Bob is, helping the scheming little bitch get ahead. And why is Anthony making her try out? It's a foregone conclusion. She's sleeping with him, for Christ's sake. Does he make her try out in bed?

The three of them walk into the studio. Riff sits down at the producer's console and starts playing with the goosenecked talk-back mic. Kathy hands Bob the mini disc player and the DATs. "Fucking DATs," Bob says. "You realize they're all deteriorating?"

"Not these," Kathy says. "I just listened to them."

"Shit," Riff says. "And they were supposed to be so great, so superior to quarter-inch tape. Once more, my man, they sold us a bill of goods."

"Yeah. All of our archives are disappearing."

"Well, everyone's backing up to CD now, anyway," Kathy says. She is moving one of the expensive leather chairs from the studio into position next to Bob. "It's not a big deal."

"Are my old shows on DAT?" Riff asks.

Bob nods. "And quarter inch. We really should transfer them," he says. "In fact, why don't you book some studio time, and we'll start doing it this week?"

"Eh," Riff shrugs. "It's radio, man, it's supposed to be ephemeral. You send it out into the ether and poof, it's gone."

"We should have been transferring them all along," Bob says. "For when we needed audition tapes."

"Like this afternoon, you mean."

"Exactly," Bob says. Maybe he should apply for the Harvard jazz gig.

Kathy looks up at her watch. "What time's your meeting?"

"Ten. I'll just hang out in here, if that's okay with you two."

Bob nods. Kathy sighs. "Sure." She hands Bob a sheet of paper. "Okay, here are the incues and outcues. We're starting with a two-way of me and Mother Teresa. It's about ten minutes in." She hands Bob one of the DATs, and he inserts it into the less finicky DAT machine and fast forwards to ten minutes on the counter. He waits a couple of seconds before he hits play. The sound is distorted and crackly. "Damn!" he says and toggles it slowly back and forth. Still distorted. He ejects the tape and gently reinserts it, hits play again. Even worse.

"What'd you do?" Kathy says, a rising note of panic in her voice. "It was fine when I just listened to it on my portable machine."

"I didn't do anything," Bob says. "I warned you these things were falling apart."

"Well, you got to make it work. Mother Teresa is hot right now!"

Riff lean his head in his hands. "Too bad you didn't land Princess Di, too."

"Oh God, I wish!"

Riff starts massaging his temples. "I don't know if I have another job change in me, Bobby. I am tired. I am old. I have seen too much. I never thought the world would get so fucked up."

Bob frowns and shakes his head to warn Riff from speaking like this in front of Kathy.

Riff ignores him. "I mean, I thought things were getting better, not worse. I thought we were entering a new age of enlightenment, that we were going to evolve into some kind of advanced race of beings, who were open minded and creative and funky and laid back."

Bob inserts the DAT into the other, less reliable, DAT machine. "Let's try this one," he says. "You never know." He hits play and the CLEANING light flashes on and off and the sound that comes out is totally distorted. "Fuck!" Kathy says. "Fuck! Stop it! It's eating my tape!"

"No, it's not." Bob puts his hand on her shoulder. "It just says CLEANING when it doesn't know what else to say."

Kathy raises her eyebrows.

"Let's put it aside for now. I'll see if the engineering department can try it on another machine. What's next?"

Kathy hands him the mini disc player. "Okay, start from the top with the nat sound. And go through my sign off, okay?"

Bob starts Kathy's piece. It opens with the sounds of a rally or demonstration, typical rent-a-mob stuff, chanting about something. He listens more closely. "Two, four, six, eight, Harvard must negotiate." Here we go again. Every four years or so the students at Harvard ally with the janitors or the food service workers or the groundskeepers and take to the street to demand a living wage. Then of course they graduate and go on to make millions in investment banking and buy themselves homes in the Hamptons and forget all about the groundskeepers who will hold patiently on until their next contract expires and a new wave of students champions their cause and takes to the streets again and the fresh-eyed reporters like Kathy go out with a mini disc player and think they are really onto something when they start their piece with the sounds of chanting. "Oh boy," Bob thinks. "I am like Riff. I have been around too long. I have seen too much."

The chanting dips and Kathy's voice comes in. I would have made the fade less noticeable, Bob thinks. "I am standing in Harvard Yard in front of the statue of John Harvard, while around me about a hundred students and as many janitors march toward the administration building." The chanting comes up full volume again, this time in Spanish. "*Dos, cuatro, seis, ocho....*" Bob rolls his eyes. Of course the Harvard students are bilingual. The next verse is probably in Brazilian Portuguese or Haitian Creole. It's not that he doesn't support the workers. He was a union worker at Harvard himself. One summer, right after college, he got a job on the grounds crew, cutting grass, blowing debris out of Radcliffe Yard. He remembers his new employee orientation, held in some cavernous hall with vaulted ceilings and walls lined with paintings of tight-lipped über WASPs, past presidents or deans he guessed, and a breakfast buffet with silver urns full of coffee and real china cups.

Some HR guy had gotten up in front of a wooden lectern and addressed the new employees. "Welcome to Harvard," he said. "You're here, quite simply, because you are the best at what you do." And Bob had to smile. *I am the best goddamned leaf blower on the planet. Finally, I've been appreciated!*

"Are you sure you want to put a reporter's piece in an audition for a talk show host?" Riff asks. "Don't you have any more interviews? Or host tapes?"

"I am just trying to highlight my best work," Kathy says. "I think it illustrates the caliber of my reporting and interviewing skills."

"But you know being a host is a lot different than being a reporter." Riff slides off the producer's chair and walks over to the console. "You got to keep the program moving, get your timing down, come in on cue, go out on cue. And most important, you got to inject personality into the show. You got to have opinions."

"Not to worry," Kathy says, "I have plenty of opinions. And the rest of that stuff, I'll pick up. Bob can you do a slow fade out of that? Then we'll fade up into the next piece."

Where do people like her get the confidence? Bob does the slow fade.

Riff checks his watch and picks up his bag. "I think I'll go put my head in the oven."

"Good luck," Bob says.

Kathy squirms in her chair. "Good luck," she says and turns back to the console.

When the door is firmly closed, Bob swivels around in his chair to face her. "So what's up? Is he getting fired?"

Kathy shrugs. "I'm not really sure."

"Shit."

"Whatever happens, it's nothing personal. Anthony actually thinks Riff is terrific and he loves jazz, by the way. It's just about the format."

Maybe he should get up right now and walk out the door in solidarity. *Let her figure out how to mix an audition tape.* But then, how will he pay the bills, the taxes, the heat? How will he take Leonie out to dinner?

Kathy picks up her edit sheet. "Hey, don't worry about it," she says, her eyes scanning the sheet. "Riff'll land on his feet. Radio people always do."

Right, Bob thinks, *until one day they don't.* He wonders how Omar is doing. He should have called him back, but he has been too caught up in the money he owes, Bryce's meditation garden, and Abigail's plan for his trees. Bet Abigail has never worried about layoffs. No wonder academics walk so slowly. "What's next?" he asks.

"Well, so far we've got Mother Teresa, a local protest. I think it's time for something light. Have you heard my piece on microbreweries?"

Bob turns back to the console. She has so much to learn. And he has so much to unlearn.

He and Mitch are struggling to get the Mother Teresa piece to play in the portable DAT player when Riff returns. "Bobby!" he says. "Bobby!" Bob turns around. He looks amused. "I got my own frigging talk show." Riff laughs. "Middays!"

Bob jumps up and gives him a clap on the back. "Whoa!"

"And guess what, man?" Riff says. "You're coming with me!"

"That's fucking unbelievable." Middays? He can work with Riff again, but stay on the day shift and see Leonie. It's almost too good to be true.

"But wait, it gets better. Irene is coming too. She's going to screen calls and do the top-of-the-hour newscast. Isn't this great?"

Mitch stands up, a Phillips head screwdriver clenched between his teeth. "Has Anthony ever heard your show?" he asks, through the screwdriver.

"Yeah, he thinks I have a great rapport with listeners!"

Bob nods his head. "Can we still play music?"

"Uh, no." Riff's face falls. "And more news, unfortunately. And frigging traffic and sports updates. And some stupid ski report."

"Hey," Bob says. "Just less time we got to fill, man."

"True," Riff says. "And there's one more thing."

"No more getting high in the parking lot?" Mitch asks.

Both Bob and Riff look at Mitch. How does he know about Riff getting high in the parking lot?

"A co-host." Riff grimaces. "Kathy."

"Kathy. Does she know about it?"

"He's telling her right now."

"You sure you want to do this?" Bob asks. "A real talk show? With Kathy?"

"What choice do I have?" Riff sinks down onto the chair that Kathy was sitting in, suddenly deflated. "Sue doesn't really work. It's not her thing. I mean, what else am I going to do. That Harvard gig? That's a long shot."

Mitch catches Bob's eye for a moment then looks back down into the DAT machine. "This is good news," he says, "for both of you. You hitch your wagon to the boss's girlfriend, and you'd have to really fuck up to get fired."

Riff nods. "But I wonder how she'll feel about co-hosting with me. I mean, she wanted her own show."

"Well," Bob says. "I'm sure she'll land on her feet. Radio people always do."

Mitch pushes the play button on the DAT machine and nothing happens. Then he tries to eject the tape. Still nothing. "Well, here's one more for the scrap heap." He unplugs the machine and gets up. "I think I have one more in the shop. If that one doesn't play it, Kathy will have to kiss Mother Teresa goodbye." He leaves the room and sprints down the hall toward the engineering shop.

"Will you look at that bastard?" Riff says. "Never so happy as when he has a screwdriver in his hand."

"Yeah," Bob says. "Some people should never get promoted. Just because you're good at one thing doesn't mean you'll be good at the next."

"Shhh!" Riff says and puts his finger to his mouth and simultaneously shakes his head. "Don't go there, man."

Mitch returns with another DAT machine and Kathy's DAT, which he has somehow extracted. "Now this one has some fast forward issue," he says, "but let's see if we can get it to play." He plugs it in and hooks up the inputs and outputs and inserts Kathy's tape into the player. Kathy's undistorted voice fills the room. *"But Mother Teresa, wouldn't all those donations be better spent on eliminating poverty than helping the poor to have a 'good' death?"*

Success! Mitch high fives Bob, who gives him a half-hearted high five back. "You better get it dubbed fast, before it craps out again," he says.

Bob opens Kathy's session and finds the spot where he left off. He rewinds the tape to the beginning of the interview, hits the record button and holds his breath. *"I'm here with Mother Teresa of Calcutta…"* Still works. He starts to dump the session into the computer. Of course, Kathy no longer needs an audition tape, but at least now she'll have a clean copy.

"There are many kinds of suffering," Mother Teresa is saying. *"Not just poverty. The suffering of no one wanting you, of being cast out. Spiritual suffering, being cut off from God's love..."*

Kathy walks into the studio, eyes shining, a wide smile on her face. She is heading toward Riff when she hears Mother Teresa's voice. "Oh my God! You got it to work!"

Mitch shrugs. "Maybe Mother Teresa is smiling down on you from heaven."

"Doubt it," Kathy says. "I really nailed her to the wall on her AIDS hospices in Calcutta. I asked her how many people got AIDS because of the Catholic Church's stand on condoms."

"I don't know," Bob says. "She seemed like a good soul to me."

Riff sighs. "It's just hard for me to square the whole 'celebrity saint' thing, you know? I mean, if you're truly selfless, then you probably labor in obscurity and no one's ever heard your name."

"Bet she was hell to work with," Mitch says. "A real ballbuster."

Everyone laughs. Mitch has actually said something funny. On the word "ballbuster" Bob involuntarily looks at Kathy, then looks quickly back at the computer screen.

"Speaking of hell to work with..." Kathy walks over to Riff, goes up on tiptoes, and gives him a hug. "Hello, partner!" she says. Riff pats her back with both of his hands, rolls his eyes at Bob. "I can't wait to get started. I've got lots of ideas, and I'm sure you do, too."

"Well, tell you the truth, the only idea I have right now is how to get some sleep. How about I go home, take a nap, then we meet up later in the afternoon? What time's good for you, Bobby?"

"Oh, we don't need an engineer just yet." Kathy waves her hand dismissively. "We can meet in my office. We're just going to brainstorm."

"Bob's more than an engineer." Riff puts his arm around Bob's shoulder. "He's our new producer."

"Really?" Kathy turns to look at Bob. She is still smiling but one of her eyelids is starting to twitch.

"Really." Riff pats Bob's shoulder. "I don't go anywhere without Bob."

"And you've talked to Anthony about this?"

Riff nods. "He's all for it."

"Okay, then," Kathy says. "Shall we rope Irene into this meeting too?"

Bob will never get used to how quickly people change tack in the work world. Wind blowing in the other way? Okay. Presto! Change-o!

They agree to meet at 4:30 in the conference room and Kathy leaves the studio with her unfinished audition tape.

As soon as the door closes behind her Bob turns to Riff. "Oh man, she's going to run right to Anthony, and she'll figure out that you're lying."

"But I'm not," Riff says. "I told him I'd only do it if you could be our producer, and engineer."

"Producer? Really?" Bob starts to smile. "You've made me into a producer? Thanks."

"Now you'll have to come up with ideas and shit," Mitch says. "Read the paper. Keep up with the news every day. Go to meetings."

"Still." Bob can't stop smiling. A producer. He can't wait to tell Leonie.

CHAPTER 25

Their first five shows are a total mess. Riff and Kathy keep stepping over each other's incues and outcues. The phone lines are curiously silent and when they do ring, Irene dumps the callers by mistake, or Kathy barrages them with rapid-fire questions. After one show, Riff tries to talk to her. "Now, Kath, you want to think of the callers as your house guests, you know, invite them in, get them set up with a drink, make them feel warm and cozy. Not like they're in an interrogation chamber."

"This is the middle of day," Kathy counters, "not the middle of the night. People are fighting their way home in traffic jams. They want a little conflict. This isn't your old audience. They aren't sitting on their couches getting stoned."

Occasionally Irene hands off to Riff, and he is not there. He is off in some daydream, maybe even asleep. When this happened on the overnights, Bob would just sneak in the music, and they would laugh about it afterwards. But now there is no music, and Kathy is not agile enough to step in and cover, so Irene repeats her outcue, which only draws attention to the dead air, one time causing Mitch to panic and thunder down the hall to make sure the transmitter wasn't off the air.

The four of them don't exactly have an easy rapport. Kathy and Riff are almost too polite to one another. And things between Bob and Irene are tense. She looks away when he speaks to her, avoids brushing him when she squeezes into their cramped office. She addresses her concerns to Riff or even Kathy and never volunteers a word during their story meetings.

Riff has not yet adjusted to the new schedule; he doesn't know when to eat, when to sleep. He has dark circles under his eyes, and in the broad daylight he looks old and tired, and if possible, even paler than before. Bob has fallen hopelessly behind. He has a stack of unread books on his desk and another on his bedside table. Who knew so many books came out in a week. On Tuesday, he caved in and bought reading glasses, on a desperate late-night run to the drugstore. And he has to keep up with the news now, which is totally depressing: genocide, famine, war, and they're trying to get rid of the only president he's ever liked. He has already gone through his favorite show ideas, in one week. Everything could be a show, it seems, or not. Work, play, leisure, movies, money, news, food. There's no escape. It's like he has homework, every night for the rest of his life. So it is not a surprise, when first thing Monday morning, Anthony summons the whole staff to a meeting in his office, a "post mortem" he calls it, as if the show were already dead.

"The first week's been a little bumpy," Anthony says, leaning back in his mahogany-colored leather chair, hands clasped behind his head. Riff, Bob, Irene, and Kathy are seated in straightbacked, beige office chairs in a semi-circle around his desk. Only Kathy has thought to bring a pad of paper. Damn! Bob thinks. I got to remember stuff like that.

"But that's only to be expected. No show sounds great right off the bat. In fact, most of them sound downright awful."

They nod their heads.

"Yeah, well, we had some technical issues," Bob says. "But we've got them all ironed out now." Why did he start there? He's not just an engineer anymore. He should have started with more of a "big picture" comment.

"Frankly," Anthony says. "I'm not worried about technical issues, Bob. I'm more concerned about host rapport right now. How do you guys think it's going?" He looks to Riff, then Kathy.

Bob flashes his eyes to warn Riff. Trick question. There is no good answer here. But Riff plunges right in, as if Anthony is his friend, not his boss. "I'm with you!" He snaps his fingers. "I keep telling Kathy, we got to get a groove going. The energy's off. We need to get our act in sync."

"You need to read the script," Kathy says.

"I have never been much of a script person." Riff gets up out of the chair and walks over to the window. "Irene and I never needed a script on the overnights, did we? We just felt our way along."

Irene smiles. "Well, I always had a script," she says. "But Riff never needed one."

"Yeah. I'm more into improv." Riff says. "You know, I came up in jazz."

Kathy rolls her eyes.

"This is good, this is good," Anthony says, sitting up. "You're coming at it from totally different angles. I had a hunch about you two. I want the sparks to fly."

Bob looks more closely at Anthony. Maybe he is not as straightlaced as he looks. In fact, some of these buttoned-down, suit-and-tie guys are the craziest motherfuckers you'll ever meet.

Anthony looks down at a legal pad on his desk. "And how do we think the interview segments are going?"

Bob clears his throat. It's his turn to answer. "Well, I think Irene did a great reporting job on the City Council. And the segment on HBO with the TV critic went really well."

"Yeah." Kathy folds her arms in front of her chest. "That's because I scripted it. And Riff did his homework, for once, and watched the shows."

"Actually..." Riff turns around and smiles at them. "I had Sue watch them for me. I hate TV."

"Whatever." Kathy massages her jaw bone, right under her ear. "It worked."

Anthony jots something down on his legal pad. "And Irene, you're screening the calls, right?"

Irene sits up straight in her chair, looks wary. "Yes?"

"What did you think about the old lady with incurable cancer?"

"Oh." She slumps back down. "I thought she had a good point about managed care."

"And you couldn't find some cute young girl with a good point about managed care? Somebody who wasn't dying?"

"Yeah, Irene, she was a real downer," Kathy says.

"I could hear radios clicking off all across the state," Anthony says.

"But we did get into a good back and forth with her." Riff turns away from the window. "She was a feisty old broad. Told her doctors to go fuck themselves. Said no way to chemo."

"Chemo!" Anthony shakes his head. "Chemo."

"Yeah, guys," Kathy says. "We're not running a social service agency here. We're in show biz."

"Sorry." Irene looks down at her hands.

"It's my fault," Bob says. "I told Irene to put her on." All eyes turn to Bob. Even Irene looks up. "I just didn't have the heart to turn the old lady away."

"That's not thinking like a producer," Anthony says.

Bob knew she would ramble, and her story wouldn't have a happy ending, but he was hoping that Riff could turn it around somehow, find the ray of light, the moment of joy, like he had done countless times before on the overnights. But the minute she started talking Bob's heart sank. Riff got melancholy; Kathy interrupted her with questions the old lady couldn't quite hear. And in the end they had to cut her short anyway, to meet the national news. "That was a bad call on my part. I take full responsibility." He looks Anthony squarely in the eye. "Sorry."

"Okay." Anthony turns his attention to Irene. "Try to think of yourself as less social worker, more talent scout, okay?"

Irene nods and turns to give Bob a smile.

"I have an idea." Anthony puts his yellow pad away, swipes some imaginary crumbs off his desk. "I have a consultant I'd like you all to meet with. She does a lot of coaching work with performers, vocalists, improv troupes." He looks toward Riff on the word "improv," but Riff is looking out the window again, his back to them. "And she's agreed to do a team-building workshop this Saturday."

Bob has plans to go to Western Mass this Saturday. He is going to show Leonie where he went to college. They have tickets for a dance performance at Smith.

"She's coming up from New York. Believe me, she's very hard to get. And she doesn't come cheap," Anthony adds.

"Sounds like fun to me," Kathy says.

"Sounds like hell to me," Riff says.

"I've worked with her before. And her results are nothing short of amazing."

"Poor Sue," Riff says. "She doesn't know which end is up. First I go on days. Now I'm going to group therapy."

"It's not group therapy," Anthony says. "It's more like acting school."

"You need me and Irene there?" Bob asks.

Anthony puts his two hands together, taps the tips of his middle fingers against each other. "You're part of the team, right? You aren't going to make great radio until you start functioning like a team."

Bob winces at the phrase, "great radio." Irene rolls her eyes.

"9 a.m.," Anthony says, dismissing them. "We'll bring in breakfast."

§

After the meeting, Riff sits in his car in the parking lot, waiting for him. Bob raps on the passenger window and Riff rolls it down, releasing a cloud of marijuana smoke. Bob opens the door and slides in. Riff offers him the joint, but he shakes his head. "I could use to get high after that session, but it's too early."

Riff shakes his head. "I don't get high anymore, just normal."

Bob laughs. "I don't think I've ever gotten normal."

"Which reminds me," Riff exhales. "Never apologize. Shows weakness."

"I thought he took it well." Bob scratches his head.

"No. Never admit you made a mistake. This guy is not your friend."

"How about you, man? Criticizing Kathy in front of him. Are you nuts?"

"You got a point." Riff takes a long hit. "Thank God my contract's almost up. This is exhausting."

"You have a contract?"

"Of course. I have a five-year contract. It's over in July. That's why Anthony is keeping me on. Cheaper than buying me out."

"And then what?"

"Who the hell knows. Sue wants to move south. She's had it with the winters. Or maybe I'll get the jazz director job." He looks out the window.

Bob feels his stomach tighten. Is this all just about lasting out Riff's contract?

Riff takes another hit and starts to cough, a hacking smoker's cough.

"That sounds good."

"Yeah, it's that chemical the feds spray on all the pot. Wrecks the lungs."

"You should watch it. Didn't Bob Marley die of lung cancer?"

"No, skin cancer."

"Really? A black guy can get skin cancer?"

"Yeah, black people get skin cancer all the time."

"I thought they'd be protected somehow."

"No, and Bob Marley was only half black anyway."

"Maybe we should do a show on reggae," Bob says, slipping into producer mode. "We could get Bob Marley's son."

"That'd be cool," Riff says. "We might as well have some fun with this show, while it lasts. And call your friend Buddy, too."

"Sure." Bob gets out of the car, waves goodbye. He watches Riff tap the end of the joint against his ashtray. He might be the last man in America to use a car ashtray for ashes.

CHAPTER 26

"Well, of course your friend would have a contract," Leonie says, as they hurry down the street, a cold rain pelting their faces. "I mean he'd have to." It's Thursday night, and they are meeting Leonie's ex and his new wife for dinner.

"Still, I wish I'd known." Bob holds an umbrella in front of them, but it's of little use. One of the struts is bent and the entire umbrella is threatening to fold inside out.

"But it makes perfect sense," Leonie says. "Your boss kills two birds with one stone. He makes Riff work out his contract, and he gives his girlfriend a talk show. Plus she gets a co-host who knows what he's doing."

"That's three birds."

"I wouldn't feel betrayed," Leonie says. "It's just work. You should try academia. There, everyone really is out to get you."

"I don't think Riff is out to get me. I just thought we were a team."

"It's not much of a team if he's got a contract and you don't."

"Well, I wouldn't even have the producer job without him. Believe me, the gulf between engineer and producer is huge. And Riff just pulled me over it."

"You really should go for that director job at the jazz archive." She squeezes his arm. Bob is too caught up in the struggle to get a show on the air to think about the jazz archive.

As they round the corner onto Mass. Ave., the wind lashes into them. "Have you ever noticed that the weather is always worse on Mass. Ave.?" he asks.

Leonie looks at him and shakes her head. "Not really."

"Maybe it's a wind-tunnel effect. Or deforestation. My father always said that the bankers wouldn't let them plant shade trees on this part of Mass. Ave. because it was where the Irish lived."

"Wow, that's paranoid," Leonie says.

"Could be true, though," Bob says. "And now you and I are suffering for it."

Leonie laughs and they turn the corner again onto a leafy side street, where the wind dies down, and the rain seems to let up. They duck into a neighborhood restaurant that has recently changed hands and reopened as the Avon Hill Bistro. "Why's everything called a bistro now?" Bob asks, as they step through the thick brown velvet curtains in the entryway. Leonie doesn't answer. She has already spotted her ex and his wife, seated at a round table in the corner. She waves to them and starts to remove her coat.

Bob looks around, adjusts his eyes to the low light. He's never been inside this restaurant before. It's warm and cozy, and they're playing an Al Green song he has always loved, loud enough to be recognizable but low enough to talk over. Long colored-glass pendants hang above the bar, and track lighting illuminates the wine and liquor bottles behind it. The walls are dark and the molding is painted with some kind of metallic bronze paint.

Bob shakes out his umbrella and then struggles to close it. He reaches to straighten out the bent strut. Amazing how cheaply they make things these days. He is tempted to dump it in the trash bucket next to the host station, but then they will have nothing. So he shoves it into an umbrella stand, next to a much sturdier, crimson and white Harvard umbrella.

Gary and his wife get up. Leonie kisses both of them on the cheek. Gary's wife has very straight blonde hair and a wide-set face and looks several years younger than Leonie, perhaps a decade younger than Gary. Up close he sees that Gary's blonde curls are shot through with gray. "You got the good table," Leonie says.

"We got here when they opened."

Gary's wife holds out her hand to Bob. "Martha," she says.

Bob shakes her hand and introduces himself. He wonders if this is as awkward for her as it is for him. He comes from the avoid-exes-at-all-cost school; Leonie meanwhile gave the toast at their wedding.

"So we finally get to meet," Gary says, once they are seated. "We've heard a lot about you."

Bob nods and smiles. Gary is younger than Bob, closer to Leonie's age. But Bob is taller and has broader shoulders. Gary does have a handsome face, though. In fact, Gary and Martha have the same healthy, just came off the slopes and applied ChapStick looks. "Are you from the West Coast too?" he asks Martha.

"Connecticut," she says. "Though I did my graduate work at Stanford." She turns to Leonie. "Hey, nice picture of you in the paper. When are they going to make a decision about that tree?"

"Not sure," Leonie says. "Now the developer is threatening to move it. We don't think it will survive."

Bob thinks guiltily about his trees. Wasn't he supposed to get back to Abigail and find out about the zoning laws from Mary Elizabeth? This working during the day leaves you no time to get things done. Now he is like the rest of the lemmings, thronging the post office on Saturday mornings, the supermarkets on Saturday afternoons, the restaurants on Saturday nights. "Shall we get cocktails?" Gary asks. "Or a bottle of wine?"

"Wine or beer for me," Bob says. "I still have work to do tonight." Kathy is interviewing a vegetarian cookbook author first thing in the morning and he has to skim through the book tonight.

Gary orders a California cabernet sauvignon. Martha asks for a cranberry and soda and the appetizer menu.

"So, Bob, we hear you're producing a new talk show?"

"Yeah, but we've only just started," he says. "It's kind of the blind leading the blind at this point."

Leonie shakes her head. "Bob, you're so self deprecating."

He covers her hand with his. "No, really," he says.

"Well, Martha and I both have books coming out this year, if you're ever desperate for guests."

"Oh really? What are they about?"

Gary looks to Martha. "You first," he says.

"Mine is about gender divergence in psycho-linguistic patterning in the sado-masochistic bondage and discipline community."

"Sounds interesting." Bob looks down at his appetizer menu, to suppress a laugh.

"And is there a divergence?" Leonie asks.

"Well it's hard to summarize it neatly, but men tend to use language or the lack thereof, for example, with the use of gags and other bondage paraphernalia, as an erotic toy, whereas women use it more to communicate commands."

"In other words," Gary says, "women talk more."

Leonie and Bob both laugh. Martha hits Gary on the arm, but she is also laughing.

"And how did you do the research?" Bob asks.

"Mostly online chat rooms," Martha says. "And…" She colors slightly. "Some field work."

"The sacrifices we linguists make," Gary says.

Bob looks at him more closely. He would prefer he did not have a sense of humor.

"And is it the same for gay and straight people?" Leonie asks.

"Ha!" Martha points her finger at Leonie. "Great question! That's my next book."

Bob looks at Gary. Does he see a hint of a smirk on his face? "And yours? What's yours about?"

"Nowhere near as sexy, I'm afraid." Gary bows his head in a show of humility. "I explore the development of neuro-linguistic pathways in religious fundamentalists."

"Oh, that is sexy," Leonie says.

"Have you ever listened to a religious fundamentalist?" Gary says. "We're not talking complex thought here. Or sentence structure. Their neural pathways are like well-worn, rutted roads. They always end up in the same place."

"My neural pathways are probably more like rotaries," Bob says. "Round and round, can't decide where to get off."

Martha looks at him appreciatively and starts to laugh.

"Funny you should mention rotaries. I've analyzed some Catholic right-to-lifers here in Massachusetts," Gary says. "Their logic and speech patterns are extremely circular."

Here we go, Bob thinks. Let's prove that all Catholics are stupid.

The waiter returns to their table with the bottle of cabernet and makes a big show of opening it for them. Bob had been a waiter his last year at college and always dreaded having to open a bottle of wine at a table. What if he applied too much pressure and broke the bottle? What if the cork fell apart? What if it just refused to come out at all? Funny how your younger years are full of these paralyzing doubts, and your older years full of scorn for ever having had them. Was there never a moment when you felt exactly right?

The waiter pours out their wine. Martha holds her hand over her glass. "None for me, thanks." She opens her menu. "But I would like to order empanadas, crab cakes, and the garlic shrimp."

Bob hopes they take credit cards. He takes a sip of wine. "This is good," he says.

"Actually, we've been to this winery." Leonie looks at Gary. "Remember the time we ended up passed out at the hot springs?"

"And I had to carry you up to the room? Now I think they have bus tours, so you don't drink and drive." Bob looks down at his menu. He doesn't want to think of Gary and Leonie in a hotel room.

"I miss California," Leonie says, sipping her wine. "Especially now, with winter coming."

"Are you going back for Christmas?" Gary asks.

Bob looks at Leonie. It hasn't come up yet. Everything is still so new. Will they spend the holidays together? What are they doing for Thanksgiving? In the past he had either gone to Mary Elizabeth's or worked extra and avoided it all together.

"I don't know," Leonie says. "Are you?"

"Definitely." He and Martha nod their heads and some communication seems to pass between them. "Actually, we're going now, because later on might not work so well." He pauses and takes Martha's hand. "We're pregnant."

Martha smiles broadly. Gary squeezes her hand.

"Oh, that's wonderful news!" Leonie jumps to her feet. She leans over the table and hugs Martha, then Gary. Martha does looks pregnant, Bob thinks, something about her face, some fullness?

"And when's the baby due?" Leonie asks.

"June," Martha says. "A Gemini. Not that we believe in any of that."

Leonie holds up her glass. "To Geminis!" They all clink glasses. Leonie takes a large sip of her wine and turns to Gary. "Your parents must be excited."

"Oh yeah," he says. "In fact, they're threatening to move here. I think my Mom has purchased her tickets already."

"And a layette." Martha laughs.

"Yeah, they've been waiting for this forever," Gary says.

Leonie blinks, takes another sip of wine. "Boy or girl?" she asks.

"We're going to wait to see," Martha says. "Even though it's hard for us. We're both such control freaks."

"Well, June is perfect," Bob says. "You'll have the whole summer off to get used to being parents."

Martha knits her forehead together, shakes her head. "Oh no," she says. "I have to write this summer. My publisher wants the gay bondage manuscript by September."

"And I've got a big paper to deliver in Zurich," Gary says, "in the fall. Afraid this summer's going to be very busy. Maybe it's good the parents are coming after all."

They laugh and turn their attention to the menus. Bob feels he has made some sort of blunder in mentioning that they'd be off all summer. But isn't that true? Leonie had told him her classes ended the first week in May. She's hoping to get back into the studio, work on a dance she started the summer before.

The waiter arrives with their appetizers. He puts four little plates in front of them and announces each dish as he puts it down in the center of the table. Martha starts piling food on her plate. "You won't believe how hungry you get." She pops an entire shrimp into her mouth. "I need to go shopping soon for maternity clothes."

Leonie looks up from her menu. She takes Bob's hand. "Maybe we should go to California for Christmas. Could you get the time off the show?"

Who is rushing things now, he thinks. Wasn't it just a week ago that she said that? "I'm not sure there'll even be a show by Christmas."

"It would be so much fun," Gary says, "for all of us to be there at the same time."

Not really, Bob thinks, as he looks back down at his menu. In fact, he is ready for this night to be over and they haven't even ordered dinner.

The rain has stopped and the sky has cleared by the time they leave the restaurant. Bob tosses the umbrella into the trash can on the corner of Mass. Ave. and puts his arm around Leonie. He is uncomfortably full and worried he won't be able to sleep. Too much wine, too much rich food. Maybe going out on Thursday night is not such a good idea. "So, do you really want to go to California for Christmas?" he asks.

"I don't know," she says. "I'm not sure I can take a blow-by-blow account of her pregnancy."

"Yeah," he says. "I was afraid for a minute there they were going to ask us to be Godparents."

Leonie laughs. "I don't think we have Godparents in California." She leans closer.

Bob tightens his grip on her shoulder. They are passing the house of the famous documentary filmmaker. There's a light on in one of the first floor rooms. On one wall are the requisite floor-to-ceiling bookcases. On another is a large abstract painting suspended by picture wires from some elaborate cove molding. In the corner there is a desk and a green shaded work light, which is lit. He can't quite make out if the great one himself is actually seated there, burning the midnight oil.

"Damn, I knew they were trying," Leonie says. "But did it have to all go exactly as planned?"

"Oh, maybe she's hatching a fundamentalist," Bob says.

Leonie laughs. "With an extremely limited vocabulary."

"And circular thought patterns. There, don't you feel better?"

"Oh, we shouldn't be laughing at her. She's actually very nice."

"Still," Bob says. "She's your ex's new wife. I can't believe you are friends at all." He puts his arm around her shoulder as they turn the corner onto Leonie's street.

That night, for the first time since they've been seeing each other, they don't make love. They undress and get into Leonie's bed and she kisses him and then rolls onto her side, her back to him. He reaches out, touches her lightly on the shoulder. "Is everything okay?"

She rolls toward him "Yes, everything's okay. I just need to sleep."

He pushes a strand of hair out of her face. "Did you and Gary try to have a baby?"

"No." She rolls over again. "He didn't want one."

Bob takes out the vegetarian cookbook. The author smiles from the back cover, the big, open-hearted kind of smile that Buddhists and holistic healers favor in their press releases. He skims through the introduction and the chapter titles. Once again, he thinks, turning to the chapter on vegan holidays, I am saved by the bad behavior of other men.

CHAPTER 27

Riff and Bob are the last to arrive for the team-building workshop. Everyone else is already gathered in the station cafeteria. Anthony's jeans have sharp creases in them, as if he had hung them up or maybe even ironed them before putting them on. His sneakers are spotless. Kathy looks slightly less made up than usual. Her hair is pulled back in a tight ponytail, and she's got a baseball cap pulled low on her forehead. It's the kind of look that is becoming on a certain brand of blonde, blue-eyed ice princess. Irene is the only one who looks better than usual. She's wearing a long black sweater that hugs her hips, and a pair of black suede clogs that make her seem taller. Her hair is pulled back and piled on top of her head. She has large silver hoops in her ears. She smiles at Riff and Bob when they enter. "Just in time for breakfast." She points to a table laid out with bagels and pastries, and thermoses of coffee and hot water. Several containers of juice, seltzer, and yogurt are half buried in a bowl full of ice.

"Nice spread." Riff picks up a raspberry danish.

Bob grabs a blueberry muffin and a coffee. Can it be that Irene has forgiven him? It almost feels like the old days, before the possibility of romance wrecked everything between them. Anthony takes a raisin bagel. "Hard to have breakfast without carbs." He pours himself a glass of orange juice.

Bob hates people who talk about carbs. He loves carbs. He is Irish, anything to do with carbs is good in his book. Potatoes, bread, pasta, rice. Bring them on.

"So where's this coach?" Riff asks.

Anthony looks at his watch. "Should be here any minute." Bob wonders if Anthony's going to stay. He hopes he's not going to have to lead him around blindfolded or do some kind of three-legged race with him. He doesn't trust him now and he doesn't want to trust him in the future. It's important for his survival that he holds onto his distrust.

The door to the cafeteria bangs open and a very large woman, with long, bright red hair, enters the room, pulling a duffel bag on wheels behind her. "I need some help here!" She lets the handle smack down on the floor behind her.

Anthony rushes to her side. "Roberta, so glad you could squeeze us in."

Roberta holds out her arms and folds Anthony in a big hug. "No problem, hon. But I thought the cabdriver was going to shoot me when I asked him to carry my bag up the stairs. And he charged me an arm and a leg."

"We'll comp it." Anthony reaches down and lifts up the handle of the duffel bag. "Not to worry." He leads her over to the buffet table, leans her bag against the wall. "Can I get you some breakfast?"

Roberta surveys the buffet table with displeasure. "Got any hot water and lemon?" she asks. "That's all I eat on work days."

Bob looks at her size and thinks, she must certainly make up for it at night.

Roberta pours herself a cup of hot water and grabs an orange slice from the pastry tray. "Got to have my citrus for the voice box." She squeezes the orange slice into her cup of hot water.

Anthony introduces everyone, and Roberta looks them up and down. "So who is it that's not getting along?"

Anthony looks momentarily embarrassed. "Oh, it's more of a matter of different styles, different strengths." He draws huge amorphous shapes in the air.

"Riff and I," Kathy says. "We're the co-hosts. Those three…" She jerks her thumb in Bob, Riff, and Irene's direction, "are thick as thieves."

"Well that must be hard for you, sweetpea, being the odd man out," Roberta says.

Kathy nods and looks in Bob, Irene and Riff's direction to make sure they heard what Roberta said.

"But," Roberta says, "you got to take that baseball cap off. It's too much of a prop, you know what I mean? Nobody gets to hide out in my workshop!"

Kathy flashes her eyes at Anthony, but quickly removes her hat. Her hair is limp and pasted down on her head. Could it even be dirty?

"Well let me get my molecules gathered here. Half of them are still back in New York!" Roberta sinks her large frame into a chair. She is wearing high heeled black boots and a voluminous skirt. "You all talk amongst yourselves." She flicks a long-nailed hand in their direction.

Irene starts picking through the fruit plate, spearing pieces of cantaloupe and melon. Bob pours himself another cup of coffee and takes a seat next to Irene. Riff breaks a scone in half and offers it to Kathy, who shakes her head. "God, no," she says. "Any idea how much fat is in a scone?"

Anthony puts his coat on. "I'm going take this as my cue to leave."

"You can stay," Roberta says.

Please don't, Bob thinks.

"No, I don't want to get in the way of the team development. I want them to function as a unit, let the creative juices flow, without management interference."

Irene leans over and whispers in Bob's ear. "Until I put on a caller he doesn't like."

Bob nods. "So how are you adapting to the new shift?"

"Okay," Irene says. "It's nice to head to work in the daylight. But when are you supposed to get stuff done? It's get up, go to work, go home, cook dinner, go to bed, get up, go to work."

"I know," Bob says. "I am falling way behind."

"Yeah," Irene says. "Who thought we'd be working this hard at this point in our lives. We should be on autopilot by now."

"We're still on the uphill slog. Probably always will be." Bob looks over in Kathy's direction. She has taken out her datebook and is hunched over it, her face screwed up in determination. Bob can see her pale scalp through her dirty hair.

"Think she'll get pregnant?" Irene asks.

"What?" Bob is startled.

"Bob, think about it. She's engaged. She's young. She's got studley at home. She'll be pregnant soon, mark my words. She's probably figuring out her ovulation schedule."

Is that all women think about? Ovulation schedules? Babies? First Leonie, then Martha, now Kathy. He can't imagine her pregnant — there is nothing soft and round about her. She is fierce though, and there is something fierce in all these women and their single-minded desire to have a child, to care for someone. Has he ever felt such ambition? No, never.

But he is happy to have Irene back. Things are so natural with her.

He doesn't have to censor himself. They see the world the same way. Riff walks over to their table and looks from one of them to the other, raises his eyebrows, makes to sit down.

"Hold on there, Biff!" Roberta says. "Don't get comfortable." She hefts her ample frame out of the chair.

"It's Riff."

"Got it," Roberta says. "Now take your shoes off!"

Thank God for dating. Bob had bought several new pairs of underwear and new socks the weekend before. Riff unzips his hipster boots to reveal two mismatched socks, one with a large hole in the toe, the other with a hole in the heel. Kathy is wearing white athletic socks with little pom poms. One of Irene's socks is on inside out. Clumps of thread mimic the pattern in the other sock.

"See, already you know so much more about each other." Roberta leaves her boots on. "Now, sit."

"Here?" Riff looks doubtfully at the floor.

"Yes, there," she nods. "Come on, you got a nice thick carpet there."

Bob sits down easily, as do Kathy and Irene, but Riff circles around like a big dog trying to find the best way to land. He finally bends his knees and leans over to touch the floor with first one hand and then the other and lowers himself down with a grunt. "I might never get back up," he says.

"You will. Now I want you all to scootch into the center and sit with your backs to each other. Touching! Yes, touching, it won't kill you to touch a coworker, Bobby."

"Bob."

"Okay, Bob." Roberta stretches out his name and lowers her voice to mock him. This would have been much worse, a month ago, Bob thinks, before he met Leonie and re-entered the world of physical contact. He can feel the heat coming off Irene's narrow back.

"Okay, Riff, you start, any word that begins with an A. Kathy next, with a B and keep going around in a circle."

"Apple," Riff says.

"Boy," Kathy says.

"Cow," Bob says

"Duck," Irene says.

"Keep going," Roberta is bending over her duffel bag. "You could be more creative. What is this, first grade?"

"Elliptical," Riff says.

Kathy starts to laugh. "Figueroa," she says.

"Galapa—"

Roberta throws a beach ball at Bob's head. He ducks to avoid it. "What the fuck?"

"Work with me," she says.

"Galapagos," he says.

"Hindenburg," Irene says.

Roberta sprays a water pistol at Riff's face. "Idiot," he says.

"Jerk," Kathy says.

"Khmer Rouge," Roberta shouts.

They all go silent. Bob looks to Roberta and feels the heat rushing to his face. Now what is he supposed to do?

"Don't let me throw you off," she says. "Improvise!"

"Am I supposed to do a K?" Bob asks.

"Up to you," Roberta says.

"Loco," he yells.

"Mean," Irene says.

"Nasty."

They keep going through the alphabet and then around again and again, while Roberta pelts them with water, tennis balls, and incendiary phrases. Finally, after Riff calls out Zoroaster, she holds up her hands. "Enough," she says. "Time for a break."

They get up slowly from the floor. Bob reaches out a hand and pulls Riff up. He walks stiffly to the buffet table, right hand on his lower back.

"So," Kathy asks. She is nibbling at the half of the scone Riff left earlier. "Are we supposed to bond now, in opposition to you? Is that the drill?"

"No 'supposed to' about it," Roberta says. "But sure, if you want to bond against me, that's cool." She is fixing another hot water and orange. This time she has also added a bit of orange juice to the mix.

"So, you do this for a living?" Riff asks Roberta, a look of disbelief on his face.

Roberta nods. "But it's different every time," she says. "Depends on what brand of asshole I got to deal with."

Riff laughs. Bob looks at his watch. 10 a.m. They've got a whole day of this nonsense ahead. What has this got to do with their struggling talk show? Is this that what all performers do? Is this what Leonie does with her Harvard dancers? Somehow he doubts all those National Merit Scholars would put up with this crap.

§

After lunch Roberta pulls a boom box from her duffel bag and leads them into the front lobby. She puts the boom box down on an end table and plugs it in. "Can someone help push the furniture out of the way?"

Bob and Irene get on either side of a couch and push. Their eyes meet momentarily. Irene starts to smile, then stops herself. They cram it against the wall, next to the table with the boom box.

"So, you all like salsa dancing?" Roberta asks.

"Oh no, please," Irene says.

"I can't dance." Bob holds his hands up, palms out.

"All God's children can dance, Bobby."

"For some reason, I'm inclined to believe Bob's the exception," Kathy says.

Roberta smiles. "Okay. Partner up. Bob and Kathy. Riff and Irene."

They line up in twos.

"Face to face. Hands out in front of you. Now hold your partner's hands lightly." Bob grasps Kathy's hands. They are surprisingly cold and clammy. Leonie's hands are warm, as are her feet. Kathy rolls her eyes at him. He shrugs.

"All right, the basic salsa step," Roberta shouts. "Watch me. Quick, quick, slow. Quick, quick slow." She steps to her front and then to her back. She is amazingly light on her feet. "Riff, can you do that?" She holds out her hands to him. "Quick, quick, slow. Quick, quick, slow." Riff glides forward and back effortlessly. "Damn!" Roberta says. "This guy's got some rhythm!"

"All right, Kathy and Bob. Quick, quick..." Bob has started going forward and so has Kathy. They crash into each other.

"Hey, one of you's got to lead. And this is Latin culture, so guess who?"

Kathy points a finger at Bob. He shakes his head. "How do I do that?"

"You don't know how to lead?"

"I told you, I don't dance. I'm a baby boomer. We just kind of flop around, and hope everyone doesn't notice."

"We do, Bob," Irene says. Kathy and Riff both laugh.

Roberta cuts in and takes Kathy's hands. "Okay, watch me," she says. "This is how you lead." She and Kathy start to move in sync. "Did you see that?"

"No."

"It's subtle. I moved first and put the tiniest bit of pressure on her hand. You try."

Bob grabs Kathy's clammy little hands. He tries to compose himself, forget that others are watching. He puts a bit of pressure on her hand and Kathy starts forward, and he follows. "Shit," he says. "I got the pressure part but I forgot to move."

"Don't think." Roberta taps herself on the head. "Just move."

Bob puts pressure on Kathy's hand, steps forward. She follows. Quick, quick, slow, and then back. Quick, quick. Is he supposed to stop in the middle? He loses count.

"Better," Roberta says. "Let's try it with music." She fiddles with the boom box. Salsa blares into the room. "Now, on the beat."

Irene and Riff start dancing back and forward, back and forward. Is Bob imagining it or is Riff rotating his stomach with the steps? Irene is smiling, having fun.

Bob takes Kathy's hands, applies pressure and steps forward and back. This time Kathy messes up. "Sorry," she says and they try again. Bob immediately steps on her toes. "Ouch!" she says. They try again and Bob forgets to go back at all. "Why don't you just let me lead?" Kathy whispers. "She won't know the difference."

"Whatever," Bob says. "I don't care."

Kathy takes the lead and Bob follows. Back and forth, back and forth, he is getting the rhythm; this is so much easier. Quick, quick, slow, it's almost fun. He has always liked salsa music, just not dancing. He imagines he is somewhere warm and bright, on vacation, and any minute now somebody will bring him a margarita, or should it be a rum and coke? I was born to follow, he thinks as he steps back and forth.

The song ends. Roberta stops the tape. "Okay now," she says. "Let me show you the side step." Bob and Kathy try to imitate her. Kathy's face is grim, her limbs rigid. There is a line of perspiration on her upper lip. Bob wonders if his own face looks as pained. "Now combine them," Roberta calls, and she counts out the steps. "One, two, three. Five, six, seven. One, two, three. Five, six, seven." Bob is wondering what happened to the four? He steps on Kathy's toes again.

"Ouch, that really hurt." Kathy lets go of his hands and walks over to the couch, plops down, takes off her shoe and starts massaging her injured foot.

"Sorry," Bob mouths. He stands off to the side and watches Riff and Irene dance. That's it. They are actually dancing, while Kathy and he could have been marching to the guillotine. He wonders if Leonie knows how to dance salsa. Maybe she could teach him? Funny but he has never actually seen her dance. Maybe he will visit her studio during the Christmas break, when the students aren't around?

"Okay," Roberta says. "Change partners!"

Bob stands across from Irene. He reaches for her hands, which are warm and strong. Irene looks embarrassed. It is the first time they have had any real physical contact since the break up. He's going to have to lead this time, and he presses her hand and steps forward. Irene steps backward. Bob steps backward and then Irene forward. She is a good dancer, he thinks. Like Riff, a natural. He forgets that he is leading and hesitates for a second and Irene starts to lean sideways. He follows her. That's better, easier. He doesn't have to keep so much in his head.

Roberta cuts in. "Guess you didn't get the hang of leading, huh?"

"Oh, I don't really care." Bob waves his hand.

"But women do," Roberta whispers. "Trust me."

He looks at Roberta to make sure he has heard her right. She nods at him and motions for Irene to jump back in. He takes Irene's hand and tries to lead and awkward as he is, Irene follows. Irene squeezes his hands and smiles. "Always knew we'd be good together," she says, and they glide seamlessly into a side step.

CHAPTER 28

———◦———

Four o'clock on a Monday afternoon and Bob, Irene, Riff, and
Kathy are gathered in their claustrophobic little office trying to come
up with a show for the next day. The guest they had lined up, a literary
critic from Amherst College, with a book on the masturbatory impulse
in Emily Dickinson's poetry, has cancelled because his mother died.
"Just our luck." Kathy shakes her head. She is standing at the large
white board that takes up an entire wall of the office, rubbing out the
critic's name.

"No, it's that poor guy's luck," Riff says. "His mother just died."

"Did she have to die today?" Kathy asks. "Couldn't she have waited
until tomorrow after the show?"

Irene laughs, looks up from scanning the local papers. "You are so
bad."

Kathy sticks out her tongue. "Gallows humor, ever heard of it?"

Irene shakes her head and goes back to the papers.

"How about if we just open up the phone lines?" Riff is leaning
back in his chair, his legs propped up on the desk that he and Bob share.
"Let the good times roll?"

"Anthony'll never go for that," Bob says. "He wants topics."

"Well, I might be able to convince him," Kathy says. "I do have
some pull, you know." She wiggles her hips as she walks over to her desk
and picks up her phone and dials. "Hi hon." She winks at her colleagues.
"Look, our guest for tomorrow just cancelled. Yeah. I know. *Really* late
notice. But his mother died. What are you going to do? Anyway, we
were thinking, just this once, would you go for open phones? Yeah.
Yeah. of course, I completely…" The sides of her mouth turn down. "But

it is after four o'clock. Uh huh. I know." She gives them a thumbs down sign. "No, I don't have anything going on tonight either." Her shoulders slump. She sinks down onto her chair. "Of course. Of course."

Bob looks away to give her some privacy in defeat. At least she tried to help. Things were starting to gel with the show. Riff and Kathy were getting to know one another, and both seemed surprised that the other was not quite the monster they expected. Irene and Bob were getting along much better, almost like the old days. She was acting just the tiniest bit flirtatious with him again. But it was different somehow. As though they both knew that nothing was going to happen, but they did share a private joke and it was perfectly harmless, wasn't it?

Irene spreads the newspaper out on her desk. "Look at this," she says. "This developer in Cambridge is planning to move this old tree. What if we did a show on that?"

"Been there. Done that," Kathy says. She turns to Bob. "Remember? I gave you the contact info for one of the organizers?"

"You mean Leonie?" Riff asks.

Irene narrows her eyes in Bob's direction, her antenna fully functional. "Oh, is that your new girlfriend?"

"What?" Kathy turns to Bob. "You're going out with the organizer?" She looks shocked and just a little bit impressed.

"Yes," Bob nods. "In fact we're going to a meeting about that tree tonight."

"But that's perfect!" Kathy jumps up from her desk. "We could put your new friend on. And maybe we could get the developer. And someone from the Zoning Board?"

"And a tree specialist?" Irene says. "What are they called?"

"Arborists?" Kathy says.

"Right, an arborist."

Bob puts his head in his hands. This is beginning to feel like *This Is Your Life, Bob Boland.* Were they going to exhume Sister Willamette and book her next?

"Though actually this developer's not too keen on speaking to the press," Kathy says, almost to herself. "If I remember correctly."

Bob holds up a hand. "Wait," he says. "I don't feel right about putting someone I am seeing on the show."

"But she's the logical person," Kathy says. "We're not booking her because you're sleeping with her. You're sleeping with her because you poached my source!"

"She's got a point there," Riff says. Irene looks down at her hands.

"And while we're at it." Kathy lets out a breath. "Full disclosure here. Anthony and I have put our names in for one of the condos."

"What?" Bob says. "You're moving to my street?"

Irene looks up. "You can afford one of those condos?"

"We both work very hard," Kathy says. "And we want to live in Cambridge." She juts her chin out.

"Okay, okay." Irene says.

Bob turns to Riff and Irene. "What do you guys think?"

Riff swings his legs over the side of the desk, stands up and stretches his back. "Well. She's in bed with the developer. You're in bed with the opposition. You kind of cancel each other out, right?" He twists to look at the clock on the wall, his hand massaging his lower back. "And it's fucking four-thirty in the afternoon. I say we go for it."

"Ditto." Irene turns to Bob. "So, what do you want me to do, boss?"

This is the first time anyone has referred to Bob as the boss. And even though there is more than a hint of sarcasm in Irene's voice, Bob has to admit, it feels good. Who would have thought it? He has never had any aspirations to be the boss. The most he dared hope for in life was to *find* a good boss. Now he's in a room full of people looking at him expectantly, waiting for him to make a decision. It's not like he's earned their respect; it's just that someone has to play the boss right now, and that someone is him.

"All right," he says. "Let's do it. I'll call Leonie. Kathy, you call the developer. Irene, could you put together a packet for Riff and Kathy? And I guess we do need some kind of tree expert. Let's see if there's someone who does Japanese maples for a living. And maybe the company that's going to do the actual moving? Who wants to do that?"

Riff raises his hand. "I can make a call or two," he says. "But let's not go crazy here, Bobby. It's only one show, after all. And it'll be over tomorrow afternoon. Then we got three more to do this week. And five more the week after that. And five more the week after that."

"And two hundred and sixty more in the next year," Irene says.

"Please stop!" Bob massages his temples. "We can't think like that or we'll go nuts. Let's agree, right now. We can only fuck up one show at a time. Deal?"

They all nod and go about their assignments. Bob sits there for a few minutes in stunned silence, finally gathers himself, picks up the phone, and dials Leonie.

The developer, Brad Sturgis, says, yes, surprisingly. Now that he intends to move the tree, he is no longer listening to his lawyers, who had all along counseled against speaking with the press. "To hell with them," he says to Bob, in the studio before the show. "Keeping silent has just made me look bad." He is a tall, well-built man with wide shoulders and a trim waist, who, Bob expects, does not have much experience looking bad. In fact, he looks like an actor playing a developer, who consulted with wardrobe, and picked out the perfectly faded leather jacket, steel-toed boots, and work shirt in a shade of blue that brings out his eyes. Both Kathy and Irene have offered to bring him coffee. Even Leonie looks a little flustered when he turns his attention her way.

"So, Leonie," he says. "We finally get to meet." He reaches his hand across the table. It is large and strong looking, but not beaten up like Rusty's. The fingernails are clean and squared off. Leonie takes his hand and smiles a hello, then looks down and starts shuffling her unruly pile of papers.

Bob walks to her side, put his hand on her shoulder. "Don't worry about all the details," he says. "You don't have to know everything. Just more than the hosts or the average listener."

"Thanks!" She shakes the pile of notes and taps the sides so that they line up into a perfect rectangle. "I didn't think I'd be so nervous."

"Pretend no one's listening," Riff says.

"Or think it's only your Mom," Kathy says. "That's what I do." She loops a strand of blond hair behind her ears and settles her headphones down securely over them.

Bob returns to the control room. Irene hands him a neatly stapled copy of the script and nods towards the studio. "The beautiful people go head-to-head. Talk about your luxury problems."

"Let me remind you, this was your idea," Bob says.

"I know," Irene says. "Just always startles me when I see these movers and shakers in the flesh. They seem to have some kind glow about them, don't they?"

She's right. Both Leonie and Brad have the glow of health, brains, and money. Leonie catches him looking at her through the glass and smiles.

"Your girlfriend's hot," Irene says. "Cambridge-style hot. Like she's about to star in a biopic about Isadora Duncan or something."

"Well, thank you, I think."

"You're welcome, I think." Irene winks and grabs her news copy and heads into the news booth.

Bob clicks on Riff and Kathy's talkback mic. "We all set in there?"

Riff and Kathy nod. "We've got Ted Swann on the line, he's the tree expert from the Brooklyn Botanical Gardens, and later on we'll have Emily Anick-Wise, the anti-driving manifesto woman."

"Why are we having her on again?" Riff asks.

"She's got a great chapter on endangered urban trees," Kathy says.

"Whatever." Riff rubs his tired eyes. "Wake me when it's over."

Irene finishes up her newscast and cues Bob, who starts the theme music — after much pleading Anthony had finally agreed to a sampled version of Sun Ra — and cues Riff in.

"Hey, Riff here, you're there, the sun's shining, the earth's below, glad to be above it one more day. Really, sometimes when the weather's turning and the days are growing shorter, don't you start thinking how much time do I have left and will I even leave a trace when I'm gone?"

Kathy looks at Bob and arches her eyebrows. Bob shakes his head. This is not in the script.

"I guess I'll leave the sound of my own voice behind, this is all being taped after all, but I hear even those tapes are deteriorating, digital or not, they're going, as we all are, you, me, Bobby, my little buddy Kathy here. I used to think it didn't matter, that this radio thing was kind of a hedge on death, it was one bright shining moment after another, you know, the eternal here and now, but now I think of it not so much eternal as relentless, the moments piling up on top of one another, crushing everything that came before."

"Jesus!" Irene runs into the control room from the newsbooth, grabs her headset and starts punching the phone lines to open them. "What the hell did he smoke before the show?"

"I have no idea." Bob looks down at Irene's carefully written script and wonders if Riff plans to use any of it.

"Like shale turns into oil," Riff says, "just from the pressing weight of it all, day after day, eon after eon." The Sun Ra theme runs out. Now Riff is musing in the clear. "And even rocks crumble to sand, right? From the constant pounding of the sea. Finer and finer bits of sand?"

Leonie and the developer exchange puzzled looks. Kathy rustles the pages of her script as if to cue Riff back to reality. The door to the control room bangs open and Anthony barges in. His eyes are wild. A lock of hair has fallen forward onto his face. "What the hell is going on here?"

"He's just warming up," Bob says. "Don't worry. He'll circle around to the topic eventually."

"Eventually? This is live radio. Get him back on script, now!"

Bob puts his hand on the talkback mic, lets his finger hover above the on button. He can't interrupt while Riff's talking. He'll have to wait for him to catch his breath.

"Even trees don't last forever," Riff says. "Sure, they outlive us. But they come down in a hurricane, or an ice storm, or rot from the inside out from some unstoppable jungle fungus. They seem immortal but really, they're just like us, finite, but with a later expiration date."

"See?" Bob says to Anthony. "He's coming in for a landing."

"And across the river in Cambridge, there's a pitched battle going on, over one beautiful old tree, supposedly planted around the Civil War. Imagine that? The Civil War! That tree has witnessed times that are even worse than now. That tree was around when we had slavery."

"Is the Civil War in the script?" Anthony asks, between clenched teeth.

"No," Bob says. "But trust me, he's going to tie this all together."

"Get him back on script."

"And just like after the Civil War, you've got this great migration, only now it's white people, flooding back into the cities. Pretty soon there won't be any black people or poor people left. They'll be pushed further and further out, to the suburbs, the exurbs, the boonies, whatever. And this tree is just like those poor people, squatting on some prime real estate, old and in the way." Riff takes a breath.

Bob whispers into his headset. "Time for the script?"

Riff ignores him. "Of course, the neighbors are freaked out about losing the tree. For them it's like losing a piece of the sky. They bought that damn view, they bought that beautiful tree. They assumed it would always be there, classing their places up, shoring up their real estate values. Because trees last just long enough, to seem to last forever."

Riff pauses again. If this were the overnights, Bob would bring the music up and give him some time to collect himself. But this isn't the overnights, there is no music, and Kathy takes the opportunity to jump in and start reading from her script. Riff leans back into his chair, unconcerned, happy, it seems, to relinquish the spotlight.

"Kill his mic," Anthony shouts. "Kill his mic. Now!"

"I can't," Bob says. "If he wants to jump back in, the audience will hear him through Kathy's mic."

Kathy barrels through the first page of the script. When she's about to bring in Brad and Leonie, Bob sneaks the faders up on their mics but leaves them off. He'll pop them in right when they are introduced. No use bringing them in early so the audience can hear Brad clear his throat or Leonie rustle her pile of papers.

Anthony turns to face Irene and Bob. "Whose idea was this show anyway?"

Bob and Irene exchange glances. Finally Irene speaks." Mine." She looks Anthony straight in the eye.

"Bad idea." Anthony turns to Bob. "And where was your judgment when you okayed it? Do you know how bad this makes the station look? How bad it makes me look? Kathy and I bought one of those condos! This is a cluster fuck!"

"I didn't know you bought one." Bob rubs his eyes. "Jesus! But hey, Kathy really wanted to do the show."

"She just bowed to group pressure."

"No." Bob shakes his head. "She was gung ho."

Leonie starts talking, but Bob hasn't opened her mic yet. He pops her in mid sentence. And then he pops in Brad. "Look." He turns to Anthony. "I got to pay attention here. I need to get the show back on track, bring in the guests. Irene's got to screen calls. We can talk about all this later, when the show's over."

"Oh we can, can we?" Anthony draws himself up, squares his shoulders, like an animal in a standoff, trying to appear larger.

Bob stands up and faces him. "Yeah, I can't have you breathing down my neck right now, Anthony. You have to leave the control room." He walks over to the door and holds it open. "Right now."

Irene's eyes widen. Anthony is stunned. He stands there in silence for a minute or so, then sighs. "In my office," he says. "After the show!" He walks out the door.

Bob closes the door behind him and returns to the producer's chair. "Can you get the tree guy's credentials up on their computer?" he asks Irene. Out of the corner of his eye, he sees her start typing, a hint of a smile on her face.

Bob speaks into the talkback. "We got the tree guy on the line," he says to Riff, who nods sleepily. "His info's up on the screen. Just let me know when you want to bring him in." His hand on the talkback mic is shaking.

Irene finishes typing, jumps out of her seat and rushes over to where Bob is sitting and gives him a high five.

Bob gives her a weak high five back and lets out a long exhalation.

"Wow, I can't believe you just kicked Anthony out of the control room!" Irene says.

"Can't believe I did either," Bob says, keeping an eye on the studio. Leonie is enumerating the reasons the neighborhood is against moving the tree. "It's historically significant," she says. "It dates back to the 1850s, when Japan was first opened up to the West."

"Japan was closed to the West?" Irene says and lays a hand on Bob's shoulder.

"Beats me," Bob says. "I must have skipped that day in history class."

"And that's why I have hired the best tree specialists in New England to move it," Brad counters. He turns to Riff and Kathy. "This group is just anti-development. They make a big deal about this tree and I say, 'All right, I'll move it,' and now they are against that!"

"Moving a tree that old would be dangerous," Leonie says. "No one knows if it will survive. And by the time we do know, you'll have extracted your millions and moved on, to another neighborhood. We'll be left to deal with the dead tree, the overcrowding, the overpriced condos."

"Hey, I don't price them," Brad says. "I let the market do that. But it's true." He nods in Riff's direction. "Everyone wants to live in Cambridge. And they'll pay a premium to do so."

"And so little comes on the market in that part of Cambridge," Kathy says. "My fiancé and I have been looking for months now. We just love it there!"

"Oh God." Bob sinks his head into his hands. He tries to get Kathy's attention, mimes slashing his own throat, the universal 'cut' sign, but she is looking at Brad.

Irene punches Bob in the shoulder. "Your house is going to be worth a fortune."

"Good, because I probably won't have a job. You better go screen calls."

"Okay, boss." Irene winks at him and pats him on the shoulder.

Leonie is watching them through the glass, her eyebrows knitted together. She turns to Kathy. "But it won't be the Cambridge you fell in love with, if he has his way."

"See," Brad says. "You people got into Cambridge and now you want to shut the door behind you, so no one else can get in."

"How about neighborhood density. And parking?"

"The condos have underground parking garages."

"And underground parking garages are not in keeping with the architectural character of the neighborhood," Leonie says.

Brad turns again to Riff and Kathy. "I can't win with these people. I even offered to sell it to them, as long as they kept it a single family, like they want me to, and they wouldn't agree to that."

"And why was that?" Riff asks Leonie. Bob smiles at him in encouragement, for getting back on task.

"We couldn't get the financing with that kind of stipulation."

"There you go!" Brad fold his arms over his chest and leans back. Now he's way off mic.

This is not going well for Leonie. Bob whispers in her headphones. "What if the tree dies?" She looks momentarily startled and turns to him in alarm. He shakes his head and repeats the question in Riff's headphones.

"So what if the tree dies?" Riff asks.

"We'll put in another specimen tree."

"That tree is irreplaceable," Leonie says.

"Everything is replaceable."

"Really?" Riff asks. "Now, I don't think I agree with you there."

"Of course it is. I'm replaceable. You're replaceable. Your staff is replaceable. This building is replaceable. With enough money, everything can be replaced."

"You can't replace the wide wood planks in my kitchen floor," Leonie says. "That wood doesn't exist anymore. It's all been harvested."

"You can get a good substitute from Brazil or somewhere."

"And when that's all deforested?"

"Look, I'm just a developer. I build houses that people really want to live in. I use natural materials. High-end fixtures. Everything is light and airy and energy efficient. I can't be held responsible for the rain forest."

"Actually, in Cambridge, I think you can." Riff starts to laugh.

Bob speaks into Kathy's headset. "Let's bring the tree guy in." She nods and starts reading from the computer. "On the line we have Ted Swann, chief arborist at the Brooklyn Botanical Gardens, and author of the book, *Actually, A Lot of Trees Grow in Brooklyn*. Ted? Is a one hundred and fifty-year-old Japanese maple tree replaceable?"

There's a rustling on the guest's line. Ted must have been drifting off. He clears his throat. "No," he says finally. "Of course not."

Leonie winks through the window at Bob. He winks back.

"This tree should of course be saved."

"And whose responsibility is that?" Kathy asks. "Is there some kind of society for the prevention of cruelty to trees?"

Irene laughs. "She's been saving that line up all day," she says.

"It's a community responsibility," Ted Swann says. "And in my mind, this community is doing exactly the right thing."

"And I'm supposed to lose my shirt," Brad says.

"Well, no," Ted Swann says. "In an ideal world, the community would compensate you somehow."

"But this isn't an ideal world. It's the real world. And I got bills to pay and subcontractors who've been waiting months to get down to work. And I have the best landscaping company lined up to move the tree on Saturday."

"But you can't guarantee that it will work," Leonie says.

"Look, Leonie, nothing in this world is guaranteed. That tree could get hit by lightning tomorrow."

Irene rips off her headset and massages her temples. "Oh God, this kind of show gives me a headache. And it's really attracting the enviro-nazis. They're ready to camp out in the tree and kill that poor developer."

"Yeah, it's exhausting, isn't it?" Bob says. "See, if we were real journalists we'd get energized by this kind of brouhaha."

"Speak for yourself. I am a real journalist." Irene starts to put her headset back on, but thinks better of it. She lays it down again in front of her. "Hey, do you think Riff has totally lost it?"

"No, but maybe the pace is getting to him." Bob thinks about the jazz archive. Now that would be the perfect pace for Riff. Or him. Dignified, stately, cresting with the occasional concert or master class, and then slowing back down to the glacial academic pace. Applications must be pouring in from all over the globe.

Bob sits up and loads the next break into the computer. He leans into the talkback mic and speaks into Kathy and Riff's headsets. "Break coming up in 30," he says. "And after that, we'll bring in Anick-Wise and go to the phones." He starts counting down at 10, then counts Riff into the break. "Stay with us," Riff says. "We'll be right back." And Bob fires off the first commercial and the irritatingly loud but catchy jingle for a national mortgage company drowns out everything that came before.

After the show, Bob walks Leonie to the front door. "So you seem really chummy with Irene," she says as they walk down the long corridor from the talk studio to reception.

"Oh yeah. We've worked together for years."

"Did something go on between you?" Leonie turns her head toward him. She is smiling but intent. "I just got a feeling."

"Oh no," Bob says. He tightens his grip on her arm. He's uncomfortable lying to her, but it seems to him that either answer is a lie. Nothing really happened with Irene. And there is certainly nothing to be gained by telling her that he considered it.

He stops into Anthony's office on the way back from saying goodbye. Anthony looks much calmer. His hair is once again in place. He gets up from his chair.

"Look, I'm sorry."

"Nothing to be sorry about," Anthony says, coming out from behind his desk. "Glad to see you're finally taking the reins, thinking like a producer. It's your show. Make something of it." He puts one hand on Bob's shoulder, shakes his hand and ushers him out the door.

CHAPTER 29

On tree-moving day, Brad has added a hard hat to his outfit. An unnecessary affectation, Bob thinks, but what does he know? No one else is wearing a hardhat. Not the landscapers, or the student protestors, or the documentary filmmaker Richard, or his crew, or the orange-robed Buddhists who have formed a human chain around the lovely Japanese maple, or Mabel and her troupe of Morris Dancers, in red and white costumes of course, who have formed another chain around the monks. "Circles inside circles," Bob's neighbor Bryce says, shielding his eyes from the sun. "Fantastic. It's like a big mandala, with the tree of life at its center."

"Or the June Taylor Dancers." Bob wonders why Bryce is not in the fray with his fellow monks. Maybe his dress robes are at the cleaners?

Leonie reaches over to extend her hand to Bryce. "I'm Leonie, by the way. I don't believe we've met?"

"Oh sorry," Bob says and introduces them.

"I must admit, I use your tapes," Leonie smiles. "Stop me if you hear this all the time, but they're great!"

"Thanks," Bryce says. "I never get tired of hearing that. Maybe you can get Bob to listen sometime. He could use a spiritual practice."

"I have a spiritual practice," Bob says. "It's called jazz."

"Jazz may be wonderful, Bob, but it's not a spiritual practice."

"We could debate that all day."

"By the way, I heard you had Pema Chodron and Robert Thurman on your show already. What's going on? You have to import Buddhists when I'm right next door? And frankly, in the rest of the country, I'm as well known as they are." He looks to Leonie who nods her head in agreement. "Maybe more so. Definitely more than Bob Thurman."

"Sorry." Bob throws up his hands. "Those shows came from Riff's wife, Sue. She reads all those books."

"I could give her a copy of my latest book, if that helps," Bryce says. "In fact, it's coming out in paperback soon. I'll have my publicist send you one."

"Oh, I'd love to read it," Leonie says.

"I'll send two."

"That would be great, thanks!" Leonie excuses herself. "Sorry, but I really need to hear this interview." She heads over to where Richard, the documentary filmmaker, is setting up a shot with Brad and Staunton Chase, the Harvard botanist. She smiles over her shoulder at Bob as she walks away.

"Your girlfriend?" Bryce squints at Bob, as if through squinting he might see him in a different light, one that would reveal why someone like Leonie would be interested in him.

Bob nods. He wishes people would stop asking that. The relationship is too new, too fragile. He doesn't want to jinx it by claiming it.

Bryce and Bob both watch Leonie walk past two Cambridge cops, who turn their heads to watch her, too. There is something about the way she moves that is hard to take your eyes off. Perhaps that's what it means to be a dancer. Not that you can learn complicated routines, or touch your foot to your head. Just that watching you move through space is totally engrossing. The larger of the two cops nods his approval in Bob's direction. God, men are such assholes, Bob thinks, but he has to admit, he is proud to be with her.

"Nice day for a demonstration, isn't it?" Bryce says, once Leonie has disappeared into the crowd around Richard.

"Too good for the bastards."

Bryce turns to him with a puzzled look. "Now what is that supposed to mean?"

"It means, that whenever these Harvard people have one of their do's, it's nice out—graduation, homecoming, the regatta. The weather just shines down on these people."

"I distinctly remember it raining for my commencement," Bryce says. "And my twenty-fifth. And this isn't exactly a 'Harvard do.' It's more of a spontaneous neighborhood uprising."

Not so spontaneous, Bob thinks. Leonie has been working the phones nonstop since Wednesday, coordinating offers of support from student councils, environmental coalitions, and students from the judge's Harvard Law School seminar, who are earning extra credit for picketing. First thing this morning, she was on the phone trying to convince the *Globe* to send a photographer. As it turns out, all they got was the *Harvard Crimson*. There's a skinny kid digging camera equipment out of a black backpack with a big crimson "H" emblazoned across the flap.

Bob scans the yard. It's an amazingly large open space for Cambridge. You could probably cram four more houses onto this lot. The Japanese maple stands right at the center, spreading its branches out in all directions, luxuriously, the way trees do when they've got no competition for the sun. Even without leaves, it is a beautiful sight. The shape, the color of the bark, the gnarled branches, which parcel off the blue and white sky. Must be over fifty feet tall. Why has Bob never seen this tree before? He's been in the neighborhood nearly all his life. This might be the only backyard he has not explored. Well, the property is forbidding from the street. There's a tall stockade fence surrounding the somewhat stingy little gray Victorian, and the whole set-up gives no clue to the grandeur behind it.

When Bob was growing up, there were fewer fences and many more kids who roamed the neighborhood yards freely, building forts, discovering secret passageways, walking quietly, single file, like Indians, through the occasional wooded lot. When it snowed they pulled their sleds, toboggans, and flying saucers up to the big houses on Avon Hill, the ones with generous sloping yards. They knew which houses to avoid — the ones with mean dogs and meaner owners — and which to flock to — the ones with old ladies who welcomed the sledders with hot chocolate and cookies.

Now most of the yards in the neighborhood are fenced off, and kids no longer roam. They are chauffeured around by parents or nannies or pushed in strollers by bored-looking black women from the islands. And after a certain age, maybe ten or so, they just seem to disappear from the streets. Perhaps they move to the suburbs, or get packed off to boarding schools, or maybe they are just locked up in their rooms dissecting frogs, studying for their PSATs, polishing their admission essays to Exeter.

Bob feels a tap on his shoulder and turns around to see Irene. She's wearing a black leather jacket and a reddish scarf that matches her lipstick. An expensive-looking camera hangs from a strap around her neck. "Jesus," she says. "What a circus!"

"Irene. I didn't expect you today."

"Oh, I wouldn't miss it. I have to find out who wins, your girlfriend or Brad." She nods in the direction of the documentary crew, who are now interviewing Leonie, Staunton and Brad.

Bryce turns to Irene. "Well, I hope you're rooting for the neighborhood against the developer. I'm Bryce, by the way."

"And I'm Irene. And I always root for the underdog." Irene smiles. She lowers her voice so that only Bob can hear. "Just not sure who the underdog is." She raises the camera to eye level and pans around the yard. "Anthony and Kathy aren't here, are they?"

"No, Kathy doesn't care if the tree lives or dies," Bob says. "She just wants an in-unit washer/dryer, and a parking space."

Irene lowers her camera. "Well to be fair to her, though it kills me, you're in a different place when you're trying to buy something. I know it from when I bought my place in Somerville. You're not comparing it to what it was like before you got there. You're comparing it to all these lousy dumps you saw in much worse parts of town. Places where they never heard of trees and still want top dollar. We can't all see into the past, like you, Bob."

Bob's not sure he likes this characterization of himself. Is that how she sees him? Holding onto the past? The documentary filmmaker has begun interviewing Brad, who is gesturing with outspread arms at the tree, and its home-to-be, twenty feet to the northeast. There is a deep, wide hole, already dug and prepped for occupancy, and now surrounded by a chicken wire fence and yellow police tape. The hole reminds Bob of the pre-dug grave at his father's funeral, covered with wood and some kind of green Astroturf, the casket surrounded by floral bouquets. Later, he told his mother he found the lumpy Astroturf disturbing. "Oh, it used to be much worse," she said. "They'd shovel in the dirt and you'd hear the stones hitting the top and sides of the casket."

But why is he thinking of death and funerals? They are transplanting this tree, not burying it. It's a beautiful day, the crew is the best in the business, and the move is happening no matter how loudly the Buddhists chant. There are two yellow front loaders parked in the driveway, one with a large bucket scoop, the other with a clawlike attachment on the front. Several landscapers are standing near the fence, armed with shovels, rope and burlap.

Bob looks at the solid tree trunk. Wouldn't it be great to have a tree like this in his own backyard? He could look out on it whenever he wanted. Hard to imagine feeling bad with a tree like this on your side. Is this the kind of tree that Abigail is talking about putting in? If so, he should just let her do it. What is he waiting for? Of course, this tree is one hundred and fifty years old, and the trees that Abigail would put in, though Bob is sure she would err on the side of generosity, would not look like this in his lifetime, or his children's lifetime.

One of the front loaders starts up. The foreman gives the cue and it rolls toward the tree. The Buddhists chant louder and the Morris Dancers link their arms and start dancing, the bells attached to their lower legs jingling The first front loader inches up to the dancers, stops, then blows its horn, which is so loud, it throws them and the Buddhists off kilter. The dancing and chanting stop. The law students brandish their signs and shout. "Stop the condos, stop the sleaze. Save our city, save our trees."

The two policeman approach the students. The shorter one tells them they have to move. A tall, red-headed kid emerges from the pack. "We have a legal right to be here, sir," he says. Can he really be old enough for law school?

"No, this is a private residence, and you don't have a right to be here." The cop pantomimes patience. "You can picket all you want out on the sidewalk."

"Actually, according to Samuelson v. Hagerty, Massachusetts Supreme Court, Judge Arthur Kapowsky presiding ..."

The cop rolls his eyes. "You can bring that up with Judge Kapowsky, but right now, sir, you do have to move."

Brad strolls over to the picket line; the film crew trails at an artistic distance. Great luck for Richard, Bob thinks, to land such a handsome villain. Leonie breaks away from Richard and Staunton to rejoin them. "Oh hi," she says to Irene. "I didn't know you'd be here." She smiles but it is not her usual wide-open smile. It is tight and forced and looks almost painful.

Brad motions for the monks and the Morris Dancers to come closer. "I know you love this tree," he shouts over the roar of the idling front loader. "So do I!" He pauses, for applause that doesn't come. "That's why we are moving it, to preserve it!"

Mabel boos. "No, what you're trying to preserve is your own bottom line," she shouts. The cameraman pivots to include her in the shot.

The protesters cheer. The monks resume their chanting. Brad waits for the ruckus to die down, looks right into the camera and smiles. "Believe me, this is doing nothing for my bottom line," he says. "I've got this entire crew here on a Saturday, I'm paying for this police detail, and I am putting in two fewer condos than originally planned. Now I didn't go to Harvard, but according to my math ..." He lets his voice trail off.

The shorter cop chuckles, nudges the other cop, who nods his head up and down. Bob wonders what they're thinking. Just another day at work? More bullshit that has nothing to do with the reality of their lives? Perhaps they have roots in Cambridge, like Bob, but can't afford to live here now. They have to commute from some far-flung suburb, to referee this showdown between the haves and the have mores, all of whom look down on them as cops. Not that Bob has much in common with the Cambridge cops. To him they are another species from on high, wielding power, demanding periodic tribute. He remembers the cops who would descend daily on his father's store, for a free cup of coffee, a package of powdered sugar donuts, a six pack of coke. At Christmas his father made sure that every cop got a good bottle of whiskey, with a storebought red bow slapped on top, and the Chief of Police got a bottle *and* a fruit basket, which Bob had to hand deliver. "Merry Christmas from Boland's," he would say to whoever answered the door at the well-appointed, single-family home, his face red with shame, then he would flee down the steps, to where his father waited in the car, readying the next delivery, to the Board of Health Inspector, or the Mayor.

"Well, I did go to Harvard." Staunton Chase steps forward, squares his shoulders. "And in fact, I chair the Ethnobotany Department there." He's wearing a turtleneck sweater, a tweed jacket, corduroy pants, and a black and crimson striped scarf. First time Bob has seen him without a bowtie. "And according to my math, this tree is nearly one hundred and fifty years old!" The crowd cheers. "And its value is incalculable. It is a nearly perfect specimen, obviously hardy and disease resistant. And going forward, it could be the subject of important horticultural research!" The Morris dancers stamp their feet, wave their white handkerchiefs over their heads.

"And that's why I am paying to preserve it." Brad sighs. For the first time, his face looks tired, his jaw line slack. Are the protestors finally wearing him down? Have they eroded his will to condoize? "And I'm going to have this tree tested," he says, "to determine just how old it really is." He shakes his head. "I really don't see that you have anything to complain about."

"I kind of feel sorry for Brad," Irene says. "I mean, he's trying to be accommodating."

Leonie frowns. "No, he's trying to destroy our neighborhood. What does he care if the tree doesn't make it? Then he'll be able to put in those extra condos. Either way he wins."

And either way, we lose, Bob thinks. This has put them all in a terrible bind. In order for them to be right, and Brad to be wrong, the tree must die. But they love the tree, right? Maybe it's time to accept that it's happening, and change tacks. Maybe the Buddhist should chant for a successful transplant, and the grade-grubbing law students should be put on a frequent watering schedule.

Bob hears sirens, at first in the distance, and then getting closer and closer. Finally, two Cambridge police cars pull into the driveway, lights flashing. The detail cops must have called for reinforcements. Four much larger, more intimidating cops emerge from the squad cars. "Oh no!" Leonie puts her hands to her face. "I can't believe this is happening."

"Where's the judge?" Bob asks. "He might need to bail his seminar out."

"Vail," Leonie says. "Had it planned ages ago."

Irene catches Bob's eye. She looks down and adjusts the focus on her camera, a wicked looking smile on her lips. She snaps a few more shots. Is Bob mistaken or is she only taking pictures of Brad?

The four new cops lumber up to where Brad, Mabel, and Staunton are standing, sandwiched between the front loader and the protestors. The two detail cops step aside. A large cop with a buzz cut and pumped up, rigid shoulders steps forward. "What seems to be the problem here?"

Brad looks at Mabel who looks at Staunton. Finally Brad speaks. "I own this lot and I am trying to move this tree, but they're blocking the path of my bulldozer."

"And I am chair of the Ethnobotany Department at Harvard," Staunton says. "This is a rare specimen of Japanese maple from 1850s Japan. We are trying to preserve it."

"You've had plenty of time to go through the courts and proper channels to do that, Professor. And although this is Cambridge..." The cop winks at Brad. "It's still America, as far as I can tell. And you can't stop a man from moving a tree on his own property in America. Unless you think it's going to endanger lives."

Staunton shakes his head. "No," he says. "It's not going to endanger lives."

"Well, I'm afraid you're all going to have to step aside and let this crew get down to work."

Staunton looks to Mabel who looks to Leonie, who throws up her hands. She shakes her head. "I don't know what to do," she says. "I wish the judge were here."

"It's the beginning of the end," Bryce says. He hangs his head.

Of what? Bob thinks, your reign in this neighborhood? It's been over for me for years. And now the powerful Harvard types are being muscled out by the big money guys, the developers like Brad, who cater to even bigger money guys. Soon even the Kathys and Anthonys of this world will be priced out.

"I never thought we would lose this one," Leonie says.

"Me neither," Bob says. "But hey, maybe it's time we start pulling for the tree."

"What?"

"Well, we want it to survive, right?"

"I can't believe you're just going to give in like that."

"I'm not giving in. I'm adapting." But even as he says this, he worries, is that what he always does? Give in, and call it adaptation? "What do we win if the tree dies?" he asks. "Nothing. We get to say we we're right?"

"We are right."

"If the tree makes it, we can say we saved it. Because frankly, without the neighborhood making a stink, Brad would have just cut it down."

"Bob's got a point there," Bryce says. He seems surprised.

Leonie nods her head and Mabel gives the cue. The protestors file out toward the street, the Buddhists slowly rise from the grass, and the Morris Dancers pack up their handkerchiefs and poles. The front loader rolls toward the tree and raises its scoop and sinks its teeth into the ground, and starts digging a large trench.

"I can't bear to watch this." Leonie puts her hand over her eyes, turns and walks toward the gate. Bob is actually curious. He hesitates. He'd like to see them wrench the great old tree from the ground.

"You better follow her, Bobby," Irene whispers. "If you know what's good for you."

"You want to come with me?"

"No, I'll stay here," she says. "Hold down the fort."

He catches up to Leonie as she is about to cross the street. The protestors have reassembled on the sidewalk in front of the little Victorian, and several cars have stopped to gawk. He touches her lightly on the shoulder and she turns. Her eyes are wet and rimmed in red. He puts his arm around her shoulder. "I'm sorry."

She looks up at him. "You have nothing to be sorry about, Bob. Sorry I snapped at you. You were just trying to look on the positive side."

"Thanks, but that doesn't really sound like me, looking on the positive side."

Leonie smiles. "Well, it's not your fault we lost. It's just so frustrating. I put so much time into this. Nothing's working out for me these days. No matter how hard I try."

Bob feels his own spirits sink. "Nothing? How about us?"

"Except us, of course."

She loops her arm around his waist, and they thread their way through the bumper to bumper cars to the other side of the street. Mr. McMahon is sitting on his front stoop, watching the traffic jam and the protestors. He stands up and waves to Bob. "So, what are the snot-nosed brats upset about this time?"

"A tree," Bob says.

"A fucking tree?" McMahon shakes his head and smiles.

"A beautiful old tree," Leonie says. "A priceless old tree. And we fought to save it." She stares McMahon down.

"All right then," McMahon says and sinks back onto the steps. He catches Bob's eye when Leonie is not looking, and winks extravagantly, but Bob looks straight ahead and pretends not to notice, his allegiance no longer clear.

CHAPTER 30

On the plane to California, Leonie reads Bob's manuscript on jazz. She's frowning. And biting her lip. And making the occasional note in the margins. Bob is trying to distract himself with the in-flight magazine, a CD of Billy Strayhorn, which he can barely hear over the drone of the engines, and a map of the Bay Area picked up at the Globe Corner Bookstore. No luck. He closes his eyes, tries to sleep, but he can feel Leonie fidgeting in the seat beside him. They are going to spend Christmas with her family and Bob is nervous about that, but not nearly as nervous as he is about her reading his treatise. What the hell was he thinking? Not letting anyone else see it for all these years? This was a really bad idea. If she doesn't respect it, how they can continue as a couple? Finally he gets up and walks to the back of the plane, turning sideways to squeeze past another restless passenger, and makes his way to the galley kitchen and asks the flight attendant for some water. On his way back, he notices a row of empty seats near the back and slips down into the one nearest the aisle, closes his eyes and tries to drift off. Let Leonie read in peace.

Already in the airplane, he feels free of winter. His gloves, still poking out of the corner of his fleece jacket, look like some curious artifact from an Arctic expedition. The weather had turned, right after they moved the tree — early December broke all records for the cold. He had vowed to walk across the street to check on it, but it was always too cold, too dark, or he was too tired; he had a book to finish, a movie to watch, a CD to listen to for the show the next day. The talk show pace never lets up. He feels his brain is morphing into something entirely new — fast acting, but shallow. He absorbs material then promptly forgets it. He can almost feel the buzz around a topic that is nearing its peak.

It turns out the tree is not one hundred and fifty years old; it had not come from the opening up of Japan to the West after all. It is a mere sixty years old, planted in the 1930s, though it's strange to think of anyone having the money to plant an exotic tree back then. Professor Chase has acted suitably chastened, and at the post-transplant meeting, apologized to the group for leading them on. "Oh, not to worry," Mabel said. "It's still a beautiful tree. And hopefully we saved it."

The group has moved on to Bob's "adapt and accommodate" position after all. And though he knows he should feel vindicated, he still wonders if he arrives at "accommodate" a little too fast. Leonie has come around to the position too, but it pains her to see the construction trucks parked on the lawn of the house, the Porta Potty in the corner, the large dumpster filling up with construction debris, and insists that they cross the street, or take an alternate route altogether, so she can avoid them.

Irene has started seeing Brad. Bob should have known she had an ulterior motive coming to Cambridge on her day off. She seems very happy though; in fact she seems ten years younger. Smiles spill out of her. At work, she is above the stress, amused by all the drama, nonchalant about the deadlines. She claims Brad's a really nice guy, soulful even — he had always wanted to play the flute. Bob still doesn't trust him. He is too good looking, his teeth too even and white. He hasn't suffered enough, even for the flute.

Bob feels a tap on his shoulder and opens his eyes. Leonie is nudging him to move to the middle seat, so she can join him.

"Did you finish?" He holds his breath.

"Not yet," she says. "But I'm far enough in to tell you it's great."

Relief spreads across his chest. "Really? You think so?"

"Really." She takes his hand. "It's fresh and new and intelligent at the same time." He starts to beam. "You have got to send it out," she says. "And, you have got to apply for that job at the Jazz Archive. You've still got time. But you'd have to hurry."

He squeezes her hand. Two different things, he thinks. He can send it out, but he is not about compete against Riff for the job.

"Harvard needs people like you," Leonie says. "And, just think, you'd have more time to write your next book."

His next book? He is not even used to calling it a book. Could it really be so easy to move into her world? Has this option always been there for him and he just didn't see it?

Gary and Martha are waiting for them at the baggage carousel. The San Francisco airport is not as gray and depressing as Boston's, and people are walking around in jeans, shorts, leather jackets, and flip flops. It makes no sense to Bob: is it cold or warm out? Is this part of the California charm, that the weather is what you want it to be?

Martha jumps up and down when she sees them and runs to embrace Leonie. Laying it on a little thick, Bob thinks. She definitely looks more pregnant than the first time he met her. She is wearing a long thermal shirt and a down vest, that doesn't quite meet around her middle. Her arms and legs still look lean and muscular and her face has a pinkish glow. Leonie hugs her back. "Thank you guys so much for picking us up." She sounds suddenly Californian to Bob's ears.

"Oh, this is fun, and it gives us an excuse to drop in on Gus and Helen early," Gary says. "We usually don't see them until Christmas Eve." He holds out his hand to Bob and shakes with a firm, assertive grasp. "First time in California?"

"Once before," Bob says. "A long time ago."

"Well, let's hope the weather holds." Gary seems suddenly Californian, too. Gone are the tweedy scarf and suede clogs. He's wearing a long sleeved T-shirt, jeans, and hiking boots. He's got sunglasses on a holder around his neck. "This is our rainy season, and it's an El Nino year," he says. Bob looks outside. The day is bright, the air suffused with a soft orangey light. He can see some shocking patches of bright green and a squat palm tree. It looks beautiful, and he is still at the airport.

The ride up to Marin is uncomfortable. Bob and Leonie are crammed into the back of a subcompact rental car. He is straddling his suitcase and his knees keep bumping into Martha's seatback. She keeps turning around, thinking he wants to get her attention and each time, he feels compelled to apologize. He had wanted to get their own car, but Leonie and Gary had worked it out ahead of time. This is what they always did. One came first, got the rental car, then chauffeured the other. As they cross the Golden Gate Bridge, he cranes his neck to see out the tiny windows. It's almost like being on the plane again. "So you grew up in Marin, too?" he asks Gary.

"No, the East Bay. But my folks have a summer place in Point

Reyes. Inverness, actually. Lots of Berkeley types flock to Inverness."

It all seem so fanciful to Bob — Inverness, Berkeley, this burnt sienna bridge, the tunnel with a rainbow-colored entrance, the houseboats, sailboats, the windswept vegetation growing sideways up the browned-out hills, the shiny unrusted cars. He looks down and picks a piece of lint off of his black fleece jacket. Funny, it had looked clean when he put it on in the pale light of a Cambridge dawn. Now it looks positively ratty. Leonie covers his hand with hers. "Now you get to see where I'm from," she says. "And meet my parents."

"Can't wait." Bob interlaces his fingers with hers, wishing secretly that they'd booked a hotel room. That is all he really wants to do right now. Check into someplace clean and anonymous, shower the re-purposed plane air off his body, crawl between the sheets, wrap his arms around Leonie, make love, order room service, then see what movies are on the in-house channel. But it is only 1 p.m. And he has a long day of uncomfortable socializing ahead.

After dinner he can barely keep his eyes open. They are seated on the deck, in comfortable redwood furniture. It's a little cold outside for Bob's taste, and he has zipped his fleece jacket up to his neck and shoved his hands into his pockets for warmth. Leonie's parents' house is modest, but open and airy with lots of windows and varnished wood. Late '70s or early '80s, Bob thinks, when wood was still plentiful and tree houses the rage. The house is perched on the side of a hill and one entire wall is made of windows. "We used to have a better view of Cascade Canyon," Leonie's father, Gus, says. "But then the trees grew in and the hill below was developed." He is a tall, handsome man, with reddish hair and beard. He looks at once younger and older than Bob had expected. His body looks younger; he's strong and upright and his shoulders are wide. He moves with a casual athleticism and strength, and his stomach is still fairly flat. But he has deep creases around his eyes, and grooves on either side of his nose and across his forehead. Reminds Bob of when his mother would say, watch out or you face will freeze like that. Gus's face has frozen like that.

Now the view is of treetops, roof decks, and satellite dishes, silhouetted against a hazy purple sky. In the distance, Bob can just make out the green peak of Mount Tamalpais.

"Tomorrow we'll go kayaking," Gary says. "I reserved three boats." Are Leonie's parents really going to kayak? They are well into their eighties, though both seem to be in good shape. He tries to picture his own mother stepping into a kayak in her sensible pumps, elastic waist skirt, and long cardigan, its pockets full of cigarettes, Kleenex, and cough drops.

"Tomales Bay is beautiful, Bob. You're going to love it." Leonie reaches over from her deck chair and takes his hand. She looks comfortable here in a way she never does in Cambridge. In Cambridge, her beauty seems aloof, her perfect posture an implied criticism. But here in California, her beauty just seems to blend into the California beauty. Her height and carriage seem natural in this land of sculpted mountains, steep cliffs, sparkling water.

Bob has never kayaked, but he assumes that Leonie has, and he will probably have the strength to keep up with two eighty-year olds and a noticeably pregnant woman. They talked a lot about the baby at dinner. Now Martha brings it up again. "We're going to have to leave Cambridge eventually," she says. "Or start saving for private school."

"But didn't you grow up there, Bob?" Leonie's mother, Helen, asks. She reaches out her empty wine glass to Gus, who pours the last of the red wine into her glass. Helen is also tall and slim. She has Leonie's dark looks and bone structure, but her hair is pure white and cut to just below her firm jaw. She wears dangly turquoise earrings and a large turquoise and silver bracelet. Her forearms and hands are tanned and covered with age spots, as is her neck. Maybe she and Gus spent a little too much time in the California sun? "Were the schools so bad then?" Leonie's parents are staunch liberals, the type who believe in public education, as long as your children get into the accelerated classes and are fast-tracked into Princeton.

"Well, I went to Catholic school," Bob says.

"And did all your family go there?" she asks. "That must have cost a fortune."

"No, there was only me."

"Really? I thought all Irish Catholics had big families," Martha says.

"My mother was over thirty when she met my father. Then she had some problems having children. She was forty when she had me."

"I'm so lucky for my age." Martha pats her belly. "After thirty-five you really do start to have problems."

Leonie lets go of Bob's hand and rises from her chair to find another bottle of red wine. Her mother watches her leave the deck, her eyebrows knotted, then changes the subject to jazz. "We hear you've written a book, Bob. How exciting! Have you got a publisher?"

"Not yet." He guesses Leonie has neglected to tell her that no one else has ever read it.

"Well, we look forward to reading it. I'm sure Leonie has told you that Gus is a big jazz collector."

Bob nods. He is worried about Leonie and wishes she would come back with the wine. Maybe it was a mistake to come to California after all?

"In fact, I'd love to show you my collection," Gus says. He is rising from his deck chair. "It's just downstairs."

Damn, Bob thinks, he wants to do it now?

Bob is trying to muster the energy to get up when Helen intervenes. She pats Gus's arm, pushing him back down into his chair. "Bob and Leonie must be tired, dear," she says. "They've been up since dawn."

"Oh," Gus says. "Right."

"And I'm really not much of a morning person," Bob says.

"Me neither," Martha says. "I wrote most of my book late at night. Of course that's when the chat rooms are hopping. I don't know when I'll work once the baby comes."

"I'm not really a night person either," Bob says.

"Then how did you ever get a book written?" Martha asks.

"I have an amazingly productive forty-five minutes," Bob says. "Right before lunch."

Helen throws her head back and laughs. She likes him, Bob can tell. Old Gus there is another story. He doesn't smile or laugh but sits there staring impassively at the treetops and the invisible canyon below.

Gus ambushes him after breakfast. Bob is feeling jittery; perhaps it's just jet lag. His mouth is dry, his stomach sour, he hasn't slept very well. He could hear Leonie's parents talking in the room above them. Leonie stayed up late talking with Gary and Martha and then crawled into bed and woke him up. They had kissed, snuggled for a while, but when Bob tentatively reached for her breast, Leonie said, "Not here."

He needs more coffee now, or maybe less, but Gus stands there waiting for him, his hand twirling the knob on the basement door. He is one *those* jazz guys, with the secret basement bunker full of records and autographed jazz photos. Bob gets up from the kitchen table reluctantly and puts his coffee cup in the dishwasher. Gus leads him down the narrow staircase, ducking under the low ceiling and switching on lights as he does so. "Been at this since I was in college," he says. He opens the door to a musty-smelling room, stacked floor to ceiling with shelves of records. "Started with Bix Beiderbecke."

Bob takes a deep breath and steps into the room. It could be worse, he thinks, he could collect guns. "I have a few Bix Beiderbecke records myself."

"Really? Would have thought you were too young for Bix." Gus examines him more closely.

"Well, I'm forty-eight. Actually." Bob imagines what Gus is thinking. *Fuck, you're forty-eight? That's too old for my daughter. Who are you anyway? What are your intentions? Something wrong with you that didn't get married before? Have you got any money? What are your prospects? You're Irish, huh? Are you an alcoholic?*

Gus nods and looks around the room. "Well, this is it." He smiles shyly and turns around three hundred and sixty degrees. "What do you think?"

"Amazing," Bob says. "How many records you got in here?"

"Thousands? I've lost count."

Bob takes out his reading glasses, the better to focus in on Gus's bounty. He might as well get comfortable. He pulls out a record at random. Louis Armstrong. "They're starting a Louis Armstrong Archive at Harvard," he says. "Did Leonie tell you that?"

"Yes. Said you might apply to be director?"

"I'm not sure I'm applying."

"Leonie thinks you are."

"Well, Leonie wants me to. But my closest friend in the world already applied. I don't feel like competing against him."

Gus nods. "Yeah," he says. "I wouldn't like that either." He takes a record off the shelf, looks at it closely then reshelves it. "Luckily, that didn't come up in my field. Statistics isn't that competitive, or glamorous." He walks across the room and gets another record and holds it out in front of Bob. "Clifford Jordan," he says. "A rare New York session. Want to try it out in the music room?" Bob nods. Gus smiles conspiratorially and leads Bob through the door, down the hallway and into another room. Gus snaps on the lights when they get in. The walls are covered in pristine-looking acoustic tiles, not like the yellowed, pockmarked ones Bob is used to seeing in radio stations. He didn't even know they were originally white. He has always assumed they came the color of nicotine. There's a worn Oriental carpet on the floor, and an overstuffed recliner positioned directly in front of two large speakers. "Sit here, in the seat of honor." Gus nods towards the chair. "I've got it all set up for the optimum listening experience."

Bob sinks down into the recliner. He wishes Riff were here. Riff actually knew Clifford Jordan. Hell, he knew Louis Armstrong. Wouldn't that impress Gus? Gus shuffles over to a turntable, takes the record out of its sleeve and drops the needle down at the edge. There's a loud crackle and pop as the needle finds the groove. Gus dims the lights, then pulls up a folding chair and sits down beside Bob. Music fills the room. Gus wasn't kidding. Everything is optimized. The sound is crisp and lush. The speakers are directly at ear level. The stereo separation is perfect. It sounds like the drummer has set up in the corner and Clifford Jordan himself is playing slightly to Bob's left. Bob looks over at Gus. His eyes are closed, lips slightly parted. His head goes up and down with the beat; his large right foot taps. Bob leans back in the recliner. Relief spreads over him, the too-much-coffee jittery feeling recedes, and even his stomach starts to unclench. He closes his eyes tightly and the world goes golden orange. He could be anywhere. He could be anyone. He could be any time. When the piece is over, Gus rouses himself, turns to Bob and whispers, as if they are in church. "Another?" Bob nods his head and settles back. Could it be he's found a kindred spirit?

Twenty minutes later, they are pulled out of their reverie by a knocking on the door. Helen's voice. "Anybody alive in there?"

Gus unfolds himself from his chair and walks over to his amplifier and slowly fades out Clifford Jordan. He sighs. "All present and accounted for." He squares his shoulders and walks over to open the door.

"Well, it's time to go kayaking," Helen says. "Leonie, Gary, and Martha have left already. We'll go in our car."

Bob is loath to leave this warm orange womb, the comfort of the recliner. He has never been kayaking but he fears it involves getting wet. It is December after all. At home they are forecasting snow. He would be checking on his supply of ice melt and sand, wondering if his winter boots needed another coat of waterproofing. "What should I wear?" he asks Helen.

"Oh, what you have on is fine," Helen says. "Once we're there, we'll change into wet suits. But do bring sunglasses. The glare off the water can be intense."

"I didn't bring any," he says. "Is there a drugstore on the way?"

Helen laughs. "Sorry," she says. "We're heading in the completely wrong direction for that."

The ride to Tomales Bay is breathtaking, on a gently winding road, over spectacularly rolling hills. The day is bright and sunny. The sky is clear blue, the hills a burnt straw color. For a while the road dips into a deeply forested area, with a stream running parallel and the occasional wooden bridge crossing the stream. To Bob, it looks like a forest for trolls. The trees are tall and grow in tight stands; the shadows are deep and black. Gus drives a bit fast for Bob's taste. He is in the back seat and can feel every swerve and sway in the pit of his stomach and the jittery feeling returns. He should have eaten more, he thinks. Maybe drunk less wine with last night's dinner. But everyone else seems fine. He doesn't want to seem like a wimp.

"I've never been kayaking before," he says, hands on the back of Helen's seat, pulling himself forward and steadying himself at once.

"Nothing much to it." Gus says. "Been canoeing?"

"Once," Bob says. Gus turns all the way around in his seat to look at him. Keep your damn eyes on the road, Bob thinks. Gus turns back around and takes another sharp corner and Bob grabs onto the door handle.

They seem to be driving farther and farther away from civilization. The hills are getting bigger and more dramatic looking, the open spaces larger. Funny no one even mentioned this drive, as though it were nothing. Back home, the drive would have been an end in itself. Right about now his parents would have begun looking for a turquoise and orange Howard Johnson's, someplace to pull off the road and calm their agitated nerves with a clam roll or a hot fudge sundae.

Finally the road ends and they come to an intersection. Gus looks right, then left. "Highway One," he says. "Coast road."

There's a funky looking general store on the corner, several motorcycles parked in front. "Hold on." Bob nods at the store. "Can we see if they have sunglasses?"

Gus makes a hard right into the parking lot and Bob jumps out of the car. He vows to ride in the other car on the way back. He walks into the general store. His legs feel wobbly, not quite connected to his feet. Two guys in motorcycle jackets are sitting at a table in the corner, drinking beers, a bag of nacho chips exploding onto the table in front of them. Behind the counter, there's a paunchy bearded guy in a *Laconia Bike Week* t-shirt. The TV blares behind him. Bob smiles. "You from New Hampshire?"

"What?"

"Laconia, New Hampshire." Bob nods toward his t-shirt. "I'm from Massachusetts. Thought maybe you were from Back East, too."

"What?"

Bob gives up; small talk is obviously not the man's forte. He approaches the counter. "Would you have any sunglasses?"

"Only these." He takes a pair of mirrored aviator sunglasses off the shelf behind him. They've got a Harley Davidson logo on the arm.

Bob looks at the price tag. "Are they really one hundred and fifty dollars?"

"They're the real deal, man. Take them or leave them."

Bob puts the glasses on. They're too tight, the arms pinch the side of his head, the nose piece digs into his skin. No wonder they are still there, waiting for a biker with a child-sized head to emerge from the surrounding golden mountains.

He hands them back to the cashier and leaves the store. "All they had were biker glasses," he says as he slips into the back seat.

"Yeah, we never stop there. It's scary." Gus backs onto Highway One without looking, swerves the car to the right, drives a few hundred yards and takes a quick left.

"Now we're heading out to Point Reyes," Helen says. "It's actually part of a separate geological plate, that drifted up from the south. The vegetation is not native to this part of California. In fact, we are coming to the edge of the North American continent. We'll be crossing the San Andreas Fault soon."

There is a body of water on the right, the sun glistening off of it. Bob wonders if there is any way to get back to civilization other than the way they just came, which was long and torturous. What if he had a stroke right now? Would he have to be airlifted to the nearest hospital? He feels his face and neck getting hot. He swallows and his ears pop.

"Beautiful, isn't it?" Helen asks.

Bob nods his head, and silently counts to ten, trying to calm himself down. It will be better when he can use his body, expend some energy. He is feeling so out of context. Who are these people in the front seat? Where is he? Can it really be Christmas? He should be home, buying gifts for his parents, no his parents are dead, he should be buying something for Mary Elizabeth's grandkids, and Mary Elizabeth herself, and maybe a CD for Riff. Riff, he would love to talk to Riff right now. He needs a touchstone. He needs a friend. He looks at his watch. 10:30. Riff will still be on the air. But he'll be coming soon to a break. He could talk for a few minutes while the commercials are running. But Kathy would be there and some guest, oh yeah, that creepy looking internet guru, he meant to read his book, but he couldn't get past his greasy hair and supercilious smile. Just to hear Riff's voice on the phone might bring him back down to reality. He looks in vain for the comforting blue of a public phone booth. There must be a pay phone somewhere in this frightful paradise. Maybe at the kayak place. He can call collect.

Gus slams on the brakes and makes a sharp right into a dirt parking lot. There are kayaks stacked up against a peeling blue shed, a nautical flag tacked over a trellis and blowing in the light wind off the bay. Gus pulls in right alongside Gary's white rental car, but Gary, Martha, and Leonie are nowhere in sight. The minute the car stops moving, Bob leaps out of the back seat and rushes inside to find Leonie, and if not her, a phone.

He steps inside the shed and can see nothing until his eyes adjust to the darkness after the bright California light outside. As his eyes adjust he picks out a counter and an older-looking blonde woman behind it. Like Gus, her body looks young but her skin looks old. She motions her head to a door over her shoulder. "They're all out back," she says. "Getting into their wetsuits. You want yours now?"

He shakes his head, almost violently. There is nothing Bob wants to do less right now than squirm into a wetsuit. "Do you have a pay phone?"

"No" she says. "But you can use our phone if it's local."

"How about collect?"

"Sure." She motions him to the wall phone behind her and slides off her chair and out behind the desk as she does so. She walks over to a chest filled with life preservers and starts to sort them. Bob dials the control room number. BJ answers, and hesitates when he hears it's a collect call. "BJ, it's me!" Bob shouts through the line. "Accept the goddamned charges!" The blonde woman looks up, startled. BJ can't hear him, and tells the operator to hold, while he confers with someone. Jesus fucking Christ. Bob can feel the sweat pouring off his forehead, running down his neck. "Is Irene there?" he shouts into the phone. The blonde woman looks up again. Finally, BJ comes back on the line and gives the operator a stiff, reluctant, yes.

"BJ, it's Bob. Put Riff on, please."

"We're on the air."

"I know you're on the air, for Christ's sake. Put him on." Bob can hear Irene shouting in the distance. "Is that Bob? How's California?" Riff comes on. "Everything okay out there?"

"No," Bob says. "I'm freaking out. I don't know what's wrong with me. I feel so out of context here. It's all so strange. The ocean's on the wrong side. Even the trees here are alien. I mean, it doesn't feel like winter or spring or summer. It's like no season at all. The sun's out but the air's cool, and there's no humidity and everything's so damned dry."

"It's called traveling, Bobby. Places are different. Weather is different. Calm down."

"And now they want to take me kayaking. In December. I want to go home."

"Oh no you don't. It's fucking snowing here. Remember that? Snow? Then it's going to change to freezing rain, just to make the driving hell. It's so dark out, I had to use my high beams on the ride in. Sue's already talking about moving to South Carolina. Says she can't take one more winter here."

Bob looks around the dark shed, the sun so desperate to get in, it pours in blinding rays through the cracks in the wall, the rips in the shades, the space under the door.

"You know," Riff says. "I had an idea. Maybe you should apply for that jazz gig."

"What?" Bob is shocked. Has Riff somehow gotten wind of Bob's interest? Did Leonie say something? He pulls himself together. "No, that's your gig. I wouldn't compete against you."

"Yeah, but what if I leave to go South? Then they give that cushy post to some Harvard guy who doesn't really need it? Hell, we might as well both throw our hats into the ring. See what happens."

"Really?"

"Really. One of us should get that fucking job. I don't care who."

Bob smiles. He has stopped sweating. The blonde woman looks over at him, cocks her head, a not-so-subtle message for him to get off the phone. "Look I'm on someone's business phone here, I got to go."

"*You* got to go? I'm on the air! Kathy is giving me the hairy eyeball."

"How's the internet guru?"

"Ripe."

"Thank God, there's no smell on radio."

"Visual's rough too."

"You only have twenty more minutes."

"This life is for the birds," Riff says. "Too much wear and tear on the body. Not to mention the psyche. Apply for the fucking Harvard job, my friend."

"All right," Bob says. "I will." He hangs up the phone and steps out from behind the desk. "Thanks," he says to the blonde woman.

"So you want that wetsuit?" She squints her eyes. "Or not?"

"I'll take it."

She walks over to where the wet suits are hanging and turns to appraise him. "Try the medium first. The changing room's out back." She inclines her head towards a screen door, facing out to the bay. Is the smirk on her face about the changing room or Bob's lack of enthusiasm for kayaking?

Bob takes the slimy wetsuit and walks over to a screen door and pauses, his free hand on the wooden crossbar. The door leads out onto a rustic-looking dock, with two Porta Potties jammed into the corner. One of the Porta Potty doors flings open and Martha emerges. She has slithered into her wetsuit and looks like a cross between a pregnant mermaid and a bondage queen. She walks over to where Gary and Leonie and her parents are standing in a circle, all of them in wetsuits. Gary is telling them something, gesturing with his arms, their heads are bobbing up and down in agreement. Funny to see them all in their wetsuits, their varying shapes and sizes. They look like a family of harbor seals, Bob thinks, about to go hunting for dinner. He looks back into the comforting dark of the shed. Surely, for someone like him, sanity lives here in the shade. But he turns around and pushes on the screen door and steps into the blinding California sun.

CHAPTER 31

Whenever Bob is flying into the airport in Boston, he thinks of the People Express flight in the '80s that overshot the runway and ended up in the harbor. The runway at Logan is too short, a challenge to land a plane on, especially on a night like this, when they are descending into a snow squall. He doubts the pilot can even see the runway, let alone the icy water beyond it. So when he feels the sudden deceleration and hears the almost hysterical pumping of the plane's brakes, he instinctively clutches Leonie's hand and braces for impact.

"Bob, stop! You're hurting me," Leonie says. "Relax!"

Bob looks down at his tanned forearm and then out into the total whiteout. The plane comes to a screeching halt and a few of the overhead bins pop open. "Thank God." He lets go of Leonie's hand. "We made it."

Leonie shakes her head and looks at him strangely. "As if there were any doubt?"

He is about to tell her about the People Express flight, but he doesn't have the energy. He is just relieved to be on the ground and home again, in Boston, a place he understands. Though, he must admit, over the week he had started to warm up to California. The weather was great, the views breathtaking, the food delicious, the pace, just a little bit slower. And Leonie's parents, and her friends, had seemed to accept him, at face value. They didn't pry about where he went to school, who his parents were, what he did for a living, how many bedrooms his house had. He is beginning to understand that line of questioning is more East Coast than West Coast.

They huddle together outside waiting for a cab. The snow is blowing in at an angle; even under the airport overhang they are getting wet. Bob fishes his gloves out of his suitcase and turns up the collar of his fleece jacket. He puts his arm around Leonie, who is shivering. "Oh my God," she says. "I can't take four more months of this!"

Bob squeezes her more tightly. "It's not four more months," he says. "Two and a half at most. By April we'll be complaining about the rain."

Leonie smiles, squeezes him back. "I was sort of hoping you'd fall in love with California."

"Give me more time," Bob says. "It takes a while to fall in love."

Later, in the cab, he watches the snowy cityscape flash by. Funny, he had never noticed how much of Boston was made of brick. And even in the snow, it looks dirty. Even the modern concrete buildings look stained and Soviet-era bleak. He is happy when they cross into Cambridge and drive along the river — the boathouses elegant, the arched bridges graceful, Harvard solid, and more brick, but stately looking in the snow. Cambridge is very pretty, he realizes. He has never been so glad to be home.

When they open Bob's front door they are greeted by an arctic blast of cold air. And the house is suspiciously silent. Has the burner gone out? It's less than a year old! Bob opens the cellar door. Usually hot air greets him, but not this time. It's as cold down there as in the hallway. "Maybe we should just go to my house?" Leonie puts her suitcase down, rubs her lower back. "Deal with this tomorrow?"

"No, we better figure out what's wrong now. Don't want the pipes to freeze."

Leonie rolls her eyes. Her face is tanned from the day of kayaking. "Even two and a half months of this is too much." She sighs. "You got any tea?"

Bob nods and heads down the cellar stairs to check the burner while Leonie walks to the kitchen. No warning lights are lit, but there is also no sound. He looks at the glass water gauge. Rusty looking but the level seems okay. He hits the emergency restart button. Nothing. He looks at the tag on the burner to see when it was last serviced. Not since he bought it, last February. The tag is dusty and covered in cobwebs. He brushes it off, takes down the number of the oil burner company and goes back upstairs to call.

Why is it always cold when your burner goes out? Stupid question, he knows, like why is it always raining when your windshield wipers stop working? He wonders if he has a service contract or will have to pay for the house call? He wishes he knew something about oil burners. His father would not have given up so easily. He would have fucked around a lot longer. He would have poked and prodded and filled up the reservoir and flicked the on and off switch and unscrewed some kind of panel and fiddled with the electrical wires, then given it a good swift kick, sworn at it, and gone upstairs to call. But Bob is afraid of the burner. It is big and noisy and involves flammable substances and fire. He is just like one of these Harvard guys, overeducated, dependent, effete. His father would be ashamed.

It is just after eleven when the doorbell finally rings. Leonie and Bob are dozing on the living room couch, wrapped up in a down comforter, the remains of Chinese takeout on the coffee table in front of them, their bags still unpacked in the corner. Bob had lit a fire, but it only seemed to make the room colder, and to make their eyes water. Maybe it is time to get the chimney cleaned? At the sound of the doorbell, Bob opens his eyes, gazes at the glowing embers in the fireplace and slowly gets up off the couch, making sure not to disturb Leonie. He looks out the windows on either side of the front door. It is still snowing, and drifts have accumulated on the front stairs and porch. At least they will soon have heat. But when he opens the door, it is not the repair man he finds but Maureen, from the apartment building behind him. She is dressed in a long down coat with a fur lined hood. Her eyes are wild, her color high. "There is a poor creature freezing to death on your roof!" she says.

A gust of cold air blows in. "Come in," Bob says. "Come in." Snow blows under the door and into his hallway. He can feel the cold air on the exposed skin between his socks and pants.

"I will not!" Maureen says. "You come out here and free the poor thing."

Bob rubs the back of his neck, which is stiff from sleeping on a plane and now a couch. "Where is he?"

"On your roof. In the back." Maureen says. "Everyone in our building is watching. The poor animal is shivering to death on your roof, in a cage."

"All right, all right. I'll call the trapper," Bob says.

"No, you have to come out and free it now!" Maureen says. "It's been there all night."

"What's going on?" Leonie has gotten up, padded to the front door, the down comforter wrapped around her shoulders.

"Your boyfriend's got another poor squirrel trapped in a cage."

"Oh, hi Maureen." Leonie says. "I met you a few weeks back."

"Please, come in." Bob says. "I'm freezing."

"Well, think about the poor animal."

"Okay, I'll go check on it. And I'll call the trapper." He starts to close the door.

Maureen wedges her foot in the door. Her eyes gleam. "I hope you die out there in a cage." She stomps off the porch.

Bob is about to put on his coat and gloves and go out and check on the squirrel when Leonie stops him. "Bob, call Rusty first," she says. "It's snowing out."

Bob nods his head. She's right. He hates ladders; he's afraid of heights and even more afraid of angry squirrels. He finds Rusty's number and dials it. It rings for a long time before Rusty finally answers. "Sorry man," Bob says." Did I wake you?"

"No, yes, whatever. Who's this?"

Bob explains that there's a squirrel trapped on the roof in the snow. "Didn't my son come by today?" Rusty asks. "To check the traps?"

"I guess not."

Rusty sighs. "All right, don't worry. Somebody'll be there soon. You can go back to bed."

Bob sighs with relief and then settles back down on the couch with Leonie to wait for heat.

The furnace guy shows up at 3 a.m. He is young and scrawny-looking with long blonde hair curling onto his shoulders. "Sorry I'm so late," he says. "Every fucking burner on the East Coast has crapped out tonight." Bob has been dozing on the couch under the comforter. Leonie has gone to bed, with her down jacket and hat on. Bob leads him down the cellar stairs, to the burner. The kid takes one look at the rusty water in the gauge and turns to glare at him. "You know you're supposed to flush this."

Bob sighs. "No, I didn't. How often?"

"I don't know," the kid says. "Before it gets like this! You got a bucket?"

Bob walks to the rear of the cellar to look for the bucket. Is it his imagination or does he hear the squirrel clawing at his trap? Or has Rusty already come and freed him and what he hears are just some branches scraping against the side of the house? He makes a mental note to go outside later and check.

Bob brings him a bucket and sits down on the cellar stairs and watches the kid work. He is in a surly mood, but knows what he is doing. His hands move confidently. Maybe I should learn a trade, Bob thinks. Forget about the jazz archive. Get really good at something. Help people out when they need it. Save lives, really. "You like this line of work?" he asks.

"No." The kid turns a nozzle and a gush of rusty sludge spurts out into the pail. "I fucking hate it. I want a desk job, like you. Maybe I'll get into the Internet."

Bob thinks there is something sad in the vagueness of the kid's dream. Or maybe he is just tired. It has been an awfully long day. He goes back upstairs to check on the squirrel.

Bob can tell by the untouched snow in the driveway, that neither Rusty nor his son has come. He plods down the driveway to the brick path and then through the garden to the fire escape. His boots need re-waterproofing. He can already feel the moisture between his toes. He brushes the snow off the bottom couple of rungs and then hoists himself up and starts climbing the ladder up to the porch roof. He can hear the squirrel scratching at the bars of the trap. So he's still alive at least. Or maybe it's a she. Funny he has never thought of a squirrel being female before. Maybe she's somebody's mother. He swings his leg over the railing and steps onto the porch roof. The sound is coming from the rear of the house, he thinks. He walks across the snow covered tar roof to the next fire escape, feeling for soft spots in the tar as he does so. He should really get this roof fixed. Maybe he should build a deck. Right, where is he going to get that kind of money? He climbs up the next ladder and steps onto the fire escape. He is closer to the scratching now, but he still can't see the trap. The roof is pitched, and there are a few inches of snow on it and he's reluctant to go any farther. He hears more scratching, louder this time. Rusty had climbed this roof in a couple broad steps. Certainly Bob could do that, too. He just had to think about getting to the peak, then all would be balanced, gravity his friend. It sounds like the squirrel is just on the other side of the peak, on the downslope. Really, if it weren't up so high he would do it in a minute. Two steps and he could grab onto the chimney. Now he can hear the squirrel crying. It's a feeble cry and he decides to give it a try. He keeps his eye on the chimney and launches himself up the roof, one big step, then another, and then half again, and he feels himself slipping backwards but grabs the chimney and pulls himself up and over the peak. Whew! Success! He exhales to calm himself down.

He looks down the other side through the snow for the trap and the squirrel. At first he sees nothing, but the squirrel rattles the cage again and whimpers and he follows the sound. The trap has rolled down the roof and lodged itself upside down in the gutter. In another two and a half steps he could be there, but there is no fire escape on that side of the house, no railing to cling to, just the gutter and a two-story drop. The squirrel will just have to wait for Rusty. Would it be dead by then? Bob wonders if he could throw his coat down and cover up the cage. Would that keep the squirrel warm? He's not exactly sure of the physics of this, but he thinks it's worth a try. He takes off his coat, bunches it up into a throwable missile, and then tosses it toward the cage. It lands on top of the cage and does a reasonable job of draping it, not completely, there will be drafts, but hopefully enough to keep the squirrel alive. In any case, it will have to do. Now Bob is freezing.

He swings his legs over the peak of the roof, grabs onto the chimney and starts to lower himself down, feet first, backwards. He looks over his shoulder and can see the railing of the fire escape and tries to touch it with his foot but he can't reach. How did Rusty get down? He can't remember that detail. Did he just let himself slide down in the direction of the fire escape? Of course he didn't do it in the middle of the night, with snow covering the shingles. Bob is loath to let go of the chimney until he has figured out exactly how this is going to work. He looks over his shoulder again and lets go of one hand and stretches that side of his body and that foot down towards the rail, but he still can't quite reach it. Maybe Rusty inched down on his butt and didn't hold onto the chimney at all?

The wind is picking up and the snow is buffeting Bob's face and neck. His thin California shirt is soaked through. He is going to have to do something, so he decides to inch down on his butt. He hoists himself back up and then turns around and aims himself in the general direction of the fire escape. But the minute he lets go of the chimney, he picks up speed and when he grabs the roof tiles to slow himself down he veers off course and flies right over the side of the roof and slams feet first onto the porch roof. The place where his right foot lands is solid enough, but his left foot lands on a soft spot and keeps on going right through the roof. The hole opens wide as he plunges through and he throws his arms out on either side and catches himself by the armpits before he falls through to the next floor. He hangs there for a moment and gasps. Jesus! He tries to hoist himself up, but his right foot is caught on something. His shoulders and armpits feel bruised and raw. He feels a wave of nausea pass over him. He's going to need help getting his leg free, and then getting out of this hole. He yells out, "Leonie, I've fallen and I can't get up." He can't be that badly hurt if he can joke, right? He calls her name again. "Leonie, Leonie!" She is in the bedroom on the other side of the house, one floor down. There's a porch roof, an exterior wall and an interior wall between them. But still she should hear him. He heard the goddamned squirrel! He calls out for the furnace repair guy. "Repair Man, Repair Man?" He's another story down and in the basement, so Bob is not that hopeful. He yells in the direction of the back apartment building, "Help, help!" The whole apartment building could hear the damned squirrel but not him? He yells again, longer and louder this time. "Maureen!"

Finally he sees a light go on in her apartment. "Maureen!" He sighs in relief. "It's Bob, up here on the porch. I'm stuck. I need help." He watches a succession of lights go on as Maureen moves through her apartment to the door. She opens her door and looks up at the roof for the squirrel first, then turns toward the porch. "Maureen!" he yells. "Over here. On the porch." She squints up toward the porch, meets his eye for a minute, then closes her door and puts out the lights, one by one.

CHAPTER 32

What kind of a sick motherfucker would let a man freeze to death on his back porch? A crazy sick motherfucker like Maureen. Is she really going to just sit there in the dark and let him die? She is, after all, the cause of all his squirrel problems. Here he thought the entitled like Abigail and Bryce were bad. But crazy people are even worse! There is a certain subset of humanity, and Maureen belongs to it, who love animals but are just plain skittish around human beings. Squirrels and dogs and cats don't notice if you can't make eye contact, or if they do they are tactful enough not to mention it, and as long as you feed them they are your friends forever. People are so much more demanding, and complex.

Bob's hair and eyebrows are matted with snow, and his teeth are beginning to chatter. His teeth haven't chattered since he was a little kid and stayed in the water until his lips turned blue. He remembers a favorite book from childhood in which the hero falls off his horse and lies there freezing in the snow. His limbs go numb, and he stops being cold, and, in fact, he feels all warm and cozy and ready to fall asleep, but he can't let himself do that or he will die. Imagine dying like this. Frozen to death on his own back porch. When his life was just starting to pick up. Leonie, the talk show, the jazz director job.

On the plane Leonie had coached him on applying for the job. "Who do you know?" she asked. "For references?"

"Riff," Bob said.

"You can't use Riff. He's applying for the job. Who else?"

"Buddy."

"Buddy would be good." Leonie nodded and moved on to the next item on her mental to-do list. "How about an African American?"

"Uh, uh," Bob shook his head. "Not going there."

"Do you want the job or not?"

"I'm not going to suck up to somebody just because he's African American and I'm white. That's against my principles."

"Bob, you can't afford your principles." Leonie forged ahead. "You must have some contacts at the magazines, or the newspapers?"

Bob always ran into the jazz critic from the *Globe* in the used record stores. He'd arrive with a shopping bag full of promotional CDs to sell. He always thumbed through the used records furtively, using his broad back to block Bob's view. He wanted to keep the good finds for himself. "I know the guy at the *Globe*," he said. "Never liked him much."

"How about clips of your previous reviews and stories?"

"Sure," he said. "I got those. Somewhere." He remembered at one point thinking they were important and putting them somewhere special, but he has absolutely no idea where that somewhere special might be. Could he have put them in the attic? Perhaps Mary Elizabeth threw them out with the Christmas ornaments?

Bob is now shivering uncontrollably, and his fingers and toes are going numb. Stupid not to wear gloves after he dragged them all the way to California and back. He wiggles his fingers to get sensation back and wiggles his toes inside his boots. "Leonie!" he yells. "Bryce! Abigail! Maureen! Tom!"

The burner shudders on and then off again, shaking the whole house. Bob can almost feel it in his bones. "White Fuel guy! White Fuel guy!" he shouts. Why didn't the White Fuel guy park in the driveway? Then he'd have to walk around to the side of the house when he got the burner running. But no, he had pulled his truck right onto the sidewalk in front of the house, flaunting his emergency responder status.

Bob squirms his legs and tries to free his foot. But the squirming just causes more of the rotten roof to give way. So he stays still. He hears the squirrel rattling his trap again and feels a certain kinship. He can't even pound on the roof or he'll dislodge himself and plunge another story down. Then again, maybe he should try to dislodge himself? Would that be so bad? Maybe he could roll to protect himself like a cat. He squirms around again and more of the roof gives, but his foot stays firmly trapped. "Leonie!" he yells. "Maureen!" He can see his own breath. It looks so warm. He blows on his hands to warm them. What the hell is Maureen doing inside her apartment? Has she gone back to sleep? He wonders how she can afford to live there. She can't make much money from her dog walking business. She is probably on her way out of the neighborhood too. Unless she'd been grandfathered in. Some Cambridge city ordinance to preserve the city's crazy people. But where could she go? Are the suburbs any more friendly to crazy people? Sure, if you have the money to own a house, far enough away from your neighbors, you can be as crazy as you want. Look at Riff and Sue. Money was really the secret to it all. If Bob had more money, he would have gotten this roof fixed years ago. Hell, he would have put in a nice redwood deck like Leonie's parents had. Of course he'd never seen a redwood deck until this past week.

A light comes on in the second floor of Bryce's house. Thank God. "Bryce!" he shouts. "It's Bob, I need your help!" The light's in the back, probably a bedroom. Maybe Bryce gets up at dawn to meditate like the Dalai Lama. "Bryce!" Funny, he just can't take a Harvard-educated, upper middle class, white Buddhist seriously. Why not? He could be the real thing. Is it any less likely that a spark of the divine would descend upon a man who shops at Whole Foods than a refugee from Tibet? "Bryce!" The squirrel whimpers again. Really, he has to hand it to the little guy. He had gotten the whole neighborhood involved in his plight and Bob can't rouse a soul.

Bryce's light goes out again. Damn, he wasn't meditating, just emptying his bladder! Maybe old Bryce was having early signs of an enlarged prostate, frequent urination in the middle of the night. Which he had to admit, Bob was experiencing himself. Only forty-eight and his fucking bladder was giving out, which reminds him, he could really use to take a piss right now. He drank a beer on the plane, always a mistake, and then a Coke to wake up near the end of the flight. He wishes he had eaten more of the Chinese food, which is still sitting in containers on the living room coffee table. A full belly would be a comfort right now. Leonie had complained about the noodles, too bland, she said, and the tofu, too slimy. Now after eating in Northern California, he understands where she is coming from. The food in Cambridge sucks in comparison. Did she really want to move back there? Who could blame her? That was home. A beautiful place to feel comfortable in. Bob wishes his own parents had migrated to California. Then he too could have taken that landscape for granted, could have woken up to that blinding sunshine and cool, dry air and felt something like peace.

A scrabbling sound on the fire escape wakes him. Has someone finally missed him? He yells, "Rusty?" But when he opens his eyes he sees a squirrel standing motionless on the top rung. He's got a peanut in his mouth. He stares at Bob. Bob stares back. What goes on behind those beady little eyes? Bob's arm has fallen asleep, and he twists to wake it up, and the squirrel starts, then freezes again, his fuzzy gray tail at attention. Bob feels a tiny bit of fear creep into him. He is stuck here and the squirrel could come attack him and he can't even run. He could gouge his eyes out! If Bob fights back then he'll plunge through the roof to his death. Calm down, he thinks. Calm down. The squirrel is more afraid than you are. He doesn't know you are stuck. All you have to do is bellow. Show him how huge you are, how much testosterone is still surging through your veins.

The squirrel takes a step. Bob yells, "Leonie, Leonie!" His own voice sounds hollow. The squirrel hops off the fire escape and onto the porch then leaps over Bob's outstretched arm to the next fire escape. He is bringing food to his imprisoned comrade, Bob thinks, as he disappears over the peak of the roof. How altruistic of him.

The snow is coming down more heavily now and starting to accumulate on his arms and hands, even his shoulders. What if he gets buried alive in the snow? Then again, maybe that would save him, insulate him from the cold? There was an often-told family story about his maternal grandfather passing out drunk in the snow. It happened right after Bob's parents got married, long before he was born. His grandfather had left a bar in Harvard Square during a blizzard, but never made it home. Bob's father drove up and down the snowy streets searching for him. Finally in desperation he pulled over and walked the route and found the old man buried up to his neck in a snow drift. He dug him out with his hands and dragged him to the car, and delivered him home, the old man pissing and moaning the whole ride about what a sanctimonious little prick Bob's father was.

He should have listened to Leonie, stayed at her house. They would be snuggled in her bed right now, sleeping off the jet lag, waking to fresh ground coffee and a winter wonderland in her sunny, plant-filled kitchen. Who cares about the pipes bursting? He would have been warm. He flexes his arms, and tests the roof gingerly. Just how rotten is it? His foot has gone numb and no amount of wiggling his toes seems to be waking it up. He decides it is time to try to plunge to the next floor. He pounds on the roof and more gives way, and he falls a couple of inches further in, but his foot is still caught and he goes no further. He tries to hoist himself out but he can't get any leverage on the crumbling roof. "Leonie! Bryce! Maureen!" he calls. "Abigail! Tom! White Fuel Guy! Anybody!"

Wouldn't it be strange to die right here, right now? Everything so up in the air. Nothing in place. Who would get the house? He had no will. Who thinks about a will when you are single and forever in the process of becoming? Mary Elizabeth was his next of kin. She could live here and fight with Abigail and Bryce and Maureen. She'd handle them better than he. She'd be more proactive. And how about Leonie, would she go back to California then? Her Cambridge chapter closed on a very tragic note? He doesn't want to do that to her. Poor Leonie! And they could have had a kid. All those wasted orgasms! What an asshole he was. How selfish! That's what you were supposed to do. Procreate, leave a next generation to soldier on, someone you could tell about your drunken grandfather who passed out in a snowbank. No, maybe that's not the kind of story Leonie would want her children to hear.

They haven't talked about the children issue in a while, though it was there in the background for the whole California trip. Fertile Martha, the world revolving around her very pregnant belly. And if they had a kid, would they only have one? Two only-children producing one only-child. He would have liked to have a sibling. They should start soon, so they could have two. He is going to suggest it as soon as he gets off this damned roof. Of course who knows if he can father a child. He has never tried. Perhaps the equipment is faulty. Which reminds him, he really has to piss. He could just let it go, at least it would be warm, but the thought of Leonie finally waking up and emerging on the porch to a stream of his warm urine, gives him the strength to hold it in.

Perhaps they should get married first? They've only known each other a couple of months, but what does that matter? They get along so well and the clock was ticking and he could be dead any minute now. Riff could get one of those Universal Life Church Minister licenses, they were all the rage in the '70s, and Bob knows for a fact that those marriages actually take, because Buddy had to hire a lawyer to get out of his.

"Leonie!" he calls. "Bryce! Maureen! Help!" He hasn't heard from the squirrel in a while. Is he still alive? Bob pounds on the roof. "Wake up, wake up!" he yells. "It won't be long now!" And the other squirrel has not come back down the fire escape. Is he holding vigil by the trap or has he leapt off the roof and onto a Norway maple to avoid another encounter with Bob?

A light goes on in Maureen's apartment. And then another. She is getting up! Perhaps she has a conscience after all. Her door opens and slams shut. "Maureen?" he yells. "Maureen!"

"I heard you the first time." She is looking up at the porch, indecisive, as if trying to make up her mind.

"I need your help," he says. "I'm stuck here on the roof."

"I'll call the fire department."

"We don't need the fire department."

"You're going to be picky? To hell with you then!" Her door opens and slams shut again and she is gone.

"Fine," Bob yells. "Whatever you want to do, Maureen. Call the fire department." But she doesn't respond, so he hangs there and waits and watches to see that her lights do not go off again, and hopes the Fire Department is on its way.

CHAPTER 33

New Year's Eve and Riff is sitting at the foot of Bob's bed in Middlesex County Hospital. "So the wacko really saved your life." Bob is trying to eat his breakfast — a cup of lukewarm coffee with skim milk, cold white toast with even colder margarine, and powdery scrambled eggs. How is anyone supposed to get better on this crap? Then again, why waste good food on sick people? Half of them have no appetite anyway.

"Yeah, she did," Bob says. "Even though she asked the firemen to check on the squirrel first."

Riff laughs. "She should have called them earlier in the night to free the damned squirrel, then none of this would have happened." He gets up and draws the curtain around Bob's bed, slightly muffling the sound of his roommate's television. "Do you mind?"

"Of course not."

"But the squirrel lived, huh?"

"Yeah, I was so happy, I told them to open the trap and free him right then and there. The little bastard hopped down the fire escape to my backyard and starting gorging on peanuts. I tell you, it's hopeless."

"You should just put that place on the market in the spring. Because man, it's trying to kill you." Riff points to Bob's bandaged foot, the hospital bed.

"You know..." Bob motions for Riff to lean in closer, lowers his voice, as though his Family Feud-watching roommate might judge him. "I haven't told anyone else this, because I don't want to sound nutty, but I got it into my head that if the squirrel died, I would die, too. That it was some kind of cosmic justice."

"For what? Trying to rid your house of squirrels?"

"I don't know. Thinking I was more important than an animal."

"You've been living there too long, man. It's clouding your judgment."

Bob changes the subject. "So what have we got going on the show this morning?" He slides the brown insulated cover back over his breakfast plate, pushes it to the edge of his tray, takes another sip of the coffee, and makes a face.

"Ah, it's stupid. Kathy's got an hour booked with an evolutionary psychologist about New Year's resolutions. Some bullshit about intentionality and brain waves or something."

"I would have vetoed that one."

"Truth is, people like Kathy's shows. The lines light up. They want to talk about fucking New Year's resolutions with an evolutionary psychologist. I am out of step with the rest of the world, I tell you. If I think it's a good idea, it probably isn't."

"No, you're just ahead of the curve."

"Maybe." Riff shrugs, looks doubtful. But unlike Bob, he really doesn't suffer from low self esteem. He lets Bob's suggestion sink in for a minute, then brightens up. "You're probably right, I am ahead of the curve," he says. "But, the trouble is, you can't be too far ahead. The media can never be too far ahead of the curve. One step, at most."

There's a knock on the door. "Bob? Are you in there?"

Leonie! "Come in!" Bob is so happy to hear her voice. He missed her last night, sleeping alone in the narrow hospital bed, hearing his roommate's strangulated snores. He has not brought up his New Year's resolution about getting married and having children yet. He will, but he is waiting for the right moment.

Riff stands up and drags his chair closer to the window to make room. Leonie rushes in and leans over to give Bob a kiss. She is so pretty. Her dark hair is pulled back; she smiles widely. He tries to pull her down onto the bed, but she resists. She's got a bouquet of flowers in one hand, a Starbucks coffee in the other. She straightens up, hands him the coffee. "Oh my God, I love you," Bob says as he takes the coffee from her. "You are my savior." Leonie looks at him. Their eyes lock. It is the first time either one of them has said the words, *I love you*, even though he was referring to a cup of coffee. He smiles and she smiles back. Is she going to say it back?

"Here, take my seat." Riff gets up out of his chair. "I got to go. Almost show time."

After Riff is gone, Leonie sticks the bouquet into the water pitcher on Bob's bedside table, drags Riff's chair up closer to the bed and reaches for Bob's hand. "I'm sorry I slept through your ordeal," she says. "I feel so guilty."

"Don't worry," Bob says. "I'm the one who keeps earplugs by the side of the bed."

"It's just that he had the oil burner going off and then on, off then on. Every time it went on the whole house shook. It was like an explosion. I could feel it in my bones. I don't know how you sleep in that room."

"You adapt." Bob shrugs. "Actually, I thought it was just me."

"Bob, it's never just you." Leonie rubs his hand between her two hands. "Anyway, I am really sorry I didn't hear you."

Would this be a good time to bring up his idea about them getting married? He is suddenly shy about it. It's not like Leonie has ever mentioned marriage. He knows she wants a child, but who knows if she even wants to get married again. She has been down that path before. What seemed crystal clear to Bob the night before when he was freezing on the porch, now seems a little questionable. She lets go of his hand. "So do you think they'll spring you tonight?"

"Hope so. I just have to wait for the grand pooh-bah to do rounds. I really don't need to be here. Now that all my fingers and toes have thawed out."

"I'll come get you. And we could have dinner. At my house? For New Year's Eve?"

"Sounds great." Bob is thinking that would be a much more romantic setting for his proposal than this crowded hospital room, the plastic vase full of flowers the only cheery note, though it is undercut by the bedpan beside it.

The doctor releases him at 2 p.m. and he immediately dials Leonie and leaves a message on her machine for her to pick him up. He gets up and changes out of his hospital Johnny and back into the horrible clothes he had on the night before and the morning before that in California. Just think, this long sleeved gray T-shirt and baggy kneed jeans have traveled back and forth across the country, been slept in at least three times, on the plane, on the couch, and on the roof – and are now probably impregnated with some toxic fear hormone. He picks up the bedside phone and calls Leonie. Again, her machine. "Could you stop by my house," he asks. "And bring me some clean clothes?"

He tells her where he keeps the spare key. All of this is forcing them to be more intimate than they really are, he thinks, her letting herself into his house and rummaging around his dresser for underwear. There is something profoundly unromantic about men's underwear. Not like women's underwear at all. He hangs up the phone and regrets that he has left this message. He wishes he could call back and erase it. He could just take a cab home. He really doesn't need to be picked up. He is not some old invalid in a wheelchair, he is a hero, who risked his own life to save one of God's creatures, though he has to admit, he is still feeling a bit shaky and bone tired.

By 3 p.m., he is getting restless. He has packed all his belongings into a plastic shopping bag, cleaned out his locker and bedside table. He has shaved, combed, brushed, and walked the corridors. He is definitely ready to get out of this place. He dials her number again, and again gets her voice mail. Can she be shopping and doing errands all this time? It's doesn't make sense. He leaves her another message, tells her he will take a cab, and see her later that night.

He forgot about the damned snow. The front walk and the stairs are unshoveled and the sidewalk has been packed down by the incessant foot traffic to Mass. Ave. He limps up the front walk and stairs and steps into the house. He looks to the coffee table for the Chinese food, but the table is empty, the table top cleaned, the cushions and pillows on the couch plumped. Leonie must have done it. Where is she? Could she have those earplugs in again? He wanders into his bedroom, to change into warmer clothes, so he can go out and shovel, but his neatly made bed beckons and he thinks, I'll lie down just for a minute, catch my breath, before I go out into the cold. He passes out on top of his bedspread.

It's dark when he wakes up. The little red light on his answering machine is blinking. Leonie has left several messages, very apologetic; she was on the other line, something important came up, she will tell him all about it tonight, around seven o'clock? He smiles and steps into the bathroom and out of his clothes and into the shower and lets the hot water pound the past two crazy days out of him.

Bob has never liked New Year's Eve. All the forced hilarity, sappy music, the stagy kisses at midnight, the New Year's Day hangover. Who cares? It has never seemed worth it. He can't remember a single New Year's Eve that was fun. Last year he worked; driving into JZY slightly before midnight, swerving to avoid drunken revelers on the road, and he and Riff and Irene and BJ had toasted the new year with mugs of champagne. Bob had taken a sip of his and thrown the rest down the drain. Who wants to drink champagne before lunch?

He has done a cursory job of shoveling, the path only a single shovel wide. His father always made Bob clear off every inch of brick sidewalk, every inch of the stairs, and salt and sand it all before he came inside. And Bob had always prided himself on following his advice, and even judged his yuppie neighbors for cutting corners. But this time, he thinks, it's good enough. He has changed into a dark reddish corduroy shirt that Leonie gave him for Christmas, not a usual color for him, but this way she'll think he really liked it. He had given her a cashmere sweater in a practical shade of beige. He likes to think he dresses in muted, tasteful colors, though one day Leonie joked that his entire wardrobe was the color of mud.

He pats his breast pocket to make sure he remembered his toothbrush, and his back pocket to check for his wallet. Funny, but they hadn't yet exchanged keys, or started leaving toiletries at each other's houses. Of course, they live so close, they could always run back and get something if it was important. But still, what does it say about them? He is getting more and more nervous about the marriage and children idea, but also more and more convinced that he should bring it up sooner rather than later. Should he spring it on her the minute she opens the door?

Leonie is not wearing the beige cashmere sweater. In fact, she is wearing the same outfit she had on that morning at the hospital: a pair of slim black pants and an oversized ski sweater. She leads Bob into the kitchen, where she is in the midst of preparing dinner. There are chopped mushrooms, onions, and garlic on the cutting board. She offers Bob a glass of wine and he is about to decline — he is feeling weak and just the tiniest bit nauseated — but then he accepts. Might make his proposal go a bit smoother.

Leonie pours them both glasses of wine and hands one to Bob and takes a sip of hers. "Let me finish chopping and then I need to tell you about my day."

Need? There is something alarming in that word. In general Bob has found that when women use the word *need*, men should be on the alert. So far the evening is not going as planned. Leonie looks a bit flushed and excited, but nervous too, and if he is not mistaken, has not even washed her hair. Not a good predictor of romantic intent.

He offers to help, and when she declines, he sits at the kitchen table and watches her chop. Leonie is a good cook in what Bob has come to think of as the California way. Everything is fresh, and seemingly thrown together, but all the details are just right: the garlic-infused oil, the fresh ground chiles, the bite-sized chunks of meat or fish, the splash of wine, the good loaf of crusty bread. Her mother had shown the same sense of unselfconscious ease in the kitchen. Could that really have only been two days ago?

When she finishes her prep, Leonie brings a bowl of marinated olives and some thinly sliced bread to the table and sits down with him. She takes a sip of wine, then pushes her dark hair off her forehead. "So I had some big news today," she says. A smile is trying to escape from her tightly held lips. She is bursting with her news.

A tenure track job, a book contract, a dance gig? Was she going to leave Cambridge now that he wanted to settle down? "Yes?" he says, trying to stay calm.

"I'm adopting!" She looks down at her beautifully shaped hands. She is smiling widely now, but can't quite meet his eyes. "There's a baby girl waiting for me in China. I'm going to leave in two weeks to pick her up, then spend two weeks over there, a week getting to know her, then another week going through this whole bureaucratic rigmarole." She shakes her head in amazement. "She's thirteen months old, and just starting to walk!" Her eyes look bright and shiny, as if she might cry.

"You're adopting?"

"Yes. I think my mother is going to come over with me. It's all happening so fast!"

"How long have you known this?"

"Just today." Leonie shakes her head up and down excitedly. "They called today, right after I got home from the hospital. My mom was the first to know. You're the second."

This is supposed to make him feel better? "But how long has this been in the works?"

"Oh, ages," she says. "I started this whole process a long time ago." She looks closely at him, finally realizes that he's upset. "Long before I met you, Bob." She takes his hand.

He pulls his hand back. "But why didn't you tell me before this?"

Her smile fades. "Aren't you happy for me?"

"Of course I'm happy. But what does this mean for us? Exactly?"

"Us?" She shakes her head, makes a dismissive gesture with her hand. "Nothing! Nothing's going to change. We'll still see each other. I mean my mother might stay for a few months, until I get comfortable, but we can work around that. I thought you liked my mother."

"Of course I like your mother." He can't believe she doesn't understand why he's put off.

"You don't want an adopted child? Is that it?" She looks at him incredulously.

"I don't know if I want an adopted child, Leonie. I haven't even had time to think about it. It's the first time I even heard about it. I can't believe you didn't think of telling me earlier."

"I told you, Bob, this started long before I met you. You don't just make a phone call and adopt, you know. There's tons of paperwork, meetings with social workers, financial considerations. Remember that weekend I went away?"

"What weekend?"

"When we first met. You left me all those messages?"

The weekend he was waiting for her to call him back. After she told him she wasn't using birth control.

"That was for a workshop with another agency. I was starting to doubt that this adoption would ever come through. I've been waiting for almost two years."

"You've been at this for two years?"

"Bob, I couldn't wait around for some guy to materialize, and then start. I had to make a decision and go for it. They don't even let you adopt after forty-five. It's now or never!"

Bob runs his hand through his hair, takes a large sip of his wine. "I know," he says, shaking his head back and forth as if he doesn't know. "But, I mean, what if we wanted to have our own family?"

"An adopted child wouldn't be your own family? Is that it?" She narrows her eyes, looks more closely at him. The sides of her mouth turn down. "Oh, no, I can't believe this. Is it because she's Chinese?"

"No, of course not!" Bob pounds his free hand on the table as he jumps up. "I can't believe this. You wanted me to get you pregnant when you had an adoption in the works? Leonie, that is so fucked up. And there I was, naïve Bob, thinking we could take our time and do it together."

Leonie tosses back a large gulp of wine. "Exactly! Take our time. I don't have time. How much longer would I have to wait? Until you finally got up the courage to apply for the Harvard job? Or when you got the guts to send out your manuscript? Or maybe when your sleeping schedule finally calmed down? After you had obsessed for years about your squirrel problem? Bob, the whole world can't move at your leisurely pace. You're forty-eight years old. When exactly were you going to grow up?"

She stops talking and puts her hand to her mouth. She seems almost as shocked as Bob by what has come out of it.

"Is that how you really feel about me?" His voice is dangerously close to breaking. He sinks back down into the chair.

"No," she says. "Not really." She props her elbow on the table, leans her forehead into the palm of her hand, and thinks for a while. Then she looks him in the eye. "Well, yes, I guess it is how I feel. You're like all men," she says. "You think the world revolves around you and your stupid battles. It's just you and your enemies. Nothing else matters."

"Hey, I wasn't the one who organized the whole neighborhood to save some tree."

"Yeah, I did, but I lost, and now I have moved on. But you never do. With you it is just one battle after another, Bob Boland against the world."

If only she knew, Bob thinks, just how far he has moved in the last months. "I was going to ask you to marry me," he says, quietly. "I thought we could start a family."

"What? I need another glass of wine for this." She gets up and brings the bottle to the table and sits down. "Well." She refills her glass. "At least when you're adopting you can still drink, not like poor Martha." She leans over to refill Bob's. He puts his hand over his glass to stop her. The wine he just drank seems to be coming back up his throat as a burning vapor.

"I'm really flattered, Bob. But I can't think about marriage right now or getting pregnant. I have enough on my plate. I've got to book my flight and my mom's flight, and a hotel room in China, and buy a crib and set up a baby's room. That little girl's got to be my priority right now."

They sit there in silence for a few minutes, Leonie sipping from her wine and chewing her lip, Bob staring out the back window, through the trees, to his house. He had left the light on in the kitchen, a mistake, but now he is glad he will not have to go home to a completely darkened house.

CHAPTER 34

It is not easy to apply for the Jazz Archive job without Leonie's help, but Bob does it. He calls Buddy for a reference. He has Mary Elizabeth edit his cover letter and pump up his resume into a curriculum vitae. He locates his previously published articles and music reviews – not in the attic, but in the cellar, in a large plastic bin covered with dryer lint and plaster dust. And one Friday night, after work, he meets Mary Elizabeth at her office in City Hall, and uses her printer to print out the final piece, an excerpt from his manuscript. They lock up her office and walk across the street to the post office to weigh and mail the now-substantial manila envelope. Bob can't believe how good he feels as he watches his application disappear into the mail slot. He is not just relieved that an onerous task is done, but also hopeful that something good might come of it. He feels light and happy for the first time in weeks.

Next he turns his attention to the jazz manuscript. He has two more copies made, mails one out to Buddy, and hand delivers the other to Riff. "Whenever you get around to it," he assures him. "No rush."

But Riff shows up to work the next day bleary eyed, and excited. "I stayed up all fucking night, man," he says. "I love it. And I totally agree. Those bastards are destroying jazz. We got to stop them!"

Riff's enthusiasm is infectious. "I know, I know." Bob shakes his head up and down. "They're so conventional. That's not what jazz is about. Jazz is about pissing people off."

"Exactly!" Riff slaps his thigh. "Man, I wish we were still doing a jazz show. I got so much music in my head today."

Bob clears his throat. "Did you, by any chance, have time to look at the Harry Truman book?"

Riff shakes his head. "Sorry," he says. "I got so carried away with your book. I'll just have to fake it."

"That's okay. I slept with Harry Truman last night."

"I'm sorry."

Bob had fallen asleep with the heavy Harry Truman biography on his chest. Several other books are rolled up in the bottom of his comforter. Others have slipped through the crack between the headboard and the wall. There are books on his night table and splayed open on the floor and under his bed. If only Leonie were still around; he would never have let it get so bad. But he is getting very good at skimming books, zeroing in on the extractable quotes, learning just enough to keep the guest talking until the callers chime in. "I'll write the intro for you," he says. "And a list of questions."

"Thanks." Riff pats him on the shoulder. "By the way, I hear there's a good jazz quartet at Lady Day's next weekend. Shall we get them on the show?"

Bob winces. "Anthony won't like it. He's trying to distance the station from its musical past."

"I'll get it past old Anthony," Riff says. "We can interview them first, then have them play a song. Normal talk shows do that all the time."

But we aren't a normal talk show, Bob thinks, as he turns to his computer to write the Harry Truman intro.

The jazz quartet Riff books has seven members, and a vocalist, who sniffs around and then declares he's allergic to something in the studio: the glue in the carpet, the acoustic tiles, Kathy's perfume, maybe the slight whiff of mildew on Riff's cardigan? He starts to cough, and his eyes get red and teary the minute he enters the room. "I can't sing in here," he says. "My sinuses are filling up. In fact, I need to get out right away or the gig tonight is off."

Irene suggests they try the conference room. Maybe Mitch could rig something up there, while Kathy and Riff fill the time with calls?

Thank God for Irene. She is happy, smart, and totally reliable. Bob has leaned on her heavily since the breakup with Leonie. She takes over and directs the show, while Bob escorts the musicians down the hall. They move slowly, erratically, as if still half asleep. The vocalist veers off to the men's room, to wash his sinuses out with saline solution. Mitch meets them in the conference room. His tie is loosened, his shirtsleeves rolled up; he's got a pile of cables, a portable mixer, headphones, and several mic stands in pieces on the floor beside him. "This is a royal pain in the ass," he says. "You want a fucking live band on the show?"

Bob holds up his hand. "Don't start." He helps him spool out the cable, assemble the mic stands, hook up the mics. Life was so much simpler as an engineer, he thinks.

The musicians eye the conference room doubtfully. The drummer forgot his carpet remnants. The piano needs a grounded outlet. The trumpet player asks if they can turn down the lights, pull the blinds on the floor–to-ceiling windows. "Too bright in here, man," he says. "Vibe's all wrong."

Bob takes out his glasses to read the liner notes on the band's CD. The Sonny Joe Burke Octet. Of course. Riff has no head for numbers. He should never have listened to him. He looks around the room at the assembled musicians, wondering which one is Sonny Joe; both the trumpet player and the pianist are black. He approaches the pianist; there is something straightbacked and regal about him. "You Sonny Joe?" he asks.

The piano player shakes his head, points to the drummer, a skinny white guy in his late twenties, early thirties, with a scraggly brown soul patch that reminds Bob unfortunately of pubic hair. He approaches him, hand extended. "I'm Bob Boland," he says. "Riff's producer."

Sonny Joe holds out his hand, knuckles first, and bumps it against Bob's hand. "I know you guys," he says. "I used to listen to the show. Jazz saved my life."

Bob smiles. "Thanks." It's so easy in radio to forget that anyone ever listens to your show, besides Anthony. "So, you think you guys can play in here?"

Sonny Joe shrugs. "We've played in worse." His eyes are half open, as if squinting against some nonexistent cigarette smoke. His skin is sallow, and there are dark circles under his eyes.

The vocalist has returned from the men's room. He enters the doorway, sniffing at the air, his nose twitching. He is holding a wad of toilet paper in one hand, his bottle of saline solution in the other. He sinks down onto one of the conference room chairs and rests his head in his hands.

"Ramon," Sonny Joe says. "You better, man?"

Ramon looks up and nods. "I guess." He looks even more Caucasian than Sonny Joe. "But." He points to the microphone and shakes his head. "I'll need a wind screen for that."

Mitch exhales loudly, mutters something under his breath. Bob offers to get the wind screen and sprints down the hallway to the engineering closet. He has never miked a live band and hopes Mitch knows what he is doing.

When he returns, Mitch is in the corner adjusting levels on the mixer and talking back and forth to Riff through a headset. The piano player is doing scales and the bassist is tuning up. Sonny Joe has taken off his coat and used it to dampen the bass drum, and Ramon is swaying to some internal rhythm in front of the mic stand. Bob slips the wind screen over his mic and walks over to Mitch. "All set?"

Mitch nods, hands him the headset. Riff is finishing up with a caller, bemoaning the loss of cheap jazz venues in the area. "I mean it wasn't supposed to be about rich people in hotel bars," he says. "All right, I think I hear the band tuning up and they are sounding really good, so without further ado, live from our studios, it's the Sonny Joe Burke Quartet!" Bob cues Sonny Joe, who taps out a light feathery rhythm. The piano and bass join in, and Ramon starts to sing. His voice is high, otherworldly. When Ramon pauses, the trumpet takes up the melody. Sonny Joe plays with his eyes closed, his head nodding. The conference room is transformed. The sound is smooth and round and slow. The piano, drums, and bass sync up like one pulsing heartbeat. Riff was right. The band is great, worth all the effort. Even Mitch is smiling. Employees from the marketing and sales departments gather at the conference room windows to watch. The sound is immediate, live, and more intimate than any club Bob has ever been to. Who knew it could sound so good in a conference room? For a minute he thinks of calling Leonie, telling her to tune in. He wants to impress her, to share this success. Then he comes back to reality. She is no longer in his life. That channel is closed. He feels the loss in the pit of his stomach.

When the band finishes their first song, the station employees erupt in applause and catcalls. Riff cuts in with a station ID, says how good they sound and asks them to play another. Bob nods at Sonny Joe who gives the sign to the rest of the band and they start into a faster, more Latin-sounding number. Ramon's voice soars higher and higher. What must it be like to have kind of instrument inside of you? No wonder he is so protective of it. Bob can't quite believe they have made this happen.

When the show is over, Riff and Bob head back down the hall to their office. "I have to admit, that was great." Bob pats Riff on the shoulder as they enter their office and heads straight for his desk. A red number 28 is blinking on his phone. Maybe Leonie heard the show. Maybe she called him. He will tell her that he misses her.

"Look at that!" Riff points. "Twenty-eight messages. We blew them away!"

Bob picks up the receiver, punches the speaker on and starts listening. The most recent message is from Anthony. "In my office, you and Riff, right now." He doesn't sound happy.

Anthony has a stack of cassette tapes and a cassette deck on his desk. He removes a pair of headphones and ejects a cassette as they walk in. "Auditioning new hosts," he says and tosses the cassette into the waste basket.

Riff follows the trajectory of the cassette and sighs and sinks into a chair. "So, what's up, boss?"

"You had a live band on the show? Didn't you pitch it to me as an interview segment?"

"Well, they were always going to play a set," Riff says.

"A set? They played for an hour straight. When was the interview?"

"Well, it didn't quite work out, technically," Bob says. "We had to move to the conference room. The vocalist was allergic to something in the studio, and there were more members in the band than we had initially anticipated." He is kind of rocking back and forth in his chair as he offers the explanation.

"An hour of jazz leading up to drive time."

"But it was fucking great," Riff says. "The phones were ringing off the hook."

"Yeah." Anthony points to a stack of pink notes. "With complaints."

"Did you actually listen?" Riff juts out his chin. "Or were you too busy trashing people's audition tapes?"

"I heard enough," Anthony says.

"Anthony, we really did plan to interview them," Bob repeats. "But it just got out of control."

"It wasn't out of control." Riff jumps up off his chair, his voice rising as he does. "It was totally in control. It was fucking great!"

"For another station maybe." Anthony has picked up another cassette tape and is tapping it against his coffee cup. "Not mine."

"Don't worry, it won't happen again," Bob says.

"What do you mean for another station?" Riff narrows his eyes at Anthony. Bob has never seem him angry before. He has always floated above conflict, unfazed, adrift on a cloud of pot smoke and jazz vibrations. But now his face is getting red, the cords in his neck are standing out.

"Another station, another host," Anthony says. "Maybe you aren't the right person for this job." He levels his gaze at Riff and holds it steady. "But we can talk about that in private."

"Fuck you," Riff says. "Fuck talking in private. Anything you have to say to me you can say in front of Bobby. And anyway, I quit!" He spins around and walks out of the office, slamming the door behind him.

Anthony and Bob sit there in silence for a moment, the door slam echoing in the room. Bob starts to get up.

"Where do you think you're going?" Anthony says.

"I'll talk to him."

"To hell with him. Hosts are a dime a dozen." He motions toward the leaning stack of audition tapes.

"I'm not doing the show without Riff," Bob says

"So, are you quitting now too?"

Bob is tempted. He has had it with the grueling pace, the pressure, the sucking up to Anthony, the bedroom full of unread books. But he needs this job. He is forty-eight years old. He can't live without health insurance. He is just paying down his credit cards. He has nothing to fall back on. "No," he says. "I'll be back." He runs down the hall to try and catch Riff before he leaves the parking lot.

Riff is waiting in his car, smoking a joint, Bill Evans playing on the CD player. Bob opens the passenger door and slides into the front seat. "I know. He's an asshole." He takes the joint from Riff, presses it between his lips and inhales. "I don't want to work for him either." Riff is looking straight ahead. Bob exhales the smoke. "But I can't quit right now, man. I'm too broke."

"I'll lend you money."

"No, it's more than that. This is a big deal for me, Riff. I finally have a good job Something to be proud of. Don't you see? I'm a producer. I just can't walk away from this."

Riff turns to face him. "I'm supposed to stay working for that insulting little prick so you can get Leonie back? Is that what this is all about?"

"What?" Bob shakes his head. "I hadn't even thought of Leonie."

"Oh, come on! She's there. In the back of your mind. You're trying to remake yourself in her image. Don't you see that, man?"

"Look, Riff, I'm begging you to come back," Bob says. "Just until I find something else. Maybe the jazz gig will come through. Maybe somebody will publish my manuscript. I'll send it to *Downbeat*, the *Globe*. I don't know. Just give me some time."

Riff takes a long hit off the joint, then stubs it out in the ashtray. He stares off into the parking lot. "All right," he says. "I'll do it for you." He punches off the CD player and shuts off the car. "But I'm only doing it for you."

They get out of the car and walk back into the station, and later in the day, Bob turns his head in a certain way, and the smell of pot smoke wafts into his nostrils but nobody else notices, or if they do, they don't mention it.

CHAPTER 35

Abigail starts leaving increasingly insistent messages on Bob's answering machine in early March. Too soon to worry about the trees, Bob thinks; there's still snow on the ground. But somebody like her probably starts planning her spring and summer projects way in advance.

He steps onto his back porch the next Saturday morning and looks out at his Norway maples. There is the usual pile of peanuts and shells under the one closest to Abigail's. They stand out in sharp relief against the white snow. And the usual squirrel tracks circling them. Which reminds him, Rusty had given him the name of a carpenter who could patch up the holes in the fascia board, and line it with metal flashing. It wouldn't be copper, or beautiful, like the rest of the neighborhood, but it would keep the damned squirrels out. He makes a mental note to call him after he calls Abigail back.

Rusty had also given him the name of a tree pruner, who could cut back the branches of the Norway maples so it wouldn't be quite so easy for the squirrels to leap onto his roof. And while he was at it, Rusty had suggested, he could thin out your trees, let a little bit of sun into your yard, and your neighbor's yard. But Bob is thinking the Norway maples just aren't worth the expense. They are weeds after all, opportunists, who sneak in when no one is paying attention. And here he was identifying with them! He is thinking he will just let Abigail take them down and see if her arborist can suggest some other kind of tree, something beautiful like the Japanese maple, but tough enough to survive in his hard, dry soil.

But Abigail is not calling about his trees. "Bob," she says when he reaches her later in the morning. "Bob, why didn't you tell me you were applying for the Jazz Archive job? I'm on the selection committee!"

"You are?"

"Of course. I'm Director of the Centre for the Arts. I'm on almost all arts hiring committees."

"Oh, right," he says, trying to recover. So that's what she does. Why hadn't Leonie warned him?

"I didn't know you were a jazz aficionado, Bob. Or that you wrote! You are just full of surprises. I'm impressed with your reviews and articles. And that excerpt from your manuscript. It's totally original."

"Really?" Bob smiles. "You really think so?"

"Oh yes. Not sure everybody else has read any of it. But I grabbed the envelope the minute I saw the return address."

"I've been working on that manuscript for years, actually."

"It shows. It really shows." Abigail pauses for a beat. "By the way, I noticed your coworker also applied?"

"Yeah. Riff. He's great. He lives and breathes jazz and knows everyone in the jazz world."

"Trouble is, it's hard to differentiate between the two of you. I mean, you both work at the same radio station, have the same, non-academic kind of background. I think some of the committee members are confused."

"Oh," Bob says. "Not much we can do about that now." Damn, he thinks, I should never have applied. I've ruined it for both of us.

"But I think your writing could really help distinguish you from Riff. In fact, I think it could tip you into the final rounds."

"Yeah?" Where is she going with this?

"Maybe I should make sure that everybody on the committee takes the time to read it."

"Oh," Bob says. "Oh." It occurs to him that she is trying to bribe him. Those stupid trees are that important to her. She'll push his application through if he'll take them down. And here he was about to let her do it. And ask her personal arborist for advice on what to plant instead.

"We neighbors have to stick together!" Abigail says.

Would it be shooting himself in the foot to tell her to fuck off? Of course it would be, more of his patented self-destructive behavior, the very thing that Leonie complained about. He thinks for a minute. "Fuck off, Abigail," he says. "I am never taking down those trees." And he slams the phone back down onto the receiver.

CHAPTER 36

In April, both Bob and Riff receive politely worded rejection letters from the Harvard Employment Office. "Overwhelming response," "strong pool of qualified candidates." The Jazz Archive job goes to a faculty member from the Berklee College of Music, a white guy, and a jazz player in his own right, something of a legend on the Hammond organ. The critic from the *Globe* sends Bob a complimentary letter about his manuscript, and though the *Globe* isn't interested, suggests he send it to a small publisher in California, and definitely use his name.

In late April, Bob and Riff attend the first day of jury selection in Omar's trial. He has an impressive new lawyer from the Harvard Health Care Justice Project. She's planning to use the "insanity-by-extreme-grief" defense. When the judge asks if any of the prospective jurors has had negative dealings with insurance companies, all raise their hands. Later, on the packed elevator ride down from the trial, Bob overhears one excused juror whisper, "I told that judge, if it's between an insurance company and a human, I'm always going to side with the human." He and Riff are encouraged.

The show is doing well and they have settled into a good rhythm. Anthony has decided to keep BJ on as the engineer, and freed up Bob to do nothing but produce. Bob relies on Irene and Kathy now to book the shows. He no longer expects Riff to read the books or write the intros, just lets him show up and improvise. Midday ratings are up, and Anthony has turned his attention to retooling the rest of the station's programming.

There have been moments when Bob has regretted that things didn't work out with Irene. She has never looked more attractive. She spends all her time with Brad these days, and is even talking of moving into one of the new condos with him on Bob's street.

Speaking of which, Bob's neighbors now supply him with a steady stream of show ideas and guests. Bryce sends him Buddhist books and peripatetic lamas. Mabel pitches a show on some powerful telescope, designed by one of her astrophysicist colleagues, who is searching for intelligent life in outer space. Even the judge drops off his prep school roommate's bestseller, on his ongoing battle with ADHD.

One warmish Sunday afternoon in early May, Bob pops a jazz vocals mix into his Walkman, puts on his headphones and goes outside to clean up after the winter. He walks around the house to inspect the damage. The mock orange has even more dead branches than last year; he should probably have it sprayed, but the thought of using poison scares him, and the rest of the bush is already starting to bud. The arborvitae in the front of the house is brown in spots and desperately in need of a trim. The grass is patchy in the front yard where the snow plow driver dumped the season's snow, ice melt, and gravel. But the lilac bushes on the side of the house are coming along better than ever before. There are even some buds developing that Bob suspects might turn into actual flowers. The bushes have never bloomed in his memory. He had assumed they didn't get enough sun or the soil was too poor or they were some sterile brand of lilac still waiting for mates. But none of that is true; all they needed was water, and since Abigail installed her underground irrigation system, they are getting plenty. Here, his trees are killing hers and she has resurrected his.

He wonders if the Japanese maple made it. He had asked Irene to ask Brad, who assured them that it was doing just fine. Of course he would say that. Bob decides to walk down the street and check it out for himself. He walks past Bryce's house, where the dogwood tree is blooming, and the birds singing. The trees along the street are just coming into their halo of bright yellow green. He can feel the heat of the day on the back of his neck. After this long hard winter, it is so wonderful to be warm! He crosses the street at Bryce's driveway. The little gray Victorian has been transformed into a condo complex, with an underground parking garage and a three-story addition hovering behind it. The original house is just a façade now, like an exhibit at Disneyland, Victorian Pavilion. They've repeated the colors and design of the slate-tiled roof in the siding and roof of the addition. The steeply sloping driveway is outlined in brick and cobblestone. There are evergreen bushes planted at fiercely regular intervals along the walkway and in-ground lighting between them. You can always tell a condo complex by the lighting, he thinks. Every path is illuminated, because every path leads to somebody's front door.

Bob walks up the brick and granite steps quickly, trying to look as though he belongs, though the condos are still empty, the stickers still visible on each of the new triple-paned, energy-efficient windows. He crosses a stone courtyard and slips around to the side of the building, where a long narrow walkway snakes between the condo and the apartment building next door. He hurries down the evenly spaced stepping stones and passes through a gate and into the back yard. It's not as big as he remembers. It seems a lot darker. The three-story building has robbed the lot of that hidden-garden-in-the-city feel. But there is still a good-sized yard and the Japanese maple stands proudly in the middle of it. Bob looks up and can barely see the top. If anything the tree looks taller than it did last fall, its crown towers over the addition, perhaps it is straining for the light? The leaves are green near the bottom and go from reddish to orange at the top, and when the breeze blows, the whole massive tree quivers with light. There are a few dead branches on the lower part of the tree, and a rather large center limb that looks to be dying. But the tree is alive, and though Bob is no arborist, he thinks it will survive.

He walks back down the street to his house. At least they did that, they saved that beautiful tree. And although Leonie was right, the underground parking garage does not fit in with the rest of the neighborhood, the addition is tasteful and painted in suitably muted Cambridge colors. Bob looks at his front yard. So hard to compete with these professional landscapers with their artfully placed stepping stones and electric green foliage. But at least he can clean up. That costs nothing.

He gathers up broken branches, crushed cigarette packs, chunks of asphalt and pulverized brick, bright bits of plastic, candy wrappers, pulpy coffee cups, and still moldering leaves and stuffs all of it into heavy-duty lawn bags which he drags to the curb. It's early in the day to put trash out, but he decides to live dangerously, flaunt the restrictions. What the hell, it's spring! He has suffered enough. He can smell the fresh load of mulch Abigail's landscapers have dumped on her garden, its not entirely pleasant tang of Pine Sol, mildew and manure, a harbinger of even better weather to come.

He is humming along to Johnny Hartman's "Dedicated to You,"

and leaning over to pick up a suspicious-looking plastic bag — had Abigail dumped a plastic bag of dog shit on his lawn when he wasn't looking — when someone taps him on the shoulder. He jumps up, drops the plastic bag, pulls off his headphones, and turns around to find Leonie's father, Gus. "Bob!" He smiles and the crevices around his eyes deepen. "I was hoping I'd run into to you." He motions for Bob to follow him over to the driveway, where there's a baby stroller parked. Gus folds his long tall body over and beams at the child inside. "My granddaughter, Maya!"

Bob squats down and looks at the little girl. For a minute he is shocked that she looks nothing like Leonie. She has spiky black hair and a very round face. "Hi, Maya." He spins one of the brightly colored plastic wheels mounted on the handlebar. She pounds her hands on the handlebar and kicks out her chubby legs in response. "She's cute," he says and straightens up.

Gus nods. "I know. My wife is obsessed."

"Would you like to come inside? Have some coffee?" Bob hesitates, looks down at Maya. "Some milk?"

"Oh no." Gus shakes his head. "I got to keep moving or she'll wail. She hates being away from Leonie."

"I know how she feels."

Gus looks him in the eye and nods. He stands there awkwardly for a moment, as though weighing whether to say more. "Hey, want to get an ice cream with us?"

"Sure." Bob takes off his work gloves, tosses them on the stoop, and rubs his hands vigorously on the front of his jeans. He could go inside and wash up, but he fears if he does so this apparition will disappear. They head down the street towards Mass. Ave, Gus navigating the stroller over the uneven brick sidewalk. They pass by Abigail's manicured yard, where the tulips are open and the rhododendrons just starting to bud. "So how long have you been here?" Bob asks.

"Couple of weeks," Gus says. "I had to meet Maya, and drag Helen home. I knew I had to intervene when she bought a down coat."

Bob laughs. "And how do you like Cambridge? It's finally getting nice out, huh?"

Gus shrugs. "It's okay." Bob looks around at the just budding trees, the trashy sidewalks, the streets crusted white with road salt. Must look awful, to a Californian.

"Been out to hear any music yet?" Bob asks. "There are a couple of really good clubs in town. In fact, you should stick around for a while.

May's a really good month for jazz."

"No, I want to go home soon."

Bob wonders if Leonie will eventually move back to California. The pull must be very strong now. Maya flings a brightly colored stuffed elephant out of her carriage and into the street. Bob picks it up then hands it back to her. She flings it again. "Watch out, she'll do that all day," Gus warns. Bob retrieves the stuffed elephant, but this time he holds it behind his back for a minute, then stuffs it in the stroller's back pocket, next to a hand carved wooden pull toy.

"Leonie doesn't know I'm doing this," Gus says.

Bob looks at him, raises his eyebrows.

"She doesn't want her eating refined sugar."

"Oh." They stroll in companionable silence for a couple of blocks. Bob had forgotten how easy it was to spend time with Gus. He wonders how he knew where he lived, if Leonie had told him?

Gus breaks the silence. "She's not always right, you know."

"What?"

"Leonie. She's not always right."

"Are we still talking about ice cream?" Bob asks.

Gus stops the stroller and turns to look at him. "No," he says. "We're talking about you."

"Well, I'm not always right either."

"That's a start." Gus resumes walking.

Business is not exactly booming at the ice cream shop this early in the season. In fact, they are the only ones there. Bob orders a coffee, then realizes he has walked out without his wallet. "On me," Gus says, with a wave of his hand. He orders a cup of vanilla ice cream for Maya and a hot fudge sundae for himself. He takes Maya out of her stroller and sits her on his lap, while Bob sets the coffee, napkins, spoons, and dishes of ice cream on the table in front of them. Maya looks from Bob to Gus and then back to Bob again, inserts her fist into her mouth and starts to cry. Gus gently pries her fingers open, one by one, and spoons a little bit of the ice cream in her mouth. Her eyes widen as she swallows. She turns to Gus and nods her head up and down. He spoons a little more in, this time with a bit of hot fudge on it. She smiles widely. "More!" She shakes her hands in excitement. "More!" Her voice goes up and she drops the "r" at the end of the word. Maya is developing a Boston accent.

Gus spoons some of his own hot fudge and whipped cream into her dish, and feeds her another spoonful and then another. The look on her face is one of pure joy. Rivulets of vanilla ice cream run down her chin and drip onto her brightly colored dress. She finishes off the ice cream and struggles to get down off of Gus's lap, then runs back and forth across the narrow store, leaning slightly forward, looking as if she might fall at any time. She pats the wall each time she reaches it, then laughs and runs back. Back and forth, back and forth she goes. When Gus finally tries to corral her into her stroller, she resists and shakes her head, until he finally gives up. "Okay, if you hold on tight," he says, wiping stray bits of ice cream and hot fudge from her chin. "You can walk with me and Bob."

They walk back down the street, and Maya is not only holding on, she is almost pulling the stroller along behind her. "Oh God." Gus looks a bit sheepish. "She's wired on sugar! She'll never go down for her nap now. Leonie's going to kill me."

They stop in front of Bob's house and Gus picks her up and plops her back down in the stroller. She starts to complain, kicks her legs forcefully a couple of times, but thinks better of it and calms down. It is like someone has turned off a switch.

"Thanks for the coffee," Bob says.

"No problem. Been wanting to get in touch."

"Stop by any time. We could listen to music. I have some records you might really appreciate."

Gus nods. "I'm sure you do." He rocks Maya's stroller back and forth over the bumpy brick sidewalk. "You might call Leonie," he says suddenly, as if it just occurred to him, but he is not a good actor, and Bob can tell that the whole encounter has been leading up to this. "I don't think she'd mind."

Bob smiles, nods his head. "I will." He reaches out his hand to shake. "Thanks."

Gus wheels the stroller around and pushes off, and Bob stands there and watches them for a couple minutes. He turns and looks at his own house. He doesn't want to go inside. He doesn't want to be alone. He doesn't want to lose this moment, to have to muster up the courage later to call. He looks back at Gus and Maya who haven't yet turned the corner onto Leonie's street. "Hold on!" he shouts. "I'm coming with you." Gus stops and waits patiently for him to catch up.

Leonie is sitting on a rocking chair on her front porch; her long legs, clad in jeans and cowboy boots, are propped up on the railing in front of her. Bob holds up his hand and waves as they approach. She looks at him in surprise, then gets up. Her face breaks into a cautious smile and she skips down the front steps to meet them. Maya starts to kick her legs and pound on the handlebars, and reaches out her arms. "Mama! Mama! Mama!" she cries.

Leonie looks from Maya to Bob and then back to Maya again. "Maya!" She holds out her arms and rushes the few steps to pick her up out of the stroller.

"Look who I found." Gus walks up the front steps, lets himself into the front door and tactfully disappears. Leonie nuzzles Maya on the neck and Maya laughs then pushes her away. Leonie turns to face Bob, and Maya turns her head, gives him a look that seems to say, who are you and why don't you just go home now?

"I should have called you earlier," Bob says.

"No," Leonie says, shaking her head. "I should have called you earlier."

"I've been selfish." Bob says.

"I've been selfish," Leonie says. "It's just that I made up my mind to do it alone. That was a hard decision to come to, but once I did, I sort of liked the idea. I didn't need to wait for somebody else to make it happen. And suddenly you came along."

"And ruined everything."

"Not at all. You made everything better."

"Really?" Bob smiles and rocks the stroller back and forth with one hand.

"Really."

Bob takes a step closer and Leonie takes a step closer. She leans in and Bob leans in. But before their lips meet, Maya sticks out an arm and pushes Bob away.

Leonie laughs. She turns to Maya. "This is Bob, honey. This is Mommy's friend. You're going to like him." She leans over again and kisses Bob on the lips. He reaches out his arm to encircle her waist, but instead finds one of Maya's chubby legs.

Leonie pulls away and Bob stands there, wondering what comes next. This is all so awkward, he thinks. This is all so good. "Can I carry the stroller upstairs for you?" he asks.

Leonie nods and he follows her up the stairs and into her house, which smells wonderfully familiar and unfamiliar, like Leonie and something new. Babies, he thinks.

ACKNOWLEDGMENTS

Thanks to the many people who helped bring *Everyone Loves You Back* into the world. To Andre Dubus II's Thursday Nighters, who listened to every word and offered me invaluable criticism and support. To the Virginia Center for the Creative Arts, the Ragdale Foundation, and The Writers' Room of Boston, where I began and finished this book, many times. To the understanding crews at *Car Talk* and *The World* for granting me time off to write. To Gorsky Press, especially editor Sean Carswell, and the members of his Publishing House course: Polette Acuna, Amanda Baxley, Courtney Derichsweiler, Heidi Dreiling, Sarah Manheim, Megan Mimiaga, Liz Olson, Douglas Peyton, Gabrielle Reiner, and Caitlin Schwanke for choosing my novel and shepherding it with such great care from manuscript to book.

Thanks also to my family, quirky Cantabridgians every one, for their love, humor, and support. To Susan Young, Richard Howard, and Linda Druker for making me and the book look better. To Jeanne Comaskey and Cindy Anderson for never giving up on Bob Boland. To Adair Rowland, Bob Steinberg, Frankie Wright, Jep Streit, Lori Ambacher, and Richard Ravin for reading one last time. To Gail Hochman for her unfailing commitment and generous advice. To the GNO for their boundless energy and enthusiasm.

And finally, thanks to my husband Jim, who always encourages me to write.